REFUGE

DAVID RICHARD SCHOORENS

To my dad, Richard Schoorens.
Dad was an avid reader of history. That was only one of the many gifts he passed to me.
He died three days after my 65th birthday, and nine days before I wrote this dedication.
I only wish he had the chance to read a draft of my first work.

A national election broken by once unthinkable laws and political violence. Tens of millions of fearful Americans demanded safety and security. The new far right president obliged, using the crisis as a pretext to declare a national emergency and pass sweeping laws that targeted political opponents and dissenters as supporters of domestic terrorism. The United States of America falls into one-party autocracy.

This did not happen because the country suffered an invasion by a foreign power. There was no natural catastrophe. There was no economic collapse. There was no military coup. Instead, out of fear or vengeance, or ignorance, or apathy, the voters deliberately chose to abandon their always imperfect democracy for promises of a return to the mythical glories of the past.

What would you do then?

Would you fight for democracy? Would you collaborate? Or would you give up?

In Saint Andrews, New Brunswick, Americans formed an expatriate dissident community. People caught away from their homes when the border closed. People who fled their homeland. People who decided to start a new life in a foreign land.

Mike and Debbie Whynot, both retired U.S. Air Force officers and leaders of their expatriate community, now face threats from the new U.S. government. Their continued fight for democracy will cost them dearly.

Across the Saint Croix River in Maine, we follow those who did not leave, but remained in service to the United States government. A few would find the moral burden of continued service unendurable.

It is a story of those who live through an extraordinary time and must find an answer to what a President long ago asked of all Americans for all time,

". . . and that government of the people, by the people, for the people, shall not perish from the earth."

It is a story of our near future that has passed from the fanciful to the possible. Even the probable.

CHAPTER ONE

EARLY SEPTEMBER

Most Every Wednesday Morning

Ease out the clutch. Depress the gas pedal an inch or so. Good; moving forward now. Shifting into second gear, then third and fourth. After decades of automatic transmissions, it was nice to do some real driving. Top down, Ray-Ban sunglasses on, wind running through where his hair used to be. Beautiful, cloudless day in the mid-60s. Or 19 Celsius for around here. *She's running pretty smooth now*, thought Mike with a smile of satisfaction. Nice, throaty sound accompanied by all the rattling parts of the typical 1969 MGB. Or any year MGB really. Best to think of the noise as a kind of mechanical music, heavy on the percussion instruments. Finally, she's restored. Deep blue paint job with chromed wire wheels and knock off hubs – spinnerets they call them, or something like that.

Mike could not believe his luck in finding this treasure. Equally lucky was having a wife, Debbie, who was as enthusiastic about the old sports car as he was. Mike had an MGB in high school, same year, and model, though in nowhere near as good a shape as this restored work of the finest British automotive engineering. To say *finest* is to admit the MG's unsophisticated, even primitive, engineering succeeded in creating a simple, affordable sports car, though of questionable reliability. The old car's Lucas electrical system sometimes lived up to its moniker, the *Prince of Darkness*.

Rescued from an estate sale, Mike, a local mechanic, and a local autobody artist, had brought this MG back to her peak. Cool, clear September mornings like today made every dollar, every hour spent in resurrecting the tiny sports car worthwhile.

If you keep saying that, someday you might even believe it, Mike scolded himself.

Moving to the traffic island's right, Mike turned right onto Harriet Street, as he had done many times before. After about a quarter of a kilometer, a left onto Water Street, then another three quarters of a kilometer before another short left to this early morning's destination, the SunRise Café. *There is no finer dish of Eggs Benedict in all the world than at the SunRise. At least in Saint Andrews,* thought Mike.

Mike was meeting George for breakfast, as he did most every Wednesday morning of late. George, Mike's neighbor at Joes Point, got off his night shift at the Saint Stephen border station about half an hour ago. He texted he'd see Mike this morning for breakfast. Mike shook his head, thinking how absolutely boring it must be for Border Services officers like George, with the border closed to everything but important commercial traffic. Despite politics, there's always essential trade and money to be made.

These breakfasts with George were mostly social. They were neighbors, and genuine friends, but Mike also found George helpful in keeping up on happenings on the border. What George saw or could say about the latest policies. Anecdotes from the other side of the border.

A couple of months ago it got a little exciting at the border. According to George, a small squad of black uniformed types with carbines appeared at the American customs building across the river in Calais, Maine. He told Mike, "Different guys, not Customs and Border Protection. They're at a lot, maybe all, the border stations now."

With the border closed, George and his fellow Border Services officers redirected their time to photographing and documenting the activities of these new American police. They would drive down the bridge, take their picture, and occasionally give them a middle finger salute.

Going back over the border, going home, was out of the question for Mike and Debbie. And for thousands of other Americans living in Canada. They were, for half a year now, and likely for some time to come, fugitives from their homeland. Not because they committed a crime, but because they had not forsaken democracy.

Such high-minded thoughts always triggered a refrain in his mind. *If you keep saying that, someday you might believe it. Or are you just trying to ease your own guilt? You're no hero. You're rationalizing. Such bullshit.*

Breakfast with Allies and Enemies

Living in Saint Andrews wasn't part of their plan. It was an accident, albeit a fortunate one, in comparison to what most of their fellow expatriates had gone through.

Three years ago, Mike and Debbie drove up in a rented RV to Saint Andrews, New Brunswick, staying a few nights at the campground on the southern-most point of Saint Andrews. They had a beautiful view across Passamaquoddy Bay. A short walk along Water Street took them into town, usually under the careful watch of a pair of deer just outside the campground.

Saint Andrews is a small, quiet town. Beautiful old homes dating back to the early 1900s, updated to accommodate the bed and breakfast tourists. Biking, something they hadn't done in decades, took them out of town along the St. Andrews Trail to the Ministers Island Bar. A tall ship took them to see minke and humpback whales, common to these waters. They sailed south from St. Andrews and past Eastport, Maine, before turning northeast, running alongside the northern shore of Campobello Island before heading north past L'Etete into Passamaquoddy Bay. Evenings ended with a dinner on a pub deck overlooking a harbor almost entirely emptied of water by the legendary Bay of Fundy tides.

And a memory stirred from childhood. From the pub deck, looking roughly to the north, Mike could make out the Saint Andrews Blockhouse, an old earthen and timber fortification. Long ago when he was a child, his parents brought him on a tour of the Maritime provinces. Mike joked it was a cultural obligation, maybe even a law in those days, for New Englander parents to take the kids to Canada in a station wagon. He remembered his parents stopped at that very blockhouse. He was startled to then learn the blockhouse was built in the early 1800s to protect Saint Andrews from, of all people, the Americans.

The nice shops, restaurants, and whale watching seemed to lead to glances at storefront realty offices. Hey, it's great here. Let's see about buying a vacation home here! And they did. Though in retrospect, it would have been a good idea to first see the place in the depth of winter.

It took a couple of return trips before they settled on a small cottage. Two bedrooms, two baths, garage, and basement, just outside the northwestern edge of the town, along the shoreline of the Saint Croix River at Joes Point. From there they could look out from the screened-in porch and deck and enjoy the views of Maine's coastline and Navy Island. Perfect for two or three weeks in the summer or fall. They could rent it out for the other summer weeks. Best thing about the house, it was all one story. An important feature that became all the more desirable as the years went by and the knees become less obliging.

In those before times, they imagined family gatherings during long summer days, with their three adult children, and eventually grandkids. A dream that now seemed quite impossible.

They never intended to stay permanently when they bought the house. True, they shared jokes about how nice Canadians were in contrast with Americans. How their politics was so less frightening than America's. How this place might be great to have if they had to flee the United States.

How the jokes became reality still bewildered them both.

That blockhouse might be needed once more.

"Great," Mike said out loud. A parking spot right out front. A good start to the day. Out of the MG and up the steps. An easier task back in high school with about eighty fewer pounds. He took little notice of the three men in the Royal Canadian Mounted Police sedan parked across the street at the Continental Hotel.

Through the door and Mike waved good morning to the owner of the café, Claude. Claude McCarthy. Fiftyish, still with a thick crop of gray tinted black hair, the product of a French-Canadian mother and his Irish-Canadian father, Sean, who sat at his usual place at the counter.

Only a dead man wouldn't notice that business was off. Half the regulars were there, and that included Claude's dad. An unfamiliar face sat alone at a nearby table, facing toward where Mike would sit. Dressed in jeans and light blue oxford cut shirt, he seemed focused on his tablet device, propped up against a heavy mug. The only other new faces were a Canadian Army lieutenant with his counterpart from the Royal Netherlands Marine Corps, enjoying their breakfast at a table near the door.

Taking his usual seat near the far corner of the dining area, Mike waited to place his order. After a minute or two, Claude ambled over. Aside from Claude, there were two waitstaff and a couple of cooks. That's all the employees the café could support these days. One cook was his longtime girlfriend. The cliché, "times are hard," rolled over in Mike's mind. Saint Andrews depended heavily on tourism, especially from the states. With the closed border, the town was going through a very troubling time indeed.

"Bonjour Claude. Ahh… J'aurai …ahh...l'habitude. Oh, merci," said Mike to Claude. To which Claude, a native speaker of French, and accented, but

4

fluent English, responded, "Yes, Eggs Benedict, coffee, and orange juice. And for God knows how many times, your French is terrible. Don't use the accent. Keep to English. You're a little better with that."

"That's a little rough." Mike said with a grin. "Just trying to fit in. Ah, George isn't here yet. Expect he'll be in a few. Hold the order until he gets here, if it's all right, *s'il te plait.*" Mike said the last part with an exaggerated American southern accent, to get Claude's goat a little. Claude grunted his acquiescence and went back to the kitchen.

Canadian Broadcast Corporation news was on with their regular segment dedicated to news of the latest political violence in the states. A congressman's district office burned. A sheriff in Idaho who hired far right militia members to safeguard his county from "communists and anarchists." A school board member's house shot up. Street protests in Portland, Oregon, violently suppressed by new federal police of unknown identity using live ammunition. An unknown number of dead. Equal treatment given to other protests in Boston, Chicago, and Atlanta. The CBC anchor summed it all up with, "Another day of violence in the United States."

Mike looked once again at the two military officers across the room. He wondered about all these soldiers deployed here in the last few months. No secret they were here. For the past two months, a company sized unit of the Canadian Army from nearby Canadian Forces Base Gagetown patrolled along the border with Maine, mostly north of Saint Andrews. Officially, they were on an extended training exercise in reconnaissance, with companies rotating in and out.

The other soldier, or more properly a Netherlands Marine Corps first lieutenant, or *Korps Mariniers Luitenant,* was with a company-sized unit of a couple hundred Dutch Marines. NATO's public announcement claimed the Dutch military concluded it was time to train these elite troops in Canada's forests. True, Mike remembered, there's little woodland in the Netherlands, *but why not Norway? Lots of trees and mountains there. And it's closer.* NATO repeatedly asserted their deployment was unrelated to the tensions along the border.

Mike couldn't buy into the official line, suspecting this had to be something more than just training. Drawing upon his own Air Force experience, Mike guessed they were trying to learn what was happening on the American side.

People around here gladly welcomed the Dutch Marines. Most took it as a sign Canada wasn't alone. And besides, the Marines spent money in their town. Their deployment was equally popular among the Dutch, according to their latest polls. The Dutch kept alive down the generations memories of

Canadian soldiers liberating much of Holland during the war. And the Dutch were not alone in their "training exercises" in Canada.

With the U.S. election, NATO faced an existential crisis. The most successful military alliance in history, the shield to western democracy, lost its linchpin member state. Contemptuous, and often hostile to the NATO allies since the opening of his campaign, again and again the new president accused the allies of corruption, of stealing the treasure of the United States. Only a month into his presidency, he withdrew the United States from NATO, using as a pretext their reluctance to meet his new exorbitant demands to fund the basing American troops in Europe. At the time, he said, "We must look to new allies, honest allies, who will give us a fair deal and who better align with our strategic needs." A port call by a U.S. Navy destroyer at Sevastopol signaled the administration's intentions to ally with the world's autocracies, as it became one itself.

Mike remembered when, as a much younger officer, he often shared in the private joke about NATO. What does NATO stand for? Needs *A*mericans *t*o *O*perate. These days, even in his most cynical moods, Mike had to admit NATO was finding itself. Staggered, NATO did not fall. After months of wrenching debate, the alliance lately seemed reinvigorated. The Baltic states held firm. Sweden and Finland, the most recent members, secured the alliance's northern flank. Defense budgets increased. The German military restored itself. Although troublesome, Turkey and Hungary stayed within the alliance.

In a major speech this past summer, the secretary general of NATO put it plainly. "NATO will not appease. NATO will defend democratic principles with all its collective might. The line is drawn." Though left unsaid by the secretary general, that line was drawn across Canada.

Publicly, NATO framed its deployments to Canada as readiness improvements necessary to counter an increasingly aggressive Russia. Mike knew this was partially true, but a message was also sent to a former ally. Just last weekend, the CBC, BBC and France 24 reported extensively on small contingents of British and French troops in Ontario and Quebec. A week ago, the British Army announced the imminent expansion of the armored British Army Training Unit Suffield, known as BATUS, at Canadian Forces Base Suffield in Alberta. More helicopters, tanks, and artillery than before. And most unusually, air defense missile batteries.

A month ago, Canada and NATO renewed low level fighter exercises at Canadian Forces Base Goose Bay, Labrador, returning permanent detachments of Royal Air Force, Luftwaffe, Dutch and Italian Air Forces. Criticism of the noise created by low level fighters seemed muted these days among the people of Labrador. Likewise, the Icelanders accepted the reactivation of the NATO air base near Reykjavik.

Since July, the NATO airborne early warning aircraft wing, out of Mike and Debbie's old base of Geilenkirchen, Germany, forward deployed three of its E-3A Sentry radar aircraft to Canada. From a ten-kilometer altitude, they saw the sky as did God's own angels.

Elements of Standing NATO Maritime Group 1, usually four frigates and a replenishment ship, patrolled near Canadian waters. According to the CBC, this had never been done before.

Would they fight if it came to that? Mike often wondered.

With NATO troops here, even if only as a trip wire force, Canadians felt a little more secure, a little less terrified of their angry and unpredictable former friend to the south. That included Americans expatriates like Mike and Debbie.

As Claude went to the kitchen, a familiar face and two strangers came into the dining room. The familiar was Roy Wilkins, a sergeant with the Royal Canadian Mounted Police, currently assigned as the RCMP detachment commander at Saint Stephen. Roy happened to live in Saint Andrews, only a couple of doors away from Mike's home. He was dressed in uniform today – his operational dress, Roy once explained to Mike. A policeman's typical hat, gray shirt, gold striped dark blue pants, short, black ankle boots, and full equipment belt, including the standard semiautomatic sidearm. If not for the RCMP patch on his shirt sleeve, the crown emblem on his epaulettes and a well-groomed handlebar mustache, Roy looked like any ordinary cop from anywhere.

No, not really, Mike thought. Sgt. Wilkins was set apart. He earned a reputation as highly professional. An effective leader if somewhat taciturn. Six-foot-two, reddish hair, and very physically fit for a man in his late forties. An expert marksman. On top of that, a nice guy who would do anything for someone in need.

"Good morning, Sergeant Wilkins, or should I say Staff Sergeant Wilkins. Congratulations on the promotion." Mike offered his hand. Roy removed his cap, secured it under his left arm, and returned the handshake, saying "Good morning to you Mike and thanks." Wilkins laid his cap on the table and then placed a recording device of some kind next to his cap. Still standing, he launched into an almost formal introduction of his two charges.

"Mr. Whynot, these two, ah, gentlemen, are special agents with the American Department of Homeland Security. Is that correct, gentlemen?" Without waiting for a reply, Roy continued. "They are here to question you and other members of your expatriate community. They claim they are here only to collect information." Roy placed a peculiar weight on the verb *claim*. "They offer their assurances that you nor anyone else they want to . . . interview . . . are part of a criminal investigation. They are not armed. You may answer their questions or not. That is your right. I am merely here as their, escort, shall we say. And to document all interactions they have with anyone, American or Canadian. Once they are done, I will return them to the border."

One of the agents put a mobile phone on the table and started his own recording.

Looks like this breakfast will be something to talk about, thought Mike.

"Yes, Mr. Whynot, I am Special Agent Williams, formerly of the DOJ National Security Division. Now assigned to the Homeland Security Corps – HSC. This is Special Agent Webb. He is also from the Department of Homeland Security, Homeland Security Corps." Both flashed their badges and identification as they spoke.

Williams continued, "Given your stature with the American community here, I want to start our interviews with you. I hope you can answer our questions."

Mike spared only a glance at their identification, keeping his attention elsewhere as the athletic looking Williams spoke. He then looked at Roy and said, "Roy, by the way, how is Marge? Feeling better I hope?" Marge, Roy's wife, had a touch of flu. Roy nodded, smiling a little, "She's doing much better now."

Mike continued with Roy, saying, "Please Roy, join me at my table. I guess this could take more than a few minutes." Roy took a chair at the end of the table.

Mike kept his eyes locked on Roy for the moment, deliberately ignoring the federal agents. Mike wanted to make sure the agents realized that he and Roy were already known to each other, even friends. Maybe Roy did too.

"Oh, and I suppose you two might as well take a seat, if you must." Mike knew this would ruin his breakfast.

Williams, who Mike judged as the senior of the two, took his seat next to Roy. When Webb tried to grab the last open chair, Mike waved him off, saying "You might want to get another chair. I'm expecting a friend for breakfast shortly."

The roll of Webb's eyes as he went off to get a chair told Mike the guy was already getting a little annoyed. *Good.*

Once Webb returned and planted his beefy frame in the chair, Williams began, "Mr. Whynot, let's start with a brief review of your history to ensure we have accurate information, and then . . ."

Mike interrupted, looking directly at Williams for just a moment. "Oh, I am so sorry gentlemen. I'm being a terrible host. Would you like coffee? Maybe a breakfast before you go off around town questioning my country-men? I can tell you they make the best Eggs Benedict in all the world here. They poach the eggs perfectly every time."

When Mike paused for a second, Williams tried to restart, but Mike called out, "Claude, Claude! Could you come over here, please? I think these two gentlemen, who are from the, ah, U.S. Department of Homeland Security and Customs and Border Protection? No, that's not right. Homeland Security Corps. Yes, HSC. Claude, I think they'd like something to eat." Mike made sure to loudly announce the identity of the agents' employers so all in the room would hear. Heads swiveled toward the agents. Nobody smiled. Audible curses followed.

Mike knew Canadians these days particularly despised U.S. Customs and Border Protection officers. Too many stories about CBP harassing, even de-taining, Canadians crossing to the south on business. And these brand-new HSC officers were held in equal, if not greater disdain.

These guys really piss off Claude. Splendid, thought Mike. The border closure ended American tourism to Canada, devasting businesses like Claude's. *Well Claude, here's your chance to get back at them.*

"And Claude, put it all on my bill. Roy, what would you like to have?"

"That's quite all right, I already ate. But I won't speak for agents Williams and Webb." Roy deadpanned the whole exchange. Mike sensed Roy was quite enjoying this.

As Claude arrived at the table, Williams tried to regain control. "Thank you, Mr. Whynot, but we're fine." Hearing Williams, Claude turned away from the table, making a show of his displeasure. Williams went on with questioning Mike, "Let's begin with your background. You were born . . ."

"Yes, that's right, I was born. In Massachusetts in 1957. February third, if I remember correctly. Sure, you guys wouldn't like some coffee? Gonna be a long day, for sure." Mike glanced around to find Claude. He ignored pro-tests from Williams. "Claude, if you wouldn't mind bringing these two gen-tlemen some coffee."

Claude turned around once again, then acknowledged Mike without a dis-cernable word of English, but a quite discernable muttered curse in French.

"Sorry gentlemen. Claude, he's the owner here and is usually more per-sonable." Mike sipped his coffee and began speaking in a more elevated tone. "But when your government closed the border last February, well, that hurt the economy around here badly. You may not know this, but Canadians don't like your administration.

"I mean, that talk from the administration about another round of trade restrictions and tariffs on Canada. Most Canadians I know think that man closed the border out of spite. Just because the prime minister spoke up in favor of democracy. That backfired on you guys, I think. Made the PM much more popular."

Mike didn't stop there. "The U.S. leaving NATO didn't help. And leaving the climate accords, again. Demanding renegotiation of trade agreements, again. Questioning Canadian sovereignty over her Artic regions. And what really got people up here mad at your president? When he did that video message of support for a Canadian far right rally. Not exactly neighborly behavior."

Again, Williams tried to get control. "Mr. Whynot, we need . . ."

Mike held up his hand toward Williams.

"Hell, people around here still argue over what to call the United States. Should it be the former America? How about FUSA, the Former United States of America? Or Fascist United States of America. Course, the *F* can have another entirely different interpretation."

"But don't worry, I'm sure your coffee will be fine." *In truth,* Mike thought, *I hope Claude pisses in your coffee. I hope they'll wonder the same when the coffee comes.*

Williams pressed on. He placed on the table a small black notebook, "You have a bachelor of science degree in history and a graduate degree in International Relations. You served as an Air Force intelligence officer for twenty years. Spent four of those years in Germany, one year in Qatar. Now collecting a military pension. Though you were living in Rhode Island, your residential address now is, I assume, in Saint Andrews. Correct?"

"Why, yes, it is." Mike then snatched the black notebook from the table, flipped a couple of pages, and said, looking back at Williams with a faux look of astonishment, "Are my eyes really brown?" Mike gave the notebook back to Williams.

Mike laughed. Even Roy, ever the professional, couldn't stifle a smile. "You two need to lighten up. Haven't you ever seen *Casablanca?* You know, Humphrey Bogart, Ingrid Bergman. It's a movie. There's this scene where the head Nazi, Major Strasser, interviews Bogart, ah Rick, the owner of the saloon, and Rick snatches the dossier and mocks the Nazi, saying, 'Are my eyes really brown?' I guess I'm Rick, and Williams, you're, the, ah . . . you know, hell, let's just say it. The Nazi major, I guess. Classic movie. Best movie of all time. You ought to watch it sometime."

Now it was Webb's turn. He leaned forward across the table. "Look, Whynot, you need to take this seriously. So cut out the bullshitting and answer our questions."

Webb, his face reddening, went on. "And what kind of name is Whynot anyway. Sounds made up."

Gently putting down his coffee, Mike grinned and said, "If you must know, it's anglicized. My German immigrant forebears found it difficult to find work in Nova Scotia during World War I. Germanic family name and all. You know, with thousands of Canadian boys dying in France and Belgium. You've heard of World War I, I take it." Mike for the first time looking directly at Webb, "And Webb, that doesn't sound made up to you?"

Two things then happened that likely prevented violence. Claude came with the agents' coffee and George walked in.

The bullshitting would continue, at least for a while, thought Mike.

"George, over here. Take this chair. We have two, what shall I call them, ah, new friends." The last part was said with all the sarcasm Mike could muster.

Claude came over to the table, and damn near dropped the coffee cups in the laps of the American agents. As a bonus, he might have said the French equivalent of assholes.

George sat down in the open chair as Mike explained to him what was going on. "These two are Mr. Williams and Mr. Webb. They're U.S. federal agents, Homeland Security Corps, in town to interview people like me. Under the watchful eye of Sergeant Wilkins of course."

Mike continued, "Gentlemen, this is George LeBlanc, a Border Services Officer with the Canada Border Services Agency, as you might have guessed from the uniform and sidearm." It was only in the last few years that all border officers were armed, a controversial decision among some in Canada at the time. Not anymore.

No handshakes were offered.

This time, Webb spoke first, and disdainfully. "Yeah, we met LeBlanc earlier, coming across the border. We got there early. Didn't matter. Seemed to take a long time to process things, even with nobody else coming across."

Uh oh, here it comes. George is a master of getting under someone's skin. Years of professional experience, Mike knew.

Speaking to Roy, George continued, smiling, not bothering to look at Webb. "So, Roy, sorry it took extra time to process their entry. You know, bureaucracy. Had to check with the higher ups to make sure these guys, I mean, agents, were who they said they were. Took time to get to the right guy on the phone. And we had to lock up their firearms, more paperwork. Take their pictures. More paperwork.

"A lot of things to do. But you know, at Border Services of Canada, we take our job very seriously and certainly don't want to assume anything about anyone. Especially, well, guys like these." Then with a wider smile, George looked directly at Webb, saying, "At least we didn't have to do a strip search, eh?"

George elbowed Webb gently, as if to say *just kidding* . . . or maybe not. Webb's mood didn't improve.

Sensing his own opportunity to annoy, Claude came over and took George's order and promised Mike his order would be put in with George's. When Williams tried to restart with Mike, Claude loudly told Williams to be quiet while he was working. Mike had to laugh.

Mike noticed that neither Webb nor Williams had taken a sip of their coffee.

Putting up his hand to get their attention, Williams said firmly, "Okay, you've had your fun. I get it. We're not welcome up here. Nevertheless, we've got a job to do, just like you do. Now let's get to it."

Williams continued without pause. "Mr. Whynot, you have a locally broadcast cable and radio show. Also streamed as a podcast. And an opinion blog. Before all that, when you were still in the states, you created a blog that was highly critical of those who would become the current administration.

"You recall the *Overseas Americans Act* passed by Congress three months ago. The act allows regulation of political activity by private Americans living abroad. Meaning you. There's great concern about any activities that may encourage or support, directly or indirectly, violence or terrorism in the United States. Frankly, the statements you've made from here in Canada are troublesome."

Mike interrupted. "What you and your kind call support of domestic terrorism, we used to call the right to protest. The rights of free speech and assembly. We can talk later about who is really behind the domestic terrorism in the states." Mike now stared intently at Williams. By now, the calm of his voice evaporated.

"Williams, looks like HSC is using their new powers to snatch political dissidents off American streets, literally. No *habeas corpus*. No charges. You just, how shall I say this, *disappear* them. And from what I've heard from people back in the states, more than a few times, political opponents have heard the midnight knock on their door. Straight out of the Gestapo, KGB and East German Stasi playbooks.

"Oh, yes, there's still the First Amendment. Free speech, but only *accepta-ble* speech. You know, speech that supports your president. Dissent supports terrorism. Say or write the wrong thing, and guys like you knock on the door. But please Williams, go on."

"Your broadcasts may be in violation of the recent Federal regulations stemming from the act. We wonder if you are trying to stir up resentment among Americans on this side of the border. Maybe both sides of the border. Resentment that might lead to plots and violence against your country. The country you once served."

That was too much for Mike.

"Yes, I served my country, though guys like you seemed to have mis-placed the United States I remember. You know, the one with the Bill of Rights. I remember my oath too . . . *to preserve, protect and defend the Constitution of the United States, against all enemies, foreign and domestic.*" Mike enjoyed empha-sizing the word *domestic*.

He then slowly said to Williams, "Of late, I am reminded that oath I took to the Constitution is a life-long oath. You two should . . . reacquaint yourselves with the oath and the Constitution. You did, didn't you, take that oath, or did that man just give you a waiver?"

Williams returned fire. "Yes, we took that oath. I like to think we're doing just that. Defending America against enemies foreign and domestic."

Undeterred, Williams continued. "May I ask you, why did you and your wife decide to stay here in Canada?"

"No, you may not." Mike wasn't going to answer that question. If he was honest with himself, he wasn't sure what the answer really was.

"Look, you two want something from me that I won't give. I'm calling my solicitor right now. He can be here in a few minutes. His office is around the corner." With that, Mike got Edward on his cell phone, quickly explain-ing that he needed legal representation *right bloody now* as there were U.S. Fed-eral agents interrupting his breakfast and asking questions.

"Mr. Whynot, you're not under arrest. You're not even under formal in-vestigation, so there is no reason to have your lawyer here." A tone of irrita-tion was quite evident in Williams.

Mike wanted to be so much more than merely irritating. "Well, I want him here. And he'll be bringing paperwork that's relevant to this . . . what shall I call it . . . conversation. Besides, perhaps Edward hasn't eaten breakfast yet."

It was Roy's turn. "Agent Williams, I must tell you that Mr. Whynot is perfectly within his rights to request legal counsel be present. The same goes for anyone you question in Canada, citizen or not. You will hold off on your questioning until his solicitor arrives. Is that clear?"

Webb looked down at the table and shook his head. *Yup, he's pissed. Excellent,* thought Mike.

George simply stared at the agents with a wide smile on his face.

Edward Donohue, Mike's lawyer, entered the café several minutes later, dressed as was his practice during business hours, in a well-fitted gray suit. In times past, Edward ran a solo practice that focused mostly on wills, contract law, real estate transactions and the like. In the last year, he began taking on immigration cases, in partnership with a lawyer from Saint John who specialized in that area. Thanks to government aid, he brought on three legal aid staffers to help the American community navigate the Canadian legal system, especially their immigration status.

After perfunctory introductions, Edward kept standing as he opened his briefcase and laid out the documents. He focused on the agents, never even glancing at Mike.

"Gentlemen, I am Edward Donohue, licensed by the Province of New Brunswick as a barrister and solicitor. I brought with me documents pertaining to Mr. Whynot's legal status in Canada. As you can see in this document, Mr. Whynot has been granted Conditional Permanent Residence Status by Immigration, Refugees and Citizenship Canada, which I am sure you are aware is a department of our federal government."

With a mocking smile, Mike flipped open his wallet to show his permanent residence card and flashed it at the agents. Then said, "And it gets me health benefits!"

Edward shot an irritated glance at Mike, as if to say, *don't interrupt me.* He continued. "Recently, parliament made such conditional status possible, necessitated by the current political situation. This special status has been granted to all U.S. citizens upon request, under the existing and since expanded Government-Assisted Refugee Program. Persons like Mr. Whynot, still must eventually complete all the normal requirements that were in place before, but in the meantime, they have the full legal protection and rights of permanent status."

Williams interrupted. "He's still an American citizen, so . . ." Edward would have none of it. "Agent Williams, may I continue? I will let you know when I am done."

Williams nodded. Mike smiled.

"Here's a copy of Mr. Whynot's application for Canadian Citizenship. I expect this will have final approval soon. Dual citizenship is still allowed. Hundreds of thousands of people on both sides of the border have it. That's been the case for years. I should add he and his wife have carefully met their tax obligations with the United States. They will continue to do so until such time as they renounce their U.S. citizenship, if they so choose.

"U.S. citizens who fear political persecution qualify for asylum. This document shows Mr. Whynot, his wife, and immediate family members in Canada, were granted asylum some time ago.

"Finally, the Prime Minister has taken the position that a citizen, or former citizen, of the United States will not be extradited to the United States unless there is a clear criminal case that is supported by significant evidence and is recognized as a crime by Department of Justice Canada. I can assure this government set a very high bar for any such evidence. In other words, we will send back a bank robber, but not a political dissident."

Edward paused for a moment, and saw that he had quite an audience among the café patrons.

"As U.S. government agents, you must know, or should have known, Mr. Whynot's legal status. You must know that he, and all others like him, has the full protection of the crown."

Edward now leaned down toward Williams. "If you think you can just walk into this country and question our citizens, dual citizens, permanent residents, or refugees, well, Canadian law has something to say about that.

"So, I ask you, why the hell are you here?"

Someone applauded.

"Allow me to answer," Williams began, struggling to keep his frustration at bay. "We're certainly aware of new Canadian laws, regulations, and policies. And I emphasize that Mr. Whynot is not presently the subject of a criminal investigation. However, under our law, his actions in Canada do give DHS and HSC reason to make inquiries."

Edward angrily shot back, "What do you mean by 'presently not under investigation?' What do you mean by 'actions in Canada?' That he has made public political opinions that are against your present government? Is that illegal now in your country?"

"DHS and the DOJ will only begin a formal investigation if the evidence warrants. We also wish to make sure Mr. Whynot understands the consequences should he continue with activities which may be violate our law. May I explain those consequences?"

15

"Political dissent will never be a violation of law in Canada! A charge based on that will fail. Have no doubt." After a moment, Edward said, "Now, say what you want to say to Mr. Whynot and be done with it."

Williams spoke directly to Mike.

"Under long standing U.S. law, you could be extradited should an investigation uncover any past or ongoing criminal activity." He then explained that under the new law, once an investigation starts while the subject remains overseas, access to all property and financial assets held in the United States will be suspended. Stocks, bonds, mutual funds, bank accounts, Social Security, real estate, everything. Including any assets or property held by a spouse or immediate family member. If the case is not resolved within six months, all such property and assets would be forfeited permanently to the U.S. Treasury.

The law also targeted military retirees living overseas. Williams explained that no matter a retirees' legal situation, remaining overseas into the next calendar year would result in the loss of military pension and veteran benefits, plus a criminal charge.

"That also means your wife Deborah. She retired as a lieutenant colonel, like yourself, correct? By January, on this provision alone, both of you will lose your military pensions – by my calculation, that is well over $120,000 a year – and face criminal extradition."

Mike, of course, knew about this. It was no secret. Nevertheless, over a thousand retired military officers chose to leave the United States for Canada or Europe. Dissent spread to the active duty as well. Since the new administration took power, over a hundred active-duty officers resigned, publicly, many of whom likewise left the United States. Many became vocal critics of the new government. All knew they could be charged with a crime for what amounted to exercising their freedom of speech. Just like Mike. Welcome to the new United States.

Yet the vast majority of military retirees stayed home. On the active-duty side, military leadership did all they could to put politics at arm's length, as they always had done. So, the few active duty who resigned were just that, a few.

Why single out expatriate military? Mike had his own hypothesis. The new president might view expat military retirees as a threat. He might suspect this cadre of dissident officers could become the leaders of an insurrection.

Williams made his summation. "In short, Mr. Whynot, you and your family may be able to live your life here in Canada, but penniless. Never seeing your granddaughter. Worrying about your sons. Always fighting extradition. Is your solicitor going to work *pro bono*? How long do you think the

Canadians will support you and thousands like you? Or you can return to the United States in time, avoid a criminal charge, keep your money and property. It's your decision."

Edward shot back at Williams, "Mr. and Mrs. Whynot will indeed make their own decision. They understand they will suffer financial and personal loss by staying in Canada. But Canada will protect their freedom. Do not doubt that." Edward looked to Mike, perhaps to reassure him.

Mercifully, Claude arrived with breakfast for Mike and George. He also saw an opportunity to needle the agents. Claude asked, "Something wrong, gentlemen? With the coffee?" The agents did not reply. Nor did they sip.

"Thank you, Claude." Mike made a bit of a show of slowly eating a bit of the Eggs Benedict before responding to Williams.

Though Mike's appetite had diminished, breakfast did give him a moment to think before speaking. *Might as well piss them off some more.*

"Gentlemen, I must say I somewhat resent your interruption of a treasured morning ritual. Not that I need to add another pound, but I do look forward to such a fine breakfast.

"Now as to your generous offer, gentlemen. I must decline. Debbie and I have talked about this possibility. We'll remain in Canada."

Webb slammed his considerable hand on the table, and then grabbed Mike's hand and held it firmly. "What's wrong with you Whynot?"

Yep, reckoned Mike. *Pissed off. Mission accomplished.*

"Do you really think these . . . Canadians . . . these friends of yours, will stand by you? Seriously, when we really push them. When we demand extradition, don't you think they'll decide it's just cheaper to send you back? If they don't, more tariffs. More sanctions. We outnumber them nine or ten to one. Their army is puny compared to ours. We'd roll right over them. These people don't have the guts to stand up to us. We'd just . . ." Webb stopped abruptly when Williams tightly grabbed his arm. Webb let go of Mike.

Roy shut down the agents. "That is enough! This interview is over. Williams and Webb, I'm returning you to the United States. Your mission is over. Not another word from either of you." Roy rose from his chair, using all his six-foot-two body to stare down at the seated agents.

"Be advised, Webb. I'm of a mind to arrest you right now for grabbing Mr. Whynot. I could arrest you for assault." Roy clearly wasn't bluffing.

"Just a moment, Roy, I don't think that will be necessary. At least not yet. But I'd like a minute to respond to Webb."

"Very well, Mr. Whynot." Roy continued to stare down Webb.

After Webb's outburst, everyone in the café focused on the show. *You don't see this every day*, must have been a common thought. Out of the corner of his eye, Mike saw the Oxford shirt guy adjust his computer tablet.

He began quietly.

"Williams. Webb. You promise, if we go back, all will be forgiven. Well, most things. The news coming out of the states says otherwise. Dissidents harassed, threatened, assaulted by these political, what shall we call them, police, gangs, militias. Terrorists?"

Now raising his voice, Mike sought the room's attention.

"Arrests without warrants or charges, confiscations, trials, imprisonments, on and on. Shooting down protesters. All perfectly legal, they say.

"How many regimes from the past did great wrongs by making those wrongs legal?

"You know, CBC does a great job keeping tabs on the states. Just before you came in, they reported on demonstrators in Chicago and Boston being shot to death by, well, maybe your people. HSC. How about you two? Shoot any demonstrators before you got here?

"Funny how your boss, that president, blames so much terrorism on his opponents. Funny how you arrest them, or shoot them, but let your kind of terrorists off the hook. Yet, the demonstrations against that man continue."

Mike took a deep breath before continuing.

"Will Canada stand by me? And people like me? Yes, Webb, I believe they will. You see, they're made of stronger stuff than you know.

"These Canadians descend from the boys and men who took Vimy Ridge from the Germans in 1917. The Canadian Corps, under Canadian officers, took a fortified position on high ground that the French and British couldn't. The Canadians lost 10,000 men, but they took it. They held it. After . . ."

Webb reacted angrily. "Look, Whynot. We don't need a half-assed history lesson!" Roy grabbed Webb's arm, twisting it behind him and then spoke in his ear. "Quiet now. Let the man speak." The pain was persuasive.

"Didn't like history class in high school, Webb? Too bad. Canada was in that war from the beginning. America didn't get into the war until near the end." Mike turned to look at the customers. "Let me ask you all. Show of hands. How many of you know about Vimy Ridge?"

Everyone raised their hands. A few swore at the American agents. Mike thanked everyone and said, "See that Webb?"

Mike then pointed to the Dutch Marine across the room. "Ask the Dutch Marine officer over there about what Canada did for Holland in '44 and '45. I'm sure he can tell you.

"I'll bet you didn't know any of this. Like most Americans, I'll bet you learned all your history from movies. You think we did it all. And I'm sure you have no idea what Canada did.

"See the older man with the blue baseball cap at the breakfast counter? That's Sean. Claude's father. He fought in Vietnam alongside our soldiers. A Canadian. Volunteered. Volunteered to serve in the United States Army. Awarded the Bronze Star, twice. Webb, 30,000 Canadians joined the American military to fight in Vietnam. Over 140 died. One even earned the Medal of Honor."

Mike then directed Webb to George, who served as a combat soldier in Afghanistan. And Roy, who went there as part of a special RCMP unit to train the Afghan National Police.

"Canada lost 159 of her soldiers in Afghanistan. Their special forces went into battle in October 2001. Their regulars and reserves fought up through 2014. Bet you didn't know that.

"Webb, you're so wrong. Canadians will defend their sovereignty with all that they have. Diplomatic. Economic. Even militarily if you people take us down that road. You see, thanks to your kind, Canadians have a cause worth fighting for. Defending democracy. Defending against a United States that threw away its democracy."

Maybe that history degree was useful after all, Mike thought.

What Mike didn't realize was that his little speech defending Canada would become known worldwide within days.

"I've said all I'm going to. Please take them away now, Roy."

The agents, silenced, left accompanied by the sound of twenty or so cheering Canadians, plus one Dutchman.

Once the agents and Roy were out the door, someone began singing the *La Marseillaise.* Mike turned, shocked to see it was Claude. *Damn, he's got a pretty good voice.* After the first stanza, Claude stopped and said, "Mike, you know, that scene from *Casablanca.* I think we just saw it happen for real. Viva Le Canada!"

As the agents were driven away, George comically waved goodbye to them from the café window, a wide grin across his face. "Next time, definitely, strip search, including body cavity, for sure."

"Mike, I'd like to meet with you in my office, say at ten. We need to talk."

"Yes, Edward, I'll be there."

Parked at the Pier

Mike finished his breakfast. It was 0915. Time to kill before meeting with Edward. He used that time to ready himself to meet his inquisitor. Mike liked Edward. His attorney focused on facts and didn't shy away from making his clients uncomfortable to get them. Even behaving more like the prosecutor than the defense attorney. Like dentistry without modern pharmaceuticals. Quite painful, but in the end, you're fixed. That's how Mike sometimes felt, yet he understood Edward was just doing his job. And Mike might just need a defense.

After seeing Edward, Mike planned to go to the studio and tape his regular broadcast for the American expat community. He thought, *how 'bout I spice it up today, throwing in my little meeting with the American agents?*

Driving out onto the town's 800-foot pier, and lucky enough to find a parking spot in the pier's lot, Mike sat in his MG and stared out over the harbor of St. Andrews. Still a beautiful, fall morning. Just a couple of clouds. The sun at his back.

He reflected on the view. *There's Maine. The United States of America. Only about three miles away, due east. Maybe this is how an East Berliner who got over the wall felt when he looked back at his former world. Grateful to be free in the West, yet grief stricken at leaving home behind. A home still so close.*

Now home was a world away. He looked to the northwest toward Joes Point. *That's the home we have now.* In almost the same glance, he could see all they lost and what they gained.

Never missing an opportunity to beat himself up, he summed up the morning. *Well, Mike, you just made things worse. For yourself, Debbie, and your kids. You humiliated two federal agents. Homeland Security Corp agents. Those bastards. Their kind won't let this go.*

Mike's hands were still shaking a little. The nervous feeling in his stomach hadn't quite abated yet. Those feelings always came to him whenever he became the center of attention. And only grew as the years went by.

Mike knew the kind of man he was. As an intelligence officer, he was cautious, overly so. He always gravitated to the tasks of data collection, its analysis, the report writing. The kind of work that is done unseen by others. He excelled at analysis, knowing that he had done all could be done. The air crews went into combat knowing all there was to know. They would kill the target and get back. All of them.

Stand-up briefings for the air crew or the senior officers, he did well. But he always had that nagging fear of being caught in a mistake in front of others. A chronic fear beyond stage fright that Mike couldn't define. Someday, someone would uncover his flaws for all the world to see. An irrational terror that he was in truth a fraud. Understanding of his fear stayed outside his reach, like in a dream when a thing is always being chased by the dreamer, but is never caught.

So, he kept to the logical and the conventional. He adopted the behaviors of the technician, compensating with hard work and long hours. An aversion to boldness that, he knew, limited his ambitions, and ability, to command.

Perhaps someone higher up deduced this weakness. Perhaps that explained his limited command experience. Why rank higher than lieutenant colonel didn't come to him. A memory came back to him again and again of what he felt when he retired. He didn't feel regret, or pride in accomplishments. He knew what it was. He felt relief.

Stop it, Mike chided himself. *You need to calm down. Get out and walk a little around the pier. Enjoy the view for another ten minutes. Then drive to Edward's office. Get there a little early. That'll piss him off,* Mike thought with a grin.

Ten O'clock

It was ten minutes before ten o'clock when Mike went up the front steps of Edward's legal office. Or more accurately his home and legal office. According to Edward, it is an example of Greek Revival architecture going back to the 1870s. What was so Greek about it, Mike hadn't the foggiest.

After passing through the wide front door, wide enough, it was said, to take a coffin with pallbearers, Mike entered the former parlor that served as Edward's legal office. Though he now had more staff to keep up with increasing legal work, he still worked alone in his house and kept his paralegals at a leased store front on Water Street. Once it was a boutique. No tourists. No shop.

Edward looked up from his desk, saying with little emotion, "You're a little early." Still in his suit, Edward always kept himself professional looking when alone during office hours. His black hair, though thinned and combed back with a prominent widow's peak, somehow added to his image as a lawyer. The legal diplomas on the wall didn't hurt that image either.

"Sorry, old habit from military days. Always arrive before you're supposed to relieve the watch."

Edward nodded and motioned to an antique chair set in from of his large oak desk, also an antique. No smiles. This was going to be serious, felt Mike.

"Thanks for coming, Mike. It's important we share our impressions of this morning. By chance, do you know if that interview was recorded? I'd like to hear the whole thing."

"Yes, Roy recorded it all. I'm pretty sure Williams did, too."

"Right. I'll give Roy a call. Shouldn't be a problem, I'd think. Mike, let me begin by asking for your overall impression of the meeting." Edward had set out a yellow legal pad for notes.

Mike didn't respond for a moment. He wanted to slow himself, analyze things as objectively as he could.

He opened with an admission, saying "I've got to be critical of myself. I did everything I could think of to provoke them, embarrass them, get under their skin. It worked, especially with Webb. Williams seems like a cooler head. Still, my behavior will likely result in them sharpening their knives.

"I expect they'll make me a subject of an investigation soon. Freeze all my assets in the U.S. And by January, Debbie and I will lose our pensions. Guess extradition after that."

Edward nodded as Mike talked, then asked, "Have you talked to Debbie since this morning?"

"No. I will. Once she's off her shift at the clinic and gets home."

Edward didn't like that response, thinking if a couple of cops greeted me at breakfast, I'd sure as hell call my wife right away, if I had one. He kept that thought to himself.

"Mike, would you review the interview before I got there, as best you can?"

After Mike's slow recitation, Edward said, "Yeah, I guess you can expect they'll come after you. Even if you were polite and cooperative, they'd still come after you. But, Jesus, Mike, you really were an asshole."

Edward paused to let that sink in with Mike.

"Do you still want to stay in Canada?"

"I'll be talking to Debbie later, but, yeah, we will stay in Canada."

"Will you continue doing these blogs and podcasts? The TV show? Stay on the Expat Committee?"

Mike's response was reflexive, even emotional. "Yes. It's a matter of duty. Hard to imagine just throwing away what I believe in."

"Right. Well, as your counsel, I am duty bound to point out it might be easier for you and Debbie to cease your podcasts and the like. Maybe that's all they're after. Though I have to say, these guys painted a target on your back. Again, it's likely that no matter what you do, they're coming for you.

"If you're going to stay here, and continue your work, you need to do some things right away. Homework. First, cash out any assets still in the U.S. and get the money to Canada. And yes, I know. Converting from U.S. to Canadian dollars means a real loss for you now, with the exchange rate."

Yeah, no shit. The exchange rate sucks, Mike thought bitterly. The U.S. dollar continued its slide down against major world currencies as the dollar lost its place as the primary reserve currency used in global trade.

China led the attack on the dollar. Seeing a weakened United States, China campaigned intensely, often ruthlessly, for the world's central banks and corporations to drop the U.S. dollar and adopt its own national currency, the renminbi, as the primary reserve currency. After all, China was now the world's one superpower. The successor to the United States. China offered the world's investors stability and safety, whereas the United States was wracked by political violence.

It worked. China set the example by selling off most of its own U.S. Treasury securities while strong arming foreign central banks to do the same. America's former allies, under domestic political pressure to punish the new autocratic American government, and from Chinese threats to withhold investments, sold significant portions of their holdings. No one was buying the Treasuries that made possible deficit spending. Drastic cuts to federal spending followed. A default on debt payments followed that.

To attract more investors to U.S. Treasuries, the Federal Reserve raised interest rates again and again, but that hurt domestic expansion and consumption. Altogether, it was a body blow to the American economy.

Raising taxes was not an option. For decades, the president's party had sown deep distrust of government. They couldn't suddenly reverse course, even in an extreme crisis, and demand higher taxes for that very same distrusted government. Politically impossible.

What did the new president do? Blame everyone else. He accused China and the Europeans of unfair trade practices and currency manipulation. He blamed "illegal immigrants" for taking American jobs. He blamed the opposition party for . . . everything else.

The American economy was a shambles, with unemployment 12% and rising. Stock market value fell by a fourth. Whatever investment accounts Mike still held in the United States, their value already dropped by a third. Maybe more.

"Ah, Mike. Mike? You listening to me? I'm not here right now just to hear myself talk."

Realizing he'd drifted off, Mike refocused. "Sorry. Got a couple of things on my mind."

"Yeah, I'm sure you do." Edward didn't tolerate clients who ignored him. "So, if I have your attention," Edward continued, "why didn't you get all of your money to Canada earlier?"

Mike thought for a minute, and then slowly said, "We've already lost so much. I guess I still hope that maybe things would get better. Maybe disposing of all our U.S. money would . . ." He had to pause, breathing deeply, "would be admitting that things weren't going to get better. That we lost. You understand?"

Nodding, Edward said, "Yes, I understand. Most expatriates I've met feel something like that. They need to hold onto something from before."

After a moment, Mike tangentially asked "Should I gift money to my kids? Maybe that's a way to shelter some of it?"

"Your two sons in the states and your daughter in Ottawa. What's the latest with them?"

"Anna's still in Ottawa. Health care worker. She got out early on. Already got all her money out. Seems her doctorate in optometry put her citizenship paperwork on a fast track.

"Robert and Matt are still in the States. No change there. Both still working. Glad for that."

"Okay. Gifting money to them might complicate things for the feds. But you might put a target on them. You need to judge that risk. Maybe it's alright for Anna, but not your sons in the U.S.

"Another thing. Put your house in Rhode Island on the market. Take the first offer."

"The family won't like it."

Never blessed with patience, Edward rebuked his client.

"Time for a little reality. Your Department of Justice won't be leaving us a lot of time. Maybe it won't be sold in time, but you should try. If it does sell, you get the money and DOJ or whoever gets nothing."

"I'll talk to Debbie." Mike said.

Edward wasn't convinced. "You don't sound like, frankly, you will talk to her. Or your kids. Look, you must face facts. DOJ is coming for you. You've stuck your thumb in their eye. They see your media work as illegal under their new laws. They'll charge you both for not returning in January. So, there are things you have to do that you will not like.

"And about your sons. I don't think it'd be paranoid to assume DOJ or FBI, or somebody, is monitoring your communications with them. And from Anna to your sons. Probably be a good idea to stay off your cell phones. Use that military intelligence experience to put together a more secure means of communication."

"Look, I wasn't a spy in the Air Force. My experience was mostly in imagery analysis and targeting, some signal intelligence, which tells me, yes, they can surveil cell phone communication. I didn't do human intelligence. But maybe I heard of a few techniques I can use, in communicating with them."

By now, Mike felt a little cornered, a little alarmed, and more than a little irritated at his lawyer. "What's next, Edward?"

"How are you fixed financially right now?"

Mike ran through their accounts at Scotia Bank, and added they paid cash for the Joes Point house. No mortgage.

"Always had a CPA do our taxes for the U.S. and for Canada. Remember that Debbie's paid for her work at the clinic here. I think we could survive even without our pensions."

In truth, Mike knew he was more a worrier than a warrior. In a safety deposit box at Scotia Bank, he kept thousands in U.S. and Canadian cash, plus thousands more in gold and silver coins, as well as copies of all their financial documents. He kept a well-stocked pantry at the Saint Joes house. Both had well prepared rucksacks ready to grab and go if they had to. Paranoia is useful if properly managed.

"Right. Good. Look, I'm not asking because I worry about getting paid. In fact, I've discussed this with my law partner, James, up in Saint John. We, and several other lawyers, will be doing *pro bono* work for American refugees. At least for as long as we can. There's talk in Fredericton about the province paying us for the work, but I don't know if that will go through. Especially in this economy. The province is strapped for money.

"I need to know how you acquired your wealth. I need this because if they drop charges on you, I'll likely be one of your defense counsels. My guess is, they'll create a tax or financial complaint, assuming you haven't been involved in criminal activity in the states." Edward said that last part as a clumsy attempt to lighten the mood. It failed.

"Alright. Eddie." Mike knew Edward hated to be called that. "Sorry, Edward. Okay, during our military years, we banked almost all my pay and allowances and lived off Debbie's pay, allowances, and professional bonuses for being a doc. No outside work or home businesses. In 2003, we both retired from the military. Pensioned since then. Debbie eventually worked in the states as a civilian doc at a community health center.

"We kept living on one salary even when the kids went through college. Not eligible for financial aid. Even so during those years, we could still save and invest, but less.

"Now about me. I found work as an analyst with a large investment firm. I prepared briefs for the senior executives on events around the world, allowing them to judge threats and opportunities. Made a good salary, but boring work actually. Ended with them last fall. Almost a year ago, matter of fact. There's a backstory to that maybe I should explain."

Edward looked up from this notetaking, saying "Yes, please do."

"August, during the last presidential campaign, I put together an analysis of political violence in the U.S., and the possible fallout for the financial sector. Did it on my own initiative. Nothing unusual in the report. Many others were doing the same and arriving at the same conclusions. That is, political violence was possible, even likely. It was already happening. Hell, even Homeland Security of that time publicly acknowledged the same."

Mike paused for a moment, looked to floor, and said, "Turns out I was right."

Looking back up, directly at Edward, Mike continued. "Well, I guess the bosses didn't like what I said. Thought it was outside the scope of my work. Would make investors nervous. They buried the report. I was asked to resign."

"You're being vague, it seems to me, about why you were asked to resign. You said, 'I guess the bosses didn't like what I said.' Come on, Mike, I think there's more to your backstory."

Edward, you really know how to make someone feel uncomfortable. That's what Mike wanted to say out loud. But he didn't.

Mike explained his report singled out right wing political violence. Among other sources, his report cited a 2017 General Accounting Office study of terrorist incidents in the U.S. from September 11 to then.

"You know what? Far right extremists committed 73% of the attacks. Islamic inspired terrorism accounted for the other 27%, though they accounted for 41% of the deaths. No deaths were attributed to left wing extremists.

"In years following, other studies from other groups came to the same conclusion. DHS agreed. They singled out white supremacists as the biggest threat. Right wing extremist are responsible for most domestic terrorism.

"Let's remember that GAO study ended in 2017. Since then, we had Charlottesville, El Paso, the Tree of Life Synagogue. We had January 6th.

"So, with all that . . . well . . . I didn't get a full explanation from my boss. I think, likely, it was because the firm's president was sympathetic to the right wing. I know he gave money to them. He believed they were better for business. Better for Wall Street. Got to wonder if he still thinks that way."

Looking for some way to pivot the conversation away from an unpleasant experience, Mike offered Edward copies of all their financial statements.

"Yes. And a copy of that domestic terrorism report if you still have it." Mike nodded. Edward paused, and leaned back in his chair.

"So, you are telling me the money used to buy the house here, you paid as cash? And all of that was from savings and mutual funds, and you paid all taxes? We have to be careful because this might be an avenue DOJ would exploit."

Mike was growing a weary with the questions. "All those records about Joes Point are here. Don't forget the realty office is here in town, plus Scotia Bank would have records of the wire transfer and conversion to Canadian dollars."

"Besides, the American dollar back then bought 1.15 Canadian, before the election. Edward, understand that for thirty years we banked and invested anywhere from four to six thousand a month from our salaries and pensions. Do the math. And we kept our spending under control."

"I see. Sorry, Mike. I'm a little unnerved myself by this morning. I don't mean to doubt you. And I don't. But I need to know, to be prepared. Trying to anticipate the next move by the enemy."

"By the way, nice little speech this morning. Not great. Nice though. I think it went over well with the breakfast crowd. Good to see a Yank stand up for Canada."

"Thanks. No worries, Edward. I appreciate that." Mike allowed a smile to his face before Edward got back to business.

"Mike, get your records in order. Get your money out. Sell that house. Here's another reason why." Edward passed a news article from a Vancouver online newspaper about the IRS auditing political dissidents and rumors of the government trashing the credit history of opponents.

"No doubt when they can't find something, they will make up something. Unless we have a detailed picture of your financial history, it'll be difficult for Canada to shield you from that kind of charge."

Edward allowed that possibility to sink in before speaking again.

"There's something else, Mike."

Spies

Roy stayed long enough at the Saint Stephen border crossing station to see Webb and Williams drive away. *Good riddance,* he thought. *But they'll be back, for sure.*

Inside the border station, Roy changed into casual civilian clothes before switching from the RCMP vehicle to a car borrowed from one of the Border Services officers. Roy turned right on Milltown Boulevard, then left and continued until he reached a coffee shop about half a kilometer away from the border. He had an appointment with a Mr. Robert LeClerc.

As Roy pulled into the parking lot, he got a call from Edward Donohue, asking for the recording of the SunRise Café interview. Roy knew Edward socially. All Roy could tell Edward was that his superiors would have to agree. And they might refuse giving the recording to a lawyer who is not yet an actual defense counsel. Edward was not pleased.

That done, Roy walked into the café, spotted LeClerc at the counter, still dressed in the same jeans and blue Oxford shirt. Almost as tall as himself, thick black hair sprinkled with bits of grey, and a somewhat softer middle. LeClerc nodded toward Roy and motioned to him to have a seat next to him.

Robert LeClerc's job that day was to witness and document as many interviews as possible the agents had with Canadians or Americans. Roy knew beforehand of his covert activity, having contacted Roy two days before the HSC agents arrived.

LeClerc was an intelligence analyst with the Canadian Security Intelligence Service. A relatively new federal civilian agency, formed in 1984, CSIS combined the duties of foreign and domestic national security intelligence gathering, extending its operations around the globe. Indeed, it could even monitor Canadians who were overseas. Yet, it had no power to arrest. Should it uncover criminal activities, CSIS would bring in the RCMP.

In the times before, CSIS closely watched the activities of extremist groups and militias in the United States and Canada. White supremacists, neo-Nazis, and others of their ilk. Canada had its share of extremists. Unlike the states, Canada had a legal means to deal with them directly. Under Canada's *Anti-Terrorism Act of 2001*, once the evidence justifies the official designation of persons or groups as dangerous extremists, they are "listed." Canada can then freeze and seize their assets of any kind and prosecute persons or organizations that lend them support. Further recruitment in Canada becomes illegal. Often, American domestic terrorist groups crossed the border to recruit Canadians to their side. LeClerc could recite most of those listed from memory. Atom-waffen, Proud Boys, III Percenters, The Base, and on and on.

CSIS could do work that their American counterparts were not allowed to do. LeClerc didn't pretend to be a legal scholar, but it didn't take a Harvard law degree to see that the American failure to establish similar laws, even since 9/11, hamstrung their fight against extremism. LeClerc often voiced his astonishment that America still lacked even a legal definition of domestic terrorism.

Now the threat to Canada came from the United States government itself, with an emerging collaboration between its government and extremists. The president himself openly supported far right groups in Canada. Even protesting the listing by Canada of his more favorite militias.

For the past four months, LeClerc and a small team augmented the Halifax CSIS Atlantic Region's office in Fredericton. They focused entirely on the emerging threat to the south. The very idea the most serious foreign threat now came from Canada's formerly closest ally deeply disturbed and sickened LeClerc. Before joining CSIS ten years ago, LeClerc served in Canadian Forces Intelligence Branch, often working alongside Americans in NATO and Afghanistan. He counted as friends several currently serving American military officers. A deep sense of loss and betrayal ran through people like LeClerc.

In his most pessimistic moods, LeClerc imagined his Primary Reserve unit, the 3 Intelligence Company, in combat against his former colleagues.

In his most optimistic moods, which lately did not come often, he hoped those past friendships might prove key to stopping such a war.

"Good day, sir. Might I suggest we talk outside?" LeClerc nodded, leaving half a cup of coffee behind and a few loonies. Not wise to allow the patrons to overhear what was to be said.

Back in Roy's borrowed car, they watched LeClerc's video recording, then listened to Roy's audio recording. After checking each other's understanding of what happened, LeClerc made the first analysis.

"Roy, don't know for sure, but I've got a strong suspicion Williams and Webb had no real interest in interviewing anyone other than Whynot." LeClerc shook his head slightly, and then continued. "Interview. No. Not the right word. Threaten. That's a better description. Perhaps they believed threatening Whynot would deter other Americans. If HSC bothers to go after a minor leader, it sends the message they will go after anyone. The list of others, that was just camouflage, distraction."

29

Roy didn't respond at once, taking a minute to think about LeClerc's hunch.

"I have to say, Robert, I think you may be right. On the ride back to Saint Stephen, Williams and Webb hardly said a word. Didn't protest their visit being cut short. Not at all." Roy added, "There's another aspect of this morning I have to ask you about." Roy briefed LeClerc on his phone call with Edward Donohue and asked, "What are CSIS's intentions for your recording?"

LeClerc said, "At least Whynot and his lawyer are thinking ahead. As of now, CSIS is simply collecting intelligence. My team at Fredericton will analyze it, offer our initial assessment, then send it along up through our chain of command. Atlantic CSIS in Halifax. I don't have the authority to do anything other than send it along."

Roy concurred. "I'll be doing the same." Then added, "By the way, the café story is already making the rounds of Saint Andrews. Got a couple of texts from people there, including a constable who heard about it from others. What Mike said to those agents will be the local gossip, at least for a while.

"Have to admit I enjoyed what he said to them. Defending Canada and all. But those Americans are going to crucify him. By the way, have you heard of DHS or HSC or DOJ questioning any other expatriates?"

"Yes, we have. Forty cases in the last week. We're still getting all the details. Only a handful are civilians. Maybe most are U.S. military. Like the Whynots. Could be more if they contacted other Americans expatriates by phone or online. Don't know yet if others in Europe were contacted, but we're looking into that."

LeClerc left part of his analysis unsaid. *They're intelligence gathering, no doubt. But are they also getting targeting data?*

LeClerc then wondered, *it would be interesting if all this somehow got out on social media. Would it spoil their plans?*

"Well, I guess we both have work to do. Have to get back to Fredericton. Thanks Roy."

Home Again, Home Again

About midmorning, Williams and Webb got back to the Coast Guard station in Eastport, Maine. On the drive back, Williams ripped Webb apart for grabbing Whynot in the café. Webb kept largely silent in response. After twenty years in the Army, he learned how to handle getting chewed out. Keep your mouth shut, except when giving a specific answer to a specific question. Admit fault, even when it wasn't yours, and promise not to repeat the same mistake.

Getting out of their car, Williams told Webb he didn't need him to write the report to HSC about their meeting with Whynot. Hired during the rushed expansion of CBP and HSC, Webb couldn't write worth a damn anyway, in Williams's opinion. Webb turned toward his trailer office.

Report done, copy printed for the files, and emailed to his HSC superiors, Williams could now hope for a quieter day.

What they would do with the report on Mr. Whynot, Williams wasn't sure. All he knew, or at least thought he knew, was HSC was building dossiers on types like Whynot.

He almost, but only almost, felt sorry for the Whynots. It was going to be hard on them.

Later that evening, HSC sent orders through the secure email, "eyes only" for Williams.

As he read the email, all he could think was, yes, gonna be hard on them.

The View Across

If I could get those trees cut down near the golf course, we'd have a nicer, wider, view of the summer sun setting over Maine. The United States. 'Course, that's not my land, with the trees. Still, we've got good views across the water as is. Settle for that. Mike remembered that one reason they bought this place was the dreamed of summer and fall evenings looking out southerly over St. Croix River and Navy Island. They treasured their summer meals in their large, screened-in porch overlooking the water.

It was half past five now. While in town, Mike finished recording the podcast and taping the evening local access TV show. Nothing to do now but get the thawed steaks out of the 'fridge and fire up the grill. Debbie would be home by six. He planned a nice meal of steak, potatoes and onions, a bottle of red wine, and a couple of corn on the cob. All locally sourced. A CBC news report from three days ago of increasing food shortages back home came back to Mike. *I hope my kids are alright,* Mike thought, before quickly moving on to the task at hand.

Debbie knew this was coming. Only now it's here. It's real. Over dinner, Mike feared a different kind of darkness would descend while the sun was still shining.

31

Mike busied himself at the grill as Debbie came in the door. Aluminum foil packets of sliced potatoes and onions were already cooking. Water in the corn pot was near boiling. In a couple of minutes, he could put on the steaks that had been marinating all day. Debbie came to him, kissed him on the cheek and cheerily asked how his day was. All Mike could do was answer with a mumbled "fine." He was distracted, disinterested, focused elsewhere.

Debbie continued the largely one-sided exchange, reviewing some of the day's cases at the clinic and the usual around town gossip. Mike half listened as he threw the steaks on the grill.

However dark his mood, Mike always managed a little prayer of gratitude to whatever gods there be for Debbie's clinic work. The province was quite happy to grant Debbie a medical license to practice. They needed help in dealing with the sudden influx of hundreds of American expatriates in Saint Andrews. She partnered with a primary care physician practicing in the area. Emergency medical care could be treated by the Charlotte Country Hospital in Saint Stephen.

Not that all was well with her clinic. Two months ago, by executive order, the new U.S. administration banned public and private U.S. medical insurance companies from reimbursing foreign medical facilities for the care of Americans known to have fled the United States. Its purpose wasn't disguised in the slightest. The new president wanted to retaliate against the dissident expatriates and their hosts.

No Canadian province hosting the American refugees was getting a dollar, making the refugees dependent on the continued largess of the Canadian taxpayer. *Perhaps Williams is right,* thought Mike. *How long would this last?*

It's a good thing experience grants primary care physicians a kind of skill set in psychiatric care. Depression and anxiety among the expats dominated Debbie's professional world. The Americans in Saint Andrews soon found refuge came with a price. An often-unbearable price of separation from the familiar and family. Among those who remained, the hurt, the doubt, the guilt, were everyday companions.

Mike and Debbie knew that agony well.

Their three adult children were scattered across the two countries. The youngest, Anna, left the U.S. for Canada months ago with no intention of going back. They had visited with her in Ottawa several times, doing their best to focus on her and not their fears for her brothers. It didn't always work. An optometrist, she secured employment in the Canadian health care system with the help of her Canadian classmates from the New England

College of Optometry of Boston. Her health care provider status put her Canadian citizenship application at the top of the pile. Mike felt confident about her future. That is, as confident as he felt about anything these days.

Their middle child, Matt, was single and an engineer in California. He was a source of pride and worry. A smart and dedicated mechanical engineer in the aerospace industry, he worked in the Bay Area of San Francisco. Matt had served as a surface warfare officer aboard a U.S. Navy destroyer. These days he held the rank of lieutenant in the U.S. Naval Selected Reserve, drilling every month and two weeks a year with a Naval Mobile Construction Battalion out of Port Hueneme. He spurned his father's advice to resign. Matt wanted to stay in the Reserves as a plan B if the economy tanked further and his civilian job disappeared. Mike still worried. *What if this president starts a war? What if Matt is recalled to active duty?*

Robert was the oldest. A high school science teacher, he married Christine, another high school science teacher. If Mike and Debbie worried about Matt, their fears for Robert and Christine were exponentially greater for no other reason than Eva, their beautiful three-year-old granddaughter.

We cannot see our sons and they cannot see us, thought Mike. He had long ago tallied the risks. If the kids tried to get to Canada, they faced arrest at the border and the likely end of their careers. Matt could even be court martialed. These things were happening.

Mike knew that he made matters worse by defying the agents. *We'd face arrest back in the U.S. It was a simple as that. What happens to our kids, our granddaughter, if we, I, continue to resist? What would the government do to them to get at us? Could we get them out? Would they want to get out?*

People went the other way too. Many of the Saint Andrews expatriates returned to the states.

Some who left had evolved into supporters of the new regime. A couple of months ago, during a party at their home for expats, Mike and Debbie met such a man. While working on his second martini, he loudly proclaimed his decision to go back. Of the new president, he'd said, "He's got no choice. If his people gotta kill some protestors, so be it. I'm okay with that. We gotta have law and order."

Mike had countered, saying, "Yeah, sure, that president wants law and order, but without the rule of law. He just wants order."

The two-martini guy wouldn't let it go. Emboldened by his own first martini, Mike had decided on the better course of action to set the man right.

He'd punched the jerk in the face and thrown him out on the lawn. Debbie had objected, saying, "Christ! Why hit the guy, Mike?"

"To save you the trouble of doing it yourself."

The next wave of returnees fell into another category. They claimed hatred for the new regime, but couldn't cope with family separation, or decided they could not make a new life for themselves in Canada. Understandable and worthy of sympathy, Mike felt. The Expat Committee made countless attempts to connect by email, snail mail, and cell phone with these last returnees. They tried known relatives. Despite all that, it was rare to learn what happened to them. And even then, any news was vague. There were only rumors, none of which ended well.

For some, their grief proved too much. In the past two months, four of Debbie's patients had committed suicide. Like Mike and Debbie, they all had children back in the States.

Mike shook himself back to the present and started setting out dinner. The meal was quite good, the view spectacular, but the conversation muted. Debbie, of course, knew something was wrong. She made the opening move.

"Talked to a local this afternoon at lunch. Don't remember his name, but he said something that was, well, odd."

"Really, what's that?" Mike found it difficult to look her in the eyes.

"This guy came up to our table, and he said, 'Hey, your husband really stood up for us this morning. At the SunRise. Tell him we appreciate it.' Didn't understand what he meant. Then others at the lunch counter said the same thing."

"Mike, you have any idea what that Canadian was talking about?"

Mike took a small bite of steak and chewed for half a minute before answering. "Yes, I do have an idea." Mike then pleaded, "But before I go into all that, let's finish dinner."

For the next ten or so minutes, it seemed like ages, they ate silently before pushing aside their plates. Cleanup could wait.

Mike refilled their wine glasses, then motioned to leave the dinner table for the two Adirondack chairs on the deck. "There's a lot to explain." He described every detail of the morning at the SunRise and his meeting with the solicitor.

Debbie patiently took it all in. Once Mike seemed to finish, she asked, "So, you spoke for me to the agents and Edward?"

Trouble coming? Mike tensed somewhat, but Debbie answered the question for him. "It's all right, Mike. We talked about all this before. And yes, I will not return. Not to this United States."

Debbie wasn't one to go wobbly. But Mike had to be sure. "Okay, tomorrow I'll make the financial moves that Edward suggested. But about the house. Do you agree we should sell our house back home?"

Three generations of her family had made the house central to their lives. A summer cottage built after the war that eventually grew into a year-round home, with a property lot that extended right to the beach. A beautiful view of Hog Island in Narragansett Bay, framed at night by the lights of the Mount Hope Bridge, a classic suspension bridge. Treasured memories of countless family gatherings. Thanksgiving, Christmas, and New Year's, of course. But also, Father's Day and the Fourth of July, watching fireworks light up the horizon up and down Narragansett Bay.

Debbie had accepted this possibility since they decided to stay in Canada. "Yes, sell it. Right away. It's no use to us now. I'd rather burn it to the ground before those fascists take it."

Her decision's coldness almost startled Mike. *Time for some more news.*

"There's one more thing that Edward said that you need to hear.

"That agent Williams said something that got to the heart of the matter. He predicted that Canadians would tire of supporting American refugees. He, Williams, used that term deliberately, refugees. So did Edward." Few expatriates accepted that word, refugees.

Mike went on. "Canada's in a tough financial situation. The border's closed. Trade stifled. New tariffs on Canadian manufactured goods and commodities like lumber and oil. And we're expensive to protect. People will start asking, why is our money being spent on people who aren't from Canada. Have them go back and fix their own damn country.

"And Edward speculated that as that feeling grows, Canadians might grow . . . apprehensive about any American's dissident activities in Canada. Like my broadcasts. Could they put innocent Canadians in harm's way? And yes, Edward has heard this from people in town."

Mike was a little surprised that he, and Debbie, had drained the wine glasses while he was talking. He got up to get the bottle, refilled the glasses, and continued while pacing near the screens.

"Here's a funny thing, Deb. Canadians I know heard about the SunRise. Then other people said they heard about it. People I don't know. I guess about a dozen or so. They all offered their support, for what it's worth. Don't know how long that'll last."

"Hail the conquering hero," Debbie said as she sipped more wine. She wasn't smiling.

Mike sat back down and for a few minutes, they looked silently across the waters. On the horizon to the east, the sun was setting over the Maine shoreline. On this clear night, he could see the lights coming on along the shoreline. Home. It used to be comforting to know that.

Debbie broke the silence, reached over to hold Mike's hand, and said something that would change their lives forever.

"Mike, get our boys out. Get our daughter-in-law and our granddaughter out. Get them here. Find a way."

Webb

While Mike and Debbie sat on their porch, Webb was likewise contemplating his future. Standing outside his trailer, off-duty and having a stress smoke, Webb ran over in his mind what happened at the SunRise. He tried to square how he saw the confrontation with Whynot with what Williams told him on the way back here. *Nothing new in getting chewed out. Twenty years in the Army, it's gonna happen more than once. And I've done my share of chewing out others. Okay, maybe I went too far by grabbing Whynot's hand. But we needed to get Whynot's attention.*

Webb's dormant resentments came forth, once again. *Typical of guys like Williams. Think they're so well educated. They're ignorant about handling people, especially criminal types. I would've gotten Whynot to talk. HSC made a big mistake when they put me as second fiddle. I should be commanding, not that lawyer Williams whose got zero cop experience. But lawyers like lawyers. Passed me over. My twenty years as an MP counted for nothing.*

Then Webb asked himself the essential question. *What do I do now?*

No answer came to mind. Even after a second cigarette.

Frustrated, Webb went back inside to hit his rack for a little light reading. But Williams called him over. "Looks like we have an operation to plan, Webb. See me at 0800. I'll explain it then. Do not tell anyone else. Is that clear?"

"Yes, sir." *Maybe that's a second chance,* thought Webb.

The SunRise Broadcast: I Fight!

The challenge was how to give these dispirited Americans a real sense of community. A community with a purpose greater than mere survival. At the same time, the Americans needed to integrate themselves into Canadian life. Getting there, Mike knew, meant finding leaders from within their community.

Forming the Expat Committee was only a first step. The local government encouraged it because they honestly needed help in dealing with hundreds of unexpected permanent residents. Being already known to some of the locals from times before and a property owner, Mike was politely "volunteered" by the municipal councillors and the mayor. Alongside Mike, four other Americans formed the committee, along with two nonvoting Canadians who served as advisors.

Communication was the next step. Early on, the Committee held town hall meetings twice a month, on alternating Tuesday evenings at the local high school. A subcommittee started writing a bimonthly newsletter. Collecting cell numbers from the expatriates enabled, if necessary, emergency communication. But Mike knew more was needed.

They needed a forum, a regularly scheduled media outlet that would share news of the day and practical advice for the expatriates. The kind of local news anyone would find familiar.

And there it was. Casually flipping through the cable TV channels, Mike came across a local access station, CHCO-TV, of Saint Andrews. It transmits on low power, focusing its range only over Charlotte County. It already offered local news for the county, as well as coverage of local events, town council meetings, school news and local sports.

Mike pleaded with the station to set aside time for the American expatriate community. It wasn't easy to persuade them. They felt American issues were already being covered well enough. But with the help of Edward and others, Mike got his hour. Every Thursday evening from five to six. The *Saint Andrews American Community Hour*. Not the catchiest of titles, but to Mike it worked well enough.

As part of the deal, the station "volunteered" Mike to be the show's host. In his first taping, Mike hadn't been that nervous since the first time he briefed a general officer in the Air Force. Still, Mike got better with experience, enough so he didn't feel the need to throw up on TV. Later, taking advice from a twentysomething, Mike got the show broadcasted online and as a podcast.

Keep to local news. Focus on practical information for the expatriates. That was the guidance provided by the ExPat Committee and the TV station. Soon the show hosted special guests who offered an increasingly robust menu of advisories, such as medical issues, immigration, finances, Canadian culture, and so on.

The show did include news from the United States. In the last 15 minutes, Mike usually led a round table discussion with two or three other community members. News stories from reputable sources, mingled with the panel's assessment and opinions. Though critical of the new administration, they strictly stayed within the rules, guiding their audience toward legal avenues of dissent. Always careful not to suggest violence or illegal actions against the new government. Always logical and conventional. And boring. Mike usually ended the hour announcing any new arrivals from across the border, if any.

Not this time.

"Well, folks, that about does it for community news. But I've got time left. And I've got something to share. Something that happened this morning, to me in fact. And I think it's important."

"Two agents from the U.S. Homeland Security Corps interrupted my breakfast at the SunRise Café. They wanted to know about me, this program, and something about many of you. They threatened . . ."

Mike went over the SunRise Café incident in detail.

"So, those are the facts. Before I forget, I want to thank RCMP Sergeant Roy Wilkins for his actions, protecting the rights of our community. I hope he doesn't mind my saying so."

"To my fellow Americans, if you have been contacted by agents of the U.S. government by any means, mail, email, phone, or in person, please, please, let the ExPat Committee know right away. If any of your family back in FUSA have been contacted, let us know."

"We've lost so much in this battle for democracy. Every one of you must make your own decision about how we go forward. I have made mine. I am done making excuses. I am done hoping that things will get better on their own. I will not wait for someone else to act. I am done retreating. Today, I fight! Tomorrow, I fight!"

"Stay peaceful. Good night."

Mike allowed himself an immediate analysis. *Well, that'll piss 'em off. I guess that indictment will be coming soon.*

In town, a solicitor named Edward almost threw a drink at his TV.

REFUGE

Listening Post

Williams had one ironclad appointment for himself each week since arriving in Eastport. Sit down, at 1700, every Thursday, and listen to Whynot's American community news program. HSC informed him of the broadcast and told him listen to it to collect intelligence on Whynot's and the Expat Committee's activities.

This evening's show, the first after the SunRise Café, did not disappoint. Williams sent a digital recording of the show along with his usual report to HSC Regional in Boston.

I fight. Well, Whynot, that indictment just got a little closer, Williams sensed.

Saturday Over the St. Croix

A beautiful late afternoon weekend day on the deck. Comfortably seated in padded Adirondack chairs, with beers in hand, Mike and Debbie settled in for a little day drinking. And thinking.

As he was taking his first swig, to his left Mike noticed George was on the deck of his own house. He gave George a little wave. Never a shy guy, George waved back and started to trot over.

"Hey, Mike! Hi Debbie!" said George as he bounded up on their deck and through the door to the screened-in porch. With outstretched hand, George said, "Hey, thanks for mowing my lawn. You really didn't have to, but thanks."

Mike returned the handshake. "No problem. Was mowing mine, and it only took a little while on the tractor to do yours."

"Yeah, still, nice to do that. Got a little long. Been busy at work. A couple extra shifts."

"Well, truth be told, I couldn't stand it any longer. Living next to a ratty house like yours." George let out a characteristic loud laugh. In truth, George kept his house immaculate. White with a dark green trim. Stunning. Three generations of his family had lived in the house, a fine filigreed old farmhouse.

"Well, have one of these and sit awhile." Mike reached into the cooler and handed George a beer.

"Wow, Sleeman! I see you've given up on those watery Yank beers."

"As it so happens, I've had Sleeman before, you just haven't seen me. Got to like it while in Germany. Knew a Canadian Air Force doc over at Geilenkirchen. He kept a whole refrigerator filled with nothing but Sleeman."

"Another Canadian stereotype fulfilled," George said and then asked, "Mind if I call Cheryl over for a beer? I'd catch hell if I didn't."

"That would be great." Debbie suggested they could do more than swap a beer or two. "How 'bout this? It's four thirty now. She'll come over. We have a few beers. Then we'll call out for pizza. We had no plans for dinner anyway."

"I'm up for that! I'll just text her. Do you mind if the boy comes over too?" Their boy, James, was George and Cheryl's only child. "But let's wait until Cheryl gets here to be sure." With a wide smile, George continued, "You know, she's in charge of things like that."

George got an immediate reply from Cheryl. She'd be over straight away. Then Debbie said, "Beautiful evening. Gonna be a great sunset I bet. Just enough clouds. But I hear the nice weather won't last. How long before the cold weather sets in?"

"Tomorrow."

Mike and Debbie both laughed. "See Mike," said Debbie, "I told you we shoulda spent some wintertime up here before buying."

Now it was Mike's turn. "Funny guy. Now, you Canadians always brag how tough you are when it comes to your winters. I gotta ask you, why is it every time Debbie and I took a Caribbean cruise in January or February, lots and lots of the passengers are Canadians. And how about all those snowbirds in Arizona?"

"Okay, you got us there. Touché. But by February, you'll want a tropical cruise too. I guarantee it." George stopped himself from saying almost all those snowbirds aren't going to Arizona anymore.

"Yeah, you're probably right. Think I'll start booking that trip to Belize now," said Debbie, as she looked at Cheryl and James coming over. Accompanying them was their dog, a black Labrador retriever. "I think I'll get something for James to drink. Doubt he wants a beer."

"Looks like the dog is on her way too. Hope you don't mind."

"Not a problem, George." Ordinarily, Mike wasn't terribly fond of dogs. Or maybe it was dog owners. Especially the little yippy dogs. But a Lab, well, Mike believed there wasn't a finer, friendlier breed around.

George and Cheryl named the dog, of all things, Spot, even though she was uniformly black. Cheryl said it was a chance to resurrect a once honored dog name, and George just liked to be contrary.

Mike and Debbie got up to greet Cheryl with a handshake and James with a high five. And a good rub for Spot. James, four years old, got his juice box. Cheryl got a beer, and the friends settled in for light conversation.

On the second round, everyone got quiet. Looking out across the river to the edge of Maine, Mike and George remarked on a couple of fishing boats headed back into Saint Andrews. Not much appeared to be happening on the

American side. Then again, there wasn't much there anyway except a few waterside homes. By sunset, the lights would appear. The faint light from Eastport would become visible near the horizon, about eleven miles south of Joes Point.

George broke the silence, leaning his head over to Mike while still looking at the far shore, and asked the question he wanted to ask for a long time.

"Mike, we've talked around the edges, so to speak, about what happened over there," pointing to the Maine shoreline. "What happened to the United States?"

George talked about Mike's homeland as if in the past tense. True enough. For George, and many of his countrymen, that America was gone. George's friends and family spoke of anger, betrayal, bewilderment. So many had American friends. American family. But most of all, to George it was like they were mourning a death of a loved one.

It took a while for Mike to say anything. "I don't know. I mean, I'm not sure. I could talk all night long about what happened. What I think happened. And I think I'd only get it half right."

George took a couple of sips in silence, regretting his question. *Christ, I embarrassed him.*

"Sorry. I shouldn't have asked. I know it's hard on you. All you Americans."

Mike took a long sip of his beer and then looked directly at George. "It's alright. It's alright, George. Thanks. Maybe another time. Not now. When we have time, I can try to explain how I feel, how I think it happened." But Mike kept talking.

"I've tried to put it all together. We've been here since January. I still don't think I have it . . . well understood. How much is factual history? How much is my own bias? Then I spent a whole lot of time distracting myself to keep from thinking about it. Might explain why I spent so much time on that MG.

"What I can say is thank you. Thanks to you and Cheryl, and Roy and Claude, and all the others who helped us. Welcomed us. Not just for Deb and me, but for all the Americans." Mike slowly drew a deep breath and said, "We broke our own society. Our own politics. We didn't control our emotions and because of that . . . because of our mistakes. Now we're causing your people a whole lot of trouble. Shame on us." Looking down, Mike said, "I am sorry."

George nodded, took a long look at Mike and tried to offer his friend a way out of a conversation he should never had started. "I don't know why you're saying 'sorry.' Nothing for you to be sorry about."

"Oh, yeah, I liked what you said at the SunRise last Wednesday. About Canada. Thanks. Made me, made us, feel better. The story has gotten around.

Lots of people, Canadians, heard your Thursday show. You may not know it, but right now you're the most popular Yank in Saint Andrews. Let's get pizza for a local hero."

The evening could've been nothing more than a fun time with friends. It certainly was that, but George's simple question lingered with Mike. *What happened?* Two words that would come back to Mike again and again, racing through his mind. *What happened?*

Quiet of the Evening

After the pizza and the beers, and after George, Cheryl, James, and Spot went back to home, Mike and Debbie sat by themselves in the living room. Mike was mostly concerned with how many trips to the bathroom were in store for him that night. Debbie had something else in mind.

"I heard your broadcast." Mike saw Debbie had that serious look on her face. *Here it comes.*

"What you say on air affects both of us. Don't misunderstand me. I support your work. I want you to keep doing it. Our community needs a leader like you. But could you let me in on what you meant by '*today, I fight*'? I mean. Goddammit! You didn't mention it at all Wednesday night when we talked."

"You're right. I should have. I'm sorry." Mike took a breath and then asked, "When did you hear the broadcast?"

"Thursday evening, like everyone else. It's taken me time to, well, think it over."

"And, so, what do you think?"

"Why say that? *I fight*. You must've known it'll only make things worse."

Mike looked away to the view out the picture window. He paused, and said, "I don't know why I said that. It just came out." Mike knew he sounded like a fool.

"It just . . . came out." Debbie, now clearly angry, demanded, "Bullshit! You could've edited it out. It's on tape, for God's sake. Why didn't you do at least that? Don't give me that 'it just came out' shit! You're not a child, you know!"

"I thought about it, editing it out, but no. I couldn't." Mike's embarrassment at being questioned suddenly turned to anger. Not at Debbie. "Those agents got me mad. At them. And at myself. Angry for always giving in, always excusing, always trying to justify why I decided to stay here, safe and sound, while others back home face very real risks. If we want our democracy, our way of life back, well, we must fight. We have to speak out, loudly. All the time. Every day."

Now softer, Debbie said, "I stayed here too, you know."

"And how do you feel about staying here, now?" Mike asked her, immediately realizing there was harshness in his voice.

Debbie got up from the sofa and walked to the kitchen, intent on finding an open wine bottle in the fridge. There being none open, she delayed answering. "I'd like a drink before I say." From the kitchen she went downstairs, retrieved a bottle of cold chardonnay from a basement refrigerator, returned to the sofa and poured two glasses, her thoughts collected.

"Mike, we're staying. Hell, or high water. Even so, since it began, I had to believe . . . things will get better. Somehow. Don't know how I could stay sane if I didn't believe that. But even if things got back to something like normal, we have to accept the fact that tens of millions of Americans enthusiastically support the guy! Remember all those flags hanging outside all those homes? They want him. Not democracy. Throw that guy out of office and those people will still be there, getting ready for the next round.

"For now, I've got my clinic work to keep me busy and not think so much about what could happen. Feel like I'm doing something important.

"Do what you think is right. But I need something from you, from here on out."

"Which is?"

"Don't blindside me again. Be honest with me. Hold nothing back about what you're doing. What you're planning." Then came a reminder, not so friendly. "And you are going to get our boys out, right?"

"I will. I'll find a way to get them out. But I need you to think about this. What if they want to stay in the U.S.?"

"Then . . . then I guess we'll have to live with that, somehow. But for now, give them the option."

"I said I will." Mike couldn't control his tone of irritation.

"Well, that's good because what you said at the café and your 'I fight' broadcast means they'll probably catch hell from DOJ. They'll go after them to get to us. So, you'd better get working on that and quickly."

"One more thing. I promised you'd know everything. The Expat Committee called me. We're meeting Monday night. They want me to explain the broadcast."

CHAPTER TWO

THE SUMMER PAST

The New Station Commander

That September morning, Lieutenant Miles sat as his desk at Coast Guard Station Eastport, Maine. Looking out the window over a collection of old, green algae-streaked trailers in the station's parking lot, he wondered again, *how the Christ did I wind up here?*

Lt. Douglas Miles. U.S. Coast Guard Academy graduate. Bachelor of science degree in mechanical engineering. First assignment at sea as an engineering officer of the National Security Cutter USCGC *Munro*. While assigned, also qualified as deck watch officer. Top marks gained him an assignment as executive officer aboard the USCGC *Glen Harris*, one of the six Sentinel-class patrol cutters stationed in Bahrain, as part of Patrol Forces Southwest Asia. Again, top marks.

With a new assignment due sometime in June, Lt. Miles hoped for another ship.

He got the word in May. Report no later than 15 June to First District headquarters for briefing on assignment as commanding officer, United

States Coast Guard Station Eastport. He was astonished and more than a little angry. *Why send a lieutenant to command a smallish, small boat station? And where the hell is Eastport?*

The answer to the first question would have to wait until he got to Boston. Google answered the second question. Home to approximately 1,400 Mainers, Eastport is the easternmost city in the United States. Nature blessed it with one of the deepest natural harbors along the East Coast, offering significant opportunities for maritime shipping from Europe. Yet, man did not bless it with rail and road infrastructure essential for Eastport to exploit that blessing. Even before the current troubles, Eastport had a chronically struggling economy marked by negative job growth and high unemployment with a slowly declining population.

At same time, Eastport is picturesque in the way tourists imagine Maine to be. Quiet, safe, and overlooked. Tourists like towns that are trapped in an imagined past. These days, it seemed doubtful the tourists would come.

Coast Guard history in Eastport goes all the way back to Revenue Cutter Service days, the agency preceding the Coast Guard. One fact, useless to the young officer, but amusing. A captain with the Revenue Cutter Service had a son born in Eastport, one Harold "Harry" G. Hamlet who would rise to be a commandant of the United States Coast Guard in the 1930s. There's a very small park dedicated to Hamlet on the grounds of the station.

With this atypical assignment, the Coast Guard knew they had some explaining to do. In the case of Miles, and another up-and-coming lieutenant slated to command Station Burlington on Lake Champlain, the explaining would fall to the admiral commanding the First Coast Guard District.

Driving into Boston over the Tobin Bridge, Miles could see a 270-foot Medium Endurance Cutter Coast prominently framed against Coast Guard Base Boston at the city's North End. Its white hull and superstructure stood out against the backdrop of old brick buildings and the downtown's skyscrapers. One might assume First District headquarters was there. A natural fit to the Base's ecosystem. And one would be wrong.

First District headquarters shoehorned itself into a bland seven-story federal government building off the Atlantic Avenue waterfront, just on the northside of the distinctive and defunct Northern Avenue swing bridge.

So, it was here that Miles and one Lt. Tosha Jackson presented themselves for a private meeting with the admiral, both in impeccable Service Dress Blue uniform.

The admiral's aide greeted them in the waiting room and advised them what the admiral was going to tell them is considered classified. That was unusual enough to get their attention.

The admiral sat at a desk that served previous district commanders. Uniform of the Day at district was the Coast Guard working uniform, classified as Operational Dress Uniform. Military style blouse and pants, in the service's trademarked blue color. Worn untucked, complete with black boots and ball cap, the ODU was a welcome departure from the old "Bender's Blues" uniform that originated decades before. The admiral greeted the two lieutenants somewhat curtly before inviting them to sit in the two chairs in front of the desk.

The admiral began by acknowledging that a chief petty officer typically commanded these small boat stations. Highly unusual to assign lieutenants to command them, but critically important now, in the opinion of the commandant. She said the commandant personally selected them based on their excellent service records and operational experience. And frankly, that they became available at the right time.

Their tour would be a minimum of one year, possibly longer based on the needs of the service. To allay concern over their careers, they would be given their choice of assignment following this duty. In addition, the commandant would place in their service records an official letter acknowledging their special service.

"Now, as to why the Coast Guard is doing this. Again, this must not be discussed with anyone.

"At both these stations, DHS will deploy a special Homeland Security Corps unit within the next few weeks. We learned of this only one month ago.

"We're not sure what their specific mission is. DHS and HSC aren't saying much. We assess it is border security and immigration, given the stations at Eastport and Burlington are near the U.S.-Canadian border."

The admiral betrayed some frustration with the situation. "We're out of the loop, frankly. We don't know how many people are in these units, how they'll be billeted, or equipped. We don't even know if we're supposed to feed them!

"All that aside, the Secretary of Homeland Security gave the order, and the commandant and the Coast Guard will comply to the best of our ability. The commandant thought it prudent to put commissioned officers there as a kind of liaison with HSC. Wouldn't be fair to leave a chief petty officer alone to deal with this . . . novel situation. Hence, you two lieutenants.

"You should know we don't have any written agreement, a memorandum of understanding, with HSC. Nevertheless, when dealing with them, make sure they damn well understand you are the Station Commanding Officer and they are a tenant command. If they need something from the Coast Guard, demand they go through you. Only you.

"Your primary responsibility. Observe and learn about the HSC unit. We need eyes on these HSC guys. Anything and everything. You find a way. Within the boundaries of law and ethics, of course. See that they don't do anything that will harm the Coast Guard's reputation, our operations, or our people."

The admiral ended by saying the lieutenants will supply daily situation reports to the sector commander and herself.

"Any questions? Please, you deserve to know as much as I know. Well, within reason of course."

An uncomfortable moment passed. Miles spoke first.

"Admiral, have the current officers-in-charge, the chiefs, been informed and will they be transferred out?

"Mr. Miles, glad you asked. Informing the chiefs falls to the CO of Sector Northern New England, Captain David Llewellyn, and his Executive Officer, Commander Mary Gonsalves. They already know the full story and will accompany you to the station. Captain Llewellyn will go with you, Mr. Miles, to Eastport. The captain served alongside the senior chief at Eastport a couple of times before. He wanted to be the one to let the senior chief know. The captain wanted to go to Burlington too, but it would take too much time. So, Lieutenant Jackson, the sector XO will go with you.

"They will be informed only once you arrive at the stations. And yes, that's an awful way to do this, but I agree with the commandant that the fewer people involved, the better. Compartmentalize it. Once I am told the chiefs have been informed, I will call them to reassure them this move is not a negative reflection upon their service.

"And no, the chiefs will not transfer out. We thought it best to have a hand around familiar with the work and area of responsibility. My advice. Let the chiefs carry on with the station as they have. Shouldn't be a problem. Both have excellent records. Officially, their service records will continue to show them as officer-in-charge."

Now it was Lieutenant Jackson's turn. "Thank you, Admiral. When do we leave?"

"In three days. You will assume command in five days. Report first to the sector commander at Base Portland. No need for a ceremony at the stations. If that's all, you'd best get packing. My aide will help you with all the logistics.

"If there are no more questions, it leaves me to say, thank you. Again, I realize this is not what either of you had in mind.

"Lieutenant Miles, stay a moment. Lieutenant Jackson, pleasure to meet you." The admiral rose and shook hands with Jackson. "Dismissed. Oh, and please close the door behind you, thank you." As Jackson walked out, she smiled at Miles.

With the admiral's office door closed, Miles, now standing, turned to the admiral and said, "Admiral, request permission to speak off the record."

"Granted!" It was a signal between the two to drop the military formalities. "Doug, so glad to see you!" The admiral was about to leap out of her chair but stopped upon seeing Miles's serious expression. "Ah, I think I know what you're thinking. That I had something to do with this assignment. Am I right?"

"Yeah, just wondering."

"No, absolutely not. I didn't know until two days ago. Purely chance, and your fine record, that you got the job. Guess I should be proud of you." The admiral paused for a moment to give Miles the chance to reply. When he didn't, she continued along a different tac. "By the way, do you know Lieutenant Jackson?"

"Yes. She's a classmate from the academy. Very, very smart. Tough. Similar career to mine, so far. Same ambition. Command. She'll be good at whatever job you give her."

"Good to hear. So, don't suppose you have time for dinner tonight. Come over to my place."

"Depends on what your aide will say about getting to Eastport, but yeah. I'd like that. Right now, I gotta to start packing. Not that I have much to pack. I'll give you a call." With that, Doug smiled and leaned down to kiss his mom on her cheek.

Dinner with Mom

The admiral's, or Cynthia Miles', or Mom's apartment was in the seaport district of Boston, one block inland from Seaport Boulevard. She told Doug it was a perfect location. Not too far from Boston's attractions, but close enough to First District headquarters that she could get to the district operations center in fifteen or twenty minutes from the phone call. Faster if Coast Guard Intelligence or the Boston Police Department were driving. So far, she told Doug, that thankfully hadn't happened.

It was a fine meal of pork chops and rice with tomato and onions, one of Doug's favorites. Paired with a nice cabernet. Of course, shop talk peppered the meal. The meal finished, clean up done, and the conversation turned more serious.

Cynthia first wanted a moment to take pride in her son. "Engineering officer and qualified as deck watch officer on the *Munro*. Then XO on the *Glen Harris* out of Bahrain. Not bad, Doug. Not bad at all. Before you go up to Maine, I want to tell you how proud I am of you. You've done very well. By the way, that's Mom talking. Not the district commander."

"I had a good role model." Doug said.

"Yes, you did. And he'd be very proud of you." Doug's father and Cynthia's husband, Lt. Cmdr. Paul Miles, died in a car accident when Doug was in high school.

"Yes. Dad. But I was also thinking of you."

Cynthia took a moment to remember her husband, smiled, then went on.

"Doug, while you were in the gulf, did you follow what was going on back here. I mean with the election and the, ah, problems?"

"Yeah, we could follow the news. Some did. I tried not to. You know all the paperwork an exec must do, even on the *Glen Harris*. Tried not to let the news distract me. Didn't want anything I said to spark any worries among the crew.

"Besides, we were operating in a potential combat zone. I couldn't let myself or the crew lose focus. Maintenance, training, navigation, intelligence. That's what I concentrated on. The skipper felt the same way."

"I understand. That's how a professional military officer is supposed to act. Stay apolitical outwardly. Keep your politics to yourself. Focus on the mission."

"I hope to stay that way. But you're asking me this, why?"

Cynthia reached for the bottle of cabernet to top off her glass. She offered to fill Doug's glass, but he demurred.

"While your answer is admirable, I personally don't find it credible."

Doug was taken aback. "Why not?"

"Because it doesn't seem credible that you, anyone, could've walled themselves off from the news. I believe you when you say it wasn't discussed on duty. But you must have internalized some of it. Jesus. Riots. Militias shooting people in the streets. The constant extreme rhetoric. The new laws. Those images of far right radical groups forming an outer perimeter of security around the inauguration, intertwined with the National Guard. Violence that continues to this day. What do you really think about all that?"

"Aren't you, right now, violating that ethic of a military officer to stay out of politics?"

Cynthia knew this challenge was coming. "No. And yes. No, I've never so much as hinted in any public statement about my politics. Never once. We can't have active-duty flag and general officers getting into politics to any degree, especially now, even though a couple have. More than a couple, I guess. Anyway, the commandant and the joint chiefs made that clear. The military, especially senior officers, will keep out of politics. I'm sure you heard what the chairman said in his speech. 'Stay in their barracks.'"

Cynthia knew that through all this the commandant, though not a voting member of the joint chiefs, was still privy to the battles within the defense department. And he kept his admirals informed.

A military leadership crisis began when the election ended. The chairman of the joint chiefs faced intense pressure from the president-elect and his party to use the military to put down the protests that exploded across the country. The chairman did as a predecessor had done before and refused to cooperate with invoking the Insurrection Act. Even after the inauguration, military leadership adamantly refused to use regular troops to put down demonstrations. Nor would it act in any way that approximated enforcement of civil law.

The active-duty military did "stay in their barracks." The chairman and service chiefs successfully argued the country's military must remain vigilant and ready to act against any opportunistic moves by foreign adversaries during this time of domestic crisis.

The new president relented. But he nonetheless extracted his price.

The president relieved the chairman. The vice chairman was sent into retirement. In solidarity, the other service chiefs also resigned. However, their vice chiefs stayed on, with the blessing of the now former chairman, to avoid of a self-inflicted decapitation of the armed forces.

Congressional opposition played up the mass resignation as a humiliation of the president. He saw it in a different light. A chance to strengthen his control. The president put senior officers sympathetic to him in key flag and general officer positions, even recalling several from retirement. Others found a new home in critical civilian leadership positions. His moves extended down into the states. Governors allied to the president put in place more compliant adjutant generals of their National Guard.

"And the 'yes' part?"

"Yes. I've my own opinions." Cynthia paused for a sip of wine to help her construct her words. "I am deeply, profoundly disturbed, angered, by what I see as a successful attack upon the Constitution of the United States. Where this new administration will take this country, I do not know for certain. But we are on a dark path. Of that, I am sure.

"We both took the same oath. *Support and defend the Constitution of the United States against all enemies, foreign and domestic; that I will bear true faith and allegiance to the same.* I believe our most dangerous enemies are of the domestic variety. And they've friends in the administration. No, more than that. They are this administration."

Doug felt they were treading on dangerous ground. "Yes, I have my opinions. Yes, the election, the violence, the national emergency. I wonder what kind of government I may be working for. But saying that, I just can't act on those feelings. You know that! And I won't ever say anything like this to anyone, other than you. And definitely not when you are acting as the admiral, not my mom."

Cynthia needed something more from this junior officer. "Explain to me why you think you've been assigned to Eastport. Explain to me what you think the mission is." In tone, now more an admiral than a mom.

"I am to observe and document HSC organization and activities at Station Eastport and report all the facts to my superiors, the Commanding Officer of Sector Northern New England and, well, you."

"Very textbook. Now why do you think the commandant put you, and Jackson, at these stations? Why do this at all?"

Doug looked away from his mom. *No, not mom. Right now, she was the admiral.* He then turned back to her and said, slowly, "The commandant must have very serious concerns about what this HSC unit might do. That its activities will harm the Coast Guard. Involve the service in possibly illegal or unethical activities. Jackson and I are there to protect the service. To act as a buffer or barrier to the HSC."

"That's better" said the admiral, nodding slightly in approval. "Imprecise, vague, but that's the best answer anyone has now. In fact, that's close to how the commandant explained it to me.

"We know very little about the HSC. You're going to help us learn." The admiral sat back in her chair, and said, "Lieutenant Miles, this might be the most important assignment we can give a junior officer these days."

One last thing from the admiral. "Until I tell you differently, you will not discuss our conversation here with anyone else. Not even Captain Llewellyn."

Then the admiral became Mom again. "Well, how about dessert."

The Bridge at Lubec

A curious event happened on the last Friday of January.

The Department of Homeland Security suddenly closed the port of entry at Lubec, Maine. A bridge there crossed the Narrows onto Campobello Island, Province of New Brunswick and to its main attraction, the Roosevelt Campobello International Park. DHS claimed the bridge was in bad shape. Too dangerous to cross. It must stay closed until the two countries could agree on how to pay for repairs.

Overnight, the border station was shuttered, orange jersey barriers and fencing placed across the bridge, and the customs officers reassigned to the Calais border station. No Americans would be visiting the former summer home of President Franklin Delano Roosevelt anytime soon.

In town, no one believed the broken bridge story. They just fixed the bridge a couple of years ago! Most decided the new president just didn't want Americans visiting the estate of an icon of the opposition. Canada protested loudly. Lubec lost tourist dollars. Lots of dollars. The administration didn't listen.

Assuming Command

At the end of that past June, Miles took command of Station Eastport without ceremony three weeks ahead of the HSC unit's estimated arrival. Together with Capt. Llewellyn, they had an expected but private meeting with the officer-in-charge, Sr. Chief Petty Officer Boatswain's Mate Brian James. Miles worried the senior chief would see this as a demotion. That they were here to take away his command.

The captain briefed the senior chief and quickly reviewed Miles's operational experience. The captain ended with assurances of his respect for the senior chief. That was when Miles saw the quality of James. He assured them he understood and didn't take it as a demotion or criticism. He agreed if this HSC unit was coming, an officer like Miles was needed at the station. He even asked the captain and Miles to remember, it was not his station. It belonged to the commandant and he could do with it what he wanted. Miles thought others might think the senior chief was a little corny, but this guy is being genuine. Indeed, Miles thought Capt. Llewellyn was more emotional about the whole thing than the senior chief, the captain's voice cracking at one time.

Miles then interjected the senior chief would in every practical sense run the station. Miles said he wanted to work closely with the chief to learn the station's operations but assured the chief that he'd focus on the HSC unit. Still, Miles knew at some level, it had to hurt the chief.

Sr. Chief James didn't show any hurt. At an all-hands meeting, the chief warmly welcomed Miles and explained the situation to the crew. The captain wisely let him do the talking. Once the chief was done, the captain told the crew, in dealing with the HSC people, he expected they would be the professionals they have always been. He went on to express his admiration of the senior chief and his accomplishments at the station. He advised them the entire situation was sensitive. If asked, beyond acknowledging the existence of the HSC unit, they were not to discuss the HSC unit's operations or activities with anyone. Anyone at all.

Then it was Lt. Miles' turn. "There's no hiding the fact that my coming here as a station commander is highly unusual. As the captain and the senior chief said, keep looking to Senior Chief James. I hope you will find that day-to-day operations around here seem normal, even with me here.

"I'm sure you'll have questions. I will answer them as honestly as I can. If I can't talk about something, I will say so. I do want to learn as much as I can as quickly as I can about your work here and about the local area."

Miles, then turned to the chief and said, "Senior Chief James, I'd like to get out on your boats as soon as possible. Let your people show me a thing or two. And what the Eastport area of operations looks like from the water."

"Aye, aye, sir. Our pleasure. How about at 1500? A patrol is already scheduled."

"Very well, senior chief."

The Captain took his cue. "Thank you everyone, but I need to get back to Portland now. Senior Chief, Mr. Miles, would you accompany me to my car."

The senior chief called his crew to attention as the captain left.

Miles then leaned into the senior chief's ear and quietly said, "Obviously, I won't be going back with the captain. My seabags, dress uniform bag, and a couple of boxes are in the back of the captain's car."

"Understood, sir. I'll get someone to take care of your gear." The chief said they could clear out an extra room for him to bunk down for now.

At the car, while a seaman got Miles' bags and boxes, Captain Llewellyn asked Miles for a private moment with the chief. Miles backed away to a respectful distance. Salutes were rendered, hands were shaken, and the chief walked back across the lot to the station.

"In case you're wondering, Mr. Miles, the senior chief and I, well, this is our third time serving together. Stories I suppose I'll have to tell you some time." He paused for an almost uncomfortable interval. "Orders are orders, it makes absolute sense, and you're very qualified for this, ah, situation, but I hated doing this. You understand?"

"Yes sir." That's all Miles could say.

"Senior Chief James is a good man. You can have faith in him." A smile came to the captain's face. "So, the 4th of July is almost here. Eastport puts on a great party. Downtown, all sorts of fun things, like a cod race. Don't ask. For I don't know how many years, the Navy or Coast Guard had a ship come here to join in. Tied up right by the station, on the Breakwater Terminal pier off Sullivan Street. Over forty feet deep there. The *Escanaba* is coming here this time. She'll pass through Canadian waters north of Campobello Island. She'll tie up at the Breakwater. Senior chief has it well in hand, so have a little fun."

The captain's smile disappeared. "I was here last year. July 4th, but starting on July 1st Eastport always celebrated what they call Independence Day. Begins with Canada Day on the 1st. Lots of Canadians came over to Eastport. Americans and Canadians always been pretty tight around here. Hundreds have family and jobs on both sides of the border. These days, those jobs, well, that's probably changed. There'd been talk of a Canadian Navy frigate coming here for that part of the party.

"No chance of that, any of that, with the border closed. Shame. Remains to be seen if the Canadians will allow passage to the *Escanaba*. They're still allowing bulk carrier merchant ships pass through to the Estes Head Terminal. I wonder how long that will continue.

"By the way, where are you billeted?"

"Senior chief is putting me in what he calls the station's guest room. Likely stay there as long as I can."

"Sounds fine. Any questions, you have my cell."

Then the captain remembered something else. "Oh, I almost forgot. I'm sure the chief would tell you, but every summer the station holds a joint training exercise with the Canadian Coast Guard and their auxiliary and our auxiliary. Last year, we did it in mid-August. Went very well. The planning is being done at sector. The chief is up to speed. He'll keep you informed.

"You should introduce yourself somehow to the Canadian Coast Guard in Saint John. Just give them a call. Maybe the exercise will still happen. Okay, we'll see you later."

With that, Miles saluted the captain and watched him drive away.

Miles reminded himself, *well, I have my first command.*

Fourth of July was a local affair. No Canadians. No cutter *Escanaba*. The Canadians refused her passage.

The Quoddy Tides: The Most Easterly Published Newspaper in the United States

On the second Friday of July, the local newspaper published a short article on the goings on at the Coast Guard Station.

Seven large trailers have been arrayed in the parking lot of the Eastport Coast Guard Station. According to the station's new Commanding Officer, Lieutenant Douglas Miles, the trailers will support an expansion of personnel coming to the station in the coming days. "However, let me emphasize, they will not be Coast Guardsmen. They are federal law enforcement officers assigned to the Department of Homeland Security. Specifically, the Homeland Security Corps. The trailers will be their temporary quarters, office space, and storage area."

Lt. Miles also said the officers are being equipped with two Zodiac type, rigid hull inflatable boats. Sailors should expect to see these boats operating in the area. He further said the Homeland Security Corps officers should arrive in a matter of days.

The Lt. explained that with the expected federal officers coming, it was decided a commissioned officer was needed at the Coast Guard station to deal with the much larger federal presence. Otherwise, he expected the Coast Guard would carry on as it always had.

Lt. Miles would not comment on the mission of the new federal officers other than to direct such questions to the Department of Homeland Security.

First Days Commanding

Done. Another report sent to Sector Norther New England in South Portland and First Coast Guard District in Boston. It noted the status of the trailers and equipment being installed ahead of the arrival of the HSC unit personnel. Miles had looked around inside the trailers as often as the contractors let him. They were probably only a few days away from finishing installation of the electrical system and moving furniture and bunks. That was the easy part.

The trailers had no access to sewer lines. That fact made the trailers' toilets, showers, and small kitchens useless. Miles pleaded with the town's department of public works to get the trailers connected to sewer lines, but they were in no mood to take on a major job with uncertain responsibility for the cost. Nor would the Coast Guard.

Somebody at HSC didn't think this through, Miles concluded. With no sign of help from above, Miles cobbled together his own solution. Out of station funds, he ordered two port-a-potties for the HSC. Miles had never experienced a Maine winter, but he needed little imagination to know that was going to be one chilly experience for HSC.

One headache no one wanted was responsibility for feeding these people. The station's Culinary Specialist was already freaking out at the possibility of cooking for double the personnel. Perhaps HSC could contract out to a nearby restaurant to cater them. The chief quipped, "Well, the local pizza joints will get a lot of new business."

One trailer looked like it was designed as some sort of rudimentary command center. At one end a separate office, telephones, file cabinets and the like. At the other end, walls and ceiling lined with heavy gauge steel mesh, metal flooring, and a matching access door. Accented by locking metal cabinets, Miles knew this space could have only one use. Weapons storage.

Overlooking the trailers was his new office. The chief had offered his own second floor office to Miles. "Senior chief, that's very gracious of you, but how about that space over there?" Miles pointed to a corner room down the short hall. "All I ask is a telephone, a decent desk and a computer set up. Maybe a filing cabinet and a couple of extra chairs."

"You sure about that, Lieutenant? I mean, as CO, you're entitled to my space. And that room in the corner. Its only view is the parking lot."

"Yes, exactly. A nice double window overlooking the parking lot. Where I can see the HSC trailers. Remember why I'm here? Liaison with HSC."

In two days, the senior chief had the new office cleared, cleaned, painted, and equipped with a desk, computer, telephone and chairs in two days. He even found a couple of framed photos of the station for the walls.

Sr. Chief James walked Miles through every aspect of the station. Maintenance, training schedules, qualification status of the crew, weapons inventory, everything.

Yes, the captain was right to trust James, thought Miles.

It's 1300. Miles imagined Jackson at Station Burlington had just sent in her own report. Miles hoped she found her new work a bit more thrilling than he did. For him, it was a bit of a come down from running a ship mounting a 25 mm chain gun and fifty caliber machine guns through the Persian Gulf at 24 knots.

REFUGE

Search and Rescue

Miles started taking watches alongside the station Officers of the Day, learning their protocols in communicating with sector. How they planned and executed search and rescue missions in a coastal environment. This was something new to Miles since his operational experience was often well away from shore.

Especially enjoyable was going with the small boat crews on their patrols and exercises. Miles cycled through each crew and talked to each crew member, asking them to explain aspects of their job on the boat and the station, and how they liked living around Eastport. All in all, aside from a few predictable complaints, the crews seemed alright.

The crews indulged their new CO by allowing him to pilot the boats, with proper oversight by a qualified coxswain. The first time with the 29-foot Response Boat-Small II, or RB-S, he pushed up the throttle and executed a hard turn to port. The boat impressed Miles. Twin outboard engines rated at 225 horsepower can bring the boat to over forty knots. An enclosed cabin with seats designed to dampen shocks from the sea, headset communications between crewmembers, digital navigation systems, excellent visibility, ballistic armor, and mounts for two machine guns.

On that first RB-S ride, Miles asked permission from the coxswain to take it full speed down the St. Croix. *Jesus, this thing is fast!* At somewhere around 35 knots, he caught himself doing his best Will Smith impression. *I gotta get me one of these!* Hardly the demeanor he usually showed as an officer, but the crew got a good laugh. Miles's had a standing joke for the crews. "Something's wrong with my assignments. I've gone from the *Munro's* 418 feet to the *Glen Harris'* 154 feet, and now to 29 feet. I'm on a downward slide, as far as ship size. What's next? A kayak?"

Station Eastport's other boat, the latest answer to heavy seas and surf as high as twenty feet, was the 47-foot Motor Lifeboat, or MLB. At a maximum speed of 23 knots, it was not as fast as the RB-S, but it could do something the RB-S could not. If capsized, the MLB could right itself in thirty seconds. When asked by Miles if she'd ever seen that happen, the coxswain replied, "Yes, sir, it's happened to me just once. At another station. Upside down. Now that was a helluva underwater search."

Almost all the early summer's search and rescue cases were routine. Overdues. Flare sightings that turned up nothing. A couple of slowly sinking yachts that were easily towed in. One rapidly sinking yacht that was left to sink once they took off the people. A couple of boat fires and a minor collision rounded out the few serious cases. Fortunately, only nonlife threatening injuries resulted. Most calls for assistance were nonemergent and could be handed off to a commercial towing company. All pretty ordinary.

Until the second July weekend. That sunny Saturday, a child slipped off a sailing vessel somewhere between Casco Bay Island and Spruce Island, in Canadian waters. Her parents didn't see her fall overboard. They didn't hear anything. They couldn't find her on the boat. Terrified as they were, they had the presence of mind to call a *Mayday* and turn back southwesterly, away from Spruce Island on a roughly reciprocal course.

Responding to the *Mayday*, Joint Rescue Coordination Centre Halifax sortied a helicopter, a highly capable Royal Canadian Air Force CH-149 Cormorant out of Canadian Forces Base Greenwood, Nova Scotia. Estimated time of arrival, 40 minutes. Still much sooner than a Coast Guard Jayhawk helicopter from Air Station Cape Cod could arrive. JRCC also dispatched a search and rescue lifeboat, the Canadian Coast Guard Vessel *Courtenay* from their base in Saint John. Estimated time of arrival at the search area was 90 minutes. Even so, with someone in the water, search and rescue planners used every resource. Once it did arrive, the *Courtenay* would start a search pattern just southeast of Head Harbor Light of Campobello, in effect watching the gate to the Bay of Fundy. Under standard operating procedure, JRCC requested assistance from Station Eastport.

Having already heard the Mayday call, Eastport Station's Officer-of-the-Day dispatched both the MLB and the RB-S. Within minutes, the station's small boats raced out at full speed into the bay north of Campobello Island. At her top speed, the MLB would get to the vicinity of Casco Bay Island, about four nautical miles out, in approximately nine minutes. At 45 knots, in that day's calm sea, the RB-S could get there in six minutes.

Getting a response underway was vital, even without all the data needed to fully plan the mission. The Officer-of-the-Day, relying on her own experience with the tides and currents in the area, mentally calculated the girl's likely drift. She ordered the MLB north of the Island, running a course roughly parallel to that of the RB-S. Meanwhile, the RB-S would search parallel to the shoreline, 0.2 nautical miles off Wilson's Beach inside Head Harbour Passage. Get the boats underway. Calculations would follow in minutes.

There was little time. With an outgoing tide, a Bay of Fundy tide, a person in the water would drift in a southeasterly direction. The little girl was headed for the ocean.

Add in the threat of hypothermia. In July, the water temperature around Eastport hovered around the mid-50s Fahrenheit. Even with a personal floatation device, an adult in waters that cold would slip into unconsciousness in an hour. A child, even faster.

After quickly briefing Sector Northern New England, the Officer-of-the-Day called JRCC Halifax to advise the station's small boats were underway and of their initial search planning. Meanwhile, sector's Search and Rescue planner set in motion the Search and Rescue Optimal Planning System, or SAROPS, which computerized SAR planning, including real-time environmental data such as wind and currents. Minutes later, sector transmitted to the station the SAROPS search pattern and coordinated the search plan directly with JRCC. Long gone were the days of paper and pencil SAR worksheets and acetate overlays on nautical charts.

Miles and the senior chief monitored the mission from the station's small operations center. During the mission, the chief quietly advised the Officer-of-the-Day on SAR protocols, but otherwise let his people do their job. Miles watched, but wisely did not interfere.

"Have a listen to this, Lieutenant." The Chief directed Miles's attention to a maritime radio broadcast about the case. "That's JRCC. Marine Safety Information Broadcast about the girl. Any luck, someone is boating around there and might see her. When the case is in their territory, JRCC handles that task for us. When I first got here, I got to tour their operations center. It's at Canadian Forces Base Halifax. Really impressive. They cover SAR over sea and land. Huge area including all of Newfoundland and Labrador. Eastern part of Quebec, too."

Only minutes into its search pattern, the RB-S radioed they spotted an orange life vest in the water less than 200 yards north of Head Harbor Light Station. They raced over. There she was. They picked up the barely conscious shivering little girl and treated her for hypothermia. It was all over in less than a half an hour.

The RB-S turned to intercept her parent's vessel, while the MLB returned to the station. As the little girl recovered, the RB-S coxswain had an inspired moment of humanity. He put the frightened little girl on VHF distress radio channel 16 so she could announce to her parents, in a quivering voice, "I'm okay."

Station Eastport alerted JRCC of the recovery of the person in the water, alive, conscious and being treated for hypothermia aboard the RB-S. The Maritime SAR Coordinator thanked the Eastport Officer-of-the-Day and then directed the Cormorant helicopter and the St. John rescue boat to return to base.

Coming alongside the sailboat, the EMT and a crewmember from the RB-S lifted the girl aboard, gently placing her in her parents' arms. Breaking his embrace with his child and his wife, the father, tears falling uncontrollably, hugged the Coast Guardsmen, almost knocking them over. More tears, more hugs followed.

Before they went back aboard the RB-S, the little girl got up and hugged both the Coast Guardsmen. Again, tears.

The RB-S coxswain advised the parents that JRCC had an ambulance waiting for them at Black's Harbor, about nine nautical miles to the east. The EMT would stay aboard the sailboat to treat and monitor the little girl as RB-S escorted them to the harbor.

Miles and the senior chief met the boat crews when they returned. Salutes and handshakes and smiles. While congratulating the RB-S crew, the coxswain directed Miles to the seaman who first spotted the girl and minutes later plucked her from the water. After Miles thanked him, he said "Skipper, there's just no better feeling."

Miles arranged for a recording of the mission and the girl's message to her parents be sent to JRCC Halifax. The station automatically recorded all missions. No doubt JRCC did the same, but Miles hoped they'd appreciate the gesture all the same.

The Coast Guardsmen, American and Canadian, carried out this mission like they always had, as professionals, acting without regard to the boundaries or politics. They were a team. Miles thought, *this team could not be allowed to fail.*

Horn Brew

The Tuesday evening after the little girl case, Miles made a request of the Chief. "I think I'm going to check out that microbrewery down the street. How about I buy you a beer?"

"Okay, skipper. Been there before. Pretty good. They've got food if you haven't had dinner yet. They're on summer hours now. Whenever you're ready, sir."

"Always ready. Sorry. No pun intended. Let's get out of the uniforms first."

A five-minute walk down Water Street. Nice little place thought Miles. A renovated old brick building. He hadn't had a chance to enjoy Eastport since his arrival, so this would be a welcome break. The weather was warm, but comfortable, so they took their beers out to a table on the deck.

Looking around the waterfront and the brewery, senior chief said, "Pretty soon skipper this place will gear up for the city's pirate festival. Lot of people. Lots of boats. We'll get a spike in cases from the boaters. Too many still think they can drink all they want and still pilot a boat." The chief laughed a little before asking, "Beer to your liking?"

"Yes. Very much so."

"Well, sir. What did you really want to talk about?"

Miles had to smile. Perceptive man. "Yeah, first I want to say how impressed I am with the crew and the little girl case. Outstanding work."

"Thank you, sir. Always a good day when it works out like that one did."

"I take it, you've had other good days, and days when the SAR case was not good."

The senior chief looked down at his beer and then out to the water. "Yes. Good days. And bad ones. I've done mostly coastal SAR in my time. It always seems the bad cases, you know, where someone dies, those get settled quick. Before we even get there. Collisions, fires, overboards. Way too many people buy boats but don't bother to learn how to operate them. That's not just me talking. Coast Guard did a study back in, ah, 2017, I think. It said about 80% of fatalities involved people who never took a boating safety or navigation course."

Then the senior chief shook his head and chuckled. Miles could tell a sea story was coming.

"Speaking of overboards, twenty years ago now that I think of it. Anyway, I went out on our 41-footer, you know, the old boat the 45s replaced. Was a seaman then, just out of boot camp. Anyway, the overboard. Long story short, this guy was out fishing with his buddies. Hot day. He got really drunk and told his buds he was going to jump in the water. Drunks can't swim well. Sank like a rock. His friends didn't know what to do. A boat nearby made the distress call."

"Turns out, the dead guy and his crew were mafia! And the guy who did the distress call, well, he was FBI. They had these drunk wise guys under surveillance!

"One less trial. That's what the FBI guy said."

"Funny, chief, funny." Miles took a sip of beer and then got to the thing he wanted to say. "Anyway, that case, I mean the little girl case, brings up a couple of things with me."

Miles explained that almost all his operational experience has been in open ocean. Even aboard the Persian Gulf. And SAR almost always involved professional merchant ship sailors. Coastal search and rescue operations focused on recreational sailors was new to him.

"Anyway, Senior Chief. I intend to keep learning your kind of SAR. I've learned a lot in the short time I've been here, but I'm still way behind you guys. So, I'd appreciate any advice, training, whatever, you could give me."

"That's what chiefs do, what they've always done. But that's not your real job here, is it?"

"You're right. It's not my real job to learn about SAR. I'm here as liaison to the HSC. But, to the public, I'm the commanding officer. If I'm answering questions from the local newspaper, or the man on the street, I don't want to sound like an idiot.

"There's a larger picture that goes beyond my real job here. The political problems between the United States and Canada could spill over into search and rescue. I saw how well our people and their people worked together on the little girl case. So, I wonder, what if that cooperation ends?

"Maybe the politics gets better. Maybe it gets worse. What if the border locks down even more? That the agreements between the U.S. and Canada were suspended. Are we, and their Coast Guard, going to lose people who could've been saved?"

Miles stopped. He looked out over the waterfront, had some more beer, and pretended to enjoy a beautiful evening. The senior chief broke the silence.

"I do my best to ignore politics. But, okay. We'll be in trouble if we can't work with the Canadians. No argument from me, skipper. And sounds like, to me, you're thinking about how to keep working with them. Even if you're told not to."

"Yeah, I suppose I am. And I suppose I would be wrong."

"Very wrong. You know the kind of trouble you'd get into? I mean, if you're told not to cross that line, but you do?"

The Lt. nodded. "No, not to worry. Probably never come to that and I will follow orders."

"Good, skipper. I'm glad to hear that. Because if you don't, it falls back on the rest of us."

Miles changed course. "Any chance I could go over into Canada and meet with my counterparts with the Canadian Coast Guard?"

Sr. Chief James answered Miles with a time-honored military response. "That, sir, is above my paygrade."

"Heard that one before, many times." Miles said with a little laugh. "Could you please elaborate?"

"Well, sir, no problem before all this politics. Just drive up across the border and down to Saint John. We did it for years. But it's different now. I'm not sure how it's done now. How you get permission. Course, haven't looked into it at all.

"Now that you bring it up, I don't think we've been hearing from the Canadians as much as we used to. We can call them, sure, but the last few times I've called to discuss a case, or to polish up our part of the August exercise, they seemed . . . nervous. Like they wanted the call to be over real quick. Does that make sense to you?"

"Yes, and no. Your suspicions may prove valid. I don't know."

"One thing Lieutenant. I'm only interested in following orders. If they order us not to rescue anyone in Canadian waters, I will not rescue anyone in Canadian waters. If you want to violate orders, that's on you. I don't mean any disrespect, but you need to know how I see it."

"Understood. Orders will be followed."

Courtesy Call

Keeping eyes on the HSC unit. That was his primary task. If Miles ever lost sight of that, he need only catch the morning news to be reminded. The latest: A local news station showed video of HSC attacking demonstrators with clubs, shields, rubber bullets, and finally real bullets. All this was done in broad daylight right in front of the New York State Capitol building.

However, spying on the HSC unit does not mean I can ignore the station's SAR mission. The rescue of the little girl reinforced that belief. They had a SAR mission, and publicly he is the commanding officer. *I have to do something to ensure high readiness in SAR, don't I?*

Miles's first step were calls to Canadian Coast Guard Station Courtney Bay and JRCC Halifax. Just to introduce himself and thank them for their help with the little girl. To Miles, they seemed receptive and pleased to talk to him. Perhaps the fact that the case turned out so well, that the girl was Canadian, and our Coast Guardsmen got her, maybe that helped break the ice. Miles wanted more though.

Miles called Capt. Llewellyn to talk about his concerns. "I have the same worries, Mr. Miles. Both sides would lose. I wholeheartedly agree we must plan for a failure in cooperation. District feels the same way. They assured me that the Commandant is just as worried, but on a much larger scale than

Passamaquoddy Bay. He's got worries about the Great Lakes and the Pacific Northwest. He's working on it, but the State Department and DHS seem to be taking a go-slow approach.

"I must make something very, very clear, Mr. Miles. Should higher authority decide to completely close the border, and end search and rescue cooperation with Canadians, we will obey our lawful orders. We will not find a way around those orders. I'm not saying that is what you want to do, or are doing, but someone else could reach that conclusion. And remember, there are careers other than your own you must think of. Do you understand me, Lieutenant?"

"Yes, sir. I understand." *An explicit warning. Am I telegraphing something I shouldn't,* thought Miles.

"Good. But the border isn't completely closed, and we're still working with the Canadian Coast Guard. We are following our agreements. Yet, we should plan for the suspension of those agreements. So, Mr. Miles, if you got any ideas, I'm all ears."

Miles made a bold play. "Captain, I'm not entirely sure a total suspension of cooperation is even possible. Notice how we talk about the border being closed, but some commercial traffic is still allowed across by both governments. Rather than total suspension, contingency planning should anticipate degrees of suspension."

"That makes sense. We have treaty obligations for chrissakes!" The captain stopped for a moment.

"If the worst happens, and I don't put the worst beyond our current politics, the recreational boater and commercial fisherman might get the short end of the stick. On the other hand, I can imagine situations, let's say a major merchant vessel casualty, where both governments have a stake in it. Say, a cruise ship with nationals from both countries. Or fuel oil pollution from a sinking vessel.

"Anyway, we're just spit balling right now. So, okay, Mr. Miles, how would you approach them?"

"Captain, I recommend we find out if our Canadian counterparts share our concerns. A face to face, informal talk. So, if it is impractical to drive there, or fly there, we can still sail there."

"Okay, you'd better explain that."

"Sir, with your permission, I'll call JRCC Halifax again. I'll request an in-person meeting, but suggest we have our RB-S rendezvous with their SAR boat. One of their Cape class motor lifeboats out of Saint John. Likely it'll happen in Canadian waters. Have the meeting before the SAR exercise. Meeting at sea means no passage through a port of entry. Fewer questions."

"You're suggesting we go behind the back of DHS." For a second, Miles feared he went too far, until the captain continued. "Still, no one has explicitly said we can't meet with the Canadians. And what would you talk about with them?"

"Captain, the first topic would be continued joint exercises. The second topic, the very same issue that worries us. Are they as concerned as us? How do we function if ordered to end cooperation?"

The captain waited a moment, then said, "Very well. I'll run this by district, quietly. Don't make that call until you hear back from me. We will not act without district approval. We will only discuss this by phone. No mention of this in your report. Clear?"

"Yes, sir." Miles felt relieved. *Maybe I didn't go too far.*

"Lieutenant Miles. You do remember your primary task there?"

Miles glanced out at the HSC officers huddled around one of the trailers. "I do sir. They've only been here a short time. They don't make it easy to forget they're here."

Smallest City

I never thought graduating from Suffolk Law would lead me here.

On his first Saturday in Eastport, Williams sat in his grimy, stuffy trailer office, using the time after lunch to reflect on his career path. He had hoped for steady, bureaucratic work in Washington, D.C., developing policies for the new administration in the Department of Justice. That's why he joined their campaign. It looked like that would happen, but then somebody claimed they saw another talent in him. Talent needed in the field. Or to get him out of sight and mind.

On the second Monday of July, Williams and his unit finally arrived at the station. Homeland Security Corps Special Unit 101, staffed by twenty-three civilian law enforcement officers, including Williams and Webb.

Born through the *Secure America Act*, HSC targeted civil unrest and protests, and domestic terrorism, both now viewed as synonymous under new administration policy. HSC's secondary mission was to augment the border patrol. A difficult bureaucratic birth, plagued with numerous organizational defects. However imperfectly delivered, the new administration now had direct control of a police agency empowered to surveil and arrest whosoever DHS determined threatened homeland security.

The scope of HSC's authority, unencumbered by such bothersome legal niceties like the *writ of habeas corpus*, never bothered Williams. His rationalization was simple. The nation was in crisis, and the president must act if he is to save the country.

Williams's HSC unit wasn't the only one in Maine. All the way up U.S. Route 1, Fort Kent has its own. The CBP sector facility just south of Houlton has two HSC units. Another unit at Calais augmented their one open CBP border station. Williams thought it odd they kept open the downtown Main Street border crossing that led over a short bridge into downtown Saint Stephen. Odd because they closed the newer and higher capacity International Avenue border crossing station that linked U.S. Route 1 to Canada's Route 1. He couldn't imagine the locals on either side were happy with all the lines of tractor trailers snaking down their narrow streets.

Once at Eastport, Williams met with the Coast Guard Station Commanding Officer to thank him for clearing space for the trailers within the station parking lot. He apologized for the inconvenience caused his personnel. It was all very polite and business like.

Though quartering in the trailers wasn't ideal, they did offer somewhat secure working spaces. However, their griminess and smell led most to believe the trailers came from a forgotten FEMA storage lot. The officers complained to Williams countless times about their workspace and quarters. He had to listen even if nothing could be done. After all, he was the unit's leader.

Once he and Webb got the officers settled in during the first few days, Williams uncovered his first doubts of the quality of his people. Naturally, the leader wants to know of their background and skills. The higher ups claimed they were the elite. However, Williams soon found that description more fanciful than accurate.

His officers' records, significantly redacted in some cases, revealed a huge and perhaps fatal problem. Except for two former CBP officers, almost all lacked civilian law enforcement experience. At least Webb spent twenty years in the U.S. Army Military Police Corps.

His people needed more training. Williams wasn't impressed by the training all HSC officers received upon their induction. He thought their "boot camp" hurried, even shoddy. His fellow trainees seemed of doubtful quality. Many showed a streak of dissatisfaction, even disaffection. Prohibited from discussing politics or their backgrounds, Williams still heard more than a few curious comments. Rumor had it that many recruits came from the able-bodied ranks of discharged military and far right militias, a rumor perhaps confirmed when Williams spotted a militia T-shirt worn by an off-duty training officer.

Williams hoped Webb with the two with CBP experience could help train the nineteen officers without experience, including himself. He organized two nine-officer squads, each under a former CBP officer. He told them to identify training weaknesses and train them on-the-job as best they could. Webb would oversee the training, offering them advice and serve as instructor when needed.

Concerning questions of qualifications, Williams knew he was the most questionable. *How did I, with no police or military experience wind up commanding this unit. Someone at HSC, probably a lawyer, thought it a good idea to have a lawyer command the unit. So, I got the command. At least, that's my personal hypothesis. Any brand-new government agency had problems, but me in command, really?*

Stop it! Never get to a better job unless I do a good job here.

Officially, Williams's unit staffed up the U.S. side of border to "prevent border crossings by illegal aliens into the United States." His people didn't take long to figure out their true mission. Deterring and arresting Americans fleeing to Canada. Outfitted in black paramilitary uniforms, Kevlar vests, balaclavas, military style helmets, radios, side arms and long guns, they'd be an unnerving sight to Americans and Canadians alike.

Conducting maritime patrols were key to their unstated mission. Northern patrols ran along the U.S. shoreline of the Saint Croix River. Southern patrols went past Lubec, on through to Quoddy Narrows, and to the Bay of Fundy. DHS sent two black rigid hull inflatable boats. RHIB or "Ribbies" for short. These were 24-foot Zodiac Milpros, with twin outboard engines and a center counsel, but no radar. And in a painful oversight, no enclosed cabin.

Only a couple of his people, Navy veterans, had the slightest experience with operating small boats. As to the rest, being good with a bass boat didn't count. So, Williams and Webb came up with yet another bare bones training plan for operating the boats. Hopefully without drowning being a training outcome.

About a week later, a squad leader summed things up for Williams. "You want us to train guys with zero LE experience, with questionable backgrounds, and on top of that, no experience on boats, and turn them into cops on the water, sir?" The only answer Williams had was, "Yes."

They began with two weeks of training during daylight, learning how to pilot and navigate the boats along the border area. Then they switched to night training for another two weeks. Meanwhile, they trained two officers to oversee boat maintenance, selecting two who seemed the least likely to screw up the boats. When not running the boats, Webb kept them focused on their on-the-job law enforcement training.

At best, Williams judged it would be a month before his unit reached minimum proficiency. In his mind, minimum proficiency meant they do not shoot or drown themselves or cause others to be shot or drowned.

Even as ignorant of boats as he was, Williams saw the Ribbies poorly matched the job and conditions. Patrolling in open boats was awful work for people unused to the water, especially at night. Without any cover or cabin, it was wet, cold, uncomfortable work. Even dangerous. They didn't even have the range for a proper patrol route. Enclosed cabin boats like the 29-footer the Coast Guard had would've been better.

Most puzzling to Williams was the fact that CBP already had its own boats and armed crews. He heard CBP deployed a 27-foot patrol vessel, with a cabin, out of the Coast Guard station in Rockland. Williams couldn't fathom why they weren't deployed here. Easy to do. It had its own trailer, for chrissakes!

Williams's criticisms were not welcomed by HSC. Requests for better boats and personnel with small boat experience, any boating experience at all, were met with what amounted to a bureaucratic, but polite "suck it up."

HSC compounded his frustration by directing that his unit, and all units like his, not train, collaborate, or consult with any of the CBP units in the area. That included any CBP agents working along the U.S. Canadian Border and the CBP officers manning the eighteen Ports of Entry in Maine. Even the CBP officers stationed at the Eastport Port of Entry!

Williams wanted to call the other HSC units. Share best practices and such. No dice. HSC prohibited the units from communicating with one another. They were effectively siloed. *Why? Was everyone having these problems?*

Then there was the delicate problem of relations with their host, Coast Guard Station Eastport. Williams made a quick study of them. There's been a Coast Guard Station here at the city pier off Sullivan Street for decades. The bigger of the station's two boats is the 47-foot Motor Lifeboat. The smaller and faster boat was 29-foot response boat. Both had their own dock within the pier. In all, twenty-two Coast Guardsmen were stationed here. Twenty-three with the lieutenant.

Williams quickly saw the border played a significant role in the Coast Guard's two primary missions here. Search and rescue and maritime law enforcement. When any boat left the docks and headed east, they were only six tenths of a nautical mile from the international border. For search and rescue, the border didn't matter. Coast Guardsmen routinely carried out SAR in Canadian waters. The Canadians reciprocated, of course. No permission necessary.

Law enforcement missions by Coast Guard or CBP in Canadian waters was another matter entirely.

If the Coast Guard wanted to enter Canadian water on a law enforcement mission, they had to get a specially trained Royal Canadian Mounted Police officer, a Mountie, to go with them. If the Canadians had a law enforcement mission in U.S. waters, a Coast Guardsmen went along on an RCMP boat.

Williams knew that there was no chance the Mounties, or even Coast Guardsmen, would be allowed on his boats. HSC was very clear about that.

HSC had very simple instructions on relations between his unit and the Coast Guard. Do not work or speak with the Coast Guard unless absolutely necessary. Work out problems on your own. You need help, talk only to us, not them.

Williams knew it didn't make a damn bit of sense. Here sat his ill-trained and ill-equipped unit, in the parking lot of a highly trained and well-equipped federal agency with a long history of maritime law enforcement and intimate knowledge of the area. And they could not ask them for help.

Feelings aside, Williams dutifully ordered his officers to keep to themselves, on the station and in town. They maintained their own equipment and ran their own communications. They planned their own missions. They arranged for their own chow. They trained themselves. If they needed help from the Coast Guardsmen on an intractable maritime problem, like figuring out the tides in a tricky area like Passamaquoddy Bay or getting the Zodiac motors to work, Williams would go to Lt. Miles as a last resort.

It only took a week before the wall of separation between HSC and Coast Guardsmen began to fall, brick by brick, chipped away by his own people. The lower ranked HSC officers began giving orders directly to the Coast Guardsmen, as if they were servants. Get me this! Fix that! The Coast Guardsmen didn't take kindly to that. Open, heated arguments quickly arose. Even a couple of shoving matches.

Their host would have none of this, understandably so Williams admitted to himself. Lt. Miles brought Williams into his office, closed the door, and told Williams in rather colorful profane terms to tell his people to knock it off. He didn't stop there.

Lt. Miles set down the rules. Whatever the issue, no HSC personnel will deal directly with Coast Guardsmen. They must go through Williams. Then

Williams will bring the matter to the lieutenant. No one else. On the other hand, if HSC is doing something unsafe, or just plain stupid, Coast Guardsmen will correct the HSC officer on the spot. Miles told Williams that his people better get used to that.

Then Miles got loud. "Mr. Williams, one of my crew spotted one of your . . . officers . . . walking around with the safety off on a loaded weapon. Get your people straight on that. If you need instruction on weapon safety, my people can help. For no other reason than keeping someone from getting shot. Happens again, I'll have the officer's weapons seized. Not a good start, Mr. Williams. It's only been, what, a week."

Miles wasn't done. He warned Williams boat crews were a danger to themselves. Williams started to object, but Miles interrupted him. "Mr. Williams, your people had no idea how to get those boats off the trailers and into the water. Christ, they tried to launch one right here, right off the pier. My people had to tell 'em about the town's boat landings and went with them to get the boats launched and then piloted them back here for you. So don't tell me your people know anything about boats."

Williams countered his team is still learning about running boats, but Miles cut him off, predicting the Coast Guard would have to save their asses someday. Therefore, new rules of operation were needed. Before HSC boats leave the dock, "once they figure out how to make them go," he demanded they check out with the station Officer-of-the-Day. They will detail their patrol route and their expected time of return. His Officer-of-the-Day will inspect their safety and communications equipment before every patrol. Only then will HSC have permission to go out.

Though embarrassed by the truth in Miles's complaint, that part crossed a line for Williams. He shot back, "We don't need your goddamn permission!"

Miles wasn't listening, saying more rules would likely follow. Summing up, Miles reminded Williams he's a tenant command. As such, he can follow the station rules or find someplace else.

Williams suspected the eviction threat was a bluff. He knew DHS and HSC wouldn't stand for that. But now was not the time to pick a fight. Williams backed off, apologized for the behavior of his officers, and agreed to the checkout rules, but told Miles the issue of permission was not settled. "We will go on our patrols when and where we want to, but would appreciate knowing of any deficiencies in safety spotted by your people."

Williams left, not waiting for Miles to respond.

REFUGE

Ironically, Williams reflected, HSC wanted minimal communications between HSC and the Coast Guard. *Looks like they got what they wanted. A frustrating and stupid policy, considering his unit's inexperience compared to what the Coast Guard could offer.*

The Coast Guard knew all there was to know about outboard engines. All Williams had was a guy who had a Boston Whaler back home. The Coast Guard had EMTs. Williams had no EMTs and most had little grasp of basic first aid. In boarding and searching boats, the Coast Guard had expert boarding officers. Williams's people where only just learning how to board from one boat to another without drowning. Even swimming. Coast Guardsmen knew how to swim, how to protect themselves in cold water, and were equipped with excellent personal floatation devices and exposure suits. Half his people couldn't swim and their lifejackets were only a step above what was found under an airline seat.

Then there's local area knowledge. Things like where the sand bars and submerged rocks were. Already, his people had run their Ribbies aground and couldn't figure how to get them refloated. When his people asked for help getting off a bar, the Coast Guardsmen seemed to enjoy their predicament, telling them to wait for the incoming tide to lift them off. That could take hours. Especially delightful during a rainy day. Civilian boats passing by really enjoyed taking pics of the helpless federal cops, which always wound up on social media.

Williams took some comfort in a simple fact. So far, no drowned HSC agents.

So far, no arrests of refugees either.

Taking stock of his unit's strengths and weaknesses, Williams saw only weaknesses. Poorly trained personnel and patrol boats ill-suited to the task. Add in poor relations with their Coast Guard host. No, worse than that. Downright hostile relations.

That day it got worse. During a call with his supervisor at the HSC regional office in Boston, Williams went a bit off track and discussed his doubts about the staffing of the unit. His supervisor wasn't amused. "Well, Mr. Williams, if you feel your unit's staffing is a problem, perhaps we could start with you. After all, we put you there to build this unit and get it operational. If you're saying you can't do the job, we can find someone else. What's your pleasure?" Williams stammered out an apology.

Yeah, thought Williams, *this was not a good start.*

The Quoddy Tides: The Most Easterly Published Newspaper in the United States
Another Second Friday

On the second Friday of August, the local newspaper published its second article on the comings and goings of the HSC at Coast Guard Station Eastport.

Recreational boats and professional fishermen, from Lubec to Eastport and from across the border to New Brunswick, have made numerous reports to this newspaper of uniformed and armed persons operating rigid hull inflatable small craft throughout the U.S. side of our waters. According to our local sailors, these persons are often seen in broad daylight carrying assault rifles and wearing tactical vests, sometimes emblazoned with PO-LICE on the back.

Digital photographs and video accompanied many of these reports. Interestingly, many locals seem to doubt the skill of these personnel on the water. A local man, who wished to remain anonymous, said he helped tow one such boat off a sand bar twice. "I don't think these guys know bow from stern, let alone how to sail these waters."

Once again, The Quoddy Tides contacted the Commanding Officer of Coast Guard Station Eastport, Lt. Miles, asking for information about these personnel. He could confirm they are not U.S. Coast Guard personnel, but instead they are members of the new Homeland Security Corps who are stationed at the Coast Guard station. One month ago, readers may recall news of seven large trailers being placed at the Coast Guard station and the impending arrival of these new federal police officers.

Lt. Miles said he could not comment on the operations of the Homeland Security Corps unit. Attempts to reach the person in charge of the Homeland Security Corps unit were not successful. Through its website, the Department of Homeland Security has issued public announcements of the HSC mission, saying they are "operating under the Secure America Act, reinforcing Customs and Border Protection and Border Patrol in their efforts to end illegal immigration and combat domestic terrorism in the United States."

The Quoddy Tides asks readers to keep us informed of the activities of the Homeland Security Corps personnel in our area.

CHAPTER THREE
WHAT HAPPENED?

Adrift

January 25 of this year. That was the last day Mike and Debbie were in the United States. They had driven up from Rhode Island to the Joes Point house to oversee repairs to the furnace. After that, they planned a quick road trip to enjoy a winter festival in Quebec City. The repairs happened. The road trip didn't.

On that day, the newly inaugurated President of the United States made a televised address to the nation declaring a State of National Emergency. Mike and Debbie watched from Canada.

Widespread street protests of his election had continued into the new year and past his inauguration. Though guilty at times of their own violence, again and again right wing counterprotests savagely met them in the same streets with clubs, gas, and guns. Far right violence vastly exceeded that of their opponents. By any interpretation Mike could make, the protests had escalated into domestic terrorism. Far right terrorism.

An outspoken liberal governor assassinated. Two opposition congressional representatives and one U.S. Senator gunned down. A massive truck bomb decimated the Atlanta headquarters of CNN. Journalists shot. Armed right wing mobs seized two blue state capitol buildings. State police and National Guard put down both insurrections, but not until a score of legislators, police, and insurrectionists were dead. Demonstrations against the new president continued in city after city.

In his address, the president blamed the violence on left wing extremists, ANTIFA and Black Lives Matter. He went further. His predecessor had incited these "radical leftist riots" and deliberately failed to quash them. At the peak of his address, he said, "This is nothing more than an attempt to use terror to overturn the election. It is an attempted coup, and I will not let that happen! I will regain control of America's streets!" Accusations, but no evidence.

Therefore, he claimed he had no choice but to act swiftly and decisively. He would do whatever necessary to save the Republic and democracy. "Unpalatable as this Declaration of National Emergency may be," he had said, "it is essential to the survival of our nation and will remain in effect until we eliminate these unpatriotic and undemocratic elements, these terrorists, from of our society and order has been restored."

A shudder went through Mike at the president's use of the word "eliminate."

The president urged governors to call up more National Guard troops, and to request the deployment of regular army troops under the Insurrection Act. He went further, warning that unless the demonstrations ended at once, and politicians and journalists voicing support for the demonstrators silenced themselves, he would suspend federal *habeas corpus*, just as Presidents Lincoln, Grant and Franklin Roosevelt did to a limited extent during previous wars and emergencies.

Mike had been stunned. He knew what that meant. Anyone arrested by federal officers would be denied the right to appear before a judge following arrest and could be detained indefinitely incommunicado. In all United States history, suspension of *habeas corpus* had never been used as he now threatened, to silence demonstrators and political critics. To "disappear" political opponents.

The president then demanded the new Congress, both houses now controlled by his party, pass emergency legislation he called the *Secure America Act*. Among other things, it would expand the Department of Homeland Security and create of a new federal paramilitary Homeland Security Corps with the mission of keeping America's streets safe and secure from radical groups and domestic terrorists. The corps was needed to "relieve the burden of fighting the violence now shouldered by our police, our National Guard, and those patriotic citizens who bravely stepped forward to defend our homes and neighborhoods. This new security force would act forcefully against the street protestors, terrorists and supporters of terrorism now threatening America's democracy, wherever and whoever they are."

Though the act would place the Homeland Security Corps within DHS, it granted the president direct authority to use HSC resources as he judged necessary to deal with the emergency. "Keeping it out from under the weight of the federal bureaucracies and empowered with new legal authority to sur-veil, pursue, and apprehend those connected to domestic terrorism will make it the effective force America needs." It was a persuasive argument to tens of millions of angry and frightened Americans.

The president said nothing about who would lead the new police force, who would be recruited to serve in it, what if any limits would exist to its power, nor how supporters of domestic terrorism would be identified.

Mike and Debbie knew what this meant. A president of the United States would have an internal, political police force with the power to arrest political enemies without warrant and detain them indefinitely. All in the cause of saving democracy, this man had just strangled democracy, justified by a threat he helped create.

The act sailed through the Congress. The president signed it into law two days later. Federal *habeas corpus* was suspended by executive order that very day. Few in Congress protested. Opposition voices were enfeebled. Like most peoples during times of crisis, when facing a choice between liberty and security, Americans chose security.

On the day the act was signed, Mike remembered a Caribbean cruise they took shortly after the election, when a guy in a hot tub loudly and proudly proclaimed to all his indifference to the election result. "I don't care what he does, as long as my 401(k) goes up."

In Mike's mind, the hot tub man symbolized the mindset of most during times of crisis. It was true that hundreds of demonstrations against the new right wing president-elect had sprung up across the country. Millions had taken to the streets again and again. Impressive though the demonstrations appeared on television, most Americans had not taken part. Most remained safe on the sidelines, and aside from ineffectual venting on social media, they had carried on with their lives. From his study of history, especially of past resistance movements, Mike knew this was to be expected, normal, even un-derstandable. Stay safe. Don't risk what you have. Someone else would do it. Wait for things to get better.

Eventually, millions upon millions acquiesced, distracting themselves with the everyday concerns of life. In the end, becoming the man in the hot tub.

Mike and Debbie had decided to stay a while longer in Saint Andrews. At least until things settled down, until the violence stopped. It shouldn't be that long. That's how they explained their decision to their adult children and friends. And rationalized the decision to themselves.

January slipped into February. The violence back home didn't abate. It wasn't getting better. By then, for Mike and Debbie, second guessing their decision became second nature. The pain and guilt of not returning home became an anger that vied with depression for dominance. Why didn't they just go home? There wasn't anything stopping them. What are we afraid of?

There was something to be afraid of. A reason to stay in Canada.

"Mike, that blog of yours. Are you keeping at it?"

Before, during and after the election Mike kept up a political blog in support of the opposition. The blog's popularity might have been the biggest surprise of Mike's life. Thousands of messages in support. But also, hundreds of threats against him and his family.

"Yes. Do you want me to stop?"

"Well, you should at least think about it. Think of our kids. This new Homeland Security Cops, or Corps, or whatever. It'll take some time for them to get going, but maybe not as long as we might think. And then . . ."

"And then, what?"

"Because of the blog, I think they could accuse you of supporting domestic terrorism. It won't matter that you never did that. You opposed the new president. You had followers. That's enough for them. We go back and you'll be arrested."

She's right, Mike knew. Dissent is still legal, but now it comes with a cost. He ended his blog the next day.

Going home became a moot point anyway. In February, the border closed.

A New Home

Mike wasn't surprised Debbie wasted no time in finding a new purpose to her life. She offered her medical services to the local health care system. They needed help in coping with the Americans refugees. Work in a good mission offered Debbie a certain relief.

Yet, however worthy the work, she couldn't relieve herself of her anguish about leaving home and staying away. She tried to keep her feelings to herself, outwardly maintaining calmness and reason, but keeping up the façade proved more painful as time went on. She was much like the functional alcoholic. Finds ways to keep doing the job and keep up appearances, but still drinking. As it turned out, many of her refugee patients suffered in the same way.

Most of her patients were suffering from things greater than physical ailments. Depression and confusion she believed came from their new status as refugees. She sought outside help. Debbie persuaded a therapist from Saint John to come to Saint Andrews once a week to help the Americans. Debbie needed the therapy as much as any of her patients.

Things got better for Debbie. Mike had a different experience.

In those first weeks and then months in Saint Andrews, Mike lacked any employment that would help occupy his mind. At first, he tried using his military intelligence experience and academic background in history to map out the events which led to their current situation, both in national politics and their personal situation. A professional examination of the facts might be the cure for what ails him, so he hoped.

It didn't turn out that way. His analysis only reinforced a hypothesis that the declaration of national emergency was likely the culmination of a well-prepared campaign. It was less a response and more an exploitation. It could have been the far right's aim all along.

Mike simply couldn't cope with this work's results. He shoved the analysis aside, sharing it with no one. He ridiculed his own work as nothing more than the doodling of an amateur. Political analysis was not his line of work. It's the work of historians. Now, if someone wanted to target a specific office in a specific building, Mike could pick out the right fighter plane to drop the right smart bomb through the right window at the right time. He'd done it many times before.

From that point on, he did anything other than come to grips with events back home. Anything to keep away the thoughts that stole away his sleep. He found distractions. Household projects, the MG sports car, and trips touring the local area. He even tried ice fishing with a new friend. He hated fishing in warm weather. Fishing on a frozen lake was exponentially worse.

Only reluctantly did Mike accept leadership of the Expat Committee, the first productive thing he did in a long time. It helped, and there was lots of work for Mike. The agony of leaving behind home, family and friends was still there. It might be there forever, but the work helped.

They could have gone home, but they didn't. They couldn't explain the decision to family and friends. Even to each other. But they knew why. They were just plain terrified to return.

They wouldn't be the last.

Downfall

George's question kept coming back to him. *What happened?*

Sunday morning. Normally Mike and Debbie indulged themselves by going out to breakfast or bringing home a treat from the local Tim Hortons. Not Dunkin Donuts, but it grows on you. This Sunday morning, Mike was up well before the sun came up. *What happened?* George's question nagged at Mike through the night. That, and for the second time a full bladder, had Mike up by two am.

Instead of turning on the cable television as he usually did when struck with insomnia, he did something he'd been avoiding. Mike got out his old financial sector report on domestic terrorism. The one that got him fired. Edward wanted a copy anyway. He also got out the informal analysis he had started after the president declared a national emergency.

He wrote the financial sector report to help clients make well informed investment decisions. Mike's report had offered a glimpse into one possible future. National politics warped by domestic terrorism committed in service to one political party. As best one could in a sleep deprived morning, Mike reasoned he could start by matching the report's predictions and recommendations against the real events that followed its writing.

Mike reread both papers. He kept telling himself he was merely trying to organize his own thoughts. Even with a degree in history, Mike knew he was far from being a scholar. He liked to say, "I know more than most, but a lot less than others." At best, Mike hoped he could write a kind of half-assed essay to himself. A way to answer George someday.

He took notes on a legal pad, trying to match the report's major points with recent political events. Bullet points matching bullet points that could be rewritten as an essay. Did any of the report's predictions pan out? Turns out, many predictions did.

Did history offer any predictive model? Mike chose the Weimer Republic of Germany. Though an imperfect lesson, Mike saw Weimer as a useful model for these times of how democracy can fail.

REFUGE

There was a souvenir of the early days of Weimer in Mike's desk drawer. A banknote from the days of Weimer's hyperinflation in 1923. Poorly printed on only one side of the note paper, it's printed value was an absurd *Zehn Millionen Mark*. Ten million Marks. In those desperate days, Germans burned bundles of banknotes in the stove to heat their homes, rather use valueless money to buy valuable coal.

He began writing.

Dear George,

You asked me the other day about what happened to my country. I couldn't answer then. I'm still too emotional about it. Let me try now. Sorry for the academic tone of this letter, but it helps me put things together. I'm going to compare some history from nearly a century ago to our world today. Please bear with me. Here goes:

At the end of World War One, an exhausted and defeated Germany, wrenched by revolution, was subjected to the punitive Treaty of Versailles. The great colossus of Europe, humiliated and broken, suddenly embarked on an experiment in constitutional democracy for which the German people had no precedent, no institutions, and no traditions.

There were a few years, from 1924 to 1929, when the republic seemed to find its footing. There was a restored monetary system, thanks in large measure to American banks underwriting the German banking system. Growing prosperity seemed to lessen civil disorder. Germany's former enemies slowly moderated their war reparations demands.

The Deutscher Republik's measurable and objective progress was forgotten when the Great Depression ripped the Weimer economy to tatters. The fact that the depression did the same to all democracies and those democracies found ways to survive and rebuild, mattered little. In the end, emotions mattered far more.

Among the German people, resentment against the Treaty of Versailles always remained high, especially among the millions of war veterans who couldn't accept the war was lost when hardly a scrap of Germany was taken in battle by the Allies. This was fertile ground for the far right to seed with the propaganda of conspiracy. The Dolchstoss myth, the stab in the back of the German warriors in 1918, wasn't created by Nazi propaganda, but they expertly exploited it by identifying who held the knife. The Bolsheviks, the socialists, and the supporters of democracy. And above all, the traditional enemy, the Jews.

The disaffected, the betrayed and the vengeful gathered to form paramilitaries bent on the destruction of the new constitutional government and the restoration of Germany to its rightful greatness.

In the November 1932 German national election, the Nazi party received only 33% of the votes, 4% less than the earlier election that past July. Though down two million votes, the Nazis still had the largest share because the remaining votes were split among a handful of other political parties. More than fifty parties if one included the truly trivial ones. The president of Germany, Gen. Paul von Hindenburg, pushed by powerful political and industrial figures who believed the Nazis could be controlled and later disposed of, reluctantly acquiesced to Hitler becoming chancellor in January 1933.

It came down to this. One third of the German electorate voted to end any hope of democracy in their country and turn their fate over to the Nazis.

With the first lines done, Mike began exploring how Weimer's history might link to the America of today. In days past, Mike recoiled at the Nazi analogy used so casually by his more left wing friends to insult to political opponents. To Mike, it trivialized the monstrous evil of the Nazis. Yet now, Mike felt parallels, however tenuous, existed between the pathway of Nazi ascension and the America of today.

What do we see today?

Viewed over history's long arc in the last century, democratic governments successfully brought prosperity out of the Great Depression and fought the Second World War to an unambiguous victory. They took the United States to the moon. Without resorting to war, Allied democracies triumphed over the Soviets after nearly fifty years of the Cold War. Victory in civil rights expanded democracy for all Americans. Unambiguous, indisputable victories. None of that mattered.

First was radicalization.

Once again, the electorate's emotions were more important than observable, measurable facts. Disaffection and distrust of government were exploited by politicians and propogandists masquerading as journalists. Disinformation based on half-truths and outright lies spread through social media at the speed of light.

For years, decades even, in a constant drumbeat of propaganda by its politicians and allied news outlets, one party demonized their opposition as the elites, enemies of the Constitution, and subverters of American culture. The liberals, the immigrants, the Black, the Brown, the intellectuals, the cities, the government itself. Claiming the mantel of the "real Americans", they whipped their followers into hatred of the others, offering the aggrieved, the cynical, the fearful, and the dispossessed a pathway to the mythical greatness that once was.

Again and again, fear, lies, and conspiratorial fantasies fueled one party's extremism. An American version of the Dolchtoss, a stolen election, gave the far right the myth they needed.

Enforcing unity of thought upon its adherents with an almost religious fervor, one party ruthlessly expelled apostates from its ranks by whatever means and replaced them

*with true believers. Loyalty to the leader was the only doctrine. An Americanized Füh-
rerprinzip.*

*And so those within that party who knew better, who were once something better, gave
in, gave up, or went away.*

*Abandoning any serious philosophy of governance, one party devoted itself instead to
doctrines of power and divisive cultural tropes. It populated itself with the grifters and know-
nothings found in all autocracies.*

*The opposition party ultimately failed to realize corruption didn't matter to tens of
millions of voters, who rationalized that all politicians are corrupt anyway. Largely devoted
to issues of rational governance and policy, the opposition simply could not understand how
the very people they tried to help could reject them.*

*The opposition party never found a way to respond. They failed to understand that lies
move with a velocity that truth cannot match. In a complex world, lies are just easier to
grasp than facts.*

At this point, Mike remembered what Debbie had said about all those
people with the right wing flags tacked onto their homes and waving from
flagpoles. These devotions were more common in the poorer, rural areas of
Maine and New England. Back then, he reacted with contempt. Do they
know they are supporting people who would do them the most harm? It took
Mike an unforgivably long time to admit his own fault. Instead of being con-
descending and patronizing, he should have found ways to reach out. He
could have but chose not to.

Next came the attack on the popular election.

*Demographics doomed the far right. They would lose election after election until they
passed into irrelevancy. Free and fair elections would be their end. Rather than allow democracy to hand over their world to people they despised, they acted to end democracy.*

*One party understood the power of state legislatures. States run the elections. By con-
vincing so many that elections as flawed, rigged, and corrupt – the American Dolchtoss –
they justified new laws and corrupt redistricting of political boundaries that together almost
guaranteed the outcome. Insisting the new voting and election laws would save elections, they
effectively suppressed voters likely favorable to the opposition. Fewer and fewer polling stations in cities. Fewer voting days. Sanitized voter rolls. Severe limits on mail-in ballots.*

*At the same time, one party granted itself the power to wholly disregard election results,
empowering their legislatures to legally nullify votes. Through elections and appointments,
they placed partisans in key positions with the power to influence the vote count. Radicalized*

poll watchers, county election officials, attorneys general, and Secretaries of State. A bewildered opposition did not counter them.

Nullification laws made it almost certain swing states would swing the right way. The strategy was simple. If dissatisfied with the popular vote, refuse to concede defeat. Claim voter fraud, call for a sham investigation and get allied county election officials and Secretaries of State to go along. Get the state legislature to nullify enough votes – throw them out – to see that electors were awarded to their candidate. It didn't have to work everywhere. Just in enough states.

The opposition party failed to pass federal legislation to protect voting rights in time for the election.

Then there were the courts.

For years, one party dominated the appointment of state and federal judges. One party ruthlessly pushed their justices to the United States Supreme Court. The opposition failed to see the consequences in time.

Sympathetic judges found in favor of the states that suppressed or nullified votes, arguing states are responsible for making election rules and the state voter laws were within the authority of the states. They found support in an obscure and once disregarded legal theory. The Independent State Legislature doctrine, created from an extremely literal interpretation of the Constitution, argued the states are the sole authority in running elections.

Opposition court challenges often went nowhere. Because they had to start with the lower courts, it worked too slowly, and these courts often refrained from granting opinions when cases were argued too close to the election date.

The U.S. Supreme Court offered only very narrow, and often insignificant, objections to the new laws that made it that far. In the end, the highest court of the land effectively ended the Voting Rights Act.

Mike stopped to get coffee. He remembered that a few weeks ago, the new president's congressional allies announced legislation to expand the U.S. Supreme Court by two justices, something they were vehemently against before. Mike knew it didn't take a rocket or a political scientist to see this would solidify the court's right wing majority for generations. The president signed the bill that month. Confirmation hearings would start in November.

All this was done out in the open for everyone to see. All this was legal.

Then came the illegal part. Then came the violence.

Long before the election, one party convinced their disciples, the true, God-fearing, patriotic Americans, of the legitimacy and necessity of political violence if the country was to be saved. In this election, politicians, pundits, podcasters and a distressing number of pastors, set them to act. Take up arms! Now is the time! Save the country! God is on our side!

And in this pursuit, there can be no sin. The ends will justify the means, any means, however corrupt, however immoral, however bloody. Whatever must be done, will be done. And remember, no matter what the right does, the left will be far worse.

The result of their rhetoric was the thousands who filled the ranks of America's militias. And the hidden numbers of new Timothy McVeighs and Dylan Roofs.

Of their enthralled millions, they needed only thousands to act. And act they did. During the campaign, opposition party offices were vandalized, often set ablaze. Journalists and campaign workers were harassed, assaulted, shot. In full view of news media cameras, right wing and white supremacy gangs waded into opposition rallies, attacking with clubs and bear spray. Bombings, large and small, targeted the right's enemies. Black churches, Planned Parenthood clinics, media outlets, LGBTQ advocacy offices, opposition party offices, and on and on.

Politicians themselves were not spared. Countless death threats to opposition politicians, culminated in the assassination of three of the opposition candidates.

On election day itself, across the country right wing organized gangs and inspired individuals, harassed poll workers, threatened voters, burned ballot drop-off boxes, and blockaded polling stations in known opposition districts. Inevitably, it was on the news. The fear spread even more. Sometimes the police acted. Sometimes they did not.

Working door to door in a voter registration drive, Mike and Debbie suffered insults and threats that left them shaken and fearful. One man pointed to a shotgun leaning against the door, saying, "That'll do my voting, so get going."

Mike remembered the harassment he and Debbie experienced as poll workers in their little Rhode Island town. Especially one late middle-aged man. Mike could still see him clearly in his mind. He screamed at Mike, "If our guy doesn't win, it's because of you and I'll come for you." When Mike told the police officer detailed to the poll station, the officer just shrugged his shoulders.

Even librarians, Mike remembered. In Texas, a librarian was gunned down. She refused to remove books the rightist town council found objectionable. A man felt inspired to act. He shot the librarian and torched the library. Mike couldn't remember if they arrested anyone for her murder.

Terrorism works. At least sometimes, Mike believed.

Fly an airliner into a building and the result is a nation unified in righteous vengeance. Yet when done on the small scale, terrorism is often successful in spreading fear. Intimidation and threats, and sometimes actual violence, against public school officials, town politicians, county, and state election officials. The terror is nearby. The terror comes from the guy down the street. The fear spreads. It didn't have to work every time. Just often enough.

The chaos and violence before the election had its intended effect. Announcements of results were often delayed for days, reportedly out of excessive caution sparked by fear. The rightist presidential candidate claimed victory on election night, well before the networks called the results.

While accepting election results that went their way, the right wing refused to concede whenever their candidates lost. There must be fraud! Cheating! Corruption! Stolen election! Their ultra-partisan election officials then went to work, setting in motion their nullification laws to shift the results their way. It was done in the open, for all to see.

Nullified votes in Michigan, Arizona, Pennsylvania, and Georgia swung the Electoral College to the right wing presidential candidate. Once again, the minority party lost the popular vote, but won the election.

The right won. Not everywhere, but they won often enough.

The opposition presidential candidate conceded. He could have challenged the results all the way to the Supreme Court. But that risked a constitutional crisis. It risked even more violence. He conceded. The violence came anyway.

Across America's cities, the election ignited hundreds, then thousands, of demonstrations against the president-elect. Far right counterdemonstrators again met them on the streets. Urged on by far right politicians, provocateurs, pundits, pastors and by not-so-subtle hints from the president-elect, QAnon cultists, radicalized Christians, Oath Keepers, Proud Boys, III Percenters, and the myriad of militia groups charged the demonstrators. Defend the election! Save the country! Save democracy! Stop the radical left! We are the true Americans! We are defending America! We are defending our freedoms! We will do whatever we need to do! God's will be done!

From the floor of the Senate, a right wing senator joined the chorus, saying "We have more guns than them. Let's use them." She was not censured. She was not held accountable.

Violence swept the country, often overwhelming the police and the National Guard. Hundreds, then thousands died.

The incoming administration saw the chaos as more of an opportunity than a crisis. Those in power always have the power to define who is a terrorist, or who is a righteous freedom fighter. The propagandizing began. Right wing allied media replayed video of burning streets and looted storefronts, again and again, exaggerating leftist violence. They romanticized right wing violence as the work of true patriots, who acted to protect American values, and laid blame at the feet of their opponents. The ground was prepared for further, more focused moves in seizing power.

Polls showed a shift among Americans toward stronger security measures, toward whatever actions would bring peace.

Passage of the Secure America Act gave the president his political police force, the Homeland Security Corps. They acted quickly. Unidentified, black uniformed police attacked demonstrators in the streets of American cities. Soon videos surfaced of unidentified police in unmarked SUVs grabbing demonstrators off the streets and from their homes across America.

Mike summed up his notes.

To the tens of millions of the far right's supporters, democracy itself was to blame for their loss of power in America. Democracy was their existential threat. Democracy had elevated minorities while diminishing whites. Democracy raised up foreign religions and atheists at the expense of their version of Christianity. Demographic trends and democratic elections would deny them power if left unhindered. The far right therefore dedicated itself to taking power by any means at its disposal, legal or illegal, to attain one-party rule.

The opposition party couldn't summon the will to fight and defend democracy. They could not keep power, having failed to understand that opponents who have no shame cannot be shamed; that those who have no reason cannot be reasoned with.

In the end, democracy in the United States of American wasn't overthrown by a cabal of angry generals. There was no military coup. Americans did not wake up to tanks in the streets of the capital or soldiers seizing the radio and television stations. The Congress didn't find itself under military arrest. A bemedaled general did not declare martial law from the Oval Office.

No, it was done by politicians. By lawyers. By citizens. Step by step, in state after state, county by county, laws were changed to make what was once illegal, legal. White robes, hoods, and militarist garb were exchanged for business suits. It was done with the support of tens of millions of Americans who voted to end their own democracy.

All on its own, America built the pathway to its downfall. It was a road open for all to see. We all watched it happen. We watched as tens and tens of millions of our countrymen took to that road. America did not lose her democracy to conquest by a foreign power. We did it to ourselves.

George, I am sorry for what happened. What we did. I am sorry for the damage that will be done to Canada.

Mike closed his laptop. He ran his hands over his face in a futile effort to ease an emerging headache. It was seven in the morning. He could hear Debbie getting up. With coffee in hand, Mike turned on CBC news. The lead story offered no comfort. The House Minority member had been indicted by the Department of Justice on charges of campaign finance corruption. The president clamored for her arrest and expulsion from Congress. Mike could only mutter to himself, "And so it continues."

American Diaspora

As his final task, Mike wrote down a few words on the history of his expatriate community. Someday, someone must write a history of the expatriates, Mike thought. Might as well get started.

From November through February, Americans fled to Canada in the hundreds, then thousands and then tens of thousands. They peaked after the holidays, perhaps wishing one last time with family and friends. Hundreds came across the border each day. By mid-February, close to 250,000 Americans voluntarily left and more were on their way out. They coalesced into communities of expatriates scattered throughout the towns and cities near the border. By the summer, there were hundreds of American expatriate communities settled into life throughout Canada. Some numbered in the thousands, like in Ottawa, Halifax, and Vancouver. Most communities, like Saint Andrews, counted in the hundreds.

At first, the new U.S. administration wouldn't admit that anyone fled the United States, as if it was a mark of their political failure. Then, in a brilliant bit of propaganda, they reversed course. They labelled those who left as the elites. People with money. Cowards afraid to face a new future of greatness. Not real Americans.

Elites. Even then, Mike knew their claim was true enough to offer legitimacy to the propaganda. The 250,000 in exile did not represent typical America. They had the wealth, or the profession, which made escape possible. Those of lesser means and wealth, those tied to the land, those who couldn't leave their work, and their family. They stayed in America.

Mike admitted to this terrible truth. We have the means, the profession, and the income. But we left family behind. Two sons. A granddaughter. We left them. What does that say about us?

The propaganda campaign worked. If the polls were right, expatriate Americans are not popular back home. Now the way was clear for the president's next move.

REFUGE

At the end of February, the president ordered the U.S.-Canadian border be "temporarily closed to all nonessential travel, by land, sea, or air, as a security measure" until all political violence ended. He accused the expatriates of fomenting domestic terrorism, done with the acquiescence of the Canadian government.

Well before the border closure, the Prime Minister of Canada had repeatedly accused the new president and his party of abandoning democracy. He openly questioned the legitimacy of the new president. He warned Americans of their fall into autocracy. At first, the Prime Minister found little support among Canadians for his bluntness. Many feared retaliations from Washington.

That changed with the border closure. Then Canadian Ministers of Parliament, business leaders and media commentators harshly and publicly objected to the border closure. They noted that the source of the political violence came largely from the president's own supporters. Speaking in Parliament, the Prime Minister predicted ". . . this economic blockade, and I use that word blockade deliberately, will ravage the economies of both nations. The White House did this in retaliation for past criticisms of its anti-democracy policies."

The Prime Minister stood his ground in the face of further threats, lies and vulgar insults from the president. The PM brought the issue to the World Trade Organization and the United Nations. He announced new measures to protect and support any American who sought refuge in Canada.

According to media reports, the Prime Minister's advisors cautioned this was a risky move. But as it turned out, among Canadians it was wildly popular. No one likes to be bullied.

Meanwhile, the president found rhetoric alone does change reality. The border could not be closed entirely. Some Americans continued to leave for Canada. After all, it is one of the longest borders in the world, running across thousands of miles of sparsely populated mountains and prairie. Even the United States did not have the resources to lock down every possible remote crossing.

Their daughter Anna was a case in point. She packed up and went to Canada in March, getting across the border with help from Canadian classmates. She later said smuggling herself in wasn't that difficult. Anna found a remote, unguarded dirt road, blocked only by a simple gate. She snapped the chain with bolt cutters and drove across. In those days, the border was still very porous. If the refugees still arriving in Saint Andrews were to be believed, it still is so.

Getting across was the easy part. But they left all they had known. They had no purpose or sense of future. So many times, the expatriates told stories of being rejected by friends and family. Now they stood accused of near treasonous actions by their homeland.

Canada never turned anyone away. She offered safety, security, medical care, and more. A chance for a new life. After they were fed, housed, medically examined, and perhaps employed, there was little else to be done. And in truth during these hard times, little more that many Canadians wanted to do.

Canada treated the Americans stuck in Canada as they are. Refugees. The Canadians could not offer to Americans refugees what they most desperately needed. Canada could not offer leadership.

The diaspora of Americans had to find leadership from their own ranks.

CHAPTER FOUR
RED SKY IN THE MORNING

Early October, Monday, 0800

Webb knocked on the door to Williams's office at 0800, to the minute. "Mr. Williams?"

"Come in. Like I said, we've got an operation to plan. Hang on a second." Williams got up and ordered the other men in the trailer to leave. After they left, he locked the trailer door.

Back behind his desk, Williams said, almost in embarrassment, "I know. That was a bit melodramatic, but these trailers aren't exactly a good place to discuss classified information."

That got Webb's attention. "Understood, sir. What kind of operation are we talking about?"

"It won't come as a surprise, but DOJ is investigating the Whynots. When, I mean, if, they uncover enough evidence, they'll be indicted. Then DOJ requests their extradition. Of course, all that isn't our concern. We come into play if the Canadian government refuses extradition. DOJ assumes that will happen. So, we've been ordered to plan for that contingency."

"Contingency, sir?" Best to let Williams do the talking for now, Webb decided.

"Should extradition fail, we'll be ordered to . . . arrest Mr. and Mrs. Whynot and return them to the United States to face prosecution. By force, if necessary. Even if that means going into Canada without the permission of Canada."

Webb was stunned. He had no idea the op would be like this. He needed time to think. For now, he decided to stick with the dumb responses. "Sir, ah, isn't that illegal?"

"No doubt the Canadians will take it that way." Webb saw a smile cross Williams's face. "But under current U.S. law and DOJ policy, arresting a suspected terrorist or a supporter of terrorism on foreign soil is not illegal, even if the foreign government is not informed or does not give its permission.

"Webb, the same law that got you a job with HSC, the *Secure America Act*, authorized DOJ to answer that question. Well, they did and now we have a new policy.

"There's precedent too, Webb. During the war on terror, DOD routinely conducted killings of suspected terrorists around the world. Drone strikes, special forces raids. Remember bin Laden? We didn't tell Pakistan we were coming."

"But they're, the Whynots, U.S. citizens. Doesn't that play into it?"

"No. Not now."

Webb looked at the ceiling, collecting his thoughts. This op better go right, or someone is going to jail. But if it works . . . time to not play dumb.

"Mr. Williams, this has to be a water borne operation. We can't just drive into Saint Andrews, even if we snuck over the border somehow. That's why DHS sent us the Ribbies. They can't order the Coast Guard or the FBI to do it. Likely they'd refuse. So, we go over the water at night. We go out like we always do, so the Coast Guard doesn't get suspicious. Whynot lives by the water, with a small beach in front of the house. We need to watch the tides, so we don't get out of the boats into knee-deep muck. We arrest him and his wife, bring 'em down to the beach, then get back to U.S. waters by the quickest route. They get picked up in one of our vans someplace along the coast, away from the station. The boats return to the station. To the Coasties, it might look like another routine night patrol. Does that about sum it up, sir?"

"Yes, well, I suppose it does." Williams tried not to show his surprise at Webb's logical and concise off-the-cuff outline of the plan. "The extradition will take time, so this op won't happen soon. But HSC directed us to have plans ready. Start planning the time, route, crews, and all the other details. I'll need to see a draft in three days. Any questions?"

"No, sir. But a couple of, ah, variables come to mind."

"Such as?"

"Weather for one, especially waves. Serious weather limits our Ribbies. And tides, like I mentioned. But there's one big problem I can see. How do we confirm the Whynots are at home?"

"Yeah. If you got any ideas on that, I'd like to hear them." Williams stopped to think before continuing.

"I guess we could try visual surveillance. Watch for activity like lights in the house." Williams realized that wouldn't work. "No, that's a bad idea. Stupid of me. We'd be spotted out on the water. We'd have to get very close to see anything with our night-vision gear. We'd be in Canadian waters. Maybe we could plant a microphone. Christ, I don't know. You think it over. Maybe we call HSC for advice.

"Again, this is classified. Do not discuss this with anyone. No exceptions. Keep any writings locked up. If there are still holes in the draft plan, details that are beyond our expertise, HSC will help us. That's all, for now."

The Committee

"Okay, Mike. We heard your broadcast. 'Today I Fight.' We understand how being questioned by those two agents would be . . . upsetting. But it doesn't sound like you followed the show's guidelines. We need you to explain what you meant by 'I Fight' and we need you to answer our questions. Clear?"

"Quite clear. Fire away."

I guess they're upset. And scared, thought Mike. They sat in his living room with Morgan, the Secretary of the Committee, taking the leadership role. It was Morgan who demanded a meeting.

Mike had nothing against Morgan. In fact, Mike thought rather highly of him. If anyone needed anything, Morgan helped in any way he could.

Questions and answers went back and forth for about ten minutes. On the good side, no one wanted Mike to resign from the Committee. At least not yet. On the bad side, they were all disappointed, even angry, that Mike didn't run his comments by them first. They were right on that point, Mike admitted to them.

Mike summed up his views. "I appreciate how you see this, but I don't back down from what I said. I will fight this new government in any way –

legal way – I can think of. No, I won't support violence. Rest assured at that. The word fight is metaphorical and purposefully dramatic. Obviously, that succeeded, otherwise you wouldn't be here. Whether people understood the metaphor, well, we'll see."

Now Mike turned the tables on them.

"Look, you need to understand something. Those agents had a list of others to be interrogated. You guys were on that list. My being an asshole stopped them from coming to your doorstep. They're focused on me. And Debbie. If they come after anyone, it won't be you guys. It'll be me. You understand what I'm saying? I saved your collective assess. At least for a while."

That quieted things for a few moments before Morgan spoke. "Yeah. Guess we've got a better understanding. In the future, please don't blindside us like that again. Run things by us, especially things like 'I Fight.' Our collective asses, as you say, are still on the line."

CSIS and the SunRise

Every Thursday, more often if needed, CSIS Atlantic Region held a secure videoconference to link together the principals of their offices in Fredericton, Saint John, and Halifax. This morning, the director of the Atlantic Region asked LeClerc to present his findings about the American agents who visited Saint Andrews.

"Sir, I'll begin with a brief on the American HSC agents and a meeting I had with an American military officer, then I will review the SunRise interview itself."

LeClerc ran down the known facts about the Homeland Security Corp special unit at the Coast Guard Station in Eastport, plus the two men in charge, Williams and Webb.

"They're running patrols in the Saint Croix River and to the open ocean in black Zodiac craft, day and night."

"Publicly, HSC says these units are to deter illegal immigration into the United States. As you know, HSC units are deploying along our border with the U.S., as well as their border with Mexico. We assess their public statements are only partially true. We suspect they are also there to prevent Americans from escaping to Canada, but we do not have definitive evidence on that.

"Once we became aware of these ops, we started a surveillance operation using various civilian boats as cover, but from Canadian waters.

"In addition, CSIS has a human asset in Eastport itself. The asset is an American who grew up in the area, lives in Eastport, and has Canadian family members. The asset's orders are to learn the structure, operations, and intention of this new group of agents.

LeClerc described how the agent gathered information. Among the asset's methods was to join in drinks at a local bar frequented by the HSC officers. Even though the officers were under orders not to discuss their work, the asset found they can become "indiscreet" after a few drinks. An example of their indiscretion was repeated disparaging remarks about the Coast Guardsmen.

The director interrupted. "So, these HSC agents are under orders not to talk to anyone about their work but are talking in a bar to our asset. Do I have that right, Robert? And exactly what, if anything, is the asset doing to encourage them to talk?"

"Correct, sir. The asset spends a good deal of time listening, but does talk directly to the HSC agents, in hopes of establishing a friendly relationship that can be exploited."

"Robert, just talking, right?"

LeClerc caught on to the director. Laughing, he said, "Yes sir. Just . . . talking. I should clarify who the asset is. He's a man well into his seventies. He has a natural, gregarious nature. Easy to talk to."

"Understood. Let's continue." The director briefly smiled.

LeClerc then reviewed the facts of his contact at sea with the U.S. Coast Guard officer, Lt. Douglas Miles. The meeting was initiated by Miles to discuss routine search and rescue coordination issues, but the meeting became something more.

"Unusually, he suggested that the meeting take place at sea. We assess he used this tactic to avoid scrutiny by U.S. Homeland Security.

"CCG informed CSIS before the meeting. I went along on our Coast Guard rescue boat out of Saint John in CCG uniform. I identified myself as a Grade 4 CCG officer who held a supervisory position at JRCC Halifax."

Being retired Navy, the director just had to ask. "How'd you fare on the water?"

LeClerc replied, "I wish we used a bigger boat." After a couple chuckles from the other attendees, LeClerc continued.

LeClerc added more detail. At the end of the meeting, Miles asked to speak off the record. We agreed. He asked us if we were concerned the current political climate would harm our joint operations. The real CCG officers agreed with him.

"Perhaps he was simply curious if we were thinking the same thing. I passed my cell number to him, saying if he wanted to discuss these concerns further, he should call me."

"Nothing significant in what he said, but interesting that a U.S. military officer would make such an approach. We do not know if he arranged this meeting with the permission of his chain of command."

The director asked, "Could he become an intelligence asset for CSIS?"

"I cannot say at this time, sir."

"That may be the lieutenant's honest concern. And, yeah, he's a relatively low-ranking officer at an out of the way posting. But he has HSC at his base. He might be an intel source on HSC. So, keep contact with this lieutenant. We need more sources. Alright, the SunRise Café. Let's continue."

LeClerc gave a brief overview of the meeting between the Mike Whynot and the American agents.

"Rather than run through the transcript of the interview, I thought, for better understanding, I'd play the video for you. I'll activate the video from my end. Nothing is required by you. If there are no objections . . ."

When the video was finished, LeClerc asked, "Any questions?"

The director spoke first. "Have you approached Whynot?"

"No, sir."

"Maybe you should. Yes, please do so. A retired intelligence officer, you say. We're using a number of retired or resigned senior U.S. military to try to get some insight into the current mindset of the American military. Maybe he could help us out in the same way. Maybe he still has contacts back in the states. That could be important.

"You also said he's head of the American community there. Let's find out if he has information about that community that could be useful to us. Now, do you know the intentions RCMP has concerning the video?"

LeClerc explained how he had asked Roy about RCMP intentions with the video. Roy couldn't say as yet.

"Why do you think the Americans were interviewing Whynot?"

Before answering, LeClerc glanced at each video frame of the attendees. Once he was sure he had everyone's attention, he said one word. "Targeting."

"Targeting. Explain that please." The director seemed a little taken aback.

"Sir, the Americans know that extradition is unlikely to succeed. Very unlikely. We know of almost forty such in-person interviews that took place in the last few days. Sergeant Wilkins told me the agents seemed not the least upset they couldn't interview anyone else. That indicates Whynot is their primary. The others were camouflage. Whynot is their target. That is the working assessment."

Now the director was getting a little nervous. "When you say targeting, are you hinting at the possibility of assassination?"

"No, sir. There's no evidence to support that. Not yet. I'm saying that we should recognize the possibility that the Americans are not done with Whynot. That they might try something . . . extraordinary."

An excruciating silence passed before the director spoke. "Very well. Well done, Robert. This will certainly be brought to Ottawa. Immediately. Your report and the video. But before I go, does anyone have any other questions, or recommendations, on what to do with this recording?"

LeClerc was hoping for this opening. "Sir, I have one recommendation, but I caution isn't without risk to Whynot, and to CSIS. It would be breaking a rule or two. And it could further anger the Americans toward Whynot and harm relations."

"Oh, Christ. Well, let's have it."

"Sir, I recommend we leak the video to CBC. With CSIS director approval of course. I suggest we leave that up to her if the PM should be informed."

"Leak it to CBC, you say." The director seemed to LeClerc to be musing over that possibility. Then, inexplicitly, the director did something LeClerc had never seen him do. He stopped the recording feature and broke into a short fit of laughter.

When that passed, the director explained himself. "Excuse me, everyone. Please forgive the laughter. Unprofessional. But I was thinking, this video will, I mean it might embarrass those bast . . . former allies . . . in Washington."

"And Robert, one could argue that the video, once public knowledge, might protect Whynot by making him a public figure. I'll pass your recommendation along to the CSIS director. Thank you once again.

"And off the record, I personally would like to pin a medal on Whynot's chest. Robert, when you talk to him, tell him, from me, great speech."

Gone Viral

Another Wednesday morning at the SunRise. CBC was wrapping up its *News from America* feature. None of it was good. After reviewing the now typical acts of political violence, they reported the arrest of a journalist with

C-SPAN, on charges of aiding terrorism. That was the third such arrest this week, according to the news anchor.

As he sat down, Mike prayed for a breakfast in peace. The Fates decided otherwise.

Edward called on Mike's cell. "Mike. We need to talk. Now. Where are you?"

"At the SunRise. I'm hoping to enjoy breakfast. A noneventful breakfast. I ordered about five minutes ago. I bet you're not going to allow me a decent breakfast."

"No, I'm not, and you can blame yourself. Because you're a troublemaker. Look, I'll be over in about five minutes. You can enjoy breakfast till then."

Mike was in no mood for that. *Like hell I'll give up on breakfast. I'm going to finish my breakfast. On my own clock. And this time, Edward can buy his own.*

Breakfast arrived just as Edward came through the door. *So, what's this lawyer got to say that's so damned important,* Mike wondered. *Bad enough he chewed me out over the I Fight broadcast . . . Don't you realize DOJ will claim that is an explicit call to violence? Didn't you listen to me at all?*

Mike had to admit that Edward had a point.

"Good morning, Edward. I hope you are well. How can I help you?" Mike carried an almost mocking tone as he dug into his breakfast.

"Help? Help me? All I can say Mike, is . . ." Edward almost seemed lost for words, a bad thing for a lawyer. ". . . is that you are the dumbest son-of-a-bitch and the luckiest son-of-a-bitch, all at the same time."

"Right. So, what are you talking about?"

"Look at this while you're eating." Edward brought up CBC on his tablet computer, maxed the volume, and clicked on a video. A video of what happened here last Wednesday. *The SunRise Café Incident.* "It's a replay of a CBC broadcast."

Mike stopped eating. So did the breakfast patrons. In a minute, Edward and Mike were surrounded by about ten staff and patrons. The tape started with the moment Roy introduced the two U.S. agents. It ended with Claude's rendition of *La Marseillaise.* For an irrational reason, Mike's first thought was, *well, at least that last part will help Claude attract French tourists.*

When the video finished, the little crowd cheered and clapped Mike on the back. All that was needed was someone to start singing *O, Canada.* And before Mike finished that thought, it already started. While the patrons struggled off key with the first verse, Edward pointed out something on the screen to Mike.

"Look at this. It's also on YouTube. Only been posted for eighteen hours. Seven million plus views. I don't know much about social media, but Mike, I think you've gone viral."

Mike's expression could forever more define the expression dumb look. The singing died down and people went back to breakfast. Except Mike.

"There's more. It's the lead story on CBC, Sky News, CNN International and the BBC at the top of the hour, coming up. Looks like people take exception to Americans cops insulting Canadians. And grabbing you. There's reporting the Prime Minister will be calling a press conference for late today. You're the reason."

Ah, shit. "What? No, this can't be. Wait. You better not be thinking I posted this. I didn't tape it. You didn't tape it. You couldn't get a copy from Roy. Anyway, Roy only made an audiotape, right? How'd it get online? Do you know, Edward?"

"The only two people I know who recorded anything are Roy and that agent Williams. Can't see why they'd post it. For Williams, makes him look bad. And Roy? No, Roy wouldn't. I gotta believe RCMP would go through channels. And not post it anonymously. I got a call into Roy, by the way."

Mike took a second look at the video, this time comparing the images to the dining room.

"It wasn't either of them. They only made audio recordings for starters. For a video recording, well, look at the perspective. Even if Roy or Williams did a video, they weren't able to video things from that perspective."

"You're right. I missed that. Too excited I guess."

"Whoever taped it, was sitting at this angle." Mike pointed from the table to the counter. "Yeah, that's about right." Mike said, "I think I know who did it."

"Now Edward, what's the fallout on me? Why am I dumb and lucky?"

Family

After finishing with Edward, Mike left a message for Debbie at the clinic. He knew it could be a while before she returned the call. Her days were a medical treadmill, with appointments every 15 minutes. She might be able to call if someone no-showed. Or her lunch time. Or maybe just a text.

Anna called from Ottawa.

"Holy shit, Dad! Was that really you . . . on the video? On YouTube? Are you okay?" Anna was both proud of her dad, and terrified. Mike winced at his negligence in not calling her too.

97

"I'm fine and yeah, it was me. It really happened." Truth was, Mike wasn't okay. He was well and truly scared.

"Look Dad. I've only got a minute before my next patient. I'll call you tonight when I get home. Love you."

"That'd be great. Love you too. Bye."

Surprisingly, Debbie called seconds after he hung up with Anna. "Mike, people in the office said you were on the news. That thing with the DHS agents. It's all over. I didn't see it. A lot of patients did. Are you alright? Was it real?"

"I'm fine. Edward has officially assured me I am fine. And yes, it's real." Mike tried to sound as matter of fact as possible. He wasn't sure it worked. "And I didn't know about this. Look, I'm sure you're busy. Let's talk tonight."

"Yes, Mike. Love you."

Texts arrived from Robert and Matt seconds later. Alerted by friends, they both saw the video. Mike texted back reassurances that he, and Mom, were fine and yes, that was him, and he'd call them tonight. That also reminded Mike he needed to work out a more secure communication plan with them.

Williams

"Sir, I think you'd better see this." The officer handed Williams his phone as it played the café interview on CBC news. Williams recognized the images. Williams gave the phone back to the officer, thanking her, and asked to shut the door on her way out. He then vomited his breakfast into the office waste basket.

That done, he went out to find Webb. Within five minutes, both were in Williams's office watching CBC online. When the video ended, Webb reached his personal best for eloquence. "Oh, shit."

Prime Minister

After taping his show, Mike went straight home. Not every day a major world leader is about to address his nation about you. Might have to redo the show after this. He turned on CBC news.

A story was running of renewed tensions across the Taiwan Strait. For the past weeks, Chinese navy warships and fighters escorting air force bombers probed Taiwanese airspace and waters with a frequency and depth not seen before. Never had the Chinese marshalled two task forces centered on their aircraft carriers. Military experts noted the air and sea fleets were too small for an outright invasion and there was no indication of amphibious capability. They speculated China was testing the resolve of a United States distracted by internal strife. The anchor suddenly broke in.

"I hate to cut you off, but we're expecting comments from the Prime Minister regarding an incident between American federal agents and a U.S. citizen, in Saint Andrews, New Brunswick. Many have already seen the video of that . . . right. Here's the Prime Minister."

"Good afternoon, everyone. *Bonjour tout le monde.*" He was speaking from the Office of the Prime Minister and the Privy Council in Ottawa, across from the parliament building. The Prime Minister stood before microphones with Canadian flags arrayed in the backdrop. Before him sat correspondents from around the world, including the United States, hurriedly brought in for this unscheduled presser. He opened with a prepared statement.

"This government is aware of the video of a very disturbing incident that happened one week ago today in Saint Andrews, New Brunswick. Millions of Canadians and millions more around the world have seen the video. This morning, it was the lead story on CBC, and quickly made its way across the Atlantic to BBC, Sky News, TV5Monde, and others. The world saw what happened.

"The video is genuine. I am assured of this by our Canadian Security Intelligence Service and the RCMP. As the video shows, an RCMP officer was present at the incident, and he has personally affirmed its authenticity."

Well, Roy had an interesting morning, imagined Mike. A call from the Prime Minister is more than a little out of the ordinary.

The Prime Minister then repeated the first part of his statement in French. This always impressed Mike. *If only I could speak a second language as well as that.* The Prime Minister then continued in English.

"As anyone can see, two American federal law enforcement agents, belonging to the U.S. Department of Homeland Security, Homeland Security Corps, questioned an American expatriate and political dissident now residing as a permanent resident in Saint Andrews. This government had granted the American government permission to interview the American only under escort by an officer of the RCMP. To say they 'interviewed' this person understates the incident."

The Prime Minister paused, and then changed to an angrier tone.

"They threatened the American, and by proxy threatened all Americans who have left their country. They threatened the American with criminal investigation and arrest because his political opinions and activities are critical of the new administration in Washington. Indeed, one of the agents laid hands upon the American and only backed down when the RCMP officer told the agent he could face arrest for assault.

"This was not an isolated incident. Intelligence confirms without doubt 39 other such interrogations. We are working to fully document the nature of the interrogations and will release further information on that as soon as possible.

"This is an egregious violation of diplomatic norms. Undoubtably, the Canadian people want to know what their government will do in response."

Again, the Prime Minister brought his Francophone audience up to speed. Then he switched back to English.

"Our challenge is this. A country who was once our greatest ally, now behaves more like an adversary. In response to this incident, this government is taking certain immediate actions."

"Americans now living in Canada will continue to have the full protection of this government. Henceforth, American federal agents will not be allowed into Canada to conduct this kind of activity. Any extradition requests made by the United States for Americans in Canada are now on hold as we develop additional safeguards protecting rights and liberty. That may eventually include a renegotiation of our extradition treaty with the United States.

"I have contacted our allies in Europe, recommending their intelligence services investigate if American agents contacted Americans within their borders. I suggested such an effort be coordinated through NATO.

"Our ambassador to the United States is now delivering a note to the U.S. Department of State demanding an explanation of the SunRise Café incident. We will await their explanation.

"I will be asking Parliament to help increase the capabilities of the RCMP and CSIS so we can better deal with such incidents.

"Finally, this government and Members of Parliament, including opposition members, have made no secret of our collective displeasure of recent anti-democratic events in the United States. Events which seem to arise daily from the new administration. Canada has a tradition of standing for human rights, for democracy. I want to assure Canadians we will not shrink from our principles. We will carry on. Canada will defend its sovereignty. Canada will defend democracy."

For the third time, he spoke in French. With that, the Prime Minister asked for few questions. Who made the video? Did the government leak the video to CBC? Have you spoken to the American who was questioned? What is the intention of the U.S. Government?

Could be a customer, someone other than the American or the agents, and we know it was not RCMP, but we're investigating. Not that I know, but that is being investigated. No. We are asking them.

Just before leaving the microphone, a reporter asked for his opinion of the American's defense of Canada to the American agents. "Oh, yes, I saw that. Magnificent. *Magnifique.*"

On Thin Ice

William's HSC supervisor called. It was not pleasant.

Over the past months, Williams developed a genuine dislike for his supervisor. No, something more. Visceral hatred. Another one of those overweight, bald bullet-headed political appointees whose personality never matured beyond that of a bully. A lawyer and a state senator from New Hampshire headed for nowhere fast, he remade himself into a hardline right wing firebrand during the presidential primary and caught the eye of the new president. Suddenly, he's a key player in the Homeland Security Corps.

"Yeah, we all saw the video. Everyone in Washington HSC and DHS leadership. And the White House. HSC hasn't heard from all concerned, but so far . . . so far, it's been negative. No, a better way to put it is this way. Do you have any idea of the shitstorm you created?"

It went downhill from there. His supervisor demanded an explanation, but when Williams tried to explain, the supervisor interrupted. Repeatedly. Yelling. Cursing.

"You let this get away from you. Whynot made a fool of you. And your second, Webb, grabbing Whynot. Didn't you go over with him how you'd handle this?" Before Williams could answer, the supervisor said, "Guess not."

"You know what's really pissing me off? The report you submitted that day. I read it. It didn't give us a full picture of what happened. Jesus, you should have included that part about the Mountie threatening to arrest Webb."

Williams simply could not speak. Or maybe it was best not to speak. Williams had never been spoken to like this. He was unnerved, to put it mildly.

"Alright. A couple things. For one, tell Webb he's on extremely thin ice. We might demote him, or even fire him. Then there's you. We'll be talking about you. I won't promise anything right now. Hell, likely this will fall back badly on me too because I am your supervisor. Goes with the territory, but right now . . ." He paused. "Williams, you let me down. But to my boss, in your favor, I pointed out that you pulled Webb back and admonished him severely in the trip back to Eastport.

"There'll be more. Right now, the White House, DHS and State are busy coordinating a response to the Canadian Prime Minister. It's not beyond the realm of possibility that you and Webb will be reassigned or fired. Honestly, I don't know what's coming. When I know, you will know. That's all."

"Yes, sir." *What else was there to say?*

The President is not Amused

The following morning, the CBC anchor led the hour with a story first reported by *The Washington Post.*

"According to their report, the American President reacted angrily to the video of the U.S. Homeland Security Corps agents interviewing an American in Saint Andrews, in what has quickly become known as the SunRise Café incident.

"Apparently, the president directed his fury at our Prime Minister, not at his own agents. He is far angrier with the Prime Minister's statement about the incident, in which the PM was very critical of the behavior of the American federal agents and the president's administration. *The Post's* reporting of the president's emotional state is fortified by an official response from the U.S. Department of State. It reads:

'Once again, the government of the United States urges the government of Canada to cease its baseless hostility toward the United States. The internal affairs of the United States are just that, internal. The actions taken by the Homeland Security Corps agents were wholly lawful. They did not arrest the subject of the interview, but merely wished to inform him of the legal jeopardy he was facing under United States law. The agents requested the subject's cooperation. He refused. Instead, the Canadian authorities, the Royal Canadian Mounted Police, overreacted. If any threats were made, they came from the RCMP.'"

The CBC anchor said, "Doesn't look like we'll be getting an apology from the U.S. government any time soon."

Mike watched the broadcast from home. *I guess I qualify as an international incident now. Wonder how I can use this in the broadcast?*

While Mike was musing about his show, across the border in Eastport an anxious lawyer got a phone call.

It was Williams's supervisor. "Well, Williams, it falls to me to tell you . . ." The man paused, deliberately, to twist the knife a bit. "You are quite fortunate. The president decided you and Webb did nothing wrong. You did your job. There will be no sacrificing lambs on the altar of diplomacy. I'm paraphrasing him. The HSC director said the president refused any suggestion to apologize. He refused any suggestion to reassign, demote, or fire you or Webb. Felt it signaled weakness. Congratulations."

Williams let out a deep sigh on the phone.

"Guess you're feeling better now. Know this though. I recommended you both be dismissed. You really screwed up. You embarrassed this agency. But . . . the commander-in-chief thought differently, so here we are."

Williams took a moment to screw up the courage to ask, "Sir, may I ask what happens now."

"What happens now? Just do your goddamn job! Do what we tell you to do. Put a leash on Webb. Get the details of that op ready. And stay the hell out of trouble." The supervisor hung up.

Could've been worse, Williams thought. He went out to find Webb.

Calling the Kids

After dinner, Mike and Debbie started calling the kids. Edward would be pleased to know Mike took his advice to be very careful in their communications with their adult children.

Was it reasonable, or rational, to believe the United States government was spying on their digital communications? On one hand, yes. Mike knew from his military intelligence training that capturing cell phone calls, emails, and videoconferencing was easily within the technical capabilities of the national security agencies. Videoconferencing apps may claim "end-to-end" encryption, but there's always a back door in. Likely they'd cooperate with law enforcement. Especially these days.

Mike had to ask himself, *why me? I'm not a leader of a great resistance movement. Even less than a minor figure. A single gnat on an elephant. Why would they waste attention on me? But they did waste attention on me. Even Debbie agrees a little paranoia right now was a good thing. Maybe they're crazy and we're not. Maybe we're both crazy. Best to take Edward's advice and put on the aluminum foil hats.*

They both knew going completely silent would only draw further suspicion. So, Mike and Debbie continued using their regular cell phones to call their kids. They sent email. They even kept up their once a week after dinner Zoom calls. Even from the beginning of their self-imposed exile, they asked their kids not to bring up politics even in the slightest degree. They kept it light with lots of videos of their granddaughter.

For what Mike and Debbie were planning, they needed a secure means to talk to their sons.

The Friday after the SunRise Café incident, Mike drove up to Saint Stephen to buy three cheap, pre-paid, stand-alone disposable phones with their own cell numbers. Difficult to trace back to the users. After the minutes are used up, throw away the phones and get new ones. Criminals used these to thwart police surveillance. A burner phone they call it. The historian in Mike remembered that effective resistance movements often borrowed the methods and tactics of criminals. Mike bought three phones. In cash. One for himself, one for Debbie, and one for Anna.

Mailing a burner phone overnight to Anna in Ottawa was no problem. He put in a short note to only use the burner for "sensitive" communications, meaning anything remotely connected with political opinions.

Anna called them on the burner phone the following Sunday. Using the burner phone's speaker, they again assured her they were fine, that the Canadian government promised them legal protection, and Edward was on the case. No worries.

"Anna, I have to say I enjoyed going after those two bastards. On the down side, I probably, no, I am certain they will try something. But I think we'll be alright. Still, you might want to watch your surroundings more closely. We know you're involved in protests in Ottawa against that man. Be careful who you deal with." Time to shift things to softer topics. "So, Anna, how are things in Ottawa?"

"Fine." The one word used by children the world over to deflect discussion. "I'm fine, Dad. But I'm worried, really worried about you two. I mean, what'll they do next?" It went on for a minute or two, Anna pouring out her fears, before Debbie gently stopped her.

"Anna, we said we're fine. We're safe. They can't touch us here. They can't touch you. We have friends here. I promise you, if things change, we'll let you know."

It was Debbie's turn to pivot to conversation. "So, any chance of us seeing you? Maybe a weekend peeping the foliage?"

Anna settled down, explaining that she's seeing more patients, including Canadians now. And she's got side volunteer work with the American community. They're planning more protests.

"I think a weekend in October will work," she said. "After Canadian Thanksgiving. My Canadian colleagues invited me to their Thanksgiving. So, I think the weekend after that. Do you want to come here, or I go there?"

"We'll come to Ottawa. We could use a little get away. See you on the Zoom call Monday? Love you."

Anna softly pleaded, "Be safe. Love you too." Debbie had the same thought as Mike. *Be safe. That's what parents always say to their kids.*

Regret welled up in Mike. He found himself weeping as his thoughts found new depths. *My kids are dispersed. Perhaps endangered. All my fault. I did this. I didn't have to do this. We could have gone along with things. Kept our heads down. Bent with the prevailing wind. Gone home.*

NO! I won't do this! Mike snapped himself back. *We did nothing wrong. We're free Americans. We spoke out. We protested. I won't allow those bastards the slightest victory, even in the battlefield of my own mind.*

The Boys Back Home

Getting his sons on burner phones was a bit trickier. He couldn't be certain that anything mailed to them from anywhere in Canada wouldn't be intercepted. He couldn't call them at their work. Texting from usual phone was open to interception. Matt and Robert needed to buy their own burners. But how do you get them to understand what to do?

Hollywood supplied inspiration. For God knows how long, movies and TV shows used product placement. Sell consumer products by placing them in a shot's field of view. Why shouldn't that work for this? For the next Zoom call, Mike put a burner phone box in the background, almost comically pointing to the box without speaking. Mike hoped they would get the message.

On the same call, Mike carefully arranged the books on the bookcases he always had in the background. He grouped them in sets representing the numbers of his burner cell phone number. Five books for the first number, seven books for the second number, and so on. A horribly stupid code, Mike knew, but maybe they'd get lucky.

It worked. Robert made a burner call on Wednesday. Matt called on Thursday. The same assurances, the same small talk about health and work. With Robert, a lot of time was spent asking with Eva, of course.

Mike and Debbie decided beforehand not to yet raise the issue of getting them to Canada. A plan wasn't in place anyway.

Mike stressed the necessity of situational awareness, telling them to assume their communications are being monitored. Know who you talk to. If something sensitive needs to be discussed, use the burner phones to reach us, or Anna, or to each other. Do not let anyone else know about the burner phones. Watch for anything unusual at home or work. Changes in the behavior of friends or acquaintances. Buy new burner phones every two weeks. In cash. At different stores.

Mike and Debbie urged them to keep their heads down. Stay away from political activities. Someday, we'll be together again.

No parent wants their child to be a hero.

CHAPTER FIVE

SAILOR TAKE WARNING

LeClerc and Whynot

The following Wednesday morning after becoming a viral video sensation, a colder and rainy morning, Mike tempted fate once more by driving up to the SunRise Café. All he wanted was a quiet breakfast with his neighbor George.

The last few days had been interesting. Interviews at home via his laptop with CBC, Sky News, *Le National*, CNN International, MSNBC and BBC. Even *The Morning Show* on Global. Also, several online news outlets from back home. Mike disciplined himself to stick to the facts and keep emotions in check. Reviewing the interviews later, he made a mental note to punch up the décor of his living room.

Funny, no interview requests from American media like ABC, CBS, or NBC. Why?

The SunRise Café incident sparked protests against the United States in Halifax, Toronto, Ottawa, and Vancouver, as well as across the pond in London and Paris. Mike and Debbie found out later that Anna spoke to the crowd protesting in Ottawa near the American embassy. Proud as he was, Mike worried the protest organizers, that is the American expatriate community there, were just using her. More worrisome, he feared agents or collaborators could be in the crowd.

Mike settled his mind on that matter. *There is always risk. I have to fight. She has to fight.*

Unsurprisingly, the news cycle moved on from him as the week went on. The last couple of days were quiet. Claude graciously had Mike and Debbie into the café for a free dinner on Sunday. But that too was a one-off. As Mike stepped in the door that morning, Claude said, "So, you expect a free breakfast now?"

Claude asked if Mike wanted the usual. As if he wanted to break a bad habit, or just irritate Claude, Mike ordered fried eggs and sausage instead. And in practiced French. Irritation won out. George came in as Mike made his order. They both took their usual seats and after the good mornings, George filled in Mike on the latest border gossip. Nothing significant.

Halfway through their breakfast, Mike looked up to see the Oxford Shirt guy coming in the café. Oxford Shirt, this time with a khaki jacket against the rain and cold, looked right back at Mike and started to walk to the counter, taking a seat at the bar and ordering coffee. A minute later, with coffee in hand, Oxford Shirt walked over to Mike and George.

"Good morning, Mr. Whynot and Officer LeBlanc. May I join you?" Mike was a bit taken aback. George just kept on eating the last of his breakfast while looking at Oxford Shirt. "Perhaps I should introduce myself, Mr. Whynot. My name is Robert LeClerc. I was here in this café when the two American agents met with you. I would like to talk to you about that."

George spoke up before Mike, acting like the protective friend he was. "Yeah, like who are you? You a cop or something? A reporter?"

LeClerc turned to George, smiling as he said, "More like the 'or something.' Here's my identification." George's eyes widened as he read the ID. He started to laugh, and looked at Mike. "Oh, boy. Well, Mike, I guess I'll finish my breakfast over at the bar and then get home. I think you two need to be alone. I'll pick up the check this time. You guys might be a while."

"Could you guys let me in on the joke?"

"I assure you, Mr. Whynot, this is not a joke. Here's my ID." LeClerc handed the ID across the table. LeClerc always enjoyed the reaction people had when they found out who he worked for. *What are you, a spy?* Even a lot of Canadians had no idea his agency even existed. He doubted CIA agents had the same reaction. More of them in the movies.

Mike denied him that small pleasure.

"Canadian Security Intelligence Service." Mike handed the ID back to LeClerc. "Right. Civilian agency. Covert and overt collection of intelligence in Canada and abroad. Advises government leaders on security matters. Established in the 80's. In '84, I think. Took over such matters from RCMP. CSIS can surveil foreigners and Canadians as well. Yeah, in some ways your CSIS has more investigative authority than CIA.

"Yeah, Mr. LeClerc, I know something about your agency. When I was a U.S. Air Force intelligence officer, always believed it was a good idea to understand the intelligence services of our allies, military and civilian. And adversaries too. Never met anyone from CSIS before, but I've worked alongside Canadian Military Intelligence. I'm sure you already know my background."

Mike took another forkful of eggs and said, "You might as well sit down."

As LeClerc sat down, Mike asked, "So, what's your job with CSIS? Why talk to me?"

"Well, first let me say I didn't expect an American to be familiar with CSIS. Well done. I'm an analyst out of Halifax Atlantic Region office. Since these border troubles developed, I've been assigned to the Fredericton office. Prior to CSIS, I was an intelligence officer with the forces."

"Don't think our paths crossed, Mr. LeClerc. You don't mind if I keep working on breakfast, do you? Anyway, as an analyst, you're engaging right now in the collection of intelligence, by meeting with me. I assume you're acting under orders from leadership."

"Quite right, on both counts."

"And you were seated at the counter when the American agents came here?"

"Yes, that is the case."

"You recorded the whole thing. And you sent it to CBC, didn't you?"

"I am not at liberty to say."

"Come on. I'm pretty sure you did record it. I saw your tablet out, camera side pointed in our direction. The video's perspective points right back to you. Don't bullshit me. Besides, this is the third Wednesday morning breakfast in a row, ruined by . . . by what I don't know."

Mike threw down his fork across the plate. The noise startled even him.

"Then, Mr. Intelligence Officer, James Bond of Canada, what are you at liberty to say?"

LeClerc ignored Mike's minor tantrum. He first reminded Mike of the Prime Minister's statement. "Mr. Whynot, the PM made clear you weren't the only American HSC interviewed that week. Taken altogether, these interviews shifted CSIS thinking."

He explained that until now CSIS did not view the expatriates as a source of good intel. Refugees were someone else's bureaucratic problem.

"That's changed. More analysis of the American expatriate communities is now warranted. Working together, American expatriates and the Canadian government, ways might be found to enhance the security of both."

Anticipating an obvious objection, LeClerc said emphatically he was not looking to use any expatriate against the United States. CSIS was not looking for agents. CSIS was merely gathering intelligence. Once the intel was collected, analysis should show if further work was worthwhile. CSIS would report its findings to the Minister of Public Safety.

Before meeting Whynot, LeClerc decided not to ask if he had any active-duty contacts in the states. People he could call. People who might provide information. Too soon, but certainly later.

Almost shrugging his shoulders, LeClerc said, "Maybe something beneficial is found for both sides. Maybe nothing." Mike thought what LeClerc said, so far, was nothing more than a vague recitation of the intelligence cycle.

Perhaps LeClerc sensed what Mike was thinking when as a first concrete step in this cooperation, he suggested allowing CSIS to meet to the Expat Committee and if they agree, start sharing information on the expatriate community in Saint Andrews.

Mike didn't respond. He kept sipping the coffee. Mike thought, *yeah, he's recruiting.*

Then LeClerc focused on Mike, explaining CSIS assesses the American agents were interested only in Mike and no one else. They were "targeting" expatriate leadership. Mike should be prepared for an extradition request, but there is a chance of something beyond that. What that could be is unknown.

"In other words, watch my back."

"Yes, that would be good advice. On the other hand, it's possible that because the video made you a public figure, DOJ, DHS, or whoever, might decide to back off. Maybe even back off on everyone they interviewed across Canada. Why? Maybe they don't want to add to your, ah, celebrity."

"You're about to explain the other, other hand."

"The video embarrassed the administration. They may react in a less than analytical, rational way. Doubling down is the correct phrase I believe."

"Well, LeClerc, I can say without any uncertainty that you have ruined my breakfast. But I have to agree with your intelligence assessment. It fits the limited intel and makes logical sense. I also agree my community could be valuable in a small way. That is, could be. But I'm not sure how they will react to sharing their stories with you. But, okay. I will take what you said back to the Expat Committee."

"Thank you."

"Let me warn you, if I think your people are trying to recruit agents from our people, the deal is off. Clear?"

"Clear. If I were you, I would harbor suspicions of my intent. It's understandable." LeClerc reached into his shirt pocket and withdrew a business card. "This is how to get ahold of me. I'd be happy to talk to the Expat Committee."

"I'll see what they say. I'll try to convince them to meet with you."

"I sincerely hope so. Really. And this is something I was told to say, but I was going to say it anyway." LeClerc paused to make sure he had Mike's attention. "Right now, our government is shielding your people from the American administration. To keep that shield up, the best thing expatriates can do is stay calm and stay within our laws.

"You see, I listen to your broadcasts. That's just basic intelligence gathering. The *Today I Fight* broadcast caught our attention. You ended with the message, 'stay peaceful.' I'm inclined to believe you want to keep things peaceful. I'm sure DHS or HSC heard it too. But I'm not sure they will interpret it in the same way.

"I think you, and the Expat Committee, need to realize that should someone in your community plot, or take, a violent action, illegal under Canadian law, that could reflect on all expatriates. It would strengthen the arguments being made by the U.S. administration, that expatriates foment domestic terrorism." LeClerc leaned in toward Mike.

"And it would put my government in an untenable situation. Violence by one expatriate could result in that shield being lowered for all. So, it would be a good idea for your community to keep us informed of any hotheads. Do you understand?"

"Yes, I do." Mike realized that warning was the real message from LeClerc.

"Good. Please pass along my message to your community. If you get any intel on illegal activity, please call me, or Roy Wilkins of course.

"I'm like a lot of Canadians right now. We don't like what happened in your country. We want to help your people. But frankly, we're scared of what might happen to us. Rather not give the Americans an excuse, ah, to do something against us."

"I'll pass along your message."

"Well, good day then." LeClerc got up, but then remembered one last thing. "Oh, yes, something more. About the video. This is off the record, but the Atlantic Region director said to tell you, from him, that he liked how you stood up for Canada. He said he'd pin a medal on you if he could."

Mike went back to the last of his breakfast, grumpily saying, "Yeah, thanks. I've heard stuff like that more than once lately."

Expat Committee and CSIS

Debbie wasn't pleased with Mike's silence during dinner. Time to spark a little conversation.

"Well, how'd it go with the committee?" In keeping with the "honesty" policy, Mike told Debbie straight away about LeClerc disturbing his Wednesday breakfast and asking for cooperation between the Expat Committee and CSIS.

"No problem making sure our people obey the law, no problem. Morgan wants that message in the show as often as possible. On cooperating with CSIS, it's a no go. They voted it down. Matter of fact, I'm the only one who voted to work with LeClerc. Guess it made them nervous. Too much risk. And no, they couldn't explain why they felt that way, but I suppose it's understandable. They're afraid."

Debbie grumbled about the committee members just wanting to bury their heads in the sand. She also had a few choice words about cowardice. "What's the next step?"

"CSIS has an office in Fredericton. That's where LeClerc works. I'm thinking of going there. Talk to him some more. Face to face. And . . ."

Debbie knew what he going to do before even Mike knew. "You're going to give him the information on our people, anyway, aren't you?"

Mike allowed a moment to pass.

"Yes. I am."

"Why? I'm not saying you should or shouldn't. But I want to understand your thinking."

"I guess it comes down to this. CSIS would interview willing expatriates to learn why they fled the states. They might be able to objectively analyze the data. All of us might gain a better understanding of why we did it and why we stay. We haven't been very good at that. You understand?"

"No, not really. I mean, it might help. But they're also looking for intel that will help defend themselves. They're looking for something more than biographies."

"Yes, you're right."

LeClerc and Miles

Somewhat timidly, a seaman knocked on Miles's office door frame to get his attention away from his morning coffee. "Ah, Lieutenant Miles? Excuse me, sir, but we just got a call from RCMP. They want to talk to you. Line two, sir."

So much for having a peaceful cup of coffee. "Thanks. I'll take it here." He punched the button for line two. Miles said, "Good morning. Lieutenant Miles."

"Lieutenant, this is Corporal Jensen, RCMP. We would like to meet with you to discuss an active criminal case we are working on. Would that be alright?"

"Of course, Mr., I mean, corporal. Where are you? Are you in Eastport?"

"Almost." The corporal seemed to laugh. "If you look out the station's windows, we are just over the border, due east of you. We're aboard one of our Coast Guard vessels. I'm calling you on a cell phone. We request permission to dock at your facility."

"Stand by one." *Christ, I have no idea if I have the authority to do that.* Miles yelled down the passageway. "Hey, senior chief, you in your office?"

"Yes, sir. How can I help?" Miles walked briskly to see the chief and told him who was on the phone. "Senior chief, this ever happen before?" The chief, somewhat amused, said, "Yes, nothing unusual, except in times past they at least phoned us ahead of time." Miles then asked, like a boy asking permission of dad, "Can I allow him to dock here?"

"Oh, yes, sir. We've done it before. Sounds like they got a law enforcement case."

Miles went back to his office. "RCMP. This is Lieutenant Miles. Permission granted." When Miles turned back to the passageway, there was the chief. "Wadda ya say, skipper, let's go meet the Mounties."

Miles and the senior chief grabbed their Foul Weather Parkas and were there to greet the RCMP as the Canadian Coast Guard vessel secured itself to the dock. A uniformed RCMP officer came off first, followed by another man in the uniform of the Canadian Coast Guard, who was suddenly familiar to Miles. The Familiar Man suggested, "Lieutenant Miles, shall we go to your office? I can brief you there."

"I have a conference room that would accommodate us better."

Once all were seated, Miles looked directly at the Familiar Man and asked, "I've met you before, haven't I?" The Familiar Man confirmed Miles' suspicion. The corporal interjected "You needn't worry, lieutenant, chief. No one's is in trouble with RCMP. This shouldn't take long. Let me allow Mr. LeClerc to brief you."

LeClerc admitted to Miles he was the man in Canadian Coast Guard uniform who gave him a business card at the end of the at-sea meeting. He then presented his CSIS identification, explaining he was an intelligence analyst, and said, "I apologize, lieutenant, for the subterfuge and false identity. We, that is CSIS, felt it was necessary because of your guests, the Homeland Security Corps. We couldn't be sure who'd be listening. Our true purpose is to share information we have about those HSC people."

At a loss of what to say, Miles stammered out a string of questions. "Who are you again and what are you doing here? What about this active criminal case you talked about?"

LeClerc decided certain preliminaries were necessary. He explained the mission of CSIS. He repeated they had intelligence concerning the HSC patrols, admitting his government had the patrols under surveillance for two months now. He then produced a USB drive.

"This drive contains a log of all our observations of the HSC patrols, plus video and digital photographs. Of course, those observations were made from Canadian territory. You may wish to compare what we logged with what HSC has been telling you.

"I am passing this information on to you, lieutenant, as a demonstration of my government's concern about these patrols. You may pass this information to your superiors, which I recommend."

At this point, the senior chief tried to excuse himself, saying this conversation seemed way, way above his pay grade. Miles asked him to stay. Without telling the chief, Miles instinctively felt he needed a witness.

"Let me try to understand this. You, the Canadian Security Intelligence Service, did I get that right? You're giving this intelligence to me. The commanding officer of a small boat station. I have to ask why. I mean, I'm kinda the lowest rung on the ladder. Why don't you send it along to our State Department with whatever protest or complaint is appropriate?"

Leaning forward in his chair, LeClerc tried to explain. "On other issues pertaining to U.S.-Canadian relations of late, we have tried that traditional approach. That hasn't worked, in my government's opinion. The U.S. State

Department does not seem to be taking our concerns on any matter seriously. We now assess that perhaps a bottom-up, local approach might be more fruitful. At least on the small things."

Miles thought to himself, appreciating the irony, *I am here to spy on the HSC unit. And Christ Almighty, a real-life spy is in my office whose been spying on them too.*

"I'll pass this intelligence along to my superiors. And the fact of this meeting. I'm sure I've no choice but to do so. Let me ask first, is there anything in there of interest to my station that requires immediate action on my part?"

"Why yes, lieutenant. Now I am not personally well acquainted with maritime operations. To put it more bluntly, I don't know much about boating. But our observations include things that might be of interest to you. Such as, HSC boat crews routinely running at night without lights. That seems unsafe, and our Coast Guard has been receiving complaints. The HSC boat crews don't wear lifejackets, like we've seen your Coast Guardsmen always wear. Doesn't take a nautical genius to appreciate their tactical vests won't keep them afloat if they fall overboard. Matter of fact, you'll find pics of one who did fall out of a boat. They got him back aboard by the way.

"We've also documented an increase in patrols with both boats running as a pair. And of late, they are practicing running their craft up on a sandy shoreline. On the U.S. side of course. We aren't sure why. Also, in the opinion of our people, these guys aren't the best sailors, but they're getting better."

Miles had to stifle a smile at that. "Have they sailed into Canadian waters?"

"No. At least, we don't believe they have done so intentionally. I understand that boats always stray over the border around here. It's called innocent passage, isn't it? That being said, if we observe them going over the border deliberately, that will trigger action by RCMP."

The RCMP corporal spoke. "Yes, RCMP will arrest them. After all, wouldn't you, if you saw a small squad of heavily armed, unidentified men in a darkened boat come into U.S. waters?"

Miles couldn't help but think, *would you arrest them, please.* "RCMP has it officers watching them, is that correct corporal?"

"I am not authorized to comment on exactly who is watching them. They should assume they are being watched for violations of our sovereignty and that we are prepared to act. As you know, your vessels, the U.S. Coast Guard, routinely enter Canadian waters while on rescue missions. Your recent rescue of the child, for example." The corporal continued.

"As you know, law enforcement missions are a different matter, requiring permission from our government if U.S. law enforcement personnel wish to enter our waters. We have written agreements to that effect."

LeClerc then admitted CSIS and RCMP was uncertain of HSC's real law enforcement mission. He added that efforts by his government to develop agreements with HSC failed.

"We have no protocols governing this situation. It is a vacuum. They say nature abhors a vacuum. Well, in this situation, trouble exploits a vacuum."

The corporal then presented an immediate concern of RCMP. "Permit me to offer a scenario, lieutenant. Suppose HSC engages in hot pursuit that takes them into our waters. What limits are there on what they can do? Fire warning shots? Pursue on to our shores? Arrest in Canadian territory?"

Miles rebuked himself. *Damn! Why didn't I think of that?*

"RCMP believes the best step to take now, to avoid an international incident, is for you to direct the HSC officers to stay well clear of Canada."

Miles needed a moment before he responded that he would inform his chain of command of their concerns. Then he'd speak to HSC. Miles knew he had little, if any, authority to direct HSC operations, but he wasn't about to admit that to the corporal or LeClerc.

LeClerc ended by thanking Miles and the chief for their time, and handed Miles his card once more. Little else was said between them as they escorted the Canadians back to their boat.

Back in his office with the senior chief, Miles closed the door and asked no one in particular, "Can someone tell me what just happened?" The senior chief suggested the lieutenant have a look at the USB drive, which he did, almost frantically. With the files up, they both said in near unison, "Holy shit."

Miles asked the senior chief to quietly get the log sheets kept of HSC departures and returns while he kept reviewing LeClerc's files. Behind closed doors, spent the next two hours comparing the logs against the intelligence files. They looked through every photograph and video. It was clear to the senior chief and Miles that where HSC said they were going often didn't match the RCMP's evidence. *HSC lied to us!*

The report to Capt. Llewellyn wasn't due for a couple of hours. This couldn't wait. After giving himself a short break to calm down, Miles called the captain, briefed him about the intel, the message from LeClerc and the RCMP, and their review of the HSC logs.

The captain, after his own holy shit moment, told Miles to send the CSIS intel files to him directly, as well as the logs on HSC boat activity, and not to tell anyone else. "And for now, don't put any of this in your report until I say to. If you haven't already, make contemporaneous notes of the meeting. Now. While it's fresh in mind. Have the senior chief do the same.

"I may be a captain, but this is new to me. Not sure how to proceed. I'll call district for guidance the second I get those files. Bet I'll run into people who are as equally clueless." The captain paused before asking, "Lieutenant, you are sure the man's identification showed he's with CSIS?"

"Absolutely, sir. senior chief looked at his ID too."

"Very well. A Canadian intelligence officer. A *foreign* intelligence officer. Right. I'm not sure of this, but I think Coast Guard Intelligence will get involved. They have a branch for counterintelligence. Don't be surprised if you have a visit from them."

"Understood, captain."

"Well, Mr. Miles, you are certainly developing a talent for complicating my day." If Miles could have seen the smile on the Captain's face, he would have felt more at ease. "I'm glad you called. You did the right thing."

The call over, Miles told the chief to keep things under wraps and start his own notes. He scanned the HSC boat logs into JPEGs and sent them with the CSIS files to the captain. As he began his own notes of the meeting, Miles looked out his window toward the HSC trailers, thinking, *Williams, you're gonna have some explaining to do.*

Company Coming

Capt. Llewellyn called Miles back two hours later, saying he spoke with the admiral, her chief of staff, and the district staff judge advocate. He didn't elaborate on the conversations. He went straight to orders.

Treat the files as classified material. Place the USB device with the CSIS files in a locked safe. Password protect the files on his laptop. Do not send the files to anyone else. Do not talk to anyone else. Tell senior chief the same.

Include the meeting in the daily report. Expect to be debriefed by counterintelligence. Routine step if a foreign intelligence officer contacts a Coast Guardsmen. Do not approach the HSC unit commander as yet. Wait until a decision is made by the commandant.

Then the captain explained what was happening at higher levels. "The admiral and her staff are evaluating the CSIS files, and the HSC boat logs. Sector is doing the same. We're checking your work before it's briefed higher, as in Atlantic Area and the commandant. If HSC has lied to you, they want to present a solid case. It is pretty certain the commandant will be briefed before he heads home today."

"Well, that's everything. I can't say when you'll hear back from me about talking to the HSC unit. I might need to be there when it happens. So, before I go, I want to ask you, what are you thinking about all this, Mr. Miles?"

"That I'd rather be at sea, sir. I should get to work on the logs and the report, if that is all sir."

"Quite right. That is more the enough." The captain ended by passing on a thank you from the district staff.

The day passed. Then Friday passed. Then the weekend passed. No one called. Miles sent in his usual reports. More than once, he fought back the urge to call the captain, deciding it was best to be patient. Demonstrate faith in the chain of command. At worst, he knew he did his job and if higher authority decided not to touch this, so be it.

The call came Monday morning at 0800. The first Monday of October. It was Capt. Llewellyn. "Lieutenant Miles, good morning. I'm about to board a HC-144 out of Cape Cod Air Station for a flight up to the Eastport Municipal Airport. A CGI agent will accompany me. And a special guest who might be familiar to you."

What? Oh, Christ! Miles interrupted, "Mom? Shit, I mean the district commander?"

Laughing, the captain said, "Yes, Lieutenant Miles, Admiral Miles. Plus, her aide. Best get things squared away. Our ETA is 0930. Have someone there to pick us up. Four people in all. Myself, the admiral, her aide and CGI. Oh, as far as anyone else is concerned, the CGI officer is just another aide to the admiral."

"And, lieutenant, if anyone asks about the admiral visiting, tell them it's just that. A visit. One stop in a previously scheduled round of visits to the district's small boat stations. The admiral likes to do this in the fall when there is less disruption to the summer operations. Operational Dress is appropriate. The admiral doesn't want any special ceremony. No formal inspection. She would rather just talk to the crew in a gather-round kind of meeting."

It struck Miles as a plausible, albeit weak cover story. Miles didn't kid himself though. Any "visit" by an admiral is an inspection by another name. Let alone a visit from your mom.

"Is the HSC commander there? Tell him to stay put. Say the admiral is looking forward to meeting him."

"Aye, aye, sir. There will be a vehicle to pick up everyone. The HSC commander, Williams, is here, he checks in with me everyone morning. If I may ask sir . . ."

"Sorry, lieutenant. No time. Gotta head to the plane."

The phone call end, Miles called out, "Senior chief! I gotta see you!"

Meeting with the Tenant

Who should pick up the admiral and her party at the airport? Senior chief had a sharp petty officer in mind, but Miles had a different idea. He was the obvious choice. After all, of all the crew at the station, he was the most redundant. Besides, the visit itself was about his spy work.

Williams didn't like being told to wait around to meet the admiral. Miles reminded Williams he was a tenant here, and the landlord was coming to say hello. It would be bad form not to attend. Williams said he could meet at 1030. If letting him pick a time to meet a flag officer satisfied his ego, fine. Miles let it go.

Miles greeted the dignitaries and steered them toward the station Suburban. The admiral got right to business during the five-minute drive to the station. They would meet Williams in the station conference room. Important to seem friendly, at least during the introductions. After greeting Williams, the admiral would leave, feeling it would allow a franker discussion. In keeping with her announced intent, she would meanwhile meet with the station crew accompanied by the senior chief.

The captain will lead the meeting with Williams. To start, Miles will discuss HSC's lack of cold weather safety gear and their intentions should the harbor freeze in the winter. Then, Miles will bring up the RCMP's complaints of safety violations. The admiral told Miles, "Try to make him think you care about the safety of his people. Offer help. Empathize. Even if you have to fake empathy."

The most serious item, lying to the station about their patrols, would be handled by Capt. Llewellyn.

No mention would be made of CSIS. The captain would use his laptop to display the RCMP evidence and then tell Williams of RCMP's intention to intercept and arrest the HSC officers should they enter Canadian waters.

Once the meeting is about to wrap up, the admiral would come back to the conference room, hopefully to witness a new understanding between the Coast Guard and HSC.

As they turned into the station parking lot, the admiral said, "I think everyone should know that the commandant was scheduled to speak with the Secretary of Homeland Security about 30 minutes ago."

As the admiral and captain entered the building, flanked by the senior chief and Miles, petty officers snapped to attention on the quarterdeck. Miles watched with admiration as she employed her well-practiced charm with the crewmembers, before going to the second deck conference room. The captain told Miles to get Williams there in fifteen minutes.

Miles returned to the conference room with Williams in tow. Miles introduced Williams to the admiral, her two aides and the captain.

The admiral greeted Williams, all smiles and pleasant small talk, explaining she was on a tour of the northern stations and thought it would be nice to meet the commander of the HSC unit here in Eastport. She invited Williams and everyone else to have a seat. Then she set the tone of the meeting. A false tone.

"Mr. Williams, Lieutenant Miles and Captain Llewellyn have some concerns about your RBI patrols in this area, concerns for your safety really. But we also must tell you about something more serious. That has to do with the RCMP." Adm. Miles paused for a moment to gauge his reaction, a blank reaction, and then continued. "I'm sure all this can be cleared up. Well, I will leave you to talk. I'm going to meet and greet the crew. Always a fun part of being the admiral! Oh, one of my aides will stay here to take notes of the meeting. Always have to have notes, isn't that so Mr. Williams? Pleasure meeting you. I'll see you again before I leave, I hope."

Capt. Llewellyn asked Miles to open the discussion. Miles, despite orders from the admiral, couldn't bring himself to fake even a smile. He had a sincere dislike for Williams. Even so, he did his level best to fake concern for the safety of the HSC officers. "Mr. Williams, winter will soon be here, and I want to be sure you and your people understand winter's implications for your patrols."

"The water is getting colder. Even in the height of summer Maine waters are cold – just above low 50s. By late November and early December, air temps will get very cold, often freezing. By January, the water temps around Eastport drops to 40. Your officers aren't equipped with survival suits. Their PFDs lack signal lights. Should someone fall in the water, they will only last minutes. The heavy tactical gear they carry won't help either.

"The harbor and the waters around here start to ice up in January. It'll stay only just above freezing in the daytime. I'm sure you realize your Zodiacs can't operate in frozen waters. Even our small boats have their limitations in ice.

"We're perfectly willing to advise your people on proper equipment, and train them in water survival techniques. I'm sorry to say we don't have survival equipment to spare, but we can help you pick out the right gear." Miles expected to be ignored. Instead, Williams reacted in an unexpected way.

"Thank you. We could use some advice on our safety equipment." Williams did not mention water survival training. Miles strongly recommended the gear be procured immediately, as well as scheduling water survival training. Continuing, Miles warned that when the water gets too cold, they should suspend their patrols until at least the equipment arrives. Williams answered succinctly, "The patrols will continue. We have to. We have our orders."

Not talking much. Miles had told the captain of the difficulty of getting much from this taciturn man.

"Then let's get the equipment ordered today. We can help you find sources. Let's talk about the ice again. Your boats obviously can't be used in ice. Have you planned for the ice?"

Should the waters freeze, Williams answered he will ask for guidance from HSC.

Damn, Miles thought. *I was hoping they would pack up and leave. I'm not getting this man's attention. Might have to try a different tactic to get a little emotion from him.* He decided to drop the concern and empathy routine.

"Now about the RCMP. They and their Coast Guard operate in these waters. And they get reports from civilian sailors. Their people, and others, have documented your boats operating without navigation lights at night. Station personnel have seen this before, and I've told you before this is an unsafe practice. Apparently, Mr. Williams, your crews are unaware, or ignoring, some basic safety practices. Why? If your people need training, we can help."

Williams said nothing.

"Your boats are not operating in accordance with the nautical rules of the road. Maybe your people aren't familiar with how to pilot a boat around aids to navigation. Buoys and such. Or even other boats. We can train you. Even your boats have to obey the rules. I've told you that before. Yet, your people continue to break the rules of navigation. That's what the RCMP reports. Why?"

Again, Williams said nothing.

"Captain, I am finished with my points."

"Thank you, lieutenant. Mr. Williams, there's a couple things I need to discuss with you." The captain's tone was noticeably less cordial than Miles.

Pissed off in other words. He opened with the logs, swinging the laptop displaying photographic evidence toward Williams.

"Mr. Williams, we're going to talk about the departure and patrol area logs your people are required to complete for every patrol. They're not accurate. How do we know this? Your boats have been under surveillance for the past two months. We're not surveilling your operations. RCMP is."

"Surveillance? RCMP?" That worked. Williams eyes widened. The captain continued,

"Yes, RCMP. They provided us, unsolicited mind you, with all their intelligence. Including night vision video and photographs. They've documented your patrols rather thoroughly. Time, place, course. All the details. Doesn't match the departure logs. The departure logs your people filled out. You and your people have lied to us."

The captain slid the laptop across to Williams to show him a night vision image of one of his crews. "We can find numerous examples in the logs saying, for example, you'll head south to Lubec at such and such a time, but the RCMP spotted your boats well up north on the Saint Croix River.

"RCMP offered a warning."

"A warning? What do you mean? They have no reason to be involved." The room was cool, but Williams was losing his. He was flushed and starting to sweat.

Now Capt. Llewellyn went after Williams. Hitting the table with his palm, "You couldn't be more wrong. RCMP has every right to be concerned when heavily armed men in blacked out commando style assault boats are running near their territory. Their warning is simple. Stray into Canadian waters and RCMP will arrest you!"

"Why didn't they just come to me? Why did the Mounties give you all this?"

"Mr. Williams, they didn't say. I can only guess they're more comfortable approaching us because they have a long history of working with us.

"So, Williams, you have a choice. Continue being irresponsible and untruthful, and you will find yourself under arrest by the RCMP, creating an international incident. Or work with us to moderate your activities so an international incident can be avoided."

Williams went back to silent mode, looking around the room as if somehow the answer would appear before him. It didn't. The captain pressed him. "What do you have to say? Come on now, I don't have all day!"

A mumbled answer. "Captain, we, ah, certainly don't want to create an incident. Ah, would it be possible, do you have the time, to discuss how, you said moderate the patrols, how we could do that?"

Miles almost felt sorry for the man. Only for a second though. Miles began to say, "I have a couple of . . ."

An HSC officer came into the conference room, handed Williams a piece of paper and left.

Williams read the paper, ignoring Miles's attempts to get his attention. He passed the paper around the table. "Captain, this is an email from HSC. We just got it. It doesn't offer any explanation, but it has a clear order. 'CONTINUE OPERATIONS AS BEFORE. DO NOT ALTER OPERATIONS IF REQUESTED BY USCG.' I guess this meeting is over." Williams got up and left the room.

Anticipating Reactions

Adm. Miles's had one question for the captain about the meeting with HSC. Did Williams know about the HSC email before the meeting started?

"No, admiral, I don't believe so. To me, Williams looked surprised when he saw the email." The captain went on. "We delivered RCMP's warning. He did appreciate the gravity of that. It shook him. But once he got the HSC email, he showed it to us and left the room."

"Gentlemen, I think we got what we came for." The admiral caught Lt. Miles' reaction to her statement and asked him, "You don't think so, lieutenant? Tell me what you think happened here."

"We didn't get Williams to comply, admiral. I'm afraid I don't understand how that is considered a success."

"Let's look at things in another way." She explained that no one, the commandant and the district commanders, expected HSC to accept any demands from the Coast Guard. The important thing is that now they know the RCMP is watching them. With any luck, they will moderate their activities on that knowledge alone. Any reasonable or rational agency would do whatever it could to avoid an international incident.

"The trouble is, HSC is not reasonable. Maybe not even rational. They are highly political, arrogant, secretive and unprofessional. And without any operational experience. We've learned a lot about them since the summer. Thanks in no small part to your reports, and those from others across districts

Nine and Thirteen. While we hope for the best, we expect the worst. I expect, in a little while, I'll get a call from the commandant. I'll brief him on this meeting, and he'll brief me on his meeting with the DHS Secretary."

The admiral allowed what she said to sink in. "Well, so I bet the question on everyone's mind is, what do we do next.

"In 72 hours, an RB-M will arrive at this Station. Four members of MSST 91110 Cape Cod will be flown in to reinforce the boat crew." Highly trained law enforcement specialists, the Maritime Safety and Security Team guys, Miles knew, were miles above the HSC officers. "The mission of the MSST team is to shadow the HSC patrols, covertly if possible.

She explained the RB-M would be a better platform than MSST's own rigged hull inflatables. More comfortable. More of a presence. Fast enough to match the HSC boats. Their deployment will last as long as the harbor and river are ice-free.

"So, if past is prologue, until January. In any event, they will return when the waters ice up."

"Now let me predict a question or two from you. We cannot say, publicly, that MSST's mission is to spy on the HSC. We have a cover story. If anyone asks, the MSST is here so that HSC can be better . . . supported. And to deal with new intelligence."

It occurred to Miles that MSST units belonged to Atlantic Area, above the district. *Just how far up does this little conspiracy go?*

"Lieutenant, I assume you can accommodate eight new personnel?" Miles answered in the affirmative, thinking that senior chief will have work to do.

"Commander Ozuka, would you speak to the intelligence prompting this deployment?"

"CGI has intel indicating increased drug trafficking across the Saint Croix from Canada. Canadian smugglers who are particularly dangerous. This team's mission is to thwart their activity. Lieutenant, here is a file on the intel. It stays in your possession, locked up. However, you are authorized to inform the senior chief, of course, and Williams. He can look at the file but cannot make a copy. It stays with you."

"Commander, I have a question about this . . ."

"You're wondering if this is real, lieutenant? My response is, 'no comment.' Anything else about the intel?"

"Thank you, no, sir."

The admiral summed things up.

"It'll start to dawn on HSC that every time their boats go out, our MSST boat goes out. When I say 'covertly if possible' it needn't be all that covert. That's acceptable. If HSC feels MSST and RCMP are always watching them, we might get the desired result. A more reasonable and well-behaved HSC."

"My final thoughts on all this. Remember, you are all following my orders. They are lawful orders."

"Now, captain, let's make our goodbyes with the senior chief and the crew. Commander, if you would please debrief the lieutenant about his visit from CSIS. We'll leave when you're done."

"Aye, aye, admiral. Lieutenant, shall we go to your office?"

"Certainly, sir." Both got up and went to Miles' office.

The debrief from CGI seemed fine. Miles reviewed once again his meeting with LeClerc and the RCMP corporal. The commander nodded politely and seemed satisfied. He left Miles with instructions to call him directly if LeClerc contacted him again. The last thing Cmdr. Ozuka said was, "And don't you call LeClerc."

As the meeting with the commander ended, Miles had a fearful moment. *Christ! It's a dangerous plan. Everyone here could lose their careers. We could all be court martialed. That includes the commandant himself. That 'lawful orders' stuff. She is trying to protect us.*

Never mind. Got work to do. I've got to talk to senior chief about the reinforcements coming. Housing, feeding, a whole bunch of things to do.

Webb's Plan

Williams wasn't pleased with how this week was starting out. More like furious.

Bastards! They're working with the Mounties. They must be. How else did they know what RCMP is doing? Unsolicited my ass! Williams remembered seeing a Canadian Coast Guard boat at the dock. That the chief and Miles met them. A Mountie and a guy in uniform got off the boat and went into the station. Didn't seem important then. Williams reached the obvious conclusion. *That RCMP cop must've complained to Miles about us. Yeah, looks like Miles would rather work with the Canucks than with Americans.*

From a folding beach chair outside his trailer, Williams watched the admiral leave the station. His thoughts came quickly. *Good, they're gone. No way I'll say goodbye. She's in on this too. Gotta report that meeting to HSC. They set me up.*

Tried to catch me on something. Thank God for that HSC email. Crystal-clear what the direction is. No cooperation with the Coast Guard at all. Period. Maybe we don't need them anymore. Maybe my guys are good enough now.

He got up from the chair to go inside his office, thinking there's no need to tell his people what happened. *It'd just confuse them. They might get angry. Maybe retaliate against the Coast Guardsmen. Got a few hot heads here. Fights won't help. What's the best course of action?*

Now he knew RCMP is out there, watching them, waiting for a chance to arrest them. No matter how he felt, he knew that couldn't be allowed to happen. It would end his career.

He decided on a half-truth for the crew. Tell them HSC's got intel that RCMP is surveilling their operations. Tell them to watch for unusual activity by other boats. Stay clear of Canadian waters. No exceptions. Give RCMP no excuse. Tell them the Coast Guard has nothing to do with this, but continue to avoid the Coast Guardsmen.

Feeling better with a plan in mind, he decided to have Webb gather them all for a meeting at 1600. The crews needed the new word before the next night patrol.

Williams was about to call HSC about getting the survival suits that Miles talked about. That made absolute sense to him. Then he spotted a pop-up box on his laptop, warning him of an incoming secure message. Nothing unusual about getting one of those.

He decrypted the message and was about to start reading it when his supervisor called. "Williams, you should have a secure email from us. Download and decrypt it immediately."

"I already have, sir."

"Good, nice to see you're up on things." Sarcasm. "Be prepared to execute the special operation in one to two weeks. An indictment and extradition demand for your target is going out today."

"Understood, sir." And just like that, his supervisor hung up. Williams wondered if he was minimizing communications to avoid detection or he was just an asshole. Experience supported the latter.

Williams went looking for Webb. He found him standing on the dock watching as their boats were being cleaned up.

"I have to talk to you. Let's go back to my office." As they started to walk back up the dock, Williams added, "Don't worry. You're not in trouble." Webb said nothing.

"Let me tell you what's going on." Williams shut the door after checking if anyone else was around. He had no intention of telling Webb all that was going on. Only what he needed to know.

"Got secure comms from HSC. We must be ready to execute the special operation in one to two weeks. In seven days, we have to be ready." HSC had already approved the Webb's plan, ordering only minor changes. "But I want to be ready in four days. Things can change, so it would be prudent to be ready earlier than they said."

Webb caught on quickly. "Agreed. The indictment coming down soon?"

"Yes. Maybe today. Certainly, tomorrow. They're not going to give the Canadians time to comply. They want to act quickly, I guess." He then asked Webb, "What do you need to do to get ready to execute?"

"Recheck the tide calculations for the next two weeks for starters. That's the most critical thing. Been using a local tide chart, backed up by a NOAA website that automatically calculates tides for Eastport. Tides at Saint Andrews aren't significantly different.

"But here's the problem. We always assumed we'd get to pick the time of execution. We need that latitude because of the tides and weather. There's easily a 20-foot difference between high and low tide. If they order us to go at a low tide, it'll be a long walk across a lot of mud to get to shore. We talked about this before. You agreed."

"Yeah, I know. Can you get me that tide data right now?"

"Give me fifteen minutes."

An image came to Williams' imagination. His boat team, in the dark stuck up to their knees in mud, with the whole Canadian Army after them.

Webb returned with his laptop in hand, opened to the NOAA website. "Based on this, the best times are October 12, high tide at 0211, October 13, high tide at 0312, or October 14, high tide at 0417. Maybe October 15, but the high tide is 0527. Fairly close to sunrise."

"Right, I'll call HSC right away to remind them of this. They approved the plan, and it did say we needed some degree of local control because of the tides here. I'll recommend the 12th or the 14th." Williams paused for a moment, then said, "On the 13th, the second Monday of October, Canada has its Thanksgiving holiday. I wonder if anyone back at HSC has considered how the Canadians will react if we crash their holiday.

"What else do you need to do?"

"Keep track of the weather. A final gear and weapons check. No long guns. Suppressed sidearms only. Plus, sledgehammers if our guy can't pick the lock. The crews are already selected. We'll need to hold a final briefing that includes intel on the targets. How much lead time will we get once the 'go' order is given?"

"According to the secure email they just sent, we'll get no less than six hours."

"Good. Plenty of time for all that." Webb looked around the office, as if he was gathering his thoughts. "Sir, about the weather. With six hours advance, we can stay on top of the forecast, no problem. But, if a storm is forecast and the waves get too much, over two feet, the plan calls for delaying the mission.

"The currents from outgoing or incoming tides could complicate navigation. Not something we can't deal with. We've trained around that problem for weeks now. How to navigate against and with the strong tidal currents and still hit a point on land. They've gotten much better at it."

"Yeah, I agree. They're doing well. Lot of credit goes to you. You trained them up well. Okay, anything else?"

"Yes. Confirming the Whynots are at home. The plan states that our guys are to cross the border and approach along the shoreline to the target, stop and observe, and then proceed. It'll be the middle of the night. They'll likely just see a dark house. After entering the house, if no one is home, they get back to the boats and leave. Yes, the doors will be broken through. Perhaps they'll, I mean the cops, will think it was a simple breaking and entering, but I doubt it.

"I take it no one at HSC liked the idea of using a drone to surveil the home. The New York Air National Guard has military drones. CBP also has them down south."

"No, they turned that down. Good idea though. But they didn't want to involve anyone else. Guess we'll just have to hope the Whynots are home. Remember, we brought this issue to their attention. They know it's a weakness in the plan. For now, I think we're covered. Anything else?"

"No, sir. That's about it. If I think of anything else, I'll come see you."

"Alright. Well, I've got something else. I need you to assemble everyone at 1600 today. I need to talk to them before the next patrol. It's important."

"Sir?" Webb had that blank look on his face.

"Webb, I learned this morning that our operations have been under surveillance for the past couple of months. That intel comes from HSC. We need . . ." Webb interrupted Williams. "You mean the Coast Guard's been tracking us?"

Williams shot back, "No, Webb, let me finish. RCMP. Royal Canadian Mounted Police! They're watching our patrols. There's no intel the Coast Guard is surveilling us!"

"But we see them all the time. You know they've run close by us more than a few times."

"Webb!" Williams yelled. He was pissed. Williams knew he had a hair-trigger with Webb, but really. "Listen to me, will you? Not much water out there. Of course, the Coast Guard is going to see us from time to time. But they did not mount a spy mission on us. The intel says RCMP. Do you understand? I need to know because I can't afford to have our guys go off halfcocked at the Coast Guardsmen."

Webb looked Williams straight in the face. "Yes, sir. I understand."

Williams slowly sat himself in his chair, for no other reason than to take time to calm down before speaking. "The intel says the RCMP will intercept and arrest any HSC personnel who navigate into Canadian waters without permission. Understand?"

"Yes, sir."

"Good. We can't give RCMP cause. I will order the crews to stay well clear of Canadian waters. We must assume RCMP is out there now. No incident that'll jeopardize our special operation will be tolerated.

"Another thing. Those departure logs Miles demands. From now until I say differently, they will accurately reflect our patrol routes. I don't want to give anyone an excuse to get in the way of our op."

"Very well sir." Webb then said, "What'll you tell our crews if they are intercepted by RCMP? What's the ROE?"

Williams blanched at Webb's mention of 'rules of engagement.' A squad of heavily armed men might not react kindly to being arrested, especially if they think they can just scoot back over the border to friendly waters. He hadn't thought that part through.

Williams asked, "What does the special operation say about ROE?"

Webb began to suspect Williams wasn't being entirely honest. "Our guys will be sanitized. No IDs. If they are confronted by local law enforcement, they are to evade and escape as best they can. They may use their weapons only as a last resort and in self-defense if their life is in imminent danger."

Webb continued, "Have to admit, there's leeway in those instructions. Can't plan for everything that could go wrong."

Williams took a deep breath, and said, "Webb, HSC approved the plan. They didn't add to the plan's ROE, did they?"

"No sir, they didn't."

"OK then, the same rules of engagement apply for our upcoming patrols. If RCMP stops our crews, they should apologize and ask to be allowed to get back to U.S. waters. If they are about to be arrested, they proceed at high speed back to U.S. waters and the station. RCMP, I imagine, has the right to pursue, but we'll leave that to HSC to sort out. If our crews are intercepted and detained, they will not use lethal force to resist RCMP. Unless their lives are in imminent danger. Again, HSC can sort that out later."

Webb had a word in mind to describe this ROE. Candy-ass. But, holding his tongue, he simply asked, "I'll wait to hear from you about your call to HSC about the tides. Is that all sir?"

"Yeah, that's it for now."

Webb made a mental note to himself. Better figure out a Plan B for going in at low tide. *Maybe bring a bunch of wood planks?*

CHAPTER SIX
TIME WITH FRIENDS

Thanksgiving Invitation

That same Monday, the sun had nearly set as Mike and Debbie sat down for dinner when someone knocked on the door. Startled, Mike went to answer the door. He'd grown fearful of surprises these days. He stopped for a second before opening the door, thinking, *should I look first?*

George and Cheryl were at the front door. "Surprise! How are ya?"

Mike, dependably awkward in social situations, stood still and silent long enough to sufficiently embarrass all present, before stammering out, "Oh, yeah, George, Cheryl. We're fine, ah, come in."

"Excellent idea!" While Mike stood aside, Cheryl chided George for the unannounced appearance before apologizing to Mike. "I am sorry for barging in like this, but George and I have something we want to ask you. Only take a minute."

"Nothing to apologize for. How can we help you?" Debbie was always better at social niceties than Mike.

Cheryl clarified. "Actually, we'd like to invite you to Thanksgiving. I mean Canadian Thanksgiving."

"Oh, that's right. When someone says Thanksgiving to us, it's a Thursday in November. Yours is coming up, ah, right, next Monday?"

Now it was George's turn. "Yep. Second Monday in October. But just about everyone does the feast on the Sunday before. Use Monday to recover before getting back to work, eh? I'm lucky this year. I've got that Sunday and Monday off. No shifts."

Mike finally said something. "We'd be glad to come over! Sounds like fun." He paused before continuing, "Really nice of you to think of us. Appreciate it. Thank you."

Debbie offered her own thanks before asking, "So, what can we bring? How can I help?"

"Just bring yourselves. Maybe a couple bottles of wine if that's no trouble." Cheryl then went on about the food. "We'll be having roast turkey and ham, lots of sides, and pies for dessert. I imagine it'll look a lot like the American version. There'll be us, you two, plus Roy and Marge, and a few other friends from around here. I've got plenty of help already."

"Best be on good behavior," said George. "You guys will be the only Yanks there!" Mike thought, *George has to be the funny guy.* And he continued to do so, "You know, we might be able to get an American football game on that Sunday. I guess you Americans watch football on Thanksgiving. You watch NFL, Mike?"

"Yes! New England Patriots, all the way! Of course, since Brady left, their record hasn't been as great. Good, but no Superbowl yet. Always rebuilding."

George laughed, "Too true! I'll see if I can get them on. See you Sunday, say about noon."

"We'll be there. Can't wait."

Debbie was smart enough to return the favor. "Cheryl, George. I want to invite you to our Thanksgiving. The last Thursday of November. Our daughter's coming with her American friends from Ottawa. We'd love for you to be here with us. We can work around any shifts, George. Maybe push it to Saturday or something."

Cheryl said, "Yes, that'd be great. Never had two Thanksgivings in one year."

October

Indictment and Request for Extradition

The U.S. Department of Justice skipped the whole notice of subject of investigation thing and went straight to indictment and extradition.

Mike and Debbie knew this was coming. Nevertheless, it was still a shock. Tuesday afternoon, a representative of the Department of Justice Canada met with Mike and Debbie at Edward's law office. There she presented a copy of the U.S. DOJ's formal request for extradition, plus supporting documentation. She went on to say that her agency had examined the request very closely, especially the supporting documentation.

"Under the existing extradition treaty with the United States, both countries must recognize the alleged conduct as a crime. The U.S. is saying you violated the *Overseas Americans Act*, to wit, your public statements give aid and comfort to domestic terrorists. Canada has an entirely different view. We do not view your behavior as criminal at all. Since we do not recognize their allegation as criminal conduct, their complaint falls flat."

Continuing, she said the U.S. DOJ would be soon notified that Canada will not issue an Authority to Proceed decision, meaning the extradition request will not be honored.

She then offered some background. Her department received the extradition petition four days ago. Forty other such petitions were made for other American expatriates. All the petitions claimed the subjects were helping terrorists in the states. "Almost the same wording in every petition."

Mike and Debbie didn't say a word. Edward spoke for them. "Thank you. My clients and I are grateful for your office's quick decision. That being said, I suspect there is something else."

The DOJ Canada representative took a letter from a file and handed it first to Edward. After quickly reading the letter, Edward gave the bad news to his clients. "Mike, Debbie, this letter states that all your assets in the U.S. are frozen. Sorry, but this wasn't unexpected."

Edward didn't wait for a reply. "Let's sum up. You're under indictment by the U.S. Department of Justice. They've frozen whatever remaining assets you have back in the states. However, the request of extradition will be officially denied by DOJ Canada. Is that correct?"

The DOJ Canada representative nodded in agreement.

"Mike, Debbie, do you understand?"

They, too, nodded.

The DOJ Canada lawyer added another item. "There's another consideration we want to make sure you understand. Please, do not travel to or through a third country. Even on your Canadian passport. Let's say you decide to travel to Mexico or someplace in the Caribbean. It's not outside the realm of possibility that U.S. DOJ would ask that you be arrested while in transit through a third country. So, stay home. Stay in Canada."

It was left to Edward to put the best face on things.

"Well, my friends, it looks like we've won this battle, but don't be surprised if DOJ tries again, on another charge. We're not done with this until they are done with this."

"Agreed." The DOJ Canada representative then went on. "I'm sure Mr. Donohue realizes this, but it is highly unusual for a solicitor from DOJ Canada to hand deliver documents like these. That was decided at the top. These are unusual circumstances."

With that, she left after accepting thanks once more from all present. She left her card with Edward before taking her leave.

Edward, back in his chair, motioned for Mike and Debbie to sit down again.

"May I ask, were you able to get your monies and investments out in time?"

Debbie answered. "All the investments and accounts stuff, yes, we got those out. But the house in Rhode Island, it was still on the market. I mean, no offers. Economy's pretty bad, I guess. We even talked to our sons about buying it, jointly, but they couldn't afford it. Wasn't enough time anyway. So, I wonder what'll happen to the place now that the bastards seized it." Debbie imagined an overweight and bald party official sitting on her deck, enjoying the view over the bay.

"I've no idea. Anyway, I want to read these documents more closely. I'll make copies and send them over to you with any other thoughts I have. Thank you for coming here."

As Mike and Debbie were leaving, Edward said, "Mike, I guess you'll have something interesting to say on your next broadcast."

Reinforcements

The four MSST members flew up from Air Station Cape Cod on a Coast Guard aircraft. They arrived late Thursday morning, ahead of the RB-M. They came with their seabags and the usual equipment, which meant weapons, ammunition, tactical gear, night vision devices, and all the other tools of their trade.

There was no hiding the arrival of the MSST from HSC. In fact, Miles wanted it that way. He wanted HSC to see the MSST members and all their gear. Especially the large, black plastic boxes that carried weapons. Miles even asked the MSST members to arrive wearing their tactical vests and helmets, which they did, as uncomfortable as it made the short trip from the airport.

MSST made a strong impression. HSC officers inside the trailers gawked out the windows. Those outside stopped dead. Miles took it all in, doubting they understood who these new guys were. *Oh, they are far better trained than any of you poor bastards,* Miles thought with a grin.

After watching the MSST haul their gear into the station, Williams came out of his trailer. He approached Miles asking, "Lieutenant, new personnel?"

Miles smiled. "Yes." Miles kept his eyes locked on Williams, hoping his curt response would annoy Williams. It did.

"I'd like to know who they are and what they're doing here. After all, my people will be working in the same area."

Miles delayed answering, knowing he'd spark a more frustration in Williams. "They're part of a Marine Safety and Security Team, or MSST if you like. MSST 91110 specifically. They're based at Air Station Cape Cod. Basically, MSST are the Coast Guard's special forces. An elite antiterrorism force. Highly trained in law enforcement, boarding, search and seizure, port security, tactical small boat operations, you know, stuff like that. I've worked with them before. They're very good at what they do."

Miles chose his next words to frustrate Williams even more.

"Instruct your people to give the MSST petty officers a wide berth, but if MSST tells your people to do something, they better damn well do it." With that, Miles started to walk away.

Williams angrily said, "Wait one damn minute. You haven't explained why they're here."

Miles turned back and walked up close to Williams, He quietly said, "I could say the same about your unit, Williams. You haven't told me what your people are doing here. What your mission is. Your real mission. And don't tell me you're here to, what is it that HSC says, 'to augment Customs and Border Protection in fighting illegal immigration into the United States.' No one believes that bullshit. You're here to keep Americans in. Stop them from going to Canada. Isn't that right, Williams?"

Williams tried to speak, but Miles interrupted him, saying, "You know, your guys might be useful to me after all." Williams didn't like hearing that, shaking his head as Miles kept talking. "Let me tell you what MSST's mission is here. You want to know?"

Miles explained there was strong intel that drug smuggling is coming from over the border, across the Saint Croix. Canadian smugglers known to be armed and dangerous. Within the hour, an RB-M with crew would arrive at the station. The RB-M crew and the MSST will patrol the Saint Croix down to the Bay of Fundy and along the Maine coastline.

"I have a file of the intel if you would like to see it, Williams. Might be helpful if your boat crews knew about this, in case they see something suspicious. And keep them safe. I'd hate to see your guys come across some real bad guys." Miles made no attempt to hide the smirk on his face.

As Miles insulted Williams, the Station Officer-of-the-Day told Miles the RB-M radioed they were about 15 minutes out. The crew of four left South Portland, thankfully during moderate weather. They came with their seabags, the usual equipment and weapons, plus spare parts for the boat.

Williams, tight-lipped, replied, "Yes, I want to see that intel." Williams didn't believe a word of Miles' explanation. He realized the arrival of these MSST commandos just days after that meeting with the captain was no coincidence. Something was up. As he followed Miles up to his office, he knew, just knew, that MSST's real job was to shadow his patrols. They would disrupt the special operation unless he did something.

The RB-M arrived as Williams headed back to his trailer. Just to tweak HSC, Miles radioed the RB-M to run by the station at full speed, 40 knots. The crew did so enthusiastically, putting on a little show until they finally slowed and entered the docks, mooring alongside HSC's little commando boats.

Message sent, Miles thought with satisfaction.

The Old Man

The old man was once a young man.

Sixty or so years ago, he graduated from Eastport's high school, near the top of his class. Though he easily qualified for college, he hadn't the money. Nor the inclination. Working on the water, as his father did, as his uncle did, was as far as his ambition took him in those days. Someday, he wanted his own fishing boat. Until then, he satisfied himself with working on his dad's boat. When his dad died a year after graduation, they had to sell his dad's boat to help out his mother. The young man worked on his uncle's boat. Hard work. The weather was too often not a friend, but the pay wasn't too bad. He had hopes. He was almost 20 when he got a second job with a marine supply store and repair yard. Combined with lobstering on his uncle's boat, he knew the day of having his own boat was drawing closer.

The young man had found what the luckiest always find. A wonderful young lady, his high school sweetheart. There was a proposal, an acceptance, and plans made for a home and family.

The Selective Service had their own plans. He knew a dozen or so Eastport boys had enlisted or were drafted. In the past year, a couple of them had been lost to the war in Vietnam. The young man was a realist. Without a college deferment, or a hardship at home, or a physical disability, or the right connections, he always knew someday the telegram would arrive.

They advanced their wedding plans. The young man had the practical, or morbid, thought that at least she would receive his G.I. insurance pay out. At least they would have had some time together.

The last working day he had on the water, he looked across to Canada with new thoughts. It would be so easy. Simply steer the boat across and ask the Canuck police if he could stay. No war in Vietnam for him.

Years later, the young man admitted to such occasional thoughts at that time. He remembered one boy in town who took that way out. As far as he knew, today that boy is still out there, living his life as a Canadian.

He would not do that. How could he? A grandfather fought in the Argonne. His father and his uncle both served in combat in the European Theatre. Only seven short years later, they lost their younger brother in Korea. Duty to country in time of war ran deep in his family story. Neither his father nor his uncle wanted him to go, but knew he had to go. As too many older men did, they understood the reality of war. They equally understood duty to one's country.

His mother and uncle saw him off to basic training, as countless other fathers and mothers, and uncles, had done in countless wars. A duality of pride and terror. The young man came home on leave after basic. He and his love married the next day. And to their profound sorrow a week later, when his mother, uncle and wife saw him off once again, this time to war.

Thirteen months later, the young man came home to his wife. His uniform bore a purple heart and a bronze star with a V for valor. As proud as he was of those bits of metal and ribbon, the thing he most treasured at that time was his discharge papers. He had done his duty. He could come home.

The years passed in a blur of work and children. A son and a daughter. They bought a house on Water Street with a somewhat obstructed view of the docks where he moored his boat. His boat. Eventually, the marine supply store and repair yard where he briefly worked before the Army, became his own.

The now older man and his wife saw their children off to college. First in their family. Their son married a lovely Canadian girl and moved to Halifax to work in investment banking. Their daughter went to Boston to work in medical research. Between them, the older man found life's greatest joy in their two grandchildren. Life had fallen into place. He believed himself the luckiest man on earth.

His love died only ten years ago. Pancreatic cancer. She lasted only a year, but she made sure they made the most of it. A couple of trips between treatments. Time with children and grandchildren until there was no more time.

Alone in their house, he could not bring himself to leave. At least not yet. Retired from the store and the water, fate offered the old man one last task. One last time of service to country.

And so, the old man walked along the Sullivan Street pier that morning, as he had for the hundredth time in his new work, taking notes and cell phone pictures of the uniformed officers and their Zodiacs at the Coast Guard Station. No one noticed or cared about an old man going for a walk. After dinner, the old man would slowly sip a glass of red wine at a bar on Water Street frequented by the Homeland Security Corps officers. The old man often regaled them with his stories of Vietnam, sometimes exaggerated, with the hope that tales of combat, combined with a bit of liquor, would loosen their tongues. It worked surprisingly often. They returned the favor with stories of their own past and new duties on the Saint Croix. And their complaints. In the evening, as he had done so many times before, he would email the pics and notes to a friend of his son, one Robert LeClerc.

The old man had purpose once more.

CHAPTER SEVEN
WITHOUT A COUNTRY

The Broadcast

It was the Wednesday before the holiday. This time Mike had a peaceful breakfast at the SunRise Cafe with George. No federal agents or lawyers. Or Canadian spies. He looked forward to taping his broadcast that afternoon. Edward was right. This one might be the most interesting of all his broadcasts.

The news on the television was not good. This morning, The *New York Times* had been car bombed. A van with explosives had been left by its building on Eighth Avenue. The bombers didn't even try to get it next to the building. They just parked it as close as they could and left. No warning. Two men, caught on security cameras. FBI investigating. Multiple fatalities. Message sent.

Since getting word of the indictments, Mike called his contacts among the expatriate former U.S. military across Canada. A few had hired on as military commentators for Canadian and European media. Mike suspected one general officer he knew went further and was actively working with Canadian Military Intelligence. *I'm not there, yet,* thought Mike.

Mike delivered the broadcast in a matter-of-fact style. He announced the indictments and explained that Department of Justice Canada denied the extradition requests. Next, he summarized what he learned from his military colleagues. Federal agents had interrogated all of them, almost to the same day. And on the same day as Mike and Debbie, all had been indicted. All faced charges of aiding and abetting terrorism. Canada denied all their extradition requests. No one told Mike they might voluntarily go home to refute the charges.

Why target former military? His contacts couldn't agree upon DOJ's intent. A few voiced no opinion, apparently preferring to find a quiet life, out of trouble's way. The rest reacted with varying degrees of anger and sadness, but none had a strong answer as to why the country they had honorably served was doing this. Mike included all that in the broadcast. Without names, of course.

Mike kept to himself his own hypothesis. Former U.S. military are targeted because of their potential to lead a rebellion. But he had no evidence to support his hypothesis and didn't know how to go about getting any. It was too speculative. Too fantastical. Maybe so, but Mike knew it was also logical.

He wrapped up the broadcast by reinforcing LeClerc's warning to stay calm and not to engage in any violence. His last words were, "Having said that, we can still legally protest and demonstrate against the autocracy that is today's the United States. We can and must continue to do that. We can and must fight. We will stay peaceful, but today, and every day, we will fight. I will fight!"

LeClerc and Whynot, Second Act

It was the Friday before the holiday. Mike reached his destination on Waggoner's Lane in Fredericton. The Canadian Security Intelligence Service. The drive was easy. Walking through the door was not.

"Do you have an appointment, Mr. mmm, Whynot?" It's a simple question, but Mike's mind left him. It's not every day you try to see a foreign spy.

"Ah, no, I don't. He knows me though. He gave me his card." Mike presented LeClerc's business card to the receptionist as if it was a secret pass into an inner sanctum. He turned the card around when he realized he was showing him the blank side. "Is he in?"

"Yes, he's in. Most people call him beforehand, but it's alright. I'll get him. Have a seat over there." Mike muttered a 'thank you' and took a seat on an uncomfortable plastic chair.

REFUGE

You know, Mike, you can still just get up and go home. No problem. Or you can stay and risk ruining your reputation. As Mike's mind raced through all the possible outcomes and consequences of what he was about to do, LeClerc came into the waiting room.

They exchanged greetings. LeClerc told him to leave his cell phone at the reception desk before he led Mike through the glass office door. They turned sharply to stand before a heavy steel door. A swipe of a key card and the door lock disengaged. As Mike stepped through the door, LeClerc remarked that they wanted a biometric scanner installed, but budgets being budgets, it would have to wait for another fiscal year. Mike took an empty seat in the middle of an empty conference room. LeClerc took an opposite seat. Mike got right to the point, explaining he was there to turn over the information on the American expatriate community.

Mike removed an envelope from his jacket and slid it across the table toward LeClerc. "Here is a thumb drive of the relevant files on our community. All of it. But I need your help in another matter."

LeClerc, seated across the table from Mike, showed little outward reaction. Ignoring the envelope, he got up to get a cup of coffee from the pot at the back of the room, slowly mixing in sugar and crème, before returning to his seat and the point of the meeting.

"Mr. Whynot, did your Expat Committee approve of this?" Mike hesitated to answer. "My guess is no. If they had, you certainly wouldn't have linked the handing it over with a favor. Well, Mr. Whynot, am I right?"

There was nowhere else to go but honesty. "Yes, you are. The committee refused my suggestion. They don't know I am here. Nevertheless, I'm willing to hand it over to you."

"And what is the favor?"

"I hope you, CSIS that is, can help me get my two sons out of the U.S."

"So let me get this straight. You're providing me with information on your expatriate community. Information that is of unproven value. You are doing this secretly. Against the wishes of your community leaders. In exchange, you want my employer to somehow spirit your sons, and their families I assume, into Canada."

Mike responded with a slight nod. LeClerc didn't respond, instead sipped his coffee, looking at Mike and then the envelope. LeClerc knew this would not do.

"Look Mr. Whynot. You're going about this all wrong. I can't accept this information. Let me explain why."

Mike started to say something, but LeClerc held up his hand. "Let's first talk about you. If I accepted this intel, CSIS would analyze it. Likely, we'd talk to select expatriates. Your Expat Committee would discover your subterfuge. They'd kick you off the committee and your value to us as an expatriate leader would go to zero. So would your community's trust of CSIS."

LeClerc stopped for a moment and then continued, "Now the larger picture. American expatriates might be a source of useful intel. Their reasons for staying in Canada, their political activities, their state of mind, their contacts in the states. We're not sure of this though. CSIS feels the best approach is proceed with the full knowledge and cooperation of the expatriates. Openly, transparently.

"Certainly, this would become news. Being open about it gives us the chance to set the story. We'd rather the media not paint a picture of us skulking around, stealing private information, trying to recruit dissidents to betray their country. Imagine the headlines. *Canadian Spies Working Secretly with American Dissidents.*"

There were reasons why Mike didn't play poker. First, he never took to gambling of any kind. Second, he couldn't keep a poker face even with a gun to his head. LeClerc could see this in Mike. A necessary skill in his job.

Leaning toward Mike across the table, he said, "You didn't expect my refusal, did you? Me, I can't understand why you didn't anticipate this."

LeClerc continued, in a more direct tone. "And regarding your request that CSIS help in, what, smuggling your sons out, that is patently not Canadian policy. Getting here, that's up to the Americans. Once here, we help them. Can you imagine the reaction of this American government if Canada sponsored a new underground railroad, an escape line, for American dissidents?"

Mike knew he was defeated. "I imagine they would react harshly toward Canada."

"Harshly? Now that is an understatement." LeClerc, against all his training and experience in interrogating human assets, allowed his anger, real anger, to surface. "Christ, do any of you Americans understand the position you put my country in? The damage you've done to us. Your extremists inspired our own extremists. Funded them too. Do you have any appreciation for the risks we are taking on your behalf? Our greatest ally is now a potential enemy. And why? Because you Americans couldn't control your own domestic politics. You unleashed something that is not only hurting your country, it is hurting us and all your former friends."

LeClerc didn't stop.

"Your little broadcast, 'Today, I Fight.' I know you don't literally mean fighting. But let's go down that road for a second. What if it did come to a fight? Would your people, would you, help defend Canada? Somehow, I doubt you people would. You'd rather let us take the risk while you guys just ran away, again."

Mike, now deeply hurt, reflexively tried to thwart LeClerc's criticism. "What are you saying? You can't really believe the U.S. would attack Canada, do you? That's absurd. Things are really bad, but . . . no, that's, no." Mike shook his head, appalled at the idea CSIS might seriously believe war was coming.

Silence. After an awkward moment, LeClerc said, "Absurd? Maybe so. I hope so. I'll leave it at that." LeClerc had said his piece, using Mike as the target for all the frustrations he felt toward Americans. He could calm down a bit now.

"Sneaking around your own people is not fighting back, at least in my opinion. You've got to do this openly, with the full support of your people. How would they react if they found a spy in their midst? Did you think about their reaction?"

LeClerc drank a little more of his coffee and turned away from Mike, if only to calm himself further, to find a way out of this exchange.

"Would you, ah, like coffee? Please, help yourself."

Mike honestly didn't want coffee, but he also saw that perhaps he and LeClerc needed time to process his failed offer.

Once Mike got back in his seat, LeClerc offered a plan. "Mr. Whynot, please take this intel back. Go back to your committee and try again. Try harder. Until they agree to working with us, we won't accept any background information on members of your group. Remember, CSIS does want to explore this avenue, but let's work together. We're doing this with other expatriate groups across Canada. Same thing in Europe too.

"Tell you what. There's an expatriate community that has agreed to work with us. They're in Toronto. Before you go, I'll give you a point of contact. They might be able to give you advice on persuading people."

"Alright. That sounds like it might be helpful. I'll give them a try."

"Good." LeClerc then had a feeling of sorrow for Mike wash over him. Poor bastard. He's in a difficult spot. Almost a man without a country. "Mr. Whynot, I know you are trying to do the right thing. Hard as it is to figure out what the right thing is these days."

Mike looked down at the table. "Did you hear of the indictment?"

"Yes, we're aware of it." LeClerc was about to reassure Mike Canada would not honor the request for extradition and he would be protected. But he waited, sensing that Mike had something he wanted to say. LeClerc asked, "How are you, ah, feeling about that?"

"As one might be expected." Mike stopped. Something was welling up inside him. Something he rarely felt. He then looked directly at LeClerc. "How am I feeling? Honestly?

"The country I served now says I am a criminal. It changed the law so that my speech is illegal, when in all our history, it wasn't. They say I am giving aid and comfort to terrorists when I spent years in the service helping to target terrorists. Real terrorists! How am I feeling?" Mike slammed his fist on the table.

Embarrassed at his outburst, Mike stopped speaking. LeClerc sat back in the chair. It was a long minute before Mike spoke again.

"I guess the reason I'm here, is that I'm looking for a way to fight back. I just don't know how. Don't know what to do. Yeah, my broadcasts. Not stopping with that. But what good are they really doing? I'm not feeling right now that democracy can win. Maybe we lost it. Maybe all we have is a facade of democracy draped over a one-party police state. What can we do?"

"Mr. Whynot, we're trying to figure that out ourselves. Maybe together we can, figure it out.

"Mike, I want to help. I should apologize for spouting off at you earlier. Wasn't professional."

"Don't worry about it."

"Look, you ought to get back home. Give that contact in Toronto a call. Then go back to the Expat Committee with a plan. Try to turn it around. Agreed?"

"Agreed."

Rain fell heavily as Mike drove back to Saint Andrews. The MGB drove almost as bad in rain as it did in snow. The tiny windshield drowned in the splash from passing trucks. Its three puny wipers fought the water valiantly, but ineffectively. It was time to either concentrate on driving, or pull over, but Mike lost himself in thought, reviewing in his mind the meeting with LeClerc. Though human intelligence was something new to Mike, even a novice like him knew what happened. He crossed a line. He was now a human asset for a foreign intelligence service. Just meeting with LeClerc in his CSIS office was evidence enough. Damning evidence.

LeClerc wasn't giving advice. He was giving orders. LeClerc was his handler. Still, Mike saw this as the only path forward.

He spent most of his drive time practicing out loud his pitch to the Expat Committee. He'd call them when he got home to ask for another meeting after the Thanksgiving holiday. Canadian Thanksgiving.

Another thing. Mike put it on his mental calendar to call the contact in Toronto LeClerc gave him. Do that before meeting with the Expat. Might be helpful.

No quid pro quo. CSIS would not help get his sons out of the U.S. He didn't have anything valuable enough for CSIS to take that risk. His thoughts summed things up. *They were on their own. So be it. It's time to lay out his plan to Debbie and then tell the boys. I'll fill her in tomorrow.*

CHAPTER EIGHT
PREPARATIONS FOR WAR AND THANKSGIVING

CSIS Teleconference

"The director started. "Good morning everyone. I have things to cover before I hear from you. Let me begin by thanking you for participating in this conference with so little notice, especially on the holiday weekend.

"After consultation with his ministers and other advisors, the Prime Minister has decided upon a response to the extradition requests made by the Americans on Monday."

LeClerc suddenly got that pit in the stomach feeling that the PM changed course. He would approve the extraditions after all. LeClerc kept his fears to himself.

"This government did not approve any of the extradition requests. Not one. The U.S. DOJ got the official reply late yesterday. So did the media. The Prime Minister emphatically said there will be no reversal of the decision because such a reversal would violate the extradition treaty itself, and thereby, Canadian law."

"Canada's position is simple. These people did not commit a crime. Therefore, they will not be extradited. It is Canada, not the United States, which is therefore in full compliance with the extradition treaty. Our reply also stated that all these individuals have this government's full protection. I doubt that went over well with the Americans."

Thank God, LeClerc unconsciously muttered.

"Yes, Robert, we can thank Him, but I also think we should reserve a measure of gratitude for the PM. It took guts, I can assure you. He's under a lot of pressure. And not just from the Americans."

Oh, Christ, they heard me. Did I really say that?

"Now, Robert, I rehearsed this as a monologue. So, if you have nothing else to say, may I continue?"

"Sorry, sir."

"Now, the sensitive part. The PM expects retaliation." The director went over the actions the PM ordered to increase security.

By Wednesday, RCMP or municipal police will begin round-the-clock protective surveillance of the expatriates targeted by the DOJ. Canadian Military Intelligence, Canadian Forces Military Police and CSIS will help them anyway they can. RCMP has deployed fast small boats wherever HSC is running maritime patrols.

Canadian Coast Guard vessels, starting with the CCG Hero-class ships, will be armed. At first, light machine guns, such as the M240. RCMP Emergency Response Teams will deploy to the ships where practical.

"You may remember a Senate committee once recommended arming these ships. At the time, a law professor came up with a memorable statement. 'The quiet authority of a deck mounted gun.' Well, we have that authority now."

"In our area, one armed ship out of Dartmouth will deploy to Saint Andrews until the waters freeze over. She'll get there Tuesday morning, following Thanksgiving. RCMP will have a team aboard."

The Director turned his attention to LeClerc for a moment. "Robert, intelligence from us, especially the Eastport asset and our covert surveillance, is essential if RCMP is to intercept HSC."

"Understood, sir."

The director ended with a review of what he called the "big picture" items. The PM quietly secured support in Parliament for a considerable increase in the readiness of the Canadian Forces. Not easy thing to do with the tight budgets and recession on. He mentioned a few specifics. More arms and munitions. Accelerated purchases of the British *Starstreak* air defense missile and more *Rapier* antiaircraft missile batteries as the Brits retired them from service. Additional Leopard tanks from Germany.

"Here's the problem. Our NATO allies must look to their own security. While we worry about the United States, they worry about Russia. Quite understandable. So, when we ask for surplus Leopard tanks, well, suddenly there's not much surplus. Production of new Leopard tanks continues, but we are competing for those with our NATO allies.

"And our U.S. manufactured defense systems are vulnerable. Spare parts are already a problem for our U.S. systems. There's been disruptions to the supply chain to us from U.S. defense contractors. Their explanations do not hold water. We know the same items are getting to other nations without trouble."

He dashed any hopes of a surge in military power. "It takes too long to build modern weapons, like fighters and frigates. Modern war is a 'come as you are party.' Other steps are planned, but our strategy is deterrence. Make the cost too high for an opponent."

LeClerc then saw something in the director he had never seen before. He seemed overtaken by a look of profound sadness.

"I never imagined that we, Canada, must prepare for action against the Americans." His demeanor changed, becoming somber, a mix sadness and fury. "I can't believe I actually said that. Something as . . . nightmarish as that. It's a feeling shared by many in this government, I can tell you. My saying this should impress upon you the need for greater action."

Restoring himself to a more proper bearing, the director continued.

"Allies. That is the key. We have allies. The U.S. does not have allies. Our diplomatic service has been tasked with making sure that doesn't change."

"This week the PM spent much time speaking with the NATO allies. Efforts are underway to increase sharing of intelligence on the Americans. That will take time. Hardly anyone has any assets in the U.S. We just never spied on them before."

"I am authorized to pass on to you a comment made by the PM to his ministers. 'We cannot view the Americans as an ally.' "

Stopping to let that sink in, he continued. "Do not share that with anyone."

The director continued with more news. To fill gaps in the Regular Army, Canadian Primary Reserve units and individuals with certain specialties are being called up, as well as volunteers among the retired military of the Supplementary Reserve. Recruitment efforts for regulars and reserves would be redoubled. In a significant policy change, foreign citizens would be recruited to the forces, including properly vetted volunteers from the approximately two hundred forty thousand Americans expatriates in Canada now.

"Some have raised not unreasonable objections. Would American recruits turn out to be double agents? Would they go into combat against Americans? Still, the idea of a Free American Brigade has a certain historical romance to it.

"The last 'big picture' item is public opinion. No one in government doubts our people's resolve in defending our sovereignty by whatever means. Economic. Diplomatic. Military. God, forbid it comes to that.

"But it is American public opinion that might be our greatest defensive weapon. A way to stop a conflict before it starts."

He explained that a media campaign was already underway. Both in the states and worldwide, the campaign aimed at undercutting public support for any further hostile actions by the United States against Canada. CBC, BBC, CNN International, and Le Monde are a few of the media outlets that signed on.

"We'll use social media. Twitter, Facebook, Instagram, Tick Tok, all of them. Even some of the right wing websites. Canadian and American celebrities and social media influencers, including those in the U.S. Play to the deep connections of heritage between Americans and Canadians. Hollywood. The NHL. How many of us here have family in the states? I do. Encourage Canadians to call their American relatives and friends."

All this triggered a memory with LeClerc of an American army officer he worked with in Afghanistan. *I wonder . . .*

The director then quickly queried each staff member for any new developments, before finally reaching LeClerc. "Robert, your group is Atlantic Region's tip of the spear, given the Eastport HSC unit. Let's hear from you."

LeClerc briefed on the arrival of the four MSST personnel at the station. He gave some background to MSST capabilities. "They're similar to our Naval Tactical Operations Groups. The MSST are supported by a newly arrived small boat, with crew, one of their 45-foot Response Boats."

"How did we come by this information, and do we have any idea of their mission."

"Sir, their arrival is no secret. Even a local newspaper reported on it. However, our Eastport asset directly observed the MSST, and the small boat arrive. We have the asset's notes and digital photographs.

"As you know, the asset shares drinks with HSC officers at a local bar and lets them talk. And talk they did. Last night, they shared with the asset their dissatisfaction, no, more like hostility, toward the MSST. Apparently, the HSC people think the MSST is out to get them."

"Do we have anything on MSST's mission?"

"No, sir. We do not. Not yet anyway. The asset is working on that. MSST could be there for a legitimate law enforcement purpose. However, the possibility that the MSST is there to surveil or counter the HSC does make a certain amount of sense. If that's the case, it means we need to figure out why the U.S. Coast Guard would do this.

"I could contact the station commanding officer and just ask him. Of course, he'd have to report my contact. And, well, my impression of him is that he wouldn't tell us. Still, he already knows we are surveilling the HSC. Seems like a logical thing for us, or RCMP, to do."

"Call that lieutenant. Better yet, go see him in person. Don't think we have anything to lose."

"I have one more local development, sir. Yesterday, Mr. Michael Whynot, the American dissident from Saint Andrews, came to my office on his own initiative. I'm sure you remember him from the SunRise Café video. He offered intel on his American expatriate community, even though his Expat Committee refused his request to cooperate with us."

LeClerc explained that he turned down the intel until Whynot's committee was fully cooperative and that Whynot asked for CSIS help in getting his sons out of the U.S. in exchange for the intel.

"Robert, that was the right course of action. But it troubles me that he wanted us to do that. Let's see what Whynot does. Let him play it out for a short while.

"Please, everything we've talked about, remember, it's sensitive. A very delicate time. If that's all, everyone, try to enjoy your holiday."

Exfiltration

Early that same Saturday morning, Mike looked out across the water. He could hardly see beyond the beach in front of the house with all the rain. Chilly, it was only in the high 40s outside. It was the kind of weather that reminded Mike of Germany. Somehow, the cold and damp got into your bones. You never felt really warm. He got a fire going in the wood stove before he started preparing scrambled eggs and sausage for breakfast.

Tomorrow's weather should be slightly better. Less rain, but just as cold. They'd be over at George and Cheryl's for Thanksgiving. *A cocktail or two, and no one would give a shit about any rain.* Mike decided to bring all his cocktail fixings to the party.

Sound came from the bedroom. Mike heard Debbie getting up and brushing her teeth. *After she'd had coffee and breakfast, then, that's when I'll brief her.*

"Morning. Jesus, it's cold in here. A fire going?" Debbie rubbed her arms to get warm a little quicker. They kept the central heating to a minimum. Heating oil was expensive in these parts.

"Yup, fire's going. Should be warm in here soon. Breakfast will be ready shortly."

Debbie went over to the coffee maker and poured herself a cup. Taking a sip, you could have heard her across the Saint Croix when she said, "ahhhh."

"Have your breakfast, get cleaned up, and then there's something I want to show you."

"You in a hurry or something? Christ, I just got up. Show me what?"

Mike didn't answer, but instead filled her and his plate with eggs and sausage, more than usual. Then he started acting really bizarre, at least so it seemed to Debbie. Mike turned up a classical music station on a radio he had put on a small table set up next to the sliding glass door. Debbie almost blurted out, *That's silly! The speaker is pointed at the glass.* Mike closed the drapes behind the radio on his way back to breakfast. Looking at her, he held his finger to his lips, and slipped her a note. It read,

Be careful what you say. Want to talk to you about getting people across the border. Have to be careful. Music helps prevent eavesdropping. Finish eating, get cleaned up and dressed. We'll talk in the kitchen. Fewer windows. Trust me. Do you understand?

Debbie looked back at him, rolling her eyes. *What is he doing?* Resigned, Debbie kept eating all the while she read the note. She surprised Mike with a brief chuckle, before nodding her head to signal, *I understand.* He then snatched up the note and threw it in the wood stove. When he picked up both their cell phones, Debbie had the frightening thought Mike would throw them in the fire too. Mike made sure both phones were power off and put them near the radio.

Mike started eating as he placed in front of her an old writing toy, one Debbie vaguely remembered from childhood, but couldn't remember what it was called. It had a red rectangular plastic frame, topped with some cartoon characters. A small clear sheet of something like cellophane covered a blackened space. A red stylus snapped into the frame. Then it hit her. She started writing on the tablet,

I remember what they used these for. Geilenkirchen!

Mike nodded enthusiastically. A story told them by a Canadian Army Chief Warrant Officer they knew from Germany. Years ago, he was stationed for a year as a security officer at their embassy in Prague. Back then, the Soviets were in charge. As a show of the worker-state's benevolence, the Czech communists provided foreign embassy personnel and their families with their own apartments. They came complete with all the modern conveniences, including the latest in Soviet designed hidden listening devices. To keep whatever private thing, they wanted to stay private, they used these toys to "talk." Smooth the clear plastic over the writing space, use the stylus to write what you want, then erase it forever by lifting the clear plastic. Easy. No paper to burn or shred.

Debbie just had to laugh. It was still a good story. But Mike knew her jovial mood wouldn't last, so he wrote out on the toy tablet,

Want to use these for border talk. Won't use them forever. Just today. Understand?

Debbie nodded, finished her breakfast in a bit of a rush, then went off to the bathroom to shower and dress. Mike did the same and met her in the kitchen twenty minutes later. He gave her a document he had typed up on his laptop at a local coffee shop and printed at the studio. He used the toy to explain the next step.

Please read. Ask questions using toy. I'm not crazy. Bear with me.

Yes.

Mike thought to himself, *"yes" to what exactly. That I am crazy or you will bear with me?* He pushed to document across the table, motioning to her to start reading.

Remember Crazy Davey? He's that eccentric guy who, on last 4th of July, fled from Maine in his 32-foot sailboat by himself. Packed his boat with everything he wanted to keep, sailed from Maine out to international waters, took a northerly course for Seal Cove on Grand Manan Island. Stopped there for a night. Tried to find Canadian Customs to check in, but nobody was there, so he continued on to along Grand Manan's eastern shore, and then straight up to the mouth of Passamaquoddy Bay, anchoring off Back Bay Harbor. I talked to him about his journey. He said it was easy.

In September, 23 people made it to our community. All drove up to the border to a deserted area of Maine, a place where there wasn't a river or bridge to cross. If they couldn't get their car across the fields or woods, they grabbed their backpacks and sprinted across. They said it was easy. But just 23.

REFUGE

In spite of the expansion of U.S. border security, it's still fairly easy to get here. That tells me something. Almost all of our former fellow citizens are staying put in the states even when escape may be easy. And no, we don't know how many failed attempts were made.

Our sons may not want to leave. It's understandable. They have a life back home. They have friends and other family. Even Crazy Davey and the 23 weren't running to Canada because their lives were in danger. Crazy Davey was fed up. Most of the 23 had just given up. Scared, but not acting on a physical or legal threat to them personally. That correlates well with most of us up here.

Our sons may decide to wait things out and hope for the best.

Helping someone to cross the border into Canada is not a violation of Canadian law. By planning this exfiltration, we are not breaking Canadian law. We are breaking U.S. law, not that it matters because we are already under indictment.

Let's imagine the boys want to, or have to, leave. Here are the options for crossing the border:

Routes by commercial air or sea are out of the question. Getting across at official ports of entry is almost impossible. Our only exfiltration options are to covertly go by land or sea.

For both options, they must travel fairly light. They can't pack their cars up with everything they own. They have to be prepared to abandon their cars on the U.S. side of the border. Also, heading north in packed up cars might tip off HSC or CBP.

By leaving for Canada, they put at risk all their financial assets. Their investment and bank accounts, retirement funds, and their homes. They will be able to take out some of it without attracting attention, but that will take time. If they decide to leave, I recommend they start to slowly turn their investments to cash. Liquidate non-IRA mutual funds. Stop contributing to 401(k)s.

By Land

We should recon all the available land routes from the Canadian side, but here's one of interest.

About ten miles north of Orient, Maine / Fosterville, New Brunswick, up to Grand Falls, on both sides, lots of fields and farm roads that get close to the border. Intel from the 23 confirms this. Simply mimic the routes taken by the 23. Drive up, get out, pack up, run. We meet them on the Canadian side.

Upside: Simplicity. Many places still open to crossing. Not as dependent on weather conditions, except snow. Less need for either of us to cross the border back into the U.S., risking our own arrest.

Downside: Patrols are increasing. DHS Blackhawks staging out of former Loring Air Force Base, plus ground detachments. Some of the dirt roads are blocked. CBP can legally set up roadblocks as much as 100 miles inland from the border. HSC can work

153

throughout the country. Traveling by car near the border may draw suspicions. Also, cell phone coverage up there is spotty.

By Sea

There are two nearby options.

First, Robbinston Maine. There's a boat dock off Elton Brooks Memorial Rest Area. Two miles from here over the water. Only half a mile from the border on the river. A small boat could quickly move to the dock, meet them, get them aboard. Would only take minutes. They come right to our house.

Second, Lubec. Wait for them on a boat at Mulholland Light, scoot across the border to pick them up at the public dock off Johnson Street. Two tenths of a mile and they're across the border. Then sail to our house.

Upside: Short distance. The towns of Robbinston and Lubec offer them good cover until they're very close to the border. For By Sea options, they could use a vacation trip as a cover. Make reservations at a nearby hotel or B&B. Also, the CBP station at the Lubec bridge is closed. No CBP officers there.

Downside: Weather and tides can be significant factors. Can't be done during winter because of ice. Therefore, the window of opportunity is shorter than the land option. We don't have a boat. Neither of us have any boating experience. Homeland Security Corps and the Coast Guard patrol our waters.

The By Sea options means sailing across the border into the U.S., putting us at risk of arrest.

I strongly prefer not to involve any others with boating experience, but By Sea options may make that necessary. Involving more people increases risk off our plans getting to the HSC.

This is not a complete operational plan. We have to think about how things could go wrong. Injury, failure of boat motor, etc. However, this conceptual framework can be updated and address such deficiencies should they decide to come here.

Questions so far? Back to the toy.

Debbie wrote, *How and when do we offer the kids this option?*

Use burner phones. Soon. Get them thinking. Warn them not to talk about it with anyone else.

It took a moment for Debbie to respond. A long moment. She wrote, *Define soon.*

On weekend following Canadian Thanksgiving.

OK, should they come out together?

Yes. If one goes ahead of other, likely draws suspicion.

That will be hard to plan.

Yes, but not impossible.

OK. Stop this for now. Pain in ass. Let's go someplace we can talk openly.

Mike picked up the papers and threw them in the fire. They let the fire burn out, avoiding talk about their plan all the while. An hour later, they were at a diner on Water Street. Mike saw there weren't many people there, but enough to make it a little noisy. They chose a booth away from everyone else and ordered coffee.

"Why couldn't we take our phones? Or talk about this in my car? Feeling a little paranoid there, Mike?" Debbie was both irritated and amused.

Mike reminded her they were both under indictment. There was a high probability their digital communications were, and have been, under surveillance. Even their snail mail back to the states. Even the kids' regular phones. Then Mike showed his truly paranoid side.

"Debbie, it's within DOJ's technical capability to listen in on our conversations at home. They can put a laser dot on our windows that can translate the vibration of the window glass into speech. Its range is limited. Maybe just over 500 meters. It could be done from a boat on the water, assuming water is calm. Or they could put someone in the woods by the golf course. It's possible."

"Christ, Mike. That's crazy. What's the chances they're doing that? From across the river?"

They stopped talking as the coffee came and waited for the server to go out of earshot.

"Yeah, well, I'm only saying it's possible. How probable it is . . ." Mike shrugged his estimate. He looked around to see that no one was within earshot. Then he looked straight into her eyes.

"I didn't think it was even slightly probable a little while ago. But something my friend in Fredericton said got me to thinking. He said Canada has its own right wing extremists. He said they're inspired and funded by Americans. What if they're recruited? Recruited to be agents for the U.S. intelligence community. So, yes, they don't need to sneak their people on a boat a few hundred meters off our house to surveil us. They'd use a sympathetic Canadian."

"So now I have to suspect even Canadians?" Debbie was about to say something sarcastic about Mike's newfound cloak and dagger obsession, when she realized he missed something.

"You forgot the Americans here. Seems to me they're more likely to find a sympathetic American here. That they planted an agent among us."

Christ I, am slow on the uptake these days. Mike realized that another reason CSIS would like our records is they're looking for American agents.

"Logical. Yup, you're right. So just be aware. But, let's remind ourselves what we went over this morning. Smuggling out of the states our sons and their families, our granddaughter. Breaking U.S. law and involving them in a conspiracy to do so. Frankly, I'd rather be as safe as possible. So, whenever we talk about this to the kids, we go somewhere else."

Debbie clearly didn't like this, but she relented. "Okay, you win. We'll do that. Guess that means when we talk to them on the burner phones, we shouldn't be in the house."

"Correct. I'm working on that."

Should I tell her that a guy will be coming to sweep the house for bugs later next week? Mike decided no, too much this morning already. Best to shut up and drink the coffee.

"I've got a couple of questions." Mike stopped sipping and put his cup down, waiting for the worst. "Are you going to ask George or Roy for help on this?"

"No. I can't. They could get into trouble. That same friend made that clear. The Canadian government will not help refugees escape. The other question?"

"Where in God's name did you get those toys?"

Of all the things she wants to ask right now, Mike thought. "A website. Sells retro toys. All sorts of neat stuff. Probably can get stuff for Eva. And retro candy too."

Peace Denied

As Mike and Debbie got ready for Thanksgiving next door that Sunday morning, Williams treated himself to a generous breakfast at a diner on Water Street. He went in civilian clothes. All he wanted was a little peace. Anonymous to the patrons and waitstaff. No HSC. No Webb. No reports. No boss. No Miles. No news.

He was in the middle of his second cup of coffee. The breakfast done, he considered asking for a third cup, but decided not to. So, he stared through a window onto the harbor, cradling the cup in his hands, nursing the last sips of coffee. Somehow, he thought, if he stayed right there, sipping increasingly cold coffee, all the bad things would go away.

They would not go away. His cell phone rattled, notifying of a text from his duty officer. HSC Regional has sent a secure email. *On Sunday morning?*

Damn them! Christ. Couldn't they just give me one Sunday morning? Constant reports. Always demanding something. And what've we done? Nothing! Aside from one arrest two weeks ago of a guy in a rowboat going over to Canada. That's it. Even that guy was not right in the head. Probably off his meds.

Williams allowed himself a dark fantasy. *If I could, I'd sink those damn Zodiacs and burn those trailers to ashes. Maybe sink one boat out there with my boss in it.*

Still, he had to admit his people had come a long way. They were borderline experts on the boats by now. Even Webb seemed sharper and more focused these days. Williams had the thought that maybe it was time to work on his own attitude.

He drained the coffee in a single gulp. He put down the cup, loudly, on the table, and shoved it aside. He threw a twenty on the table and got up to leave.

"You okay, son?" The only other patron in the diner that morning was an old man. Williams had the feeling he'd seen him before. But it's a small town. Stay here long enough and he'll probably know everybody.

"Sorry, sir. Just a thing from work. Didn't mean to disturb you." Williams put on his coat and started to walk past the old man's table to the door.

"No apology necessary. You're not from around here, are you? I think I know everybody for miles around. Tourist?"

"Ah, no, I mean, in a way." Williams wasn't comfortable with telling people who he worked for.

"Well, that's an interesting answer." The old man smiled, held out his hand, and Williams reflexively took it. "I'm all retired and everything, so I don't have to answer to anyone. No bosses. Now that I think about it, I really haven't worked for anyone else. Ran my own boat here, fishing, lobstering. Owned the marine supply store and yard on Sullivan Street. Nice not to have a boss."

Williams didn't leave. He stood there not knowing why. Instead, he asked the old man, "You say you fished this area?"

"Now you've done it. You asked an old guy to start telling stories. Maybe you should sit down for a few minutes." The old man pushed a chair in Williams's direction.

He knew shouldn't stay. There was an email waiting. Could be important. Williams sat down.

The old man called to the waitress for more coffee. "Yup, I worked these waters since the sixties, before and after I got back from Vietnam. Married, raised a couple of kids. They've gone on with their lives." The old man stopped himself from mentioning his lost wife. "Something you want to know about fishing around here? You're a little late for the striped bass season."

"Nah, ah, just curious. About that life. Must have had its good points. And its bad points."

"Huh, good points and bad points. Yeah, it did." The old man went on to tell a couple of stories about how beautiful it could be out on the water, especially the sunrises and sunsets in calm weather. To balance it, he told how miserably cold it could get and how backbreaking the work could be.

"There're easier ways to get by, but guess I was born to it. Never really wanted anything else."

Williams slowly prepared his coffee, and took a sip before saying, "Born to it. Your own boss. Yeah, I think I understand why you stayed with it." Williams took another sip before continuing. "Well, I hope I can find that someday. What you had."

A smile of satisfaction crossed the old man's face. "You know, son, sometimes I wonder if it, life, worked out for me. So many things could've been different. Had more than a few close calls. Around here, I mean. Not just in Vietnam. But I guess it worked out." The old man looked Williams in the eye, and said, "I've found that we're more in charge of our lives than we think. Maybe not so much 'in charge.' Maybe 'responsible' is a better way of putting it. Sometimes the wind and the current, you have to fight them to stay on course. Sometimes they help. Life is like that."

The old man took a little more coffee, then looked at Williams. "Thanks for what you said. Nice for an old guy to hear."

Not entirely sure why the old man thanked him, Williams said, "Quite alright."

"Nice talking to you, son. I'll bet you've got something to do."

They shook hands as Williams left up Water Steet to his shabby little trailer.

Five minutes later, the old man followed the same route up Water Street to his home. Later that morning, he'd walk the pier, and as always, take his notes and pictures, and send them on to LeClerc.

GO

For now, Williams and Webb agreed to keep to themselves the special operation authorization message, the "GO Signal" they called it. With the signal in hand, Williams wanted to get everyone ready then and there, but Webb persuaded him otherwise.

"If we tell them today about the op, on a Sunday, that gives two days for word to leak out. I'm not saying any of them would drop a dime to *The Washington Post*, but you don't want to give them too much time to dwell on things. Besides, if we text them all to get back here from some time off, the Coasties would probably notice that and think something was up."

Williams, though anxious, agreed to hold off the briefing until Tuesday morning. "Yeah, you're right. For now, we'll act as if nothing is going on. Nothing in the message saying the crews have to know today. Why did they send it out on a Sunday?"

"Who knows why? Doesn't matter." Webb wasn't one to question things from on high. He thought, *Christ, this guy doesn't have his head in the game.*

Thanksgiving Sunday

Turned out to be a better day than forecast. That small gift pleased Mike as he looked forward to the food, friends, and with a little luck, football.

Roast turkey, baked ham, stuffing, mashed potatoes, corn, squash and the most important element of the feast, gravy. Then the treat Debbie brought. She told Mike, "I know Cheryl said to just bring ourselves, but we can't just do that." Meat stuffing, a family recipe that combined finely diced onions, mashed potatoes, Bell's Seasoning, ground beef and ground pork. By itself, an entrée. Pumpkin pie with whipped cream or vanilla ice cream rounded things out.

Mike brought his cocktail mixing kit with all the ingredients. Shakers, strainers, and stirrers. Orange and lemon slices and peels, orange bitters, black cherries, and olives. Ginger ale and cola. Small batch vodka, genuine Kentucky bourbon, dark rum, champagne, and Irish cream. Hosting the bar, Mike served up martinis, white Russians, plus old fashioneds and bourbon highballs.

And then the friends. New friends. In all, twenty-one people. George graciously introduced Mike and Debbie to his family and friends. "Hey, I want you to meet the Yanks from next door."

It was splendid. George found a streaming service for the New England Patriots. That part was not splendid. They lost in a close match. A few guests must have wondered about the cheering and moaning Americans.

159

The dinner and desert finished, the table cleared, Mike completed his duties as bartender by serving Irish cream aperitif. George joined him at the bar with a deadly concoction. Moose Milk.

Pointing to the punch bowl of Moose Milk, Mike said, "Jesus George, are you trying to kill everyone with that?" A surprised George said, "You know about this stuff, Mike?"

"Sure do. From Geilenkirchen. A staple of any party at the Canadian detachment. I tried to get the recipe, but they claimed it's a Canadian military secret. They said if they told me, they'd have to kill me." George laughed at that and then divulged the secret. The key ingredient, booze. Lots of booze.

While everyone was comfortably sipping, Roy came over to Mike and Debbie to discuss something more serious, guiding them away from the others.

"Guys, I'm glad to see you here. It was great. And, I have to tell you, it saves me a task I was to perform tomorrow."

Debbie was quicker than Mike to understand where Roy was headed. "RCMP kind of task?"

"Yes, exactly. Let me start by saying, you needn't worry. I do want to discuss your personal and home security here. May I ask you a few questions?"

"Sure," Mike replied.

"Does your home have a security alarm? Outdoor lights? Security cameras and motion detectors? Do you have a firearm?"

"I think you're going to say we should keep the alarm and the lights on. But our system doesn't have motion sensors or security camera. And we do not have a firearm."

"You should seriously consider having your security system upgraded. Call whoever you wish on Tuesday. If you have trouble getting them out here right away, call me. As to a firearm, we'll discuss that at another time, except to say that as permanent residents, you can legally own a firearm. If you do decide to buy one, I or George can help you out. That's the free advice from Roy."

"Also, in three days a constable will be posted at your home, for your protection."

Almost at the same moment, Mike and Debbie said, "What!?"

"I would've liked to start it sooner, but RCMP is somewhat stretched these days as far as our personnel goes, and the decision to do this, yeah, I just got the word this morning. RCMP is concerned, given the U.S. indictment and denial of extradition by the Canadian government . . . that the Americans might try something. Something, well, extraordinary."

"Extraordinary? Care to explain that?" Mike felt his good mood slipping away.

"The honest answer, RCMP does not know. We do know the U.S. Department of Justice is furious over the extradition refusals, but our government doesn't have any hard intelligence on their next move. Very little intelligence actually. But we do not trust our old friends. So, we're being cautious, perhaps to a fault. I'm awfully sorry about all this."

They thanked Roy and rejoined the party, knowing he was only looking out for them.

Pouring himself a glass of chardonnay he really didn't need, Mike went back to Roy, motioning him to step into another room. "Do you know a Robert LeClerc, CSIS?"

Mike could see a startled look in Roy's face. "Yeah, I know him. Why do you ask?"

"I met with LeClerc, twice. He said much the same as you, about what the Americans might do. Even used the same word, 'extraordinary.' But I think RCMP and CSIS have a better idea than you or LeClerc are letting on."

"Now hold on there, Mike. You don't . . ."

Interrupting Roy, Mike said, "Please, I'm not doubting your, or anyone's, intentions or integrity. But I am saying they're thinking about certain scenarios. That's what intelligence types like LeClerc do, but don't want to discuss them with us. No intel of any certainty. Don't want to unnecessarily alarm us. That's perfectly understandable and appreciated, but . . ."

"I can't comment on CSIS thinking. But you've got something you want to say."

"Roy, I have very high regard for you. You're a friend. It's just that, when RCMP says they will have a constable watching over us, at our home, one of those scenarios is the Americans will come and attack us. Something like that."

"Maybe you should ring up LeClerc and discuss your concerns with him. RCMP is only acting on their recommendations. Please understand." Mike knew Roy well enough to know he was genuinely concerned.

"I'll do that."

"Good. Jesus, I really spoiled the party for you guys, didn't I?"

"No worries. Let's get back to the party." That wasn't entirely true, as borne out by Mike's somewhat sleepless night.

CHAPTER NINE
THE STORM IS HERE

A Warning to Miles

Monday morning. 0730. The official day of Canadian Thanksgiving. The Officer-of-the-Day called up to Lt. Miles to say he had a visitor. A Mr. Robert LeClerc. Miles asked the petty officer to repeat the name. "Very well, I'll come down." Miles wondered how interesting this day would get.

"Good morning, lieutenant. How are you? I hope you remember me." LeClerc stood casually on the station's quarterdeck and extended his hand.

"Yes. Mr. Robert LeClerc" Miles said as he returned the handshake, without smiling. *What Is this man doing here?* "Shall we talk in my office? I don't think you just dropped by to say hi."

"No, you're right. Wanted to say more than just hi. Before we go to your office, could I drop by the latrine, I mean, head, you call it, and then get a cup of coffee first? It was a long drive from Fredericton. Then we could go up to your office, away from prying eyes and ears, eh?"

Miles didn't really want him hanging around in sight of the crew. "Sure, I'll wait here. Then we'll go up to my office. I'll have coffee brought up to us. How do you take it?" LeClerc answered, "Cream or milk, two sugars."

Once in the office, Miles closed the door, motioning to LeClerc to take a seat. As Miles sat, he got right to the point. "Why are you here? You understand that I have to report this contact to our intelligence people."

LeClerc smiled as he sat down, taking as relaxed a posture as he could muster. "Yes, I understand. Feel free to take out your mobile phone and record this meeting. Have your chief petty officer join us as a witness if that makes you feel more comfortable. I shouldn't need more than fifteen minutes of your time. Besides, its Thanksgiving Day back in Canada. I'm supposed to have the day off."

Miles took a moment to consider getting the senior chief but decided against it. He did set his phone out to record. "For the record, now that this is being recorded, Mr. LeClerc, you came here unannounced without any advance notice whatsoever. And I did not call you to set up this meeting. Is that correct?"

"Yes, lieutenant, that is all true" said LeClerc, chuckling a little. "Consider yourself covered. Of course, like you've said before, I'm a spy and I lie for a living." A knock on the door. "Coffee's here."

LeClerc prepared his coffee, nice and hot. Miles was getting hot himself. "Again, Mr. LeClerc, I have to report this. Don't appreciate you being so flippant." LeClerc spread his hands, offering an apology. "You're right, sir. I am sorry for that crack. An inside joke of the trade. Shall I get to business?

"RCMP has observed the arrival of new personnel and a new rescue boat, a rather large one. I saw it as I drove up. What do you call it?"

"A Response Boat, Medium."

"Yes, of course. Anyway, the boat doesn't concern us, but the personnel who arrived by vehicle Thursday last do concern us. They don't appear to be regular personnel, being equipped with all sorts of tactical gear and such. We've already seen them operating on the Response Boat. Rather well armed. Your boat has mounted a light machine gun. The RCMP felt our government should know the reason why a new heavily armed team of Coast Guardsmen is operating near our territory. They are Coast Guard, right? Can you explain? Oh, forgive me, I meant to say that Corporal Jensen was unable to come with me."

"First you explain to me why I have to explain anything to you."

"Good question. If I were you, I'd take the same position." LeClerc sipped a little coffee, before answering with a half answer. "Suppose we reverse roles. A heavily armed Canadian military team is patrolling just off your station. I imagine you'd demand an explanation."

Miles knew LeClerc was right, judging that not answering would only get them more curious. Miles explained the new Coast Guard personnel were part of a MSST and their mission is a pursue intel the Coast Guard had on drug smuggling in this area being done by some particularly dangerous people. Miles thought, *now who is the liar?*

"Very well. That sounds reasonable. Canadian drug smugglers? I wish Corporal Jensen was here. Have you passed this information along to RCMP?"

Miles lied. "It's my understanding that district did."

LeClerc finished his coffee before coming to the heart of the matter. "I'll check up on that. We knew they were MSST. Sounds routine. That being said, there's an alternative explanation I'd like to run by you. The Coast Guard sent the MSST here to keep watch on the HSC unit. Care to comment on that?"

"I told you what they are doing. That should be enough."

"Not really. You see, if we are correct, that your service feels the need to watch over the HSC, that indicates a level of distrust between Coast Guard and HSC. Distrust that must exist at a much higher level than this station. Distrust that might lead to, let's say difficulties between your agencies. Difficulties that might manifest themselves very close to our border. Difficulties involving heavily armed personnel. At CSIS, we see that as a possibility. A reasonable possibility."

LeClerc disposed of his pleasant demeanor to deliver his message.

"Prudence dictates my government increase its security forces in response. On Tuesday, a Canadian Coast Guard ship, the *Corporal Teather*, will arrive at Saint Andrews. She will be armed with light machine guns. On board, RCMP will deploy an Emergency Response Team. Unlike you, we are at least showing you the courtesy of alerting you beforehand of this new deployment.

"When you report this contact to your Coast Guard superiors, I strongly suggest you include word of our deployment. The other involved party here is the HSC unit. We suggest you tell them of the arrival of the *Corporal Teather*. HSC is our main concern here. Although this MSST team is unusual for this area, we view the U.S. Coast Guard as disciplined professionals. You are a known. We do not view HSC in the same way. Not at all. They are an unknown."

"I will. Anything else?"

"No. I've delivered the message. Do you have anything you want to ask me, Lieutenant?"

"Yeah, I do. How did you get here, I mean get across the closed border? And how did you know about the MSST arriving?"

"I have a diplomatic passport. One of the perks of my job. They can't stop me at the border. As to the other matter. Come now. I'm a spy and you wouldn't want me to give up our little secrets, would you?

"Actually, we read the local paper, *The Quoddy Tides*."

Miles had to smile at that one. *I'm beginning to like this spy,* he admitted to himself.

"How about you walk me out to my car, Lieutenant."

Miles escorted LeClerc out to his car. LeClerc stood at his opened car door. "I want you to know something. In intelligence, we take information, and we try to discern capabilities. From that, threats and intentions. We make predictions of what an opponent might do. Sometimes we get it right. Sometimes not. You follow?"

"I'm not unfamiliar with the use of intel."

"No doubt. We're aware of your record of service. And no, we didn't snoop into your records. The basic biography is open source. The *Munro*. The *Glen Harris* in the Persian Gulf. Impressive. Maybe we should see about getting you a commission in the Royal Canadian Navy."

LeClerc saw the startled look on Miles's face. "Don't worry, Doug. I'm joking." *No, not joking really,* LeClerc reminded himself. *For now, the seed is planted. And we need good officers.*

"CSIS has assessed that HSC is about to take action. We do not know what it is. As yet, we can only describe it vaguely. 'Extraordinary' is the word we settled on. Possibly extrajudicial. We're working with too few facts. Too many unknowns.

"I think we both want to avoid problems between our governments. Soon both of us will have well-armed, highly trained personnel in close proximity. Possibly in opposition to each other. That is an inherently dangerous situation. The last thing we want is someone to get hurt, or worse, because of a misinterpretation of the situation.

"From here on out, I want to believe we could work honestly with each other. That we can supply each other with enough knowns as to avoid a regrettable event. Here's my card, again. Call me if you would like to discuss this further."

LeClerc got in his car, not waiting for a reply, and drove away. Miles looked at the card, not sure what to do with it. He turned, walking back to the station front door, almost absent mindedly put the card in his front shirt pocket. His mind was racing. *Have to call someone. CGI. Got to write notes first on what LeClerc said. Make a transcript of the recording. Got to call someone. Gotta make notes.* Without thinking, he had sprinted up the stairs to his office.

CCGS Corporal Teather C.V. Arrives

At daybreak, Williams and Webb, plus a few other HSC officers, were standing on the Sullivan Street pier, watching through binoculars as a large red and white steel ship passed by Eastport on her way to Saint Andrews.

Williams knew the ship to be the Canadian Coast Guard Ship *Corporal Teather*. Yesterday, Miles told Williams of her expected arrival and her intentions. To Williams, Miles seemed almost gleeful in telling him to keep his people far away from the border and the ship. "You know, I think the Canadians are really after you. Remember, they've got an RCMP team on that ship."

As the Williams watched, the Coast Guard RB-M left its dock on what looked like a course to intercept the Canadian ship. *Christ, first our Coast Guard. Now the Canucks.*

The *Corporal Teather* was barely moving as the RB-M met her almost due east from the station. She suddenly let loose a series of horn blasts. Williams didn't count how many. A fainter horn, from the RB-M he guessed, replied in kind.

"That's our boat, Mr. Williams." Startled, Williams turned to see Senior Chief James right behind him, broadly smiling. Williams and company were so fixated on the *Corporal Teather*, they didn't notice the senior chief had walked up the pier.

"Lieutenant Miles went out on the RB-M to greet the Canadians. A matter of courtesy. He'll be coming back soon. Nice ship, isn't she, Mr. Williams."

"I wouldn't know, chief."

"I wouldn't expect you to." The senior chief wasn't about to tell them anything about the ship.

Webb interrupted. "Chief, any idea why the Canucks got a machine gun mounted on its deck?"

"Do they now? You know some Canadians don't like that term 'Canucks.' And its 'her,' not 'it.' Why is there a gun mounted? That's above my paygrade. Besides, Webb. We got the same guns. Anyway, maybe you guys ought to do what the skipper said, stay the hell away from them." With that, the senior chief turned and walked away.

Williams waited until the senior chief was far enough away before telling his officers to head back. He then turned to Webb and said, "This doesn't matter. I called HSC Regional about this yesterday. Mission is still on. We still brief our people at 1400."

Miles had made one mistake yesterday, letting it slip that the Canadian ship couldn't dock at the Saint Andrews pier. Too big for the pier. Needs deeper water, especially with the tides. She would anchor off the western side of Navy Island, two, maybe three kilometers from Joes Point. Only radar could spot his boats at night from that distance.

Yesterday, they modified the op plan to take into account the *Corporal Teather's* radar. He remembered being told that the Zodiac boats had a low radar signature, but to be sure he called HSC Regional. Yes, the boats have a low radar signature, but they were quick to say that low doesn't mean invisible. Radar could pick up the framing, engines and cockpit. Though neither Williams nor Webb were radar experts, they knew it operated on line of sight, something they could use to their advantage.

Their boats would hug the Maine coastline northward until they were well up the Saint Croix River, at a point just north of Saint Croix Island. They'd done that route before many times, day and might, so their route should seem like a routine patrol to RCMP. Webb drilled the crews in piloting the boats using night vision goggles. Williams and Webb estimated two hours to get there at a slow and quiet eight knots.

At the designated GPS coordinates, they would turn east directly toward the Canadian shore. Saint Croix Island's northern shoreline should help hide them from the Canadian ship's radar for those critical minutes as they approached the Canadian side of the Saint Croix River. Then they'd move south, eventually rounding a point off the golf course. They'd stay close to the shoreline to blend in with the radar return from the shore. About four nautical miles. Going against the incoming tide would take about almost another hour. Their estimated time of arrival at the target should roughly coincide with the 0417 high tide.

Moving slowly, quietly, with no lights, relying on night vision goggles, staying close to the shore, combined with their low profile, they hoped they would pass unnoticed by ear or eye or radar to the target. Landing the boats on the beach in front of the target, the two boat pilots would stay in position, engines idling, ready for a quick return. Eight officers would go over the breakwater, using the wooden stairs on the Whynot's property. Two of them would take covering positions at the top of the stairs.

Two teams of three would approach the house. One officer had some skill in picking locks, so they might be able to enter fairly easily. If not, they'd use the sledgehammers to bash in the deck door locks. Any alarms would be ignored. They would rely on speed.

After the subjects were arrested, zip tied, gagged, and black bagged, they would retrace their steps, securing the subjects with one man on each side, and a third man covering them. Once all were onboard, the boats will follow the same route back, sticking close to the Canadian shoreline, back across the northern side of Saint Croix Island and across the border.

Returning southerly along the Maine shoreline, the boats would meet one of unit's SUVs at the Elton Brooks Park dock and hand over the subjects. The SUV team would drive to the CBP facility in Houlton and lock them up. The boats should get back before the 0750 sunrise. To the Coast Guardsmen, it would look like they went on the usual patrol.

If detected in Canadian waters on the way to Joes Point, the boats would speed directly back over the border. Let HSC do the explaining afterward. Sorry, Canada. Just an error in navigation. A weak lie, but it only has to work for a little while.

If spotted in Canada with the targets aboard, get back to U.S. waters as fast as the boats can go.

To deal with Miles and his crew, Webb had a plan to deceive them. Illegal, but Williams and HSC thought it a good idea. The fact that it authorized committing a felony was, as Williams put it, a trifling matter.

Another series of horn blasts from the *Corporal Teather* brought Williams back to the moment at hand.

Tired of watching the Canadian ship, Webb walked back to the trailers, telling Williams he had work to do. Williams remained for a few more minutes. He debated whether he should wait for Miles to return aboard the RB-M but decided there was nothing to be gained. As the RB-M docked, he started back.

"Oh, hello, good morning son. How are you today?" Williams was almost halfway back down the pier, but not really looking where he was going when he almost bumped into an old man, standing in his path. He was the old man.

"Ah, yeah, ah, you're the, ah, man from the diner. Sunday."

"Yes, I guess I am. Good morning." The old man greeted Williams with a wide smile and open hand. "What brings you out on the pier? Watching that ship, son?"

Williams blurted out, "Yeah. Something to see. Not much else going on around here."

"Nothing ever goes on here." The old man took a moment to glance over Williams's uniform before saying, "Now I know something about you. You work for that new border police outfit, don't you?" When the old man sensed Williams's hesitancy to answer, he said, "Don't worry, son. I don't involve myself in politics. Too old for that."

Somehow, Williams felt more at ease with the old man. "Actually, sir. I'm in charge of this group. Homeland Security Corps."

"Oh, yeah. Well, impressive. Once in a while I see you guys going out on those black Zodiacs."

The two endured an awkward moment of silence as the Coast Guard RB-M crew and Miles, walked past them on their way to the station, carrying sidearms, a rifle, and other gear. Miles couldn't resist a dig. "Morning, Williams. Like I said, there's the *Corporal Teather*. You keep your people away from her, right?" Miles didn't stop to wait for a reply.

Once the Coast Guardsmen were out of earshot, the old man shook his head in disapproval and said, "You know, I remember the days when the Coast Guard didn't carry weapons all the time. When we knew their job was to save our lives. Now . . . helluva world we live in, isn't it?"

Williams didn't reply.

"Just my opinion, son, but I think that lieutenant ought to treat you with a little more respect. You know, as a fellow commander and such."

"Yeah, well, maybe so." The old man saw Williams's mood hadn't improved since Sunday. "If you excuse me, sir. I need to get back to my office." As Williams started to walk away, he halted, feeling a pang of guilt over his ungraciousness. "Hope to see you again for breakfast sometime. Maybe we'll have more time for stories. Have a good day." Williams gave a slight wave as he walked away.

The old man stayed on the pier for another ten or fifteen minutes, finishing his usual walk to the end and back. He took the usual pictures and notes. At the end of the pier, he called LeClerc on his cell. "I made contact again. Did you get it all?" LeClerc replied, "Yes, it's recorded." They hung up.

Briefing

Tuesday, October 14. A wind was blowing to the southeast, forecasted to stay around 5 to 10 miles per hour. Temperatures would decrease from 43⁰ F to mid to low thirties by the early morning. Skies would be clear.

Inshore seas calm. High tide at the target would be at 0417 Atlantic time zone. Nothing in the weather forecast to impede the operation.

At 1400, Williams gathered the officers inside one of the trailers. He had them turn in their cell phones.

"Everyone, I want to assure you that what we are about to do is legal. DOJ has studied this issue very carefully. As I mentioned to Mr. Webb before, even under the Obama administration, we didn't ask Pakistan for permission before going into their territory and killing bin Laden. That's the precedent."

Opening with a warning that the op was classified, Williams then walked through the operation step by step, minute by minute.

"Finally, with the Canadian Coast guard ship here, you must maintain light and noise discipline. Follow the plan and we can defeat their radar. Any questions?"

Williams could see the officers glancing at each other, as if they had the same thought. *You first.*

Then a question from the back. "Mr. Williams, you covered what we are to do if the Whynots aren't home. Get back in the boats and return to base. I get that. But I'd have thought we could have done something, like technology wise, to confirm they are home."

"Good question. Yes, HSC looked into using military drones with high powered night vision and infrared equipment, but that was rejected. HSC doesn't have those drones. CBP can't to redeploy them from the southern border. DOD won't loan us the drones either.

"However, we do have the means for confirming they're home. I can't tell you right now, it's classified, but you needn't worry."

Not the best answer. In fact, a lousy answer and Williams knew it.

"If there are no other questions, recheck your equipment, study the plan again, and then make sure you get some rest. You must stay in your trailers. You'll be awoken at midnight. Dress warmly. You'll be out on those boats for a while."

As a last task, he had everyone advance their watches one hour to put them on Atlantic Zone time.

Once the officers had left the room, Williams asked Webb to meet him in his office.

"I got word on confirming the Whynots are at home." Williams took out a chart of the target. "Once you come around Joes Point, where the golf course is, if the Whynots are not home you will receive a code word, repeated three times, *Take a Knee*. Response is *Loss of Down*. If they are home, the code is *Forward Pass*. Respond with *Safety*. It will come over our secure frequency. Don't tell the other boat captain until they are about to get underway."

"Very well. *Take a Knee*, abort the mission. Response is *Loss of Down*. *Forward Pass*, execute. Response is *Safety*. Got it." Webb looked at Williams with a smile on his face. "Looks like somebody is a football fan. I guess they got an . . ." Webb was about to say *an agent* but caught himself. "Never mind. Need to know." And need to know when to shut up.

Refusal

"Mr. Williams, we have a situation."

"Let's have it, Webb. What now?" Williams leaned back in his chair, doing his best to hide his own nervousness over what was about to happen that night.

"The leader of boat team two, Officer Schroeder, told me he won't go on the special op. He's refusing orders."

"What? Why?"

"He believes this op is illegal."

"But I told them it was legal. Completely legal."

"He doesn't believe you."

Williams looked at his watch. Seven hours till midnight. *Think! What does this mean to the op?*

"Where is he? Where's Schroeder right now?"

"He's outside this office." Williams told Webb to bring him in. As Schroeder stood before him, Williams asked him what was wrong. Schroeder confirmed what Webb told him. Williams knew he had few options and little time.

"Schroeder, give Mr. Webb your weapon and equipment belt. You are relieved of duty." Schroeder complied. Williams took the handcuffs from Schroeder's belt, handing the cuffs to Webb.

Williams asked Schroeder if he'd spoken to anyone else. "No, sir. Just Webb."

"Keep it that way. Do not talk to anyone else about this. Sit down outside my office." Schroeder, head down, sullenly complied.

With the office door closed, Williams whispered to Webb. "Take Schroeder to the Eastport Police Station. Just you. I want him away from our people. Right now. Use cuffs once you get him in the van. I want him in custody at least until tomorrow morning."

"Will they, the cops, do that? I mean, what's the charge?"

"Tell the cops that Schroeder is a federal prisoner . . . no, wait. He's acting strange. Irrational. We're worried about him. Tell them he may do harm to himself, or others. We can't have him around here with access to weapons and we don't have anything near a proper facility for him. We'll have HSC pick him up tomorrow. I'll call the Eastport PD right now."

"Alright sir. I get it. But what if he talks? Tells the cops about the op?"

"I guess we'll have to hope they think he's crazy, delusional."

"What about the op? How do we execute without a boat team leader?"

"Webb, you're boat team two's leader now. You go."

Williams was somewhat surprised Webb didn't object. *Hell, he even seemed quite pleased,* Williams thought.

The Prisoner

"Handcuffs? What do you think I am? Where you taking me?" Webb didn't answer.

"Goddamn it, Webb, answer me! You have any idea why I refused? Do you have any idea of the shitstorm you guys are going into?" Schroeder kicked the driver's seat from behind as hard as he could.

Webb got himself in the driver's seat and started the engine. Schroeder kicked again. "That op is a crime! You can't do it!"

This time, Webb spoke. "Knock it off, Schroeder! Sit there and shut up. Do that again and I'll . . ."

"You'll do what, you fat prick!"

Webb took the van out of the lot, a little fast, taking a hard left turn on Water Street for the one-minute trip to Washington Street and the police station. Webb parked in front, got out and opened the side door by Schroeder. Webb hauled Schroeder out. *Fat prick, huh?*

"Schroeder, we're bringing you here because you're not, ah, well. You're irrational. Maybe suicidal. We told the cops here we can't safely keep you. You're being put in protective custody. They agreed to help."

Then Webb got close to Schroeder, their faces only inches apart, and whispered to Schroeder, "Say anything about the op, you'll face charges for divulging classified material. I don't think the cops will believe you anyway. We'll put you in a real jail if you're not careful."

For good measure, Webb grabbed Schroeder by the hair and slammed his head against the door frame. Webb brought Schroeder into the station for processing.

In ten minutes, Webb was back at the trailers. He hustled boat team two together to break the sad news about Schroeder.

The Asset and CSIS

The old man spent much of the afternoon watching the HSC from his home's second-floor observation post. He saw little activity, except when all the HSC officers went into one of the trailers around two o'clock. They came out about an hour or so later. A short walk to the waterfront an hour before sunset found both of their boats still there. They hadn't moved all day. Nothing terribly unusual in that.

Nobody at the bar that evening but a couple of locals he really didn't consider friends. In a way, the old man looked forward to talking to the HSC guys. He was self-aware enough to realize maybe he just liked talking to anyone these days. He wondered, *am I just getting old?*

"Slow night tonight, Mac?" The bartender, whose name really was Mac, said, "Yup, have to agree, but it's Tuesday. Never really gets busy on Tuesday night. Course, it's still a little early. We'll see."

The old man ordered his customary after dinner glass of red wine. He sat at the bar, sipping it slowly. Maybe some of them would come by.

An hour later, the old man gave up on finding company at the bar. *Mac the bartender is a decent enough guy*, thought the old man, *but any dog is a better conversationalist.* He walked back home, deciding that he would try to stay awake for a while, maybe watch a favorite movie, maybe two. Let's see what the night might bring.

Chase

Colby felt something wasn't right. Boatswain's Mate Second Class Colby had the duty. With recreational boat traffic down this time of year, the station went from two watchstanders on duty to just one. In an emergency, extra hands could be called down from the crew berthing.

Colby believed he had gotten to know a few of the HSC officers. *No, that isn't right.* Colby corrected himself, admitting he only knew them well enough to see when something was a bit off. Like the two officers who came in just before midnight to log in their departure and patrol area. Tonight, Colby saw that these two were unusually excited.

HSC's departure log said the HSC boats would head south to Lubec, then continue to Quoddy Head, and possibly to Hamilton Cove along the Maine coast. Both their boats. Estimate time of return to the station at approximately 0600.

One officer asked Colby for the latest weather report. He replied, "Not bad. Overcast. No precipitation forecast for tonight. Winds, out of the northwest at five to ten knots. Seas calm at least until Quoddy Head. Then waves, one to two feet. Wind higher past Quoddy, ten to fifteen knots. Temps, no better than mid to high thirties. Water temp in forties. You know, typical Down East Maine. But your boats ought to be able to handle it. Gonna be damn cold though. Long patrol for you guys. Dress warm."

The officers quickly thanked Colby and left. Colby wondered, *what's the rush?*

Standing orders now required that when the HSC departed, the watchstander must advise the MSST team leader, no matter the hour. The team leader would then decide if further action was warranted. The team leader said he'd be down in a minute.

Colby went to a window. He saw the HSC crews walking down the docks to their boats. The HSC guys were only about 140 feet away and bathed in the station's floodlights. Now Colby knew something was off. *Sledgehammers? What are they doing with sledgehammers? No long guns either. The HSC guys always liked to show off their guns. No POLICE placards on their jackets. All with black balaclavas. And they were supposed to wear their new Stearns personal floatation devices, not just carry them.*

The MSST team leader, Maritime Law Enforcement Specialist Petty Officer First Class Dillon, joined Colby at the window, dressed only in pants and undershirt. He asked, "Do you see what I see?"

"If by that you mean no police thing across their backs, no rifles or shotguns, but two big sledgehammers, yes, Petty Officer Dillon, we see the same thing."

"They don't usually do this, do they Colby?"

"No, they don't. Since you guys got here, they'd have their PFDs on before they got in a boat. This time, no. Another thing. The HSC guys who filled out the departure log seemed in a hurry. Nervous."

"Colby, keep watching them. I'm getting my team and the RB-M crew up. Call the senior chief. I'll wake the lieutenant too. Ahh, looks like they've started their engines." Dillon ran topside.

Colby reached the senior chief at home. After apologizing for the late call, Colby told the chief what he saw. "Colby, I'll be in as quick as I can."

Dillon was back at the window fully dressed. His team and the RB-M crew were scrambling to get all their gear together.

"There they go, Colby. This time, they've got their nav lights on. Sledge-hammers? Any ideas why they would take those?"

"Petty Officer Dillon, senior chief is on his way in. The sledgehammers? Nope. Got no idea why they've got the hammers. We both saw them. The lieutenant?"

"He's getting dressed. Colby, they've turned. Headed south. Lights still on. What's their departure log say?"

Colby read the log out loud as Dillon continued to watch the HSC boats as they disappeared into the darkness save for their navigation lights.

Miles, now down on the quarterdeck, in uniform and holding his foul weather coat, asked for an update. Dillon answered, keeping his eyes locked on the boats all the while. "They've got both boats out. Went east from the docks, halfway to the border. Then turned south. They had their nav lights on. At moderate speed. Colby reported a couple of unusual things.

"HSC didn't bring any long guns. They usually do. Their jackets lacked the police identifier placard. They usually Velcro those across their vests and jackets, front and back. All had on black balaclavas. Like they want to be as invisible as they can. They carried a couple of big sledgehammers."

"Sledgehammers?"

Dillon smiled. "Had the same reaction, sir. I can't imagine why they brought those, but they must have a reason." He handed Miles the departure log. "The log says they plan to head south."

Miles quicky read the log entry, then turned to Dillon. "You know, since your team got here, HSC has kept to their log entries. Granted, not a long time since you arrived. Your surveillance has spotted no deviations whatso-ever, correct?"

"No deviations, sir. They do what they say they will do."

Colby said, "I think they turned their lights off. Or they rounded Buck-man's Head and are out of our line of sight. Can't see them anymore."

Miles considered the facts. *You use sledgehammers to drive in large tent stakes, break things, pound things. Guess we'll find out later what they needed those for. But, no, I don't trust them.*

"Very well. We'll follow them from well behind. We'll go south first. Through Lubec Narrows to Quoddy Narrows. Six nautical miles roughly. Go dark about one nautical mile south of the harbor. Use our night vision goggles. Keep them on radar and the FLIR. They're working, right?"

The RB-M coxswain, Boatswain Mate Second Class Powell, who unbeknownst to Miles, was standing behind him, answered. "Yes, sir. It's all working." Miles thanked him. And winced a bit as he hoped the coxswain didn't think he was questioning the readiness of his boat. He thought, *Good to know the FLIR thermal imager was working. Might be more useful than radar for this mission.*

"I can't be sure they're not lying to us again. Dillon, Powell, we go south first, and if we don't see them, we go north. I'm going with you. Understood?"

"Yes, sir. But when we leave, whoever is behind at the trailers will let them know."

"That's true, Powell. Not much we can do about that. Anyway, like been said before, if they know we're watching them, they're more likely to keep to the straight and narrow. Let's get underway."

Senior chief arrived just as Miles was last out the door. "Hello, skipper. Going somewhere?"

"Hello to you, senior chief. It's such a lovely night. We all got the urge for a midnight cruise. I think Colby can fill you in."

Deception

There's no point in my going along with the boat teams, Williams decided long ago. First, if he was seen going on a boat, it might draw too much attention. Second, he would likely be a hindrance. Third, he gets seasick.

His job now was to watch. He watched his boat teams get underway and saw them leave on their feint to the south. About 15 minutes later, he watched the Coast Guard leave and head south. He watched them until he couldn't see them anymore.

So far, the deception was working. His boats put their navigation lights out half a nautical mile south of the station and turned east, straight across the border to Campobello Island. By the time the Coast Guard left the dock, his boats had already made a lazy kind of U-turn north, running dark and silent in Canadian waters. Now his boats were already north of Eastport. But still too far south for the *Corporal Teather* to catch them on radar.

Williams tried to remember that line from the old song about two ships passing in the night. The Coast Guard's still heading south, and we're heading north. He got a text from Webb saying they were headed to Dog Island, just north of Eastport. From there, they'd stay close to the Maine coast.

Williams knew they needed more than a lie on the departure log to fool Miles. True, it was working, but that won't last. HSC had other options for dealing with the Coast Guard. Williams had one officer dropped off at the closed CBP station in Lubec, where he could see any boats passing under the bridge to Campobello Island. He'd call Williams if and when the Coast Guard boat passed by.

A second officer sat in one of the unit's SUVs, parked by the old lighthouse down at Quoddy Point State Park. The officer would use the VHF-FM radio installed in the SUV to broadcast a Mayday distress call on channel 16 to pin the Coast Guard to the south. The guy Williams chose had amateur acting experience, so that should help sell the Mayday call. *Help, I'm in a sailboat halfway between Maine and Grand Manan! I'm sinking! Yada, yada, yada.*

False distress calls are illegal. Very illegal. Six years in jail. And very hard to catch people doing it. But once the Coast Guard heard the distress call, they'd have no choice. They must respond. *They'll have to start a search further to the south, away from our op.*

Williams wasn't troubled by committing a felony. HSC assured him that he and his people would never face prosecution. *The op had to be done. He knew it was his ticket out of here.*

If the Mayday option didn't work, there was the final option. Williams would call the command center for HSC Regional in Boston. They'd call the Coast Guard First District operations center, ordering them to cease MSST operations in Eastport and withdraw to Joint Base Cape Cod. Williams imagined the fuss that would create.

The Asset

The old man stayed awake after all. Coffee and the need to deal with a full bladder helped. He checked the docks from his perch every ten minutes. Just after midnight, he saw the HSC boats leave. *It could be nothing. Then again . . .*

He called LeClerc to report the boat movement and finally went to bed.

LeClerc passed the intel on to the captain of the *Corporal Teather*, saying "Don't have any details other than both boats left. Could be nothing really."

CHAPTER TEN
SOMETHING EXTRAORDINARY

Are We Good?

Now sailing east, they passed the northern shore of Saint Croix Island. Webb stood alongside the boat pilot. Leaning close to the pilot's ear, Webb said, "It's working." At first, the pilot only nodded in response. Then he leaned over to Webb, cursed the cold and said, "Can't we go a little faster and get this over with?"

No point in responding to that. Webb couldn't blame him. He mentally calculated they had crossed the international border. *They were criminals now. But only with the Canucks. And who cares about that?*

In minutes, they'll begin their turn south, staying somewhere around 50 yards from the Canadian shore. Crouching low, he went forward and tapped the team member near the bow who was scanning with the night vision googles. Webb asked, "Anything? Are we good?"

"Nothing on the water. Just occasional house lights on shore. We're good."

Webb ordered the pilot to turn south, signaling the second boat to follow. "Incoming tide, so punch up the throttle a little to maintain speed." He checked his watch. 0245. Another hour and they should be at the target.

Response Boat – Medium

While the HSC boats turned south along the Saint Croix River's Canadian shore, Miles and the RB-M were just south of West Quoddy Head Lighthouse. Miles considered whether to continue southerly along the Maine coastline. They saw nothing. Radar, thermal imaging, night vision goggles, bare eyeballs and ears didn't pick up the slightest hint of the HSC boats. Nothing through Lubec or the Quoddy Narrows. Six nautical miles and one hour of nothing.

HSC lied. Williams lied. Again. Furious, Miles relished dark fantasies of what he was going to do to Williams. *I'll . . . what. What can I really do?* HSC worked for Homeland Security and after that meeting with Williams, it's clear leadership favored Homeland Security Corps over the Coast Guard.

Miles slammed his hand on the navigation chart table behind the coxswain station. *Not the best demeanor for an officer*, Miles admitted to himself. Taking the seat at the third navigation station on the starboard side, he donned the headset. He called to the coxswain, "Powell, get us back to Eastport. Balls to the wall." Miles then turned to Petty Officer Dillon, and said, "We're going to look north now. Just like we planned."

Then a nautical mile southwest of West Quoddy Head Lighthouse, the RB-M turned back north. Powell hit the throttle to take her well over 20 knots. Even at that speed and without the headsets, to Miles the RB-M was a comfortable craft. No more cabin noise than anyone experiences as an airline passenger. It didn't hurt either that the waves were barely half a foot. They were almost halfway to Lubec Channel Lighthouse when the call came.

"MAYDAY, MAYDAY, MAYDAY. I'M SINKING. I NEED HELP, PLEASE."

The signal blasted across VHF channel 16. As Powell grabbed the mike. A MSST team member in the cockpit remarked, "Christ, this guy in the next room or what? Gotta be close by." Powell brought the RB-M's engines to an idle.

"VESSEL CALLING MAYDAY. VESSEL CALLING MAYDAY. THIS IS UNITED STATES COAST GUARD. WHAT IS YOUR POSITION AND NATURE OF DISTRESS? OVER." Powell repeated the call on channel 16 twice more. Then came the reply.

"COAST GUARD. I NEED HELP. I'M SINKING. I'M SOMEWHERE BETWEEN GRAND MANAN AND MAINE. I NEED HELP! I'M SINKING!"

Powell wasn't surprised the caller couldn't offer a precise position. He'd seen that before. Powell continued trying to get the caller back, asking for the number of persons onboard, if he had personal floatation devices, the vessel name and description. He advised the caller to fire a distress flare or shine a strong light to help determine his position.

No response except a repeat of MAYDAY and SINKING.

Even someone new to these waters could see from a chart that there's not a lot of water between Maine and Grand Manan Island. Maybe ten nautical miles across at most. The other day, a station crewmember had casually mentioned to Powell that on a clear day you could see the northern end of Grand Manan Island from Lubec.

Miles told Powell to reverse course back to the Quoddy Narrows. "No choice. It's a Mayday." Off they went, with Powell hitting the siren and blue rotating lights. Miles asked Powell for the radio detection finder bearing when the Mayday call first came in. The Mayday call transmitted along a bearing of almost 185 degrees from their position. That line ran over the eastern most edge of West Quoddy Head.

Enroute, Miles conferred with Dillon. "Well, what do you think?"

"We've got no choice, sir. But kinda funny we get a Mayday right when we get headed back to Eastport." Miles nodded in agreement.

"Lieutenant, Petty Officer Dillon, I have a suggestion."

Miles didn't know Powell but for a matter of days. He judged Powell as fairly shy. Awkward with others in the station. Yet, once in the coxswain chair Miles saw Powell left no one doubting his ability to command.

"Very well, Powell, let's hear it."

"We have one bearing. We keep trying to get the guy back. Get another direction finder bearing. We'll be out past Quoddy Head in seconds. I'll bet radar and FLIR pick up nothing. Could be a fake call. He's close by. Seen this before."

"Very well, Powell. Take us half a nautical mile south of the lighthouse."

Using a secure radio link, Miles contacted Station Eastport, telling them of his intentions and suspicions. "Get the RB-Sierra going in case we need it. Have it stand off Eastport harbor for now and use their radar to spot HSC."

"Coast Guard 608, Eastport. Transmitting SAROPS pattern from Sector."

"Very well." Miles knew sector had no choice. Until they found evidence, real evidence, they had to conduct a search. *Christ, I hope they don't waste a helo from Cape Cod.*

A moment later, Powell downloaded the search orders. Appearing on the screens of all three navigation stations, the search pattern overlayed a scalable digital chart of the area, with tides, currents and winds already calculated in.

Powell started on the first leg of the pattern, running south along the Maine Coast for 13 nautical miles. One leg alone would take them nearly an hour.

Powell had another crewmember relieve him of calling out on channel 16. He had a couple of other things to concern him. Miles stood aside as they called again and again, trying to reach, or provoke, the distress caller.

"COAST GUARD, JESUS! CAN'T YOU FIND ME? WATER PRETTY CLOSE TO THE SIDES. I MIGHT HAVE TO GET IN MY LIFE RAFT!"

"Got him!" Powell yelled. Now barely two nautical miles into their first leg, the radio detection bearing went as Powell expected. "Sir, that bearing goes right back over Quoddy Head Light."

Powell went back to channel 16, trying to get the distress caller to give his position. No reply. A third radio bearing would nail this guy for sure.

Miles double checked Powell's chart display. *Even with just two bearings, we got him.* He grabbed the secure comms mike. "Eastport, Coast Guard 608. No sightings of distressed vessel. Have a second radio bearing on the distress caller. We have high confidence the two lines intersect at West Quoddy Head Lighthouse. Advise Sector of possible fake distress call. Also, call the Lubec Police. See if they can send a cop down there. Will continue on search pattern until district suspends. Over."

"Coast Guard 608, Eastport. Roger that. Be advised Lubec does not have a police department. Will call Maine State Police. Over."

"Eastport, Coast Guard 608. Understood. Have someone check to see if both the HSC Suburbans are still parked in their spaces. Over."

A minute later, Station Eastport responded. "608, Eastport. Sector awaiting decision from district. RB-Sierra is standing off Eastport harbor. State Police dispatching an officer to the lighthouse, but ETA unknown. And both HSC vehicles are not at home. Over."

After acknowledging the station's last transmission, Miles leaned over to Dillon. "If district suspends the search, which I think they will, we'll shoot up to Eastport and points north as fast as we can. In the meantime, the RB-S is standing by. I hope we didn't get you out here for nothing."

"Lieutenant, may I ask you why you inquired about the HSC vehicles?"

"I think you know why." Miles considered not answering but relented. "Williams had his people lie on the departure log. They went someplace, just not south. Did they go north? Or did they go right up Passamaquoddy Bay on their own little invasion of Canada? I don't know. Now we have this distress call. Their vehicles are gone at the same time. I think I remember seeing radio antennas on their vehicles. Like you said. Kinda funny how that call came in just as we turned back north."

Dillon, quiet for a moment, said to Miles "I wonder if there are any other surprises in store for us. Lieutenant, I really hope you're wrong about the distress call. That federal officers would commit a felony like that, well . . ."

"Coast Guard 608, Eastport. Active Search Suspended. Active Search Suspended."

Miles acknowledged the station and, smiling to Powell, "Get us back to Eastport, Powell. Put us off Loring Cove, here. We'll see what we find."

Target in Sight

The HSC boats rounded the sandbar at the end of the golf course, keeping as close to the shore as they dared. A little too close. Webb's boat started to slide across bottom sand. He ordered the boat pilot to stop and reverse the engine. It crept off the bottom. Webb was terrified he would have to order his men out of the boat to push it off the bar. He calmed down as the boat inched its way off the bar. Now free, they got back on course.

Webb sighed in relief. *Thank God it wasn't rocks. Sinking was not part of the plan.*

The words *Forward Pass* came over the console speaker, repeated three times. Webb cursed himself for leaving the speaker on so loud. He grabbed the mic, checked the radio panel to make sure he was on the secure frequency, and said, "*Safety, Safety, Safety.*"

The subjects are at home.

CCG Corporal Teather C.V.

That early morning hour, a boatswain crewman aboard the *Corporal Teather* monitored the ship's surface search radar. All quiet. Nothing on radar. At times like this, it seemed to her that she was the last living person on earth. Ships like hers, a 140-foot Hero-class Canadian Coast Guard ship, needed only a crew of nine. Only her and one other crewmember were on watch. The rest of the crew were asleep in their racks. Of their four special guests, the RCMP Emergency Response Team, three slept while another remained awake in the galley.

Her job that watch was to monitor any vessel traffic, using the radar and the night vision equipment. As dedicated as she was to her job, at times she found herself in a refrain recited by deck crewmembers since the first moment man stepped aboard a ship. It's cold. It's boring. And I've seen nothing. Even the fishermen have the sense to get some sleep.

Their briefing before leaving Dartmouth, Nova Scotia, and the heavily armed RCMP guys, hinted that they were not looking for illegal fishing activity. Part of her wished something would happen.

It did. At 0350, the radar screen picked up something. A couple of little dots, moving slowly along the shoreline outside of Saint Andrews, as if they had just rounded the point up there. Two kilometers away. They intermittently appeared and disappeared over the next few minutes. Something was there. Two images, then one, then none, then two again. She called over the other crewman on watch to see if he saw the same thing. He did.

She rang up the navigation officer, who, after a little grogginess, came up to the bridge to look for herself. "Yeah, might be something." She zipped her coat against the cold and stepped out from the bridge, using her binoculars to see what might be there.

"Night vision show anything?"

"No," replied the seaman.

"Let's keep looking. No need to bother the RCMP or the captain yet. We're not even sure there's anything there."

A minute later, the boatswain told the navigation officer, "Whatever they, or it, are, it seems to have stopped. They're gone now."

West Quoddy Head Lighthouse

I need another line of work, HSC Officer Fawkes muttered to himself, sitting alone in the Suburban. Williams explained this little acting job was a felony, but he shouldn't worry. Williams promised nothing would happen to him. Fawkes could've turned down the assignment, but he didn't, admitting to himself that he needed to get away from that place. Especially this night.

The amateur actor in him even enjoyed this chance at playacting. On center stage, the role of the drowning boater.

He was only too happy to be left out of the boat teams. *I'm warm and dry here. I'm no damn commando. But those guys will get all the medals, or whatever they get. Certifiable Homeland Security Corps heroes. At best, I might get mentioned in some sort of email. So, yeah, turns out a law enforcement career was not for me.*

From inside the vehicle, he saw the Coast Guard boat with its blue light racing south by the point maybe half a mile away. After his second fake call, it followed the shoreline in kind of a southerly course. Then it reversed course and headed back north. Fawkes decided maybe the game is up. His character had drowned in a sinking yacht. No further transmissions. Leaving the Suburban running, he walked out to the chain link fence surrounding the old lighthouse grounds to check on the Coast Guard boat, thinking it best to be thorough. Also, he wanted to stay away from Eastport as long as possible.

He stayed at the fence until he couldn't stand the cold and wind any longer. Seeing nothing, he walked back between the two old buildings and was about to open the Suburban's door when the world filled with swirls of blue lights.

Oh, Christ! Police. He couldn't move, stuck standing by the driver's door, gawking at the quickly approaching police cruiser. The cop got out of his car, ordering Fawkes to stay where he was and keep his hands visible. *The cop's gun was out! This is just like in COPS,* a somewhat amused Fawkes thought.

"Maine State Police. Place your hands on the hood of the vehicle." The trooper said it twice, loudly. Fawkes wondered, *what's this guy so upset about? Oh, wait, he sees a guy with a gun.* When Fawkes turned his head toward the trooper to speak to him, the trooper's high intensity flashlight temporarily blinded him.

"Officer, please, I'm with Homeland Security Corps. I'm here to surveil the coast, watching for illegal immigration. Please, put your gun down." That was the line Williams told him to say if police stop him.

The trooper came behind him, seized Fawkes' sidearm and kicked his feet apart before backing up a couple of steps. "Use your left hand and drop the equipment belt. Now!" Almost before the belt hit the ground, the trooper began searching Fawkes. Protesting that all this wasn't necessary, Fawkes repeated he was Homeland Security. The trooper didn't say anything as he grabbed Fawkes arms, pushed him into the fender, and cuffed his hands together behind his back.

Good technique, I guess, supposed Fawkes. The trooper leaned Fawkes on to the Suburban's hood, face on the hood, keeping him off balance. Fawkes told the trooper his identification was in his wallet, and he was welcome to take it from his back pocket. The trooper had his wallet before Fawkes finished talking.

Then the questions began. What is your name? When did you get here? What were you doing here? Were you using the VHF marine radio in your vehicle? He ignored Fawkes pleas to be released from the handcuffs.

"Mr., ah, Fawkes, we have a complaint from the Coast Guard that someone's been making false distress calls. That's pretty serious. You were here when those calls were made. You have a VHF radio. I looked inside the vehicle. The radio is on. The Coast Guard's direction finder pretty much points to this location as the origin. You were here. No one else. Got anything to say about all that?"

"Hey, man, I mean officer, trooper, I'm just here doing what they told me to do. Watch for illegal immigrants. The distress call? Wasn't me. Must have come from someplace else. Hell, maybe they were real distress calls. I don't know about all that." Fawkes stopped talking for a moment, thinking over what to say next. The trooper didn't react. Fawkes thought of something else.

"Officer, I do not doubt a distress call was made. I can assure you I did not make the call. My word as a fellow police officer." An appeal to the fraternity of law enforcement officers.

At that, the trooper started laughing. "Well, speaking as one cop to, well, I guess maybe another cop, that is the biggest crock of shit I've heard in a long time. And I've been around a long time."

"Fawkes, you're under arrest on suspicion of a felony. Making a false distress call. I'm going to put you in the back of my vehicle and take you to our holding facility in Ellsworth. It can be all sorted out there. Now, let me tell you about your rights." While the trooper read Fawkes his rights, all he could do was think, *hey, this is just like on TV*.

"Ellsworth? I know where that is. How'd you get here so fast?"

The trooper wasn't really surprised by Fawkes irrelevant question. Another dim bulb who can't focus on the important things. Like being arrested. "Glad to know that you're so familiar with the area. Must be my lucky day. Just happened to be near Lubec, doing traffic on 189. Guess I should thank you for getting me out of a boring duty to come out here to arrest your sorry ass."

Once Fawkes was settled into the back of the State Police vehicle, handcuffed and behind a seat belt, the trooper contacted his field office, briefing the desk officer on his status and the incoming guest. "Oh, and you should call the Coast Guard in Eastport about what I found."

On the Beach

Four in the morning. *Why does Spot always need to go out at four in the morning?* To George, it always seemed Spot waited for a night when he really needed some undisturbed sleep. And just the right hour to make it difficult to get back to sleep.

Dressed in winter coat, pajamas, and unlaced rubber soled boots, George took Spot toward the thick stand of trees on the edge of his property. He dutifully kept Spot on a leash, making sure there were still poop bags in the handy little dispenser attached to the line. As fastidious as George was about his home, he was borderline fanatical when it came to his lawn and lot. Always trimmed grass and bushes, always clear of fallen branches and leaves. The very thought of leaving dog turds on his lawn almost sickened him.

"Oh, and Spot, thanks for choosing such a cold night," George quietly said to Spot. The dog was in the middle of doing what he needed to do when George heard a boat engine. Outboard engine, or engines, close by. *Kinda a strange time to be out and about on a boat.*

After struggling a bit to open the plastic bag, George picked up after Spot, and decided to do a little investigation of the noise. He walked around the water side of his home and opened the door to their sheltered porch to leave Spot and the bag inside.

Walking toward the rock fortified shore, George heard more sounds. He hunched lower and started to walk quickly. Not just boat engines. Voices, muffled, but voices. Then, breaking glass. From over at Mike and Debbie's house. Then he saw them.

Human figures, moving, illuminated by the house floodlights. Noises, coming from inside the house. Crashing, yelling. An alarm. George had enough. He ran back to his house, not noticing the loss of his unlaced boot. Leaping up the stairs to the bedroom, he shook Cheryl awake.

"Something's going on at Mike and Debbie's. Men are breaking in. Be quiet. Call 911. Get you and James in the basement. Lock all the doors behind me. Now. Please."

George didn't wait for her. Cheryl was about to demand some clarity when she saw him reach up into the closet to the weapon safe where he kept his service pistol. George entered the code with a shaking hand and retrieved his pistol and three magazines. He took his service equipment belt. On the way down the stairs, he noticed his missing boot, ignored it, and went to the rifle cabinet where he kept his deer rifle and shotgun. Unlocking it, he took the telescopically sighted rifle and a box of shells as Cheryl and James came down the stairs.

"George, I called 911. They're coming. Please, George, be . . ."

"Don't worry. Get downstairs. I'll be fine."

George wasn't fine. He was scared. He hadn't used a firearm in anyway remotely like he may be about to do since Afghanistan. Maybe to calm himself more than Cheryl, he said again to her, "Really, it'll be fine." George forced himself to walk, not run, out the door.

George thought he must be a ridiculous sight. Pistol, gun belt, rifle, and pajamas. One boot off.

He trotted to a large boulder that was halfway to the shoreline and marked the property line with Mike's. He crouched low, and loaded the rifle, one round at a time. From the rock, he could see their entire backyard, down to the stairs leading to the water.

People moving, coming out on the back deck of Mike's house. Two men held someone. *Mike? Debbie?* They held someone wearing pajamas, bare feet, a dark bag over their head, walking together off the deck, a man on both sides. Then another pair with someone else, also with a black bag. George saw their hands were bound, held out front. A second later another two men followed. *They have Mike and Debbie. That must be them.*

All dressed head to toe in black, the men spoke in low tones. In the background, the house alarm kept squawking. Two men stood by the stairs that lead down to the beach. George wondered why they hadn't put out the deck lights.

George looked down at his rifle in his hands. *I don't have a shot. Never so good I could take one now. What can I . . .* George moved down toward the shore, hoping he wouldn't be seen. He took position behind a bunch of beach roses and a pile of basketball sized rocks.

George had a clear view of the boats, their bows resting on the short stretch of sand and illuminated just enough by the house deck lights. One man in the cockpit of each boat. *Do something. Now.*

"POLICE! STOP WHERE YOU ARE! PUT DOWN YOUR WEAPONS!" In all his years in Border Services, George realized this was a first for him. He'd never said such a thing before. He wasn't even sure they heard him.

The figures didn't respond but kept hustling their captives to the stairs.

George sighted in the nearest boat's outboard engines. Just enough light to make out the engines with the scope. He worked the bolt to chamber a round. *If I can't hit the bad guys, I can at least keep them from getting away.* He fired. George couldn't tell if he hit the engine. He fired again and again until he could see the guy in the cockpit hitting the deck, then crawling back to the engine.

George yelled again, "POLICE! FREEZE!" *Christ, this is awkward. I sound like a TV cop.* He reloaded the rifle with the last three rounds from his pocket. He shifted his fire toward the second boat. He could hear police sirens. *They're close by.*

CCG Corporal Teather C.V. and the RCMP

Just as the seaman came into the bridge to report a kind of popping noise coming from the north, the RCMP team leader appeared. "Got a call from RCMP. We're to dispatch immediately and head north up the St. Croix. Trouble involving armed men. They request the ship get underway." Two other team members headed for the rigid hull inflatable craft already moored alongside. The fourth was busy uncovering the deck machine gun.

The navigation officer now abandoned, and regretted, her earlier caution. "Very well." She lifted the intercom phone to the captain's quarters. "Captain, we have a situation." The captain said he was on his way to the bridge.

As the captain came onto the bridge, the navigation officer briefed him on the situation.

"Captain, RCMP is dispatching to an incident involving armed men less than two kilometers north of us. Joes Point, Saint Andrews." She pointed to Joes Point on the digital chart. "RCMP requests we get underway."

"Very well. Let's go. Sound the alarm. You start hauling the anchor. I'll fire up the engines."

As the boatswain sounded the alarm, the captain and the navigation officer started preparations for getting underway. It would take roughly ten minutes to do so.

The captain quietly asked the navigation officer, "How long ago did this start? Is RCMP away yet?"

The sound of the RCMP roaring away from the ship answered the second question.

"Captain, ten minutes before I called you, the boatswain asked me to look at a radar image appearing to round Joes Point, moving from the north. We, no I, couldn't be sure something was there. The image stopped for a minute off the point, then seemed to flicker along the shore before it disappeared. Nothing seen by binoculars or night vision. I stayed on the bridge. But something did happen.

"Captain, I should have called you earlier. My fault. My fault entirely."

The captain cut her off. "We can talk about that later. Right now, we need to get moving and put that guy with the machine gun in a more useful position."

Finality

Mike desperately tried to call out to Debbie, but he couldn't. They had shoved a plastic gag in his mouth and strapped it around his head before he was black bagged and zipped tied. The last thing he saw before the bag went over his head was Debbie suffering the same treatment. At least she got out a string of curses before they gagged her. He tried to fight them as best he could, refusing to move, dragging his feet down the stairs, until something very hard slapped his right elbow. He screamed in excruciating pain, almost passing out.

Suddenly he was outside. He felt the cold air and the near frozen ground on his bare feet. Thoughts came quickly. *Grass. I'm on the lawn. Two men, one on each arm.*

They said little, mostly grunting and swearing. Mike heard something . . . shots! *Somebody was shooting!*

Maybe it was the cold air and ground. Maybe it was pain. Mike understood what was happening. *I am being taken. Debbie is being taken.* And it filled him with rage. *No, I will not go!*

Mike twisted, struck out with his right leg, hitting something, someone else's leg. A knee? The man on his right lost his grip. Mike twisted to his left and spun away, moving forward.

A third HSC officer, a step behind the two holding Mike, thought he saw something by the rocks. Someone. Someone with . . . a rifle! The officer reflexively leveled his pistol and fired twice. Mike kept moving.

The first round missed. The second one struck Mike below his right ear, passing explosively out his left eye, carrying with it blood, bone, and brain. And his life. Mike fell to the ground. He was gone.

CHAPTER ELEVEN
MISSION FAILURE

Chaos

Webb didn't hear the lethal shots. He didn't see one of the subjects fall dead to the ground. Webb stayed at the top of the stairs, covering the officers holding the second subject, the woman, as they started down the stairs to the water. Now, looking to his right, he saw a man shooting at them from behind a rock pile.

He saw the pulsing blue and red lights of police cruisers on the other side of the house. People were coming around both sides of the house, moving toward him.

"Webb, boat one is out of commission! Engine shot up!"

Webb had no idea who told him that, but he yelled to all the others, "Get the subjects on boat two. Everyone else too. Move!"

"Boat two's hull's damaged!"

Webb wasn't listening. "Get moving! Get her out of here! Now! Go!"

Delay. Have to delay the cops. Give them time to get away. Only needed a few minutes. The idea of firing on the cops passed quickly out of his mind. *Maybe the guy by the rocks. No. We're done. We failed.* He knew that. Killing a cop would only get his own people killed. Pointless.

I can scare them though. Webb unscrewed the suppressor from his pistol, clicked the safety off, and fired three rounds into the air before moving to his left. He knew it wouldn't stop them. And might even get himself killed, but it would buy a minute or two. *That'll be enough.*

Webb looked behind toward boat two. In the dim light, he could see it moving off, faster and faster. He flopped on his back, fired two more rounds into the air, almost vertically. Looking toward the house, he could make out at least four cops coming toward him, pistols at the ready, in flanking teams of two.

He saw two of his men lying face down on the ground halfway between the house and his position. He saw more cops cuffing them. Webb looked left and right. The flanking teams were still approaching, yelling at him to drop his weapon and surrender.

Webb turned his head to his right across the ground and saw a man above him in pajamas. A man with a pistol pointed at his head. Webb thought, *I am about to die at the hands of a man in pajamas.* Webb let go his weapon and laced his hands over the back of his head.

George screamed at Webb, kicking him in the hip. "I know you. Webb. American. I know you Webb. Where's Mike? Where's Debbie? What've you done, you bastard!" George kicked him again, forgetting his foot was bare. Webb didn't say a word.

In Custody. In Death

As George kicked Webb for the second time, an officer descended upon Webb, cuffing and searching him for weapons. A second officer carefully moved George aside, taking away George's pistol. He put his arm around George as he led him away, asking "Officer LeBlanc, George? Are you unharmed?"

George didn't respond right away. Then he shook his head no and turned to the RCMP officer and pleaded, "Mike? Debbie? I saw them. They're being . . . kidnapped . . . by these men. I tried to stop them. Stop it from happening. Where are they? Are they alright?"

"I know you did, George. You did all anyone could do." It was Roy. He'd come directly from his home when Cheryl called. Roy led George slowly away from the scene and then did something he rarely did. Roy embraced George tightly, holding him in an almost loving way. Roy finally released George, but still held him by his arm around the shoulders.

"George, we got three of them. No ID, but I recognized that man Webb. They must be American Homeland Security. We've got one of their boats. We got them because you called. Because you shot out one of their boats. If you hadn't, well, they would have gotten away completely.

"I want to ask you a question, George." When Roy judged he had George's attention, he asked, "In what direction and at what did you fire your rifle? And did you fire your pistol?"

"Roy, what about Mike and Debbie! Tell me!"

"Listen, I need you to first answer those two questions. It's important. Trust me, please, George." Roy still gently held George by the shoulders.

"Ah, yeah. Give me a moment." George looked back at the rock pile. An RCMP officer stood there holding the deer rifle George left there. "I fired my rifle, maybe, not sure, maybe six times, at the boat engines. Only the boat engines. When I approached Webb, I had my pistol out, but I did not fire it. Not once."

"Listen, something bad happened." Roy paused, as his chin started to quiver. George could see tears welling up in his eyes. "George, Mike is dead. He suffered a gunshot wound to his head." Roy stammered out, "I, ah, I don't know how, how it happened exactly. We suspect one of these Americans shot him. I asked you those questions so, so you wouldn't . . . you'd know it wasn't caused by your gun."

George turned himself away from Roy, walking a couple of steps before falling to his knees, crying like he hadn't cried since he was a little boy. Roy walked to his friend, knelt down and put his hand across George's back. Another officer came over, whispering to Roy if there was anything he could do. "Yes. Please go next door and get George's wife Cheryl. Tell her what's happened and ask her to come here and help bring George back inside. Thank you."

Roy stayed with George until he saw Cheryl coming out with the RCMP officer. He helped George to his feet, only releasing him when Cheryl enveloped him in her arms. After motioning to the officer to see them safely home, Roy stepped back from George, watched them walk slowly, unsteadily back to their home. Roy turned and walked over to Mike's body. *My God, what have they done to you?*

Debbie. Where are they taking Debbie? Is she still alive? Roy stepped away from the body. He needed to get a handle on himself. He just lost a neighbor and friend, but another was still unaccounted for. There was a job to be done. And likely he was the senior officer present.

Roy called out to the RCMP officers to secure the crime scene and preserve evidence. From the beach to the house. He ordered two officers to sweep the house and the yard in case any other of those Americans were left behind. And to look for Debbie. Two others kept custody of the American prisoners. He dispatched one officer in a cruiser to block unauthorized traffic from coming down Joes Point Road. More officers were on their way from his command, the Saint Stephen Detachment.

He quickly queried the other officers if they had seen someone else being taken by the Americans. None could say they saw another person being taken, but several said the Americans where descending down the beach stairs when they arrived. Roy called his detachment, updating the duty officer and ordered him to update the RCMP on the *Corporal Teather* that the Americans may have a hostage and had fled the scene in boats.

Roy went to the arrested Americans. Three of them, all kneeling on the ground, their hands cuffed behind their backs. He saw Webb. He grabbed Webb from behind, hauled him to his feet, shoving him away from the others before sending him back to the ground. Roy flipped Webb on his back, putting his knee on Webb's shoulder.

"Where is she, Webb? Where is Deborah Whynot?"

Webb stared straight up at the night sky, silent.

Roy repeated the demand. Webb said nothing.

One of the other prisoners spoke. "She should be alright. They took her on the other boat. Look, we didn't come here to shoot anyone. It was an accident. We came here to arrest them. It's all legal."

Roy ordered an officer to take away the protesting American and keep him away from the other two. On his cell phone, he called RCMP J Division Headquarters in Fredericton directly, briefing them on what he knew. "Mrs. Deborah Whynot, wife of the man killed, was likely taken by the Americans by means of a Zodiac type boat, perhaps some fifteen minutes ago."

"Staff Sergeant Wilkins, this is the Assistant Commissioner." Roy hadn't met the new Division Commanding Officer as yet. "We know where she is. RCMP ERT and the United States Coast Guard intercepted the second boat. We expect the *Corporal Teather* to arrive on scene in minutes. We are monitoring developments there. Right now, they are all straddling the border. We're awaiting word from ERT as to Whynot's health and the status of the American officers. It's pretty fluid right now. What do you need?"

"Sir, a forensics team. Someone to handle press inquiries. That's sure to come. We need to pass word to Border Services that one of their officers was involved. Officer George LeBlanc is a friend and next-door neighbor to the Whynots. He saw something happening and confronted the Americans. Used his deer rifle to disable one of the American boats. Heroic, if you ask me."

"Understood. We'll get you what you need. I'll be down there by daybreak. Do all you can to preserve the scene." The assistant commissioner instantly regretted his last. "Sorry, I didn't need to say that. I'm sure that's already underway. Thank you."

Debbie's alive. Thank God for that. Roy realized he needed to let his wife know about Mike and Debbie.

Between Two Countries

Miles stood beside RB-M coxswain. Time to evaluate the interesting situation facing him.

The RB-M and the RB-S intercepted the HSC boat just as they passed into U.S. waters and ordered it to halt. They complied at once, even happily waving to the Coast Guard. Miles had the RB-M come alongside the HSC boat and secure it to the RB-M. The RB-M's digital navigation chart showed they were positioned less than ten meters inside U.S. waters. The men in the boat loudly identified themselves as HSC officers. Miles ordered the MSST team to disarm and secure the men in the boat.

Miles knew they were Homeland Security Corps. He recognized the boats and even their faces. For now, though, he decided to keep that to himself. MSST reported the men had no identification whatsoever. Neither did their boat offer identification of any kind. No emblems on the side. No flag. *What does one do with armed, unidentified men in flight from another country?*

And then there is the unidentified female, dressed in pajamas, bound by zip ties, gagged, and her head covered by a black bag. Petty Officer Dillon had the RB-M's EMT treat her. She was injured, seriously perhaps. Multiple contusions, possible broken ribs and a fracture of her right foot that could become a compound fracture. Likely in shock. When the EMT recommended medical evacuation to the nearest trauma center, Miles ordered she be brought aboard the RB-M.

Straddling the border was a Canadian Coast guard RBI, piloted by a Canadian Coast Guardsman. Accompanying him were three RCMP officers, outfitted in tactical uniforms and armed with submachine guns. Their RBI had launched from the *Corporal Teather*, which now approached the scene with all sorts of powerful floodlights that turned night into day.

Only a minute before, Miles radioed the RCMP team, requesting clarification of their interest in the men in the Zodiac. What Miles learned did not endear the HSC officers to him.

RCMP told Miles they were in hot pursuit of an unknown number of "terrorists" who had crossed from the United States into Canada to kidnap two Americans who were also dual citizens with Canada. One of those Americans was dead. The injured woman is the deceased man's wife. RCMP demanded the woman be evacuated to a Canadian hospital and the unidentified men be turned over to them to face arrest.

Over the secure comms from Station Eastport came interesting news. Miles recognized the senior chief's voice. "608, Eastport. Be advised, State Police arrested an individual they believe made false distress calls from West Quoddy Head Lighthouse. Right where we suspected. State Police identified the suspect as an officer with Homeland Security Corps, by the name of Fawkes. Over."

Miles acknowledged the message. His first thought was, *why am I not surprised?*

"Eastport, 608. Inform sector of the arrest. We will be here for a while longer. Out."

First things first. Miles knew the nearest medical trauma center was Canadian. In Saint Stephen. With the woman on board the RB-M, being treated by the EMT, her gag, black bag and zip ties removed, Miles told her he would get her to a proper medical center immediately.

"Ma'am, I am Lieutenant Douglas Miles, United States Coast Guard. I am the commanding officer at Coast Guard Station Eastport, Maine. May I ask your name?"

"Debbie Whynot. Where's my husband? Where's Mike?" EMT had covered her in a couple of mylar blankets before whispering to Miles that she may be in shock.

"I do not know, Mrs. Whynot." Miles lied. "Please excuse me for a moment."

Miles went back to the VHF radio. "RCMP, Coast Guard 608. We need to MEDEVAC the injured woman to a medical trauma center. Saint Stephen is closest. We'll transfer her from this vessel to our RB-S, with our EMT. Recommend you also transfer one of your officers to the RB-S. Can you arrange for an ambulance to meet the RB-S at a dock in the Saint Andrews area? Over."

"U.S. Coast Guard, RCMP. We will arrange for the ambulance and have an officer will go with the casualty on the RB-S. Over." Miles radioed back his agreement.

Miles had Powell radio the RB-S, instructing them to come alongside. Within minutes, the RB-S, with Debbie and an RCMP officer, were headed to an ambulance dispatched to the docks of the Saint Andrews Aquarium just north of the golf course.

The *Corporal Teather* had taken position on the Canadian side of the border. Miles saw they had a deck mounted machine gun on the port side facing them.

Now, for the second issue at hand, thought Miles. "RCMP, Coast Guard 608. Would you send an officer aboard our vessel, so we can address the men we have detained? Over."

"Roger that" came the reply from the RCMP. Within a minute, they were secured to the RB-M.

"Officer, I am Lieutenant Miles, are you the senior RCMP officer here? We need to talk about those men in the boat on our port side."

"I am. Corporal McCloud. Talk? We want them. Now."

Miles deliberately softened his tone, speaking as calmly as he could to McCloud. "Corporal, I do not doubt what you told me, about what happened to Mrs. Whynot. I do not doubt you were engaged in a lawful pursuit of these men that took you across the international boundary."

Miles continued. "Mrs. Whynot asked me about her husband. I didn't tell her. Hope that was the right thing to do. Now as to those men, I want to show you something."

After adjusting the scale, Miles placed his finger just below their position on the digital chart display. "Petty Officer Powell, I make us six meters on our side of the international boundary. Do you agree?"

Powell adjusted his own display. "Yes, sir. I agree."

"Thank you. Keep me advised of our position relative to the border."

Overhearing, McCloud exploded. "Hey, don't you think for a second you're keeping those terrorists!"

"Corporal, please. Allow me to explain.

"We were a little more into U.S. territory a moment ago. I know that because this system is very precise. If you check this part of the display, it shows the current wind velocity and direction. It also takes into account the tidal currents, which are now outgoing. We will soon drift across the border. Do you understand what I am saying, corporal?"

"I don't understand why you're giving me a goddamn navigation lecture!" The corporal was still angry. "Let me say it again, we want those men! My team will not leave here without them! And you won't leave. Do you understand me?"

"Corporal, I understand. I am sure I'd feel the same way. By the way, I imagine the *Corporal Teather* has some pretty sophisticated navigation technology. You may want to contact them to confirm what I am saying."

"Lieutenant, the nav display now puts us four meters from crossing the border. Almost within its margin of error."

"Very well, Petty Officer Powell."

"So, corporal, please hear me out. We have only moments before we drift across the border. So, I guess we need to reach some sort of resolution to this, ah, problem. As I see it, part of the problem involves jurisdiction since we are within, but barely within, U.S. waters. We want to be sure we do this correctly since this kind of thing doesn't come up very often. We'll both have to answer to our higher-ups, right? So, perhaps you should contact your chain of command. And I will do that same. Do you, ah, get my, ah, drift, corporal?"

Corporal McCloud's mood suddenly changed from anger to one of astonishment. "Lieutenant, are you . . . never mind. I'll make that call. Give me a moment. Please."

While the corporal contacted his superiors, Miles took out a pen and scribbled notes about what he would say to sector.

"Lieutenant, we have crossed into Canada."

"Very well." Miles had the impression that Powell understood exactly what was going on.

"Lieutenant, RB-S reports they've reached the dock and are transferring the casualty to an ambulance."

"Very well, Powell. Thank you."

Once McCloud finished talking to the *Corporal Teather*, Miles told him of Mrs. Whynot's status and asked him to be patient while he contacted his own chain of command on the secure channel. Briefing Sector Northern New England's duty officer, he kept to the facts. At least, most of them, before announcing his intentions.

"RCMP engaged in a lawful hot pursuit of the suspects. RCMP demands custody of the suspects we intercepted and detained. As per our past agreements with Canadian authorities, I will comply with the RCMP demand. More details will follow as RCMP continues its investigation."

The sector duty officer asked a few questions to clarify his understanding, but ultimately advised Miles that undoubtably there will be other questions as he briefs the sector commanding officer and the district. Miles confirmed sector was aware of the arrest of the HSC officer in connection with the fake distress call. At that point, the transmission ended.

"Lieutenant, the *Corporal Teather*. They confirm our position as within Canadian waters."

"Then, Corporal, it's a clear case. The United States Coast Guard detained seven suspects in a serious crime that was committed in Canada. Your team is in a legal hot pursuit of these very same men. As we are now in Canada, there is no question of jurisdiction. On my authority, I turning them over to you, with all the evidence we have gathered. The MSST team can help you in the safe transfer of these men to the *Corporal Teather*. Agreed?"

Still a little bewildered by how events unfolded Corporal McCloud said, "Agreed. Can you take us alongside our ship, the *Corporal Teather*?"

"Yes. Petty Officer Dillon, keep those men in the Zodiac. Powell, contact the *Corporal Teather* and take us alongside her to transfer the suspects." Within minutes, it was done.

About to disembark the RB-M, McCloud turned to Miles. "I'd like to ask you a question, privately please." Miles steered McCloud to the stern of the RB-M.

"Off-the-record. You deliberately let this boat drift back over the border, didn't you? Was that really necessary?"

"Corporal McCloud, I have no idea what you are talking about. I'm just glad things could end, well, peacefully."

"I hope your higher ups agree. Good luck, Lieutenant Miles."

"Thank you, Corporal." *Yeah, I'll need all the luck I can get. For my court martial.*

"Petty Officer Powell, Petty Officer Dillon, let's get back to Eastport."

Return to Base

Williams stood on the pier, watching as the RB-M with Miles tied up at the docks. The sun was just coming up. Senior chief met them on the dock. Williams saw the senior chief talking to Miles, but he was too far away to hear.

The special op failed. Horribly. Williams did know that, if little else. Why it failed was the unknown. The boat's last transmission laid out the essential elements of the disaster. Someone fired at them on the subject's lawn. One subject dead. One boat out of action. RCMP arrested the three men left behind, including Webb. Second boat intercepted by the Coast Guard. Then the comms went dark.

Before sunrise, at the waterside park in Robbinston the four-man custody team in the suburban could only watch the unfolding fiasco. With a clear line of sight, they reported to Williams on the activity roughly east of their position. "Looks like a couple of Coast Guard boats, U.S. ones that is, and that big Canadian ship. They all got their blue and red lights going. We think we see our guys, but difficult to be sure. Doesn't look good, sir." This went on for a while, until Williams ordered them to return to base once the boats dispersed.

Not a word from Fawkes. There was no sign of his surviving boat crew.

Williams, looked at the dock where Miles was assembling his crew. He prepared for a confrontation. As Miles started leading them up the dock's gangway, Williams went to the top of the gangway and stood there. Once Miles came close to him, Williams started screaming. "Where are my people? Miles, dammit, what happened to my people? What did you do?" He continued, question after question, now peppered with profanity, something new to Williams. Miles came on slowly, stone faced.

Miles didn't answer with words. When Miles reached the top of the gangway, Williams suddenly found himself turned and propelled backward against the pier's safety rail. Miles held Williams there, forcing his back over the rail. For good measure, Miles slapped Williams across the face with the back of his right hand.

The Coast Guardsmen, with the senior chief in the lead, continued up the gangway. Startled, shocked, there was nothing for them to do but keep walking toward the station. The senior chief did not follow but grabbed Petty Officer Dillon by the arm.

Miles started to lose control.

"WHAT HAPPENED TO YOUR PEOPLE? YOU WANT TO KNOW WHAT HAPPENED?" Miles slapped him again. He cocked his arm, ready to land a magnificent punch straight to Williams's face, when he was manhandled away by his Coast Guardsmen.

"Easy, lieutenant, easy. Come on now." It was the gentle voice and powerful arms of Petty Officer Dillon. He held Miles tightly from behind, pinning back his arms, pulling him back, away from Williams. Senior chief got between Williams and Miles, broke into a wide smile, and said, "Lieutenant, you gonna be good now?"

Miles nodded. He turned his head back around, to assure Dillon he was alright, and asked if he would release him, please.

Standing before Williams, Miles said, "RCMP arrested your people. They seized your boats and all the equipment they had. Your man Fawkes, who made those fake Mayday calls, is under arrest. You might get a call from the State Police about him. You ordered him to make those calls to take us away from your little operation. Didn't you?"

Williams, as was his way, stayed silent. Miles did not.

"Your people murdered someone! Michael Whynot. Dead. Murdered! His wife is at a trauma center in Saint Stephen!" Miles was again screaming at Williams. Senior chief and Dillon remained at his side, ready for a repeat performance. Miles went on. "Fawkes must have acted under your orders. The man Whynot is dead because you ordered this raid. You killed that man. Just as if you pulled the trigger." Miles started to walk away.

Williams, straightening himself, finally said to Miles, "It was legal. Homeland Security said it was legal. They were both under federal indictment. We were following . . ."

Miles would tolerate no more. "STOP! ENOUGH WILLIAMS!" Miles turned fully around, waving his arms. "ORDERS! That's what you were going to say? 'I was only following orders.' When have we heard that before, Williams? Huh? Maybe at Nuremburg?"

Indictment? What does Williams mean by that? Miles didn't betray his confusion on that point, but instead moved on.

"My people are going to get some chow and sleep. I think you should call a lawyer. If anyone is going to be indicted, it'll be you."

Miles left Williams standing by the rail as he walked backed to the station. It was senior chief who spoke first. "Well, lieutenant, you sure know how to make the day interesting." Miles turned toward the senior chief. With half a smile, he said, "Yes. Interesting. I get that a lot."

Williams went back to his trailer office. He had a phone call to make.

An old man continued his walk along the pier.

Calling the Boss

Williams expected fury. Insults and threats. Instead, his supervisor seemed calm, measured. He asked Williams only a few questions before summing things up. When the call seemed about done, Williams ended with "If any new information comes in, I will call you immediately. Do you have any other questions at this time, sir?"

Williams didn't mention getting smacked by Miles.

"No, Williams, I do not right now. But I do need things from you. Send us a report by secure email on everything known to you. Right away. We'll need a list of those officers now in Canadian hands, of course. And box up all their personal items, too."

"Yes, sir. What else do you need?"

"Let's see. What else do I need, Williams?" Williams braced himself for what was to come. Yet, the supervisor continued in his almost fatherly approach. "Well, Williams, I'm sure there'll be much more as the day goes on, especially as this is briefed up the chain. I mean, this is bad. Really bad.

"I'm not sure what our bosses will say. But it doesn't take any imagination to think an investigation will happen. You don't know this, but tonight we ran the same kind of op in ten other places. We arrested and returned eight subjects. But yours is the only op that ended with people dead, and our guys arrested.

"Look Williams. After you make that report, gather in one place all the materials, emails and such, you have about this operation. You're a lawyer. I'm sure you understand the preservation of evidence."

"Yes, sir. I will do that. Sir, I am sorry for the outcome of the operation."

Williams could hear the supervisor take a deep breath. His demeanor changed. "Sorry? Williams, this morning I wanted to hear about the successful arrest of two indicted traitors. Instead, we have a disaster. An absolute goddamn disaster. You and your people failed!

"Sorry? That's precisely the wrong thing to say to me right now! Look, there's consequences coming to you. We're done." The supervisor hung up.

Hands shaking, Williams put the phone back in the receiver. *Where did it all go wrong?*

Crime Scene

By daybreak, the RCMP forensics team was scouring the Whynot's home and yard. Other RCMP officers collected detailed reports from Roy Wilkins and the other local constables that responded. A public information officer from RCMP was handling the battalion of media held up the road. Border Services investigators sat with George in his house, getting their reports done.

George became almost inconsolable once the notion crept into his mind that Mike would still be alive, under arrest, yes, but alive, if he hadn't fired upon the Americans. He kept saying, "It's my fault, it's my fault." Cheryl, Roy, his wife Marge and other RCMP officers offered their assurances that he was not at fault, but it was clear George needed more time.

Bastards killed my friend Mike. They took my friend Debbie. They hurt my friend George. Roy may have seemed the calm professional to others, but below the surface he raged, wishing for his own vengeance on the Americans. *No,* thought Roy. *By the book. Use the law to get these bastards.* Though Roy would have enjoyed interrogating the prisoners, he knew his friendship with Mike and Debbie would make that unlikely, at best.

Now on scene, the new assistant commissioner walked over to Roy. A helicopter had landed him at the nearby golf course, well away from the crime scene.

"Staff Sergeant Wilkins, good to meet you finally, although I wish the circumstance were different. I apologize for not having done so earlier." The AC offered his hand. Roy thanked him, waived off the apology as unnecessary, and then began to brief him on the facts of the crime scene. The AC listened, asking no questions.

"Staff Sergeant, I have a couple of things to pass on to you. I'll start with the American prisoners. The three taken here and the seven taken from the boat. They're being processed at the Saint Stephen Detachment. As soon as that's done, they will be transferred to an army base. CFB Gagetown. Army military police and engineers are putting together a holding facility in a warehouse on the base. We'll do the full interrogations there.

"We could hold them at other places. Civilian facilities. To use CFB Gagetown, that decision was made by the prime minister himself. This wasn't the only kidnapping action by the Americans. So far, it's happened in at least eleven places. Including here. We're still getting details. Looks like the Americans were successful in eight instances."

Stunned, all Roy could say was, "Mother of God. I didn't know that."

"Well, all the country will know soon. By the way, this was the only place where we got prisoners. And this is the only case where someone died." The AC stopped, placing his hand on Roy's shoulder, and softly said, "I understand the victim here, Mr. Whynot, was a friend of yours. Roy, I am sorry."

Roy nodded. "Mike was my friend, and a friend to many people here. Especially George LeBlanc, the Border Services officer who fired upon their boats. He's Mike and Debbie's neighbor, over there." Roy pointed to the LeBlanc's house. "He's rather upset by all this."

"Yes, I imagine so. I was briefed on his role in all this. Bloody hero, if you ask me. Of course, that's my personal view." Roy nodded his understanding.

Allowing a respectful moment for Mike and George to pass, the AC continued. "Given the extraordinary actions by the Americans, the PM wanted these prisoners held at a military base, surrounded by hundreds of our soldiers. His feeling is if they, the Americans, did this, they are capable of other actions. I can't say what all the government is planning in response, because I am not privy to such things, but I can say RCMP is putting on duty every single officer it has."

"Seems we're on the front line."

"Quite agree. Now let's get back to local issues. Mrs. Whynot is at the hospital in Saint Stephen. She's being treated and a full recovery is expected."

Roy interrupted. "Does she know about Mike? Her husband?"

"Yes, she does. She was in shock when she got to the ambulance. It was thought best to wait until she got to hospital before telling her. Do it properly. Doctor, officer, and chaplain. But someone must have said something, and she overheard. That's speculative on my part. I'm sure you know how letting someone know that a loved one died . . . how difficult it can be."

"Yes. Once I am satisfied the crime scene is properly contained, I'd like to see Deborah in hospital."

"Absolutely. Please do. How long until you think you'll be done here?"

"Forensics is still processing the scene. The American boat here will be trailered out soon. Forensics will want to examine that, too. So, maybe by this afternoon at the earliest."

"Here's an idea. I'm not unfamiliar with overseeing a major crime scene. You take my helicopter and fly up to the hospital. Now. See Mrs. Whynot. The helicopter will wait for you and bring you back when you're ready. I'll watch over things until you get back."

"Sir, ah, that's very generous, I am, ah, with respect, this is my crime scene."

"Go, Roy. Go now. I'll be here. You might want to first call ahead to the hospital, to see if they will allow visitors."

"Thank you, sir. I won't be long." Roy turned and walked away a couple of steps, but then turned back toward the AC. "Exactly where is your helicopter?"

Notification

Hospital security ushered Roy directly from the helicopter landing pad through the trauma center to Debbie's room. At first, the doctor objected to a visitor, but the RCMP badge carried the day. The doctor, an orthopedic surgeon, explained the surgery to reset the fracture of her right ankle was successful and had not required general anesthesia. Sedation to keep her calm and a spinal block sufficed. There was a previously undiscovered dislocated shoulder, as well as treatment for multiple cuts and scrapes. Several broken ribs, but no evidence as yet of internal injuries. Debbie was still awake, though groggy.

"Sergeant, if you must talk to her, please keep it brief. She needs sleep. Later, we'll have a grief counselor see her. Keep in mind that her recollection of what happened may not be complete. Maybe the questions could wait." The doctor looked for acknowledgement from Roy. He nodded, then asked the doctor, "I'm not just a police officer. I'm a friend and neighbor. Mike was her only family around here. She has a daughter in Ottawa. Anna. I want to ask Debbie about how to reach her."

Christ, we need to call Anna before she hears it on the news, thought Roy. Word of the American raid was quickly spreading. Roy heard it from the hospital security staff, in the conversation of staff and patients. On his way to her room, Roy glimpsed a CBC broadcast on a lounge television. He saw the stares directed to him and the fear in their faces.

Perfectly rational fear, Roy knew. If they would do this, what else would the Americans try. The hospital locked down when Debbie arrived. An RCMP officer was stationed outside her door, with Debbie the only patient in the room.

Notification of next of kin. Roy had personally performed this painful duty more times than he wished to remember. He remembered them all too well. There is no duty performed by an officer that is more difficult. You meet a complete stranger, identify yourself, and give them the worst news imaginable. Roy still remembers almost every detail of every notification. Sometimes you walk away in complete admiration of their stalwart behavior. Other times, they blame you. They break down into a wrath that rips your soul.

And once it is done, every messenger anguishes over one question. *Did I do it right?*

Roy remembered one notification in particular. Arriving that early autumn morning at a home in suburban Halifax, he and another officer knocked on the door. The door opened. An older woman, dressed in a housecoat, greeted them. Roy and his fellow officer identified themselves, asked the woman for her name and asked that they might speak to her. There was an awkward, painful few seconds as they stood in the foyer. Roy still remembers distinctly the look of foreboding on the woman's face. Roy stood straight, placing his cap under his left arm, and then said the words that no parent ever wants to hear. Your son was killed in a traffic accident last night. We are so sorry to tell you this.

The mother's gaze broke for only a moment before looking back at Roy, before she kindly invited the officers to please be seated while she telephoned her husband. Her voiced quivered but did not break. After she hung up with her husband, she asked if they would like coffee. Not entirely sure what to do, Roy accepted.

She did not collapse in tears, as most forgivably would. She held firm until her husband came home with a friend. As he embraced her, the tears did come, but quietly. The husband released his wife to step toward Roy and the other officer. Roy and his partner stood as the husband, through his own tears, thanked them both and said he wished they'd met under different circumstances.

Every time, you wonder how you would react to such news. The unexpected death of someone you loved. Should it ever happen to him, Roy hoped he could summon the dignity and grace he saw that morning.

When Roy entered Debbie's hospital room, he saw a different woman, somehow older, wholly vulnerable, her dignity torn away by the necessities of medicine. Her upper body was slightly elevated, one or two IV lines in her arm, cardiac monitor leads fixed to her chest, and her right leg elevated off the bed. As he stood there, she turned her head to face him. She smiled. In a raspy voice, she said "Hi, Roy."

"Hello, Debbie. May I talk to you?" Roy felt an immediate, almost overwhelming wave of emotion. She was his friend. He had seen her and Mike at a party only two days before. He wanted to embrace her. Tell her everything would be alright. Vow to her the men who did this would face justice. The IV tubes and the monitor wires meant Roy could only hold her hand. And everything would not be alright. Maybe never.

"I understand you've been told about Mike?" She nodded and said 'yes' through building tears. While not breaking the grasp of her hand, Roy pulled a small stool by the bed. He grasped her hand with both his hands as she began to shudder. Roy felt his own tears. Yet, within seconds she restored her control and asked Roy a question.

"Can you tell me what happened? I mean, we were both asleep. Heard a crash. We got out of bed. Those men saw us coming from our room. I remember them grabbing me. They put something in my mouth. I couldn't speak. They put a bag over my head. I couldn't see Mike. I couldn't tell him. Tell him . . ." She broke down.

Roy let her cry for a while. When she seemed to calm herself, he told her. "Those men are Americans. Homeland Security Corps, from a unit stationed at Eastport, Maine. We have them in custody. All ten. They came in by boats. Landed at your beach and came in across your lawn. Smashed in the doors with sledgehammers. There's something you might not know. Can I continue?"

She nodded. Roy handed her a tissue before continuing. "George heard something happening. He heard your house alarm. Cheryl called 911 and then me at home. George grabbed his hunting rifle and shot out the engine of one of the boats. He stopped them. He made it possible to rescue you."

"And Mike? How did he . . ."

"He, ah, he died from a gunshot wound." Roy paused for a moment to let that sink in. "We do not know exactly what happened. We do know that one of the Americans fired his pistol twice. He confessed to that. He was walking near Mike as you both were being taken to the boats."

"Did they . . . did they mean to . . . to assassinate him?"

"No, I don't believe so. Could be an . . . accident. The American who confessed said their plan was to take you, and Mike, back to the U.S. for prosecution. And this happened at other places in Canada. All involved persons under indictment for the same charges as you."

"How is George? Is he okay?"

"Ah, yes, he wasn't hurt. But he believes he, he only made things worse. I can assure you that George did not accidentally shoot Mike if you are thinking that. He's not really listening to that. George is blaming himself. He's in a bad way right now."

Her tears started again. With a quivering voice, she said, "Tell him from me, thank you. Tell him I think he did all he could. That he helped rescue me. And that we love him. We love Cheryl and James. Will you do that for me, Roy?"

"Yes, I will. Straight away."

"Anna doesn't know."

"We want to send officers over to where she lives. I know this might be a lot to ask, especially right now. Can you tell us her cell number and her address?"

Roy needn't have worried she wouldn't remember. She gave Roy her number and address. Roy excused himself for a moment to call the AC. Once he ended the call, he sat back down by the bed and took her hand again.

"Anna will know very soon. I just talked to my assistant commissioner. He'll call RCMP in Ottawa. They'll send officers to tell her to call me. I will tell her, if you wish. At least, I am someone who is not a complete stranger. I will stay with you until then. Unless you . . ."

Debbie nodded and said, "Thank you, but I think I should be the one to tell her that her father has died. And Rob and Matt."

"Alright." Roy wanted to say more but was having his own difficulty. He waited.

"When she calls, if she asks for any details about what happened, I can do that. I can tell her what RCMP is doing. And I'm sure she'll want to get here as quickly as she can."

A minute passed before Debbie spoke. "I guess RCMP will want to talk to me more about all this. You know, an investigation."

"Yes, but that can wait until you're more rested."

Agonizing minutes passed. Tears and awkward smiles.

Roy's cell phone rang. On the other end, an RCMP officer explained to Roy she was with Anna before handing the phone to her. Once more, a duty to be performed.

"Anna, this is Staff Sergeant Roy Wilkins of the Royal Canadian Mounted Police. I am the commander of our detachment office in Saint Stephen. More than that, I am a friend of your mother and father."

Anna interrupted and said in a shaky voice, "Yes. I remember meeting you before, at my mom and dad's place. What's happened to them, please?"

Roy paused, taking a breath before continuing.

"There was a serious incident at your parent's home. I am with your mother at the Charlotte County Hospital in Saint Stephen. Your mother is being treated for injuries. Serious injuries, but she will fully recover. She wants to talk to you . . ."

"Is it about my dad?"

"Here is your mother." He handed the phone to Debbie and moved away to give her a measure of privacy but stayed in the room.

Roy did his best to not hear anything as they talked, but it was inevitable. Debbie told Anna that Mike was dead. She told her what happened. Roy heard Anna crying. There was anger. More crying. Debbie brushed away tears, telling Anna to stay on the phone because Roy wanted to talk to her. She ended by telling Anna she loved her.

"Wait, Mom! What about Rob and Matt?"

"I'll call them. I'll call them after you've talked to Roy." She looked up at Roy and said, "I guess I'll borrow Roy's phone." Roy nodded that was okay, but Anna had another idea.

"Look, Mom. I'll call them. I can't imagine you're in great shape right now. I mean you're on meds and you need rest. Please. Let me call them."

Debbie struggled to answer. To think through what she should do. *That's my job. I'm their mother. It should be me who tells my sons their dad was killed.* But then, her pain and anguish took control. She started to cry again as she realized Anna was right. *I'm not in good shape. I'm not sure I can do that. Telling Anna. That hurt so much.*

Anna heard her mom sobbing. Fighting her own emotions, she pleaded, "Mom, please. Let me help you."

Debbie began nodding before speaking. "Yes. Okay. It'd be a help to me right now. Go ahead. I'm so sorry."

"Roy, here's your phone. Thanks. Anna said the officers will stay with her awhile. She's going to come out as soon as she can catch a plane. Not sure she wants to hear anything about how he died."

Roy took his phone and slipped into his policeman persona. He offered Anna his condolences and asked if she wished to hear the details of what happened. Anna said no. "No, not now. I . . . I need a little time. I need to get a flight, to see mom. Is my mom, is she safe?"

"Yes, Anna. She's safe. RCMP has an officer at her door. She is safe. When you can, call me and we'll talk. Call me when you get a flight. Someone will pick you up." Anna agreed. They ended the call.

"When she gets here, somebody will pick her up at the airport. Marge, I think. No, better to send one of my officers with Marge.

"I should go now. I'm sorry. I have to get back to the, well, you know, your home. There will be an officer stationed outside your room. Hospital security and RCMP is screening everyone coming in. You're safe. Please rest. I'll see you soon."

Roy released himself from Debbie and slowly, quietly backed away from her. As he grasped the door handle, she called out to him. "Roy, wait."

He stopped and turned toward her. "Debbie?"

"You got the men who did this? You got them?"

Roy nodded. "We got them. Ten in all. And we'll get anyone else involved."

Debbie turned away from Roy to look out the window. "Good. Make sure they pay, Roy. Make sure they pay."

He left her room, nodded to the RCMP constable by the door, and started to walk down the corridor, but unsure what to do next other than wipe away his own tears.

He was only a dozen or so steps down the corridor when he heard someone call his name. He turned. It was Robert LeClerc.

CBC Lead Story

"We are monitoring a developing situation in Saint Andrews, New Brunswick. Early this morning, at about four, American authorities attempted to arrest two American permanent residents at their home in Saint Andrews. The action ended in the death of one of the Americans and serious injury to the second. Their identities have not been released by authorities. Here is the truly incredible part of the story.

"Both individuals were under indictment by the United States government. Their extradition back to the U.S. was, only days ago, denied by Canada. It is known the two Americans were political dissidents, in opposition to the current U.S. administration.

"It looks like the Americans attempted a seizure, maybe kidnapping is a better word, of the Americans in violation of Canadian law and sovereignty. RCMP has released a statement confirming the American perpetrators, ten in all, are in custody. And incredibly, they are officers in the United States Homeland Security Corps. U.S. federal law enforcement officers. They crossed from the U.S. to Canada in high-speed boats, armed, in darkness, across the Saint Croix River. The Americans acted, in the words from the RCMP statement, 'without permission, without legal pretext and without justification.' To repeat, the men under arrest are United States law enforcement officers who entered Canadian illegally.

"It is unknown at this time how the one American died.

"We are also getting reports of similar incidents happening at other places in Canada. Obviously, this a major story. And we expect more details to emerge."

LeClerc and Wilkins

Roy and LeClerc sat in a quiet corner of the lounge listening to the CBC story. Roy shared with LeClerc all facts of the crime he knew. In turn, LeClerc briefed what CSIS knew so far of the larger picture.

"I got a call from our office in Halifax. They got word of all this through channels. RCMP to CSIS. And, of course, now media reports. Came down here from Fredericton as quick as I could. Called ahead to your detachment. They said you were flown here. I got here, I guess, just as you came out of Mrs. Whynot's room. How is Mrs. Whynot?"

Roy filled him in on what the doctor said. And went through the notification of Anna. LeClerc tried to say something sympathetic about Anna. And to Roy about having to tell her what happened. Roy wasn't listening.

"Can you confirm the Americans did the same thing in other places? That's what my AC told me this morning."

"That's correct. All timed within hours of each other."

Both looked up to the television screen. CBC had shifted to a live broadcast from its reporter on the scene at Joes Point. Much of what the second reporter said was redundant.

"Roy, let's run through this a bit. The raids came only days after the extradition requests were denied. The raiders were U.S. federal officers. They were equipped with pistols and suppressors, with special commando boats, and with night vision. Their route was complex. They hit the Whynot's right at high tide." LeClerc paused, then asked, "What does all that say to you?"

Roy went to the heart of the matter. "The bastards planned this long ago. Long before the extradition requests."

"I should caution you, and me too, that we do not have all the facts. A proper, by the book analysis is needed. But, yeah. The bastards had this planned all along."

LeClerc made a request. "Saint Andrews stands out because this is the only place where we have prisoners. CSIS would like to interview your prisoners, after RCMP had done what they want to do."

Roy interrupted to say, "They're at CFB Gagetown, or on their way there. The AC told me."

LeClerc nodded. "Yeah, we know. CSIS wants to go through all the forensic evidence too. I'm sure the request will come down through official channels."

Roy didn't respond but looked up to the television. CBC was announcing this afternoon the prime minister will be at Parliament to speak live to the nation about what his office called a "criminal violation of Canada's sovereignty."

"There's something else you should know. Mike Whynot came to us, to me actually, unannounced, at Fredericton, to hand over some intel. Pretty low-grade intel, on his expatriate community. I met with him before that to suggest CSIS and his community work together. The first step would be getting information on who was in their community. Their experiences, why they stayed in Canada, you know, stuff like that. We hoped . . . "

"You were recruiting him as an intelligence asset then." LeClerc nodded his ascent.

"I just hope that didn't have anything to do with him getting killed." Roy's demeanor changed. There was anger in his voice.

"Maybe I shouldn't have mentioned it, but I thought it best."

Roy stayed quiet for the next few minutes, until he softly said, "I just saw the two of them, Mike and Debbie, at a Thanksgiving party, next door to their house. At George LeBlanc's house actually. The guy who fired at those Homeland Security people. I told them to be careful, keep their house alarm on. I told them an RCMP officer would be stationed nearby them to protect them. That the officer would be there probably by Wednesday. Meaning today." Roy exploded.

"WEDNESDAY! GODDAMMIT! WE WERE LATE! TOO GOD-DAMN LATE!"

LeClerc didn't know Roy well. They were professional colleagues at most, and not for very long at that. But he had never seen Roy this emotional, this angry. He decided not to say anything, let Roy work it out himself. After all, he just lost a friend, and another friend lies in a hospital bed down the hall.

Roy recovered himself minutes later. "Sorry about that, Robert." Roy then explained himself. "We, no, I, was late in assigning a protective detail, and not just because we don't have enough officers. I didn't put enough urgency behind it. I could've put officers there within hours. I could have done that. Just order them there and figure out the rest later on. I could've pushed to have Border Services guys put there, or even soldiers. Hell, I could have stayed with them myself. I live round the corner! But . . . but, it was the holiday. I didn't want to spoil things for people. I didn't want to be inconvenient.

"I didn't want to believe something like this would happen. That they would do this."

LeClerc placed his hand on Roy's shoulder, startling Roy. "Roy, don't take all this on yourself. Please. The Americans did this. They killed Mike. If there is any fault on our side, it's that we didn't appreciate their ruthlessness. Well, we're not going to make that mistake twice."

The SunRise Café

Claude was at the café that Wednesday morning to prepare breakfast. Routine. He'd done this so many times that he had no idea how many times. Tables to be double-checked for cleanliness and utensils. Bathrooms checked. The fixings for the more popular dishes to be set up. The computer system spun up. At times, Claude felt he could do it all in his sleep.

An hour before opening at six, Claude was getting the crates of eggs ready to go when his dad appeared through the back door. For the past few years, in exchange for a little bit of light set-up work, Claude compensated Sean with the breakfast of his choice. An indulgence easily justified, thinking it gave the old man a reason to get up in the morning. Besides, at least Claude knew he got one good meal a day. Claude greeted his dad and knew right off something was wrong.

"Claude, maybe you've heard, but something's going on a Joes Point. Sirens. Heard lots of 'em last night. Went by there on the way here. Lots of cops there. TV trucks too." Claude always winced a little whenever his dad of eighty-two years talked about driving. "So, you see anything else?"

"No, just lots of cops. Claude, doesn't your friend, the American, the one who told those other Americans to go to hell, doesn't he live out there?"

"Yeah, so? I'm sure everything's fine." Claude forced a smile. "Dad, let's get things ready."

As the breakfast crowd came in, the goings on at Joes Point was on everyone's lips. Claude, distracted by the talk, realized he'd forgotten to turn on the television. He selected CBC.

Claude, his father, the cook, the waitstaff and the half dozen or so customers sat or stood frozen in place. Silent, as they tried to understand what the CBC anchor was saying. It was Sean who broke the spell, putting his hand on Claude's shoulder, saying, "I guess we still have work to do, right son?"

As he went from customer to customer, slowly, at times bewildered, Claude checked back at the television for any news, again and again. And the clock. He couldn't help but think, *Mike came here Wednesday mornings. He was late. The news said one American was dead. Mike was late.*

212

Claude hadn't noticed that Sean had gone outside to talk a constable friend of his. Sean came back inside and took his son away from a customer's table to the kitchen.

"Claude, I just talked to Pat outside there." Claude knew Pat was an auxiliary constable in town. Claude could see him through the café window. There he was, in uniform. "Pat didn't want to say, but I got it out of him."

"It was Mike. It was Mike. I'm sorry, son. He's gone."

Claude looked down, shaking his head. "Dad, we just saw him at the Thanksgiving party. We just saw him." His voice strained. His hands started to shake.

Claude looked at his dad, then thought the better of it and looked away. "I see. Dad, I've got some things to get out of the closet. Maybe I'll close up early today."

In the next hour, the news confirmed the death of Michael Whynot, Lieutenant Colonel, United States Air Force, Retired. Claude turned the door sign to *Closed* and when the last customer left, he started putting up the decorations he always had for Remembrance Day.

In the restaurant's big window, he hung a large Canadian Flag. He would notice that by noon the Maple Leaf, hundreds of them, hung from almost every home and business in town.

Miles Reports

"You did what?" In his briefing to Capt. Llewellyn, Miles had reached the point of slapping Williams.

"Yes, sir. Had senior chief and Petty Officer Dillon not stopped me, well, I would have hit him again."

"As I have said in the past, you make the day interesting." Miles didn't know what to make of the captain's deadpan delivery.

"Alright. Let me tell you my first impression of the case. Up to the point of hitting Williams, I agree with all you did. Williams's people lied to you, they made a false distress call, a felony, to take you off their track. They crossed into Canada on an unsanctioned law enforcement mission that was in violation of, well, it's a long damn list. The RCMP engaged HSC in hot pursuit from their territory, which they have every right to do. We, meaning you, intercepted the HSC boat, Medevac'd an injured woman they held, detained seven armed men who had no identification and turned them over to RCMP.

"Okay, drifting across the international boundary was a bit theatrical, but those men ended up being arrested in Canadian waters. Clear jurisdiction, as you said. You upheld our end of our law enforcement agreements with them. And no one, yourself included, had any idea the two expatriates were under federal indictment.

"And Mr. Miles, like you I would also argue handing them over to RCMP avoided a more serious international incident. As you said, RCMP might have engaged us in a direct confrontation. Judging from the news, the Canadians are furious. Absolutely ballistic. At the same time, it seems likely the White House will be furious at us because we handed them over, judging from the right wing media coverage."

"Thank you, captain."

"Don't thank me yet. You're going to face questions, a lot of questions, from a lot of different people. Coast Guard, DHS, HSC. Someone will say we shouldn't have handed them over to RCMP. Slapping Williams will complicate things. They'll conveniently forget the false distress call by a, Jesus, I can't believe I'm saying this, a federal law enforcement officer.

"So, stay out of sight. Don't answer questions from the press. Tell your people to refer all media questions to, oh, Christ, I'm not sure. I'll ask district what they want us to do. I'll call them in a couple minutes."

"Aye, aye, sir. I'll await your call."

"Put all you've told me in the daily report. Step by step, minute by minute. Get the MSST team leader to write a report, as well as the RB-M coxswain. Also, add any activity that's going on with that HSC unit this morning."

"Oh, and one last thing. Off the record. If I was a young Lieutenant again, yeah, I would've clobbered that bastard too."

Fallout for HSC

Williams sat in his office, mid-morning on the day after, wondering about his future. Twelve officers lost. One quit. Schroeder. He's probably still at the Eastport Police Department. One arrested by Maine State Police. Fawkes. Ten held by RCMP. Including Webb. Twelve in all. One more than half the unit. Both boats. Gone. One Suburban. Gone. Seized as evidence by the state troopers when they arrested Fawkes.

And one man dead.

I am so screwed.

His phone rang. It was his supervisor.

"Williams, I'm calling to let you know that no decision has yet been made about the future of your unit or yourself. This is going all the way up the chain to the White House. I've been told to tell you to secure your remaining equipment and not run any more missions. No patrols." Up until then, the supervisor kept a polite tone. Then the sarcasm returned. "Not run any patrols. As if you could. You lost both your boats, one of your vehicles, and half your people."

"Sir, as you directed earlier, I've seen to it that the personal items of the team members in RCMP custody are boxed up. I've also collected all documentation connected to the special op."

"Well, that's nice. Someday you'll make a nice clerk somewhere. Any press there yet?"

"Yes. There's a couple of TV station trucks with satellite dishes set up off the station property. Looks like they're local media from Bangor or Augusta. They've tried to enter the station, but at least for now they are being kept away by the Coast Guard."

"Tell your people to keep their mouths shut if the press or anyone starts asking questions. Direct the reporters to HSC Public Information Office here in Boston. Just stay inside, out of sight. You follow? You can at least do that?"

"Yes, sir." The supervisor hung up.

I am so screwed.

Refused Service

Minutes after his supervisor's call, two of his HSC officers knocked on Williams's office door to ask permission to go to a nearby diner and get takeout breakfast for the remaining team members. Though reluctant to let anyone out, Williams acquiesced with the warning not to discuss the special op in any way. Go in civilian clothes. Stay off the streets. Get the food and get back.

The officers changed into civilian clothes before taking the surviving Suburban for a quick ride to a coffee shop just down Water Street. They parked it out front of the shop. They forgot about the government license plates.

As they stood behind the counter waiting to order a dozen breakfast sandwiches, from across the room another patron asked them, "Hey, you guys from that Homeland Security bunch up the road? I see those U.S. government plates on your truck. Well, are you?" There was real anger in his voice.

The officers turned and tried to smile. They said nothing.

"I guess that says it. So, you guys murdered that man over in Canada." The patron got up and left through the door, cursing.

The owner came out from the kitchen. He went to the window and saw the SUV and the plates. Walking over to the officers he said, "Yeah, I recognize you guys. You've been in here before."

"Everyone in town heard about what happened last night. What you guys did." He waited for a response from the officers. Hearing none, he said, "Well, you can get your food from someplace else. But I gotta tell ya, good luck with that. You guys ain't too popular around here. Weren't before. Definitely not now."

The officers left without a word. They tried another diner just down Water Street. No luck. Word was getting around. A trip to the IGA supermarket was more successful. Apparently, they hadn't watched the news.

And so began the siege of the Homeland Security Corps of Eastport.

CHAPTER TWELVE

CONSEQUENCES AND CONFLICT

Returning to the Scene

oy left the hospital in the helicopter and flew back to Joes Point. The AC brought him up to speed on the crime scene. Forensics teams were still working. More officers had arrived to help secure the area. The AC met with the press to keep them informed and at bay. Border Services was there helping to secure the scene and be with George, more for counseling him than anything else. A team of Canadian Army military police from CFB Gagetown was enroute. In fact, there was word that the forces would be making a larger show there very soon.

The coroner retrieved Mike's remains. To Roy, all seemed well in hand.

"I think it'd be best that I get back to my office. You know how too many cooks spoil things. Unless, of course, you feel I should stay."

"I think you're right, sir. Best that you get back. Thank you for taking over here for a bit. I will certainly keep you informed of any developments here."

"How is Mrs. Whynot?"

Roy kept to the facts of her medical condition. "She's too foggy from the painkillers to interview her about the case. I'll see to that later." There was no need to mention anything else that was said between them. He then informed the AC of CSIS's appearance at the hospital, leaving aside a retelling of his own emotional lapse.

"We shouldn't wait too long before interviewing Mrs. Whynot. Memories get foggy, too. And I think I'll assign another officer to that task. I think, perhaps, you're too personally involved. You may accompany that officer, even be in the room if it will help Mrs. Whynot be at ease. But I'd ask you not to take part in the questioning."

Roy didn't like to hear that, but he could see the AC's point. He'd do the same thing if he were the AC.

"I understand. I'll remain here as long necessary." Offering his hand, Roy thanked the AC again for allowing him to see Debbie.

With the AC on his way, Roy went to see George and Cheryl to let them know about Debbie. His cell phone rang as he was about to enter the house. It was Anna.

"Mr. Wilkins. I've listened to the news. But I understand you are at my parent's house, where it happened. Can you, please, tell me what happened?"

"Yes, Anna. I'll tell you all I can."

Pointing Fingers

It was eleven a.m. when Miles walked out to the station's front gate to deliver a statement to the media. CNN, FOX, CBS, and MSNBC represented the national cable channels, with WABI from Bangor and Portland's WMTW rounding out the local news outlets.

Miles recognized the editor of the *Quoddy Tides* in the crowd, standing all by herself. He made a mental note to grant her time for an interview later on, when the big media left. Might be useful to pay attention to the local audience.

An hour earlier, the National Command Center at Coast Guard headquarters sent Miles the press statement he was about to read. It came from the commandant himself. Adding to the drama, the vice admiral commanding the National Command Center, with the rear admiral commanding Coast Guard Legal Division, called Miles directly to make sure he knew what to say. And what not to say. Miles hadn't any sleep for going on 30 hours by then, but a conversation with an admiral tends to restore one's vitality. The coffee, cold shower, and shave before going out didn't hurt either.

REFUGE

After calling the reporters together, Miles introduced himself and explained he had an official statement from the Coast Guard regarding the incident in the Saint Croix River.

"At approximately 0500 hours this morning, the U.S. Coast Guard intercepted, detained, and disarmed seven armed men aboard an assault style boat that was sailing at high speed from Canadian waters. The men bore no identification whatsoever. The Royal Canadian Mounted Police were engaged in a hot pursuit of these men in connection with a crime that resulted in the shooting death of a resident of Saint Andrews, New Brunswick. The detainees were turned over to the RCMP, in accordance with long standing law enforcement agreements between the United States and Canada.

"The RCMP has informed the Coast Guard that three additional armed men were taken into custody at the Saint Andrews crime scene. These three, and seven from the assault boat, are part of the Homeland Security Corp unit that staged from Coast Guard Station Eastport.

"A permanent resident of Canada, who is also an American citizen, was found in the same assault boat. The woman is the spouse of the man shot to death in Saint Andrews. She was bound and gagged, with a black hood over her head. She was seriously injured. The Coast Guard, in cooperation with the RCMP, facilitated a medical evacuation of the injured woman to a trauma center in Canada.

"In addition, the Coast Guard can confirm the arrest of another Eastport Homeland Security Corps officer by the Maine State Police. The arrest was made at the approximate time as the HSC operation in Canada. This HSC officer is being charged with making a false maritime distress call on VHF marine channel 16, the distress channel, from the VHF marine radio in the HSC unit's vehicle. The arrest was made on the grounds of the West Quoddy Head Lighthouse, south of Lubec, Maine. The Coast Guard thanks the Maine State Police for their assistance.

"Other than being a tenant command here at the Station, the HSC officers in custody have no connection whatsoever with the U.S. Coast Guard. The Coast Guard had no knowledge, offered no support to, and in no way a participated in last night's Homeland Security Corps operation.

"The Coast Guard has started a formal investigation into the incident. I will now take your questions."

A wave of questions followed. Miles responded as ordered. Please direct your questions to the Department of Homeland Security, Homeland Security Corps. We can only confirm the details of the Coast Guard response to the incident. Miles went off script only once when he was asked if he was personally involved. "Yes, actually. I was aboard our 45-foot boat, our Response Boat – Medium. I was the senior Coast Guard officer present. I ordered the HSC personnel turned over to the RCMP. I followed the protocols in effect, that is, protocols relating to hot pursuit."

After thanking the reporters, Miles went back inside. He called the National Command Center to report the statement was delivered. Now, the next priority. Sleep. As he started into his rack, it occurred to him that HSC isn't going to like what he said. *No, what the commandant said, through me.*

Miles didn't get more than half an hour sleep before senior chief woke him. Beyond merely groggy, Miles looked up at a face telling him he needed to get up. *Oh, yeah, senior chief. Something's happening outside.*

"Lieutenant, you need to get up. Get dressed. We got some locals causing trouble. Brought our crew inside the building. I've called Eastport PD."

Eastport PD. That snapped Miles awake. At least a little more awake. He sat up, slapped on his uniform as if the ship's general quarters alarm sounded. Once dressed, the senior chief brought Miles to his office's second-floor window overlooking the Eastport Port Authority parking lot. A small gathering of maybe a dozen or so people were at the lot's entrance.

"What do we have?"

"They're going after the HSC trailers. Throwing rocks. Shit like that. Ah, looks like the police are here. State police. Pretty quick response from those troopers. And there goes the TV crews."

"Are they throwing rocks at us?"

"No, sir. Just at HSC. Those guys buttoned up in their trailers. Guess the people around here don't like what happened last night. I just hope they don't get too excited."

"HSC or the locals?"

"Both, sir."

"Yeah, let's make sure of that." Miles went to his office and called Williams. No answer. "Chief, I'm going to walk over to see Williams." Miles's imagination took a dark turn. Undisciplined and scared HSC officers with guns. Miles bolted downstairs.

Miles was nearly at the door of Williams's trailer when he heard a loud bang. A bang that came from inside that sounded like someone hit sheet metal with a hammer. He started pounding on the door, yelling, "Williams, let me in! This is Lieutenant Miles! Williams!" Miles screamed his demand again before an HSC officer unlocked and opened the door. "Jesus Christ!

Ambulance! We need an ambulance!" The HSC officer kept yelling. Miles went to Williams's office.

Williams sat in his desk chair. Head down, chin on his chest. A good deal of what was Williams spattered the wall behind him. He had shot himself. He was dead.

Question Period for Prime Minister

Sitting alone in an RCMP vehicle, Roy streamed CBC live on his smartphone. Earlier, George told him the Prime Minister would be speaking in Parliament about what happened here. "He'll use the Question Period. At 2:15. Never watched more than a couple of minutes of that before. Guess I will today. You can watch it in here if you wish, with us." Roy said he had to stay out at the scene, available to the officers. "Besides, I can get it all on my phone."

George seemed better, or so Roy supposed, or wished. *What's the cliché? He'll need time. Hell, I'll need time too.*

He got the video streaming just as the members of Parliament started singing '*O, Canada.*' Roy knew this was customary, having watched Question Period quite a few times. This time though was different. This time the members sang with greater heart than he could recall.

A memory came to Roy. At Mike and Debbie's home one warm summer weekend. Mike passed his phone to Roy. It showed a looping video of Question Period. Like many Americans, the very idea of having the chief executive speak directly to the representatives of the legislative branch, in full view of the public, was both amusing and captivating. "God. Imagine our president doing that? Getting questioned by opposition politicians right out in the open. And having to answer them then and there. I wish we did that. At least, it would mean we'd have to elect presidents who had something on the ball. Never gonna happen though. Too bad."

Mike seemed like a child to Roy at that moment. Showing the grownups what he discovered all on his own. Outwardly, he shared in the humor. Underneath, he was irritated at Mike. *Those Americans believe they're so sophisticated, so superior. They do everything better than everyone else. How quaint of these Canadians!* As time passed, Roy learned to let such little American faux pas pass by. They mattered little and were best disposed of before they spoiled friendships.

Once the applause in the House of Commons ended, the speaker remained standing and called for oral questions, in English and French, before introducing "The Honourable Leader of the Opposition." More applause from the members of his bench. The conservative member stood and faced the speaker.

"Mr. Speaker, all the members, indeed, all Canadians, are by now well aware of the events that played out across our country early this morning before daybreak. All are particularly aware of the incident in Saint Andrews, New Brunswick, which resulted in the death of an expatriate American, an American political dissident. All are aware that American federal agents carried out this . . . this atrocity. I have no doubt the vast majority of our citizens see this action by the American agents as an attack, yes, I say attack, on Canada itself. It is quite reasonable to suspect these American agents acted on orders from the administration in Washington. I ask the Prime Minister. How shall this government respond?" To the applause of his party members, he sat down.

As was customary, the speaker then called on the Prime Minister. "The Right Honourable Prime Minister."

The Prime Minister waited until the applause died away before standing, as if wanting to signal the gravity of the moment. "Mr. Speaker. Yes, I wish to outline for the members, and all Canadians, how this government will respond. I beg the indulgence of the speaker and the house to grant me extra time, beyond what is customary, for an opening statement. Following my remarks, I will remain here to answer questions."

The Prime Minister then turned slightly, and with an open arm, said, "I beg the Right Honourable Member and Leader of the Opposition to grant me those few, but essential, extra minutes." There was no applause from the Prime Minister's bench, nor the opposition bench. Only silence.

The speaker called upon the Opposition Leader. "Mr. Speaker, the opposition offers no objection whatsoever." There was an immediate round of "hear, hear" accompanied by muted applause.

"Very well. The Right Honourable Prime Minister."

"Mr. Speaker, and all members of the house, thank you. I will tell you of what we know happened. Following that, I will tell you of the actions underway in response, and what we are planning to do."

"Let me say first, I must agree with the Right Honourable Leader of the Opposition. This was an attack! An attack without any shred of legality, without any provocation or justification! The most serious attack on Canada and our sovereignty since the second world war!"

The house was stunned into silence, but only for a moment. Applause spread from one member to another, from one bench to another, reaching a crescendo of applause and cheers that almost seemed to catch even the Prime Minister by surprise. Once the applause diminished, the Prime Minister repeated his dramatic opening statement in French. Applause followed once again.

"And let me be absolutely clear. We do not say America attacked us. We do say the agents of the current administration, this anti-democratic administration of doubtful legitimacy, attacked Canada."

The Prime Minister then reviewed the basic facts of the eleven attempted kidnappings by the Americans. Eight attempts were successful. Three others failed. RCMP's investigation was ongoing in all cases. He then focused on the Saint Andrews case.

"Mr. Michael Whynot, and his wife, Doctor Deborah Whynot, both permanent residents of Canada, were seized from their home by the Americans agents in the dead of night, at approximately 4 a.m. You may recall Mr. Michael Whynot. American agents interrogated him this past September, at a café in Saint Andrews, a recording of which appeared widely on social media.

"It was only in Saint Andrews that a death resulted. I must sadly confirm the death of Mr. Whynot. He was a retired officer in the Air Force of the United States. He was a political dissident. He was gunned down.

"The agents broke into their home. They gagged them, tied their hands, put black bags over their heads, and manhandled them out to assault boats waiting to take them back across the Saint Croix River to the United States.

"Though a forensic investigation is still underway, we are certain Mr. Whynot did not die by shots fired by any Canadian. I can report that Mrs. Whynot, Doctor Whynot, is now undergoing medical treatment in Canada for injuries suffered while being dragged across the rocks and beach near their home.

"I am pleased to report that as a result of actions by the RCMP, and especially the bravery of a Border Services officer who lived next door to the Whynots, we have in custody the entire American raiding party – ten in all – plus all their equipment. Assault boats, night vision devices, sidearms with suppressors. The lot!"

Thunderous applause from both benches.

"These prisoners are now being questioned by RCMP and the Canadian Security Intelligence Service. This morning, the Department of Justice Canada has announced these men will be prosecuted under our laws. We will follow the evidence. We will follow the law." More applause. In a lower tone, the Prime Ministers then continued.

"Since this morning, the United States Department of Justice, their State Department and the president himself, have demanded the return of these so-called law enforcement officers." The Prime Minister paused and looked around the house, before turning back to the speaker.

"Let me assure all of Canada, these kidnappers, these terrorists, will not be returned! They will face justice!"

All the members stood, cheering, tossing stray papers in the air. All the while, the Prime Minister stood quietly and remained focused on his notes he held in his hands.

"Only a week before, Mr. and Dr. Whynot were indicted by the U.S. Department of Justice on charges that were so without merit, so flimsy, this government rejected the accompanying request for extradition. Indeed, many other expatriates faced the same charges and we rejected them all.

"I would ask all the members to examine the timeline of events. Only one week before, the extradition requests were refused. The Americans made no request for this government to reconsider the decision. No, instead, they executed a complex, and completely illegal, operation that must have been planned weeks, months, in advance!"

Again, the members called out their support of the Prime Minister from both benches.

"Our investigations are ongoing. More details will emerge as the days go by. This government will share our findings promptly. Now I must tell you of our response to this outrage. This attack.

"This government's response will cross the full spectrum of diplomatic, economic and security measures. I beg your patience as I go through all the things we are doing."

On the diplomatic front, the Prime Minister announced the recall of Canada's ambassador to the U.S. and a meeting planned for that evening with the American ambassador to Canada to demand an explanation of the raids. He also detailed the European Union member states that planned the same action.

"Canada has demanded an immediate convening of the United Nations Security Council to discuss this extrajudicial action by the United States. Canada will also present its grievance before the World Court. In addition, at this government's behest, the European Union will begin discussions of legal and economic sanctions against the United States."

On the economic response, the Prime Minister announced an immediate suspension of talks renegotiating existing trade agreements. He cautioned the members to be patient with other economic sanctions as given the intimate ties between the two economies, "this government wants to be sure that measures taken in punishment toward the United States will have the desired effect."

Applause again.

"Now, as to our security. The American actions last night clearly showed that the current U.S. administration cannot be trusted to follow legal or diplomatic norms, nor even laws or treaties."

"Some will say, we should learn to live with the new reality. We should accept the fact of an immensely powerful and possibly hostile United States.

"Some will say, no matter the righteousness of her cause, Canada simply cannot stand up against the might of the United States." The Prime Minister paused, lowering his voice. "We should not confront them. We must not provoke them. We should . . . appease."

Now the Prime Minister unleashed anger.

"I say no! NO! This government will not follow the counsel of the appeasers!"

The members of Parliament of both benches leaped to their feet cheering. The Prime Minister stood stone-faced in his place. A full minute passed. He continued.

"Let me remind all here and all who can hear my voice. In these times, Canada has one thing the United States does not have. We have allies. They do not! Canada is not alone. It is the American president who stands alone!

"Together with our NATO allies, Canada will use every resource it commands to defend itself, in every conceivable way. Economically, diplomatically, and yes, militarily.

"In the dark days after Dunkirk, when liberty and democracy were nearly lost to fascism, when Great Britain, and Canada, stood alone and together against Nazis, Winston Churchill forecast that the British Empire, and I quote, 'would carry on the struggle, until, in God's good time, the New World, with all its power and might, steps forth to the rescue and the liberation of the old.'

"Now, history presents an opportunity for the Old World. To step forth to the rescue of the new. And they are!"

The Prime Minister announced that the following day NATO will begin formal consultations on an invocation of Article Five of the NATO treaty.

"Members of this house may also remember that the first and only time NATO invoked Article Five was in support of the United States of America, one day following the horrendous attacks of September 11. Canadian Armed

Forces were on the ground in Afghanistan by the next month, fighting alongside our American ally.

"Now, in an awful irony and tragedy of history, Canada must now ask for its allies to help defend us from a government of the United States. An ally that is now more an adversary. And that aid is coming!" Again, applause, but somewhat less enthusiastic, as the possibility of conflict had now come out from the shadows and into the open.

The Prime Minister detailed the NATO forces already operating in Canada and in her waters. He assured the house that even ahead of any formal invocation of Article Five, the United Kingdom and France, and others, had promised to dispatch of ground, air and naval forces. A substantial increase of the armed forces and the national security apparatus was expected from Parliament. He then announced a limited mobilization of the Primary Reserve of the Canadian Armed Forces.

"In summation, this government is committed, absolutely, to the defense of our sovereignty, our democracy, our people. We will not give in to the enemy of democracy our former friend has become. That is the real tragedy. A nation, a great nation, *chose* to discard democracy.

"I, and I am sure all the Members in this House, know that Canadians will *never chose to abandon democracy!*"

Both benches stood applauding, many chanting, "Never! Never!" The Prime Minister in turn raised his hand, saying he had one final thing to say. He waited until there was near silence in the House.

"We still cherish the inspiration all of us here, indeed all of humankind, still find in the American Declaration of Independence. 'We hold these truths to be self-evident, that all men are created equal, that they are endowed by their Creator with certain unalienable Rights, that among these are Life, Liberty and the pursuit of Happiness.'" Pausing for a moment, the Prime Minister emphasized the next passage.

"That to secure these rights, Governments are instituted among Men, deriving their just powers from the consent of the governed."

With that, the Prime Minister carefully sat down, unsmiling, exhausted. The leader of the opposition rose. Neglecting the formality of being called upon by the speaker, he walked across the aisle to embrace the Prime Minister. Other members followed their example, until a single member, known for her exquisite voice, sang the Canadian anthem once more, alone at first, and then joined by all.

CHAPTER THIRTEEN
THE FIGHT GOES ON

The Homefront

Released from the hospital that Saturday morning, the RCMP brought Debbie and Anna home to Joes Point. Their home. The RCMP's crime scene. A line of media waited, out of sight from the house, kept at a distance by the constables. Debbie and Anna kept looking straight ahead as they slowly drove through. *Be patient*, Debbie thought. *You'll get something for the news shows in a little while.*

As the car came to the house, Debbie saw three large, four door pick-up trucks, flat green color, parked near the house, alongside two police cars. Canadian Army. And the Mounties. The car came to a stop by the front doorsteps.

"Did I mention how I hate these goddamn boots?" Debbie remembered how many times she prescribed these Bledsoe boots for patients and how they always, always, complained about trying to walk in them. Or sleep in them. *Karma*, Debbie admitted to herself. *Now I got the boot. And I hate it. This cold drizzle isn't helping either.*

"Yes. More than once." Anna replied in a quiet voice, doing her best to be patient with the patient. She helped Debbie get out of the RCMP sedan and up the steps to the front door. "How about the cane?" It was still in the car.

"I hate goddamn canes as much as I hate goddamn boots." Anna left her mom standing at the door and turned back to get the cane. Cpl. Jenkins had already retrieved it and their bags of personal items. "Ma'am, I think you might need this," the officer said as he put the cane in Debbie's hand. "Let me help you folks inside."

To either side of the door, there were dozens and dozens of cards and cellophane wrapped bundles of flowers. Debbie saw them, making a mental note to write thank you cards. Sometime later. When she was up to it. Anna could help with that.

Once in the foyer, Cpl. Jenkins helped Debbie out of her coat and guided her to a chair with a footrest. Anna sat down beside her. Now in her home, in her chair, the horror of that night came back to her. She felt herself slipping away, falling downward in her grief. *My God, what they did to us. Mike . . . Mike . . .*

Corporal Jenkins brought her back to the moment at hand.

"Mrs. Whynot, again, there will be RCMP officers here round the clock. Including myself. And you'll also see a squad of Canadian Army military police cycling in and out of here. They will do everything they can to respect your privacy. By the way, the forensic team is done with their work, so they won't be here. You will be safe and secure."

"Thank you, constable, ah, I'm sorry, I'm still a little foggy from the hospital. Three days in a hospital, well, doctors don't make good patients. I don't remember your name."

"Quite all right. It's Jenkins, David Jenkins. And it's Corporal. Are you comfortable, well, as much as can be expected? There's a couple of things I want to talk to you about."

"Oh, yeah, ah, Corporal. The police and soldiers. How long will they be here? And I hope they won't have to spend all that time outside. In the cold and rain, I mean. It's perfectly fine if they want to come in here."

"Very gracious of you, ma'am. I'll put that to them, but I think most of the time they will be outside watching the perimeter."

"Okay, Corporal Jenkins. Thank you ever so much."

"Let me apologize for the plywood over the deck door. Someone will be out tomorrow to replace the door with something more permanent. They'll do their best to match the color and style. I hope you don't mind our taking the liberty of arranging for it. We thought it necessary for your comfort. And your security. Right now, your alarm system won't work with just plywood there."

Debbie wasn't quite sure how to react to that news. "I guess that makes sense. They needn't have troubled themselves, but thanks."

"Yes, ma'am. I must discuss another security matter. Please make sure your mobile phones are always charged and always with you. Here is a card for a mobile phone number being used by the RCMP stationed right here. Also . . ." Jenkins produced from a small satchel a portable two-way radio and charger. "I'll set up the charger and set it to the right channel. This is the very same hand radio we use. Any trouble, use this. Police and soldiers stationed here are on the same channel. Probably not necessary, but we feel it's best to have a back-up." Debbie and Anna thanked him.

"Another thing. Marge Wilkins. I am to call her once you got home. She's wanting to come over and lend a hand, if that's alright. So will Cheryl. You know, cooking and such. And before I go, I'll bring in all the flowers left by the door."

"Yes, I'd like to see them, Marge and Cheryl I mean, but in a little while. I guess, maybe in an hour or so would be fine."

Jenkins laid the flowers and cards on the kitchen counter, covering the counter completely. He then made his goodbye. There was no need for the "sorry for your loss" speech. He had already done that at the hospital.

A sharp pain struck Debbie in her left side as she tried to shift to a more comfortable position. Three fractured ribs. No jogging for a while. She couldn't even remember how that happened. The docs offered stronger painkillers, but she refused, saying acetaminophen and ibuprofen would be enough.

Anna got up, saying she would make them both a cup of tea. But Debbie reached up to grab her daughter's hand, pulling her back next to her. They looked at each other. The tears came. And came. It would be a while before the tea was done.

It was an hour before Cheryl and George, together with Marge Wilkins, came by, carrying multiple, unidentified but delicious looking casserole dishes.

Marge took Anna by the hand to start the tea and a casserole. It was Debbie who broke the awkward silence. "George, are you working today or tonight?" George said no, he was on leave for another week. "Good, then do something useful. I know it's barely after twelve but go mix us some cocktails. I want something more than goddamn tea. The liquor cabinet is in the armoires over there."

George laughed. Laughed hard. "For sure! What would everyone like?"

Vodka martinis, with lemon twists for Debbie and George. Anna, of course, pleaded with Debbie to keep it to only one, thinking to herself at least she's not on any strong pain meds. Anna kept to tea, knowing she had a job to do in a little while. Marge went for a gin martini with olives. Cheryl settled for white wine. "Hey, can't have too much. After all, someone has to take care of our kid." She explained James was at home, being watched by her mother.

There were more smiles than tears. After a lunch of hamburger casserole, and fortified by a martini, Debbie felt she was ready to say something.

"I know this is difficult, very difficult, for all of you. I am so grateful. And George, I have to say, and I don't mean to embarrass you, but you saved me. I'd be in an American jail right now if you hadn't done what you did."

"But, Debbie, if . . ." George stammered. Debbie sensed where he was going. She looked him directly in the eye and spoke sternly to him. "George, don't you go there! Don't blame yourself. At all. Ever. I won't goddamn hear it. Mike loved you. I love you. But I won't put up with any blabbering from you. George, you're a hero. A goddamn hero. Is that understood?"

"Absolutely, ah, colonel." For the moment, George shook loose from grief and started to laugh again, with everyone else joining in.

"Good, that's settled."

Someone knocked on the door. Debbie checked the clock on the kitchen wall clock. Two o'clock. That would be Edward. Right on time. "Well, everyone, that'll be Edward. I called him on the way back from the hospital. We have things to discuss. So, if you want to do more drinking, we'll have to do it later.

"Seriously, I need to start planning . . . things. Private things, with Edward. I can't thank you enough. I really, ah, really, love you guys. I'll see you tomorrow?"

Plans and Politics

Anna walked out the front door with Edward at her side. They headed for the collection of television trucks and damp reporters.

"It would be raining, wouldn't it?"

Edward held an umbrella over Anna, regretting his suggestion that they walk all the way out to the media line. "We'll be fine, Anna. You'll be fine."

As they neared the reporters, Edward reminded Anna of what they were about to do. "Don't worry. Say hello to them. Thank them for being here. Then you can read the statement we've prepared. Word for word, if that makes you comfortable. Say what you wish about your father and mother. Answer any questions they have. Don't be embarrassed if you, yeah, if you get, ah, emotional. If you want, I can take over at any time. Remember, this is the first step."

Standing before the reporters, their cameras and microphones, Anna held the printed statement in her hand, folded tightly in her clenched hand. She motioned to Edward to take away the umbrella.

She introduced herself and thanked the reporters for respecting her family's privacy. Anna said her family offered their "most sincere and deepest thanks to all the Canadians who took us in, who befriended us, and now, who defend us. Our neighbor and friend, of Border Services, who risked his life to stop this crime. The RCMP officers who rescued my mother. The Canadian soldiers here safeguarding us. And all those who are supporting us in this moment of trial and loss."

Then she spoke the same words in fluent French. Quebec French. Until then, Edward had no earthly idea Anna spoke French. He smiled. *Debbie knew. Well done, Debbie. This will play well.*

"My father and my mother served their country as officers in the United States Air Force, with honor, with distinction. They, and I, were fortunate to find a new life in Canada. Sadly, my mother must now carry on without her husband, Michael. We trust a full investigation of what happened here will be made and those responsible will be held to account under Canadian law, our law. As believers in our homeland's founding ideals, we were especially moved by the Prime Minister's recitation of a passage from the Declaration of Independence in his speech to Parliament."

As Anna repeated the words in French, Edward reminded himself that the true purpose of the statement was about to follow.

"We are planning my father's funeral." Anna stumbled for a moment, needing a moment to regain her composure before continuing. "He was a good man. I loved him . . ." A shudder of grief came to Anna. She paused once more as Edward put his arm around her shoulder. Restored, she gently released herself from Edward and continued. "Details of the service will be released soon, but we wish to have the service here in Saint Andrews, among our friends.

"But our family is incomplete. My two brothers, Robert and Matthew, cannot come here to mourn with us. Like all Americans, they are being held at home by the inhumane closure of the American-Canadian border to all nonessential travel. No exceptions are granted by the United States even for family tragedies."

Anna said her family's calls to the American Embassy in Ottawa in intercede went unanswered. Likewise calls to congressional offices.

"So now we ask the help of the people, on both sides of the border, to push the U.S. State Department and the Department of Homeland Security to relent and allow Robert and Matthew to help bury their father. Thank you."

Once the last was said again in French, they started walking back. Anna didn't want to answer any questions. Edward was very pleased. She didn't even use the written statement. Did it entirely from memory.

When they were far enough away to not be overheard, Edward just had to ask. "Anna, so how did you learn to speak French?"

"Don't you? Anyway, started taking it in middle school, then high school, a few courses in college. Helped that we lived overseas once. On trips to Belgium or France, Dad and Mom always used me for translating. Took trips to Quebec, too."

"I see. It'll make a good impression on Canadians. And no, my skill in French is, ah, at the level of sucks."

"Edward, this was a political thing, the statement, wasn't it?"

"I thought I made that clear. We need to create pressure to get your brothers here. This was as good a time as any, I suppose. Anna, take a look around town. Everywhere you look, there's a Canadian flag. The news says the same is happening all over Canada. You know, after 9/11, people around here hung American flags. And look at the protests in Canada and Europe."

Since Wednesday, large protests appeared in all of Canada's major cities. Vancouver, Halifax, Ottawa, Calgary, Toronto, Quebec City, and Montreal. Even Saint John's, Newfoundland. Every Provincial capital city. In Ottawa, the American Embassy was almost under siege. Protests spread to almost all the major cities of the European Allies. Even to the American embassies in Australia and Japan.

"You know, a fisherman client told me he sailed yesterday down past Eastport and Lubec. They're two little border towns in Maine, down the Saint Croix River here. Anyway, he saw Canadian Flags being flown on both sides of the river. Both sides! He lost count of how many. If the news coming out of the states is right, that's happening a lot, especially in the American border towns."

Edward directed her to a seat on the covered porch. "Here's more evidence." He handed her a copy of a newspaper. "The Quoddy Tides. It's printed in Eastport. Read the part I highlighted."

'We find ourselves, inhabitants of an often forgotten, always peaceful rural seaside community, at the center of a frightening international incident, pitting the North Atlantic Alliance against the United States. And a once unthinkable question is being asked by many around here. Will we see hostilities between Americans and Canadians?

In the opinion of this editor, the answer must be no. A thousand times no. Since the appearance of this HSC unit in our town, we have seen a steady rise in tensions. The President's border closure continues to cause economic and personal hardship to the people of both countries. We cannot allow this to go any further. So many of us count Canadians among our friends. So many of us include Canadians among our families.

The Homeland Security Corps raid on Saint Andrews was wrong. It was a crime. Our government must own up to that simple fact. Indeed, the inflammatory rhetoric from our government, from the President in particular, must stop. It must stop now.'

Anna couldn't hide her surprise. "You think that's how they really feel back there? I mean, I didn't expect that."

"Public opinion on both sides of the border might be with us. So, like I explained to Debbie, we need large venue for the funeral. As big as we can find. Lots of people want to come. That's why I want to call the New Brunswick Community College here in town. Use their gym. The churches are just too small."

"We're using my dad. You're turning him into a martyr."

Edward stopped a few feet before the door and turned toward Anna. "Yes, Anna. But look at it another way. We're helping your father continue the fight. A fight he joined in. Let's give him a chance to finish the fight."

Left unsaid by Edward was a harsher viewpoint. *You damned Americans caused this. You did not fight for your country then. Why should anyone believe you'll fight now. And now Canada's paying the price. We need every weapon at our disposal. If that means using your father, so be it.*

The Station

Miles finally got back after midnight Sunday, driving all the way from Washington to Eastport in a single shot, stopping only for gas, fast food, and coffee. Lots of coffee.

It'd been a long few days. Miles spent the past Friday and Saturday morning at Coast Guard headquarters, undergoing questioning by senior officers and lawyers who constituted a formal board of investigation examining the Saint Andrews raid.

The chief investigator, a civilian and Deputy Chief Counsel, zeroed in on the drift issue. "Lieutenant Miles, it's fairly clear RCMP could have arrested those men in any case, under our agreements with Canada relating to the pursuit of criminal suspects across the border. But allowing the boat to drift, what concerns did you have at that time? Why do that at all?"

"Sir, I agree. RCMP had every right to arrest those men regardless of our relative position to the border. However, HSC already violated agreements by conducting the raid. That gave me reason to believe HSC or DHS would continue to violate agreements and refuse the RCMP demand, using our position on the U.S. side of the boundary as justification.

"Had HSC refused RCMP, I judged it possible, even likely, RCMP would use force to take custody of the HSC officers. To put it plainly, RCMP's blood was up. There was a need to defuse the situation. Allowing the RB-M to drift across the boundary left no doubt as to RCMP jurisdiction. It was my decision."

When he arrived at the station, the watchstander asked if he wanted the senior chief to come in. No, said Miles. "Just tell me if anything has happened in the last few days."

"The MSST team went back home. The RB-M's already back at Portland. All the HSC guys are gone. A bus came down here and took them all away. And all their personal gear, equipment, and weapons. Wouldn't tell us where they were headed.

"Just as well they're gone. The locals are pretty pissed. Almost all the trailer windows are broken. Rocks. Someone used a paint ball gun on them too. They're pretty much wrecked. We don't know if they're going to haul them away. At least, nobody torched them. Thank God for small favors.

"Good news is nobody's bothered our people."

"That's a relief. Anyway, saw more than a few Maple Leaf flags out there on the way in."

"Yes, sir. I guess people around here, they're with Canada in all this."

Now imagine if I didn't hand those HSC guys over to the Canadians, thought Miles. I'll bet those rocks would have been smashing our windows too. Tomorrow, I'll put all that in my report.

Sheer exhaustion from the investigation and the long drive was the only reason he got any sleep last night. Even so, sleep proved difficult. Inevitably, thoughts of an ignominious end to a promising career ran through his mind at night. Again and again, his mind would not let him forget he was under investigation. *Get yourself ready. Someone in DHS, some political appointee, will blame you. You're the easiest target.*

Miles didn't dare call his mom. It would put her in an awkward position. *She ordered the MSST team there. Are they investigating her too?*

Funeral

Debbie asked that a recording of *Shed a Little Light Together*, by James Taylor, be played in the minutes before the funeral began. Mike was never particularly religious, but Debbie and he loved James Taylor. So, a good choice.

From the front of the gymnasium, a bagpiper then played *Going Home*, signaling the beginning. All stood. Television broadcasted the ceremony live.

A bearer party of eight Canadian Army soldiers entered the gymnasium, carrying the casket of Lt. Col. Michael Whynot on their shoulders, advancing in the precise movements of the slow march. All were in Full Dress Ceremonial Uniform, with white gloves, without headdress, arranged in ascending shoulder height. The flag of the United States of America draped the casket.

The officer commanding the funeral detail followed. Falling in behind her were the headdress bearers and two reserve pall bearers.

Limping, Debbie followed the military funeral party down the center aisle created within the gymnasium. A Canadian Army captain escorted her, holding out his arm to steady her as she kept pace with the bearer party.

As is the privilege of U.S. retired military, Debbie wore her Service Dress Uniform, with medals, one pants leg pinned just above the medical boot she wore. She used no cane.

As she made that walk, that awful walk, Debbie struggled to keep her mind focused on the moment, and no further. Even to the point of counting her steps. She knew herself well enough that her best defense against a very public emotional collapse was to not think about what was to come. She had practiced. She was prepared.

Anna, together with Robert and Matt, followed behind her, each escorted by a Canadian soldier. Matt, a lieutenant in the United States Navy Reserve, wore his Service Dress Uniform Blue. His uniform bore the Surface Warfare Officer insignia. He walked uncovered, having left his service cap in the foyer. Robert carried under his arm his father's service cap. Anna and Robert both wore the red poppy of Remembrance Day.

The pressure campaign worked. Under severe criticism from Canada and her European allies, as well as media across the world, the U.S. State Department relented and granted Robert and Matt passage across the border. However, there were conditions, more notable for their cruelty than compassion. They could not cross the border until 48 hours before the funeral. They had to return to the U.S. no later than 48 hours after the funeral. Also, they could not bring anyone in their immediate family. This provision appalled Robert. He could not bring his wife and child when he truly needed them.

Out of compassion, and to metaphorically twist a knife in the President, the Prime Minister announced the dispatch of two Royal Canadian Air Force VIP transport aircraft to pick up the sons the day before yesterday. One flew to San Francisco and the other to Boston. The Prime Minister went further, announcing the offer to the family of official military honor guards.

Edward was right to prepare for a well-attended funeral. From her home to the community college, Debbie saw people and Canadian and American flags lining the streets that clear, cool Sunday morning, now ten days since Mike's death. They filled the gymnasium to standing room only. Remembrance Day, a day memorializing the end of World War I throughout the British Commonwealth, would not be for another nine days, yet many here wore the red poppy.

Nobody would say it, but everyone knew. Politics was as much a part of the funeral as the casket holding Mike's body. The Premier of New Brunswick and the Prime Minister were already inside. They had seats in the row of chairs behind those reserved for the family. So was the leader of the opposition. The mayor of Saint Andrews and her husband sat beside the Premier. In deference to Debbie's wishes, they would not speak. She felt it crass to grant time to politicians who never knew Michael. Their attendance alone was a sufficient measure of respect. And to others, an acknowledgement of their failure to safeguard the nation. To Debbie, now hardened to a new reality, the funeral was all those things, and also an opportunity.

Debbie recognized many of her American patients and friends among the seated guests. A few dabbed away tears or held their hands over their hearts as the casket passed. Several of Michael's military retiree friends, now expatriates in Canada, were seated nearby, also in their service dress uniforms. Near them were others in uniform. Different uniforms. She recognized a few. German, French, British. She would later learn they were military attaches from the NATO member embassies in Ottawa.

No dignitary or representative of any kind from the U.S. embassy attended.

Near the front on the other side of the aisle, she saw an elderly man wearing a somewhat loose-fitting uniform of the United States Army from another era. Unmistakable though were the medals. Bronze Star and Purple Heart. The man stood rigidly at attention as the casket passed. Claude stood next to him.

REFUGE

The bagpiper finished. A recording played of a work by John Williams, *Hymn to the Fallen*. As she walked steadily behind the bearer party, Debbie suddenly remembered that Mike had once said his favorite song was *Somewhere Over the Rainbow*. She smiled at the thought of soldiers carrying Mike to the voice of Judy Garland. *Maybe we'll play that at the reception.*

The bearer party approached the platform prepared to receive the casket, and in commands and movements reflecting traditions inherited from the British Empire, they laid Michael down. The bearer party then silently moved in formation to the side of the hall while the escorts guided Debbie and her family to their seats. Robert went forward and placed his father's service cap, facing forward, on a small table set beside the casket. Robert, Anna, and Matt followed their mother to their seats.

George and Cheryl were seated in the front row to Debbie's right. She made sure everyone would see they were invited to a position of honor.

Resplendent in their iconic red tunic uniforms, two RCMP officers came forward to flank the casket. They stood at attention. Debbie saw one was Roy.

Framing the temporary pulpit, stood the flags of Canada, the United States, the Province of New Brunswick, and in a surprise to Debbie, the flag of the U.S. Air Force.

The service began with a Catholic priest offering a prayer. The mourners were then asked to be seated. The priest informed the mourners of the events that would follow.

Debbie glanced to her children and nodded her head. It was time.

Anna, Robert, and Matthew rose from their seats, forming a single rank line before their father. They stopped for a moment, bowing their heads, before moving together to the podium.

Robert went first, beginning with a conventional acknowledgment of the dignitaries present, then thanking all those in attendance. He talked of his father, sharing memories from his childhood, the trips his family took while in Europe and a couple of his dad's favorite stories.

"When I last saw my father, before these troubles, we talked about his life. I don't remember what sparked our talk, but I do remember it well. My father said he was, in his words, 'an ordinary man.' I reminded him of his military service, that he was a respected air force officer and provided well for his family. I remember what he said next. 'Nothing I ever did would earn so much as a footnote in any history book. No, so many others had done so much more. I'd prefer anyone just say, 'he's a good man.'

"Then he looked at me. He said . . ." Robert faltered at that moment, fighting through his emotion. "Dad said, 'the greatest gift I've had is your mother. My greatest accomplishments are you, Matthew, and Anna.'"

Then it was Matt's turn. He placed a sheet of paper on the podium.

"I am Matthew Whynot. My family wishes to offer words familiar to all here. Words we hope are well suited to this occasion and these times. Words we offer in thanks to their adopted country and home. Words from the pen of Lieutenant Colonel John McCrae, of the Canadian Army of 1915." He read the lines with the greatest care.

In Flanders fields the poppies blow
Between the crosses, row on row,
That mark our place; and in the sky
The larks, still bravely singing, fly.
Scarce heard amid the guns below.

We are the dead. Short days ago
We lived, felt dawn, saw sunset glow,
Loved, and were loved, and now we lie
In Flanders fields.

Take up our quarrel with the foe:
To you from failing hands we throw
The torch; be yours to hold it high.
If ye break faith with us who die
We shall not sleep, though poppies grow
In Flanders fields.

Matt stepped back from the podium as Anna stepped forward.

"I am Anna Whynot. We find ourselves struggling to deal with our grief while celebrating the life of a good man. Once more, we will rely upon the words of a poet known to Canadians. Robert Williams Service, to help us respond to the circumstances of his death and my father's work left undone. To help us carry on." Anna recited the three stanzas of *The Quitter*. She raised the tone of her voice at the third stanza.

It's easy to cry that you're beaten -- and die;
It's easy to crawfish and crawl;

But to fight and to fight when hope's out of sight --
Why, that's the best game of them all!
And though you come out of each gruelling bout,
All broken and beaten and scarred,
Just have one more try -- it's dead easy to die,
It's the keeping-on-living that's hard.

Anna translated all she said into French.

Their task done, together they left the podium, walking past the casket, touching the flag as they passed, once more aligning themselves before their father, bowing their heads before returning to their seats.

It was Debbie's turn. She stood, limping to the podium. As she passed her husband's coffin, she gently brushed her open hand across the flag. At the podium, she took out her printed remarks. Holding herself steady with one hand on the podium, she looked out upon all those in the hall.

She began by recognizing all the dignitaries present and thanking all present for their support. Debbie shared a couple of funny stories of her and Michael. When they first met. A couple of vacations with the kids. She thanked Michael for standing by her side as she endured the sometimes agony of medical school and residency. She continued by thanking the Canadian people for all they had done for her family.

What she said next was unexpected.

"Canada has become our refuge. We have made many friends here in Canada. Close friends. Over time, I think I have come to realize the question that they would ask of us, but out of politeness or worry, do not ask us. What happened? What happened to your country?

"We could not answer because we did not know. We did not understand. I can tell you, it troubled Michael greatly. I recently ran across an essay he was preparing that he hoped would answer that question. I will not go through here all the points he raises, but I think I can now answer that question. What happened to the country we both served?"

Pausing, she lowered her eyes for a few seconds, and then continued in forceful voice.

"We Americans did not lose our democracy to a natural cataclysm or invasion by a foreign power. We openly and deliberately decided to discard democracy. We did it to ourselves. Every step toward authoritarianism was taken in the open, in full view. There should have been no surprise.

"We made *legal* . . . *we made legal* what was once thought unthinkable, unpatriotic, and immoral. We gave in to our worst demons. We surrendered reason to fear. We surrendered tolerance to racism. We replaced discussion and debate with terrorism and violence. We abandoned once dearly held principles to corruption, to lies, to greed, to power, to cynicism.

"We did it to ourselves. We did great harm to Canada. We did great harm to every democratic government in the world. No longer is there a superpower standing for human rights, helping nations to build democratic institutions, promoting the rule of law, facing down the dictators. That moral leadership and power no longer exists in the United States. Now, *this* United States, is more interested in helping governments which rule their people, rather those which serve their people.

"Now, we know this United States will murder its own.

"Is it time to ask, is the American experiment over? Has 'government of the people, by the people, for the people' perished from the United States?

"No. No. NO! I will not accept that end. We Americans here, we Americans everywhere, cannot accept that end. Democracy, humanity, must prevail. Our campaign will continue. We will not surrender to darkness and tyranny!

"My husband Michael is only the latest loss. There were many before him. There may well be many after him. Yet, I have faith in the righteousness of our task. But in this moment, allow me to suggest what will happen if we do not act. The United States will not be the last democracy to fall. Emboldened, the forces intolerant to freedom and liberty and modernity, will grow in strength and ruthlessness. They know democracy anywhere is a mortal threat to the legitimacy of autocracies everywhere. These forces will cut through other lands across this continent and across the Atlantic.

"I know what I have said is not the usual fare for bidding farewell to a loved one. I know I have made many of you uncomfortable. I imagine many will be critical of what I said here today. But I am done crying. I am done evading the challenge of our times. And we are running out of time.

"Neither I, nor any American, has the right to ask for help. Yet, I must. I must ask for the help of others. But, if that help is not forthcoming, I shall understand. I shall continue. And if necessary, alone."

Debbie ended with thanks to all, left her speech on the podium, and walked back to her seat, once again to pass her hand over her husband. She did not notice the hundreds of mourners in the hall who rose to stand silently.

As the bearer party reformed and began taking Michael slowly down the aisle, a local choir sang the hymns *Amazing Grace* and *On Eagle's Wings*. Debbie knew Mike loved those songs. Exiting the building, Debbie, Robert, Matt, and Anna followed behind their father. The Prime Minister and other dignitaries followed them. Hundreds of people watched from the campus grounds as they moved to the waiting hearse.

An RCMP honor guard lined one side of the walkway. On the other, an equal number of Dutch Marines. The honor guard raised a hand salute as the casket, the family, and the Prime Minister passed.

The hearse bore two flags on its fenders. One Canadian. One American. Preceded by a police sedan, and together with funeral cars for the family, the dignitaries and friends, the long procession began to move away on the short drive to the cemetery. They slowly passed down Water Street, hardly more than walking speed, past all the shops, before turning onto Harriet Street, then Champlain, and finally Cemetery Road.

Debbie kept her focus straight ahead, battling for composure in what would be the most painful episode of this morning. Robert kept his arm around Anna, in a sometimes-futile effort to comfort her and himself. Matt looked instead up and down the streets of Saint Andrews. There were people. Hundreds more, maybe thousands, lining the sidewalks, standing outside their homes. Canadian and American flags hung from windows and often makeshift poles. Here and there, he saw men and women, some in military uniform, saluting as they went by.

The Last Post

The graveside ceremony proceeded with characteristic grace and majesty. The military bearer party kneeled as they placed the casket over the grave. The Whynot family was seated to the side, under a large tent. Slowly the bearer party came off their knees, stood to attention, turned and marched a few feet away. Before the bearers moved away, they placed a wreath of flowers upon the casket.

The priest offered a short prayer, and then ended with words of the fourth stanza of a poem from Laurence Binyon's *For the Fallen*.

They shall grow not old, as we that are left grow old.
Age shall not weary them, nor the years condemn.
At the going down of the sun and in the morning
We will remember them.

The bearer party returned to the casket. Flanking the coffin on both sides, as one they kneeled, removed the American flag from the casket, stood, and began to fold it in the style of the U.S. military. Thirteen folds to form a precise triangle. The officer-of-charge presented the flag to Debbie.

A rifle detail a short distance away volleyed three times. A bugler followed with a haunting *The Last Post*, a tradition in military funerals of the Commonwealth nations. Then in a departure from those traditions, and in deference to the American service of Michael, the bugler played *Taps*. Matt rose from his seat, stepping out from the tent toward his father, saluted and held his salute until the last note.

The bearers knelt to grasp the heavy straps arrayed under the casket, stood once more to gently lower him to this final place. At the last, the bearers marched away. It was over.

Debbie and her children went a spot away from the grave. She held the flag, while Robert and Anna held her. There was no need for words.

Matt moved a little away, facing the foot of the grave, and came to attention. He rendered a slow funeral salute. It would be his last salute in this uniform.

A Request

Claude arranged for a reception at his restaurant. He hoped Mike would have appreciated the irony of having his funeral reception at the SunRise Café. After all, it was here this whole thing had started.

Debbie wanted a small, intimate gathering to follow the burial. Still, she allowed for the dignitaries to make a brief visit. And so, they, and Claude, and George and Cheryl, met the Prime Minister and his wife. And the Premier. And the leader of the Opposition. Respectful, gracious, and brief. And perhaps useful.

Debbie invited the entire military honor guard, including the Dutch Marines and the RCMP officers. She would not abide the slightest neglect of these soldiers and police officers. Earlier, as they began to leave the cemetery, she walked over to greet and thank every last one, making clear to their commanders that she expected to see all of them at the reception. They came to the café but didn't stay long enough to enjoy a little food.

Soon the gathering at Claude's diminished to family and close friends. Funeral receptions are necessary for the mourners to offer thanks to all who came, but they served another vital purpose. To release the anxiety and tension of the day. As Debbie said to no one in particular, "I'm relieved that it's over. I thought it went well." She turned to her children. "You guys, you were magnificent."

Debbie decided it was time. She called out, "Well, Claude, how 'bout it?" Claude understood. He announced it was time for cocktails.

With whiskey and soda in hand, Matt went over to talk to Roy. After introducing himself and thanking him for his service in the ceremony, Matt asked Roy if he would like something more substantial than a glass of ginger ale.

"Thanks, lad, but no. In uniform, on duty. You must know how that is."

"You know, today, I made my last salute. To my father, at graveside."

"Beg pardon, Matt?" Roy sensed something was coming. Something that might make him, and everyone else uncomfortable. He reconsidered. *Maybe I'll have that drink after all.*

"Staff Sergeant Wilkins, would you be the senior Canadian official present in this space?"

Oh, Christ. This is almost comical. What does he want? He looked at Matt curiously and put his soft drink down on a table. "Alright. Lieutenant, I imagine I am. You are asking, why?"

Matt put down his drink and brought himself to attention in front of Roy.

"I will not be returning to the United States. I wish to remain here, in Saint Andrews or elsewhere in Canada. I therefore request asylum. I guess that's the right word. I cannot return to a country that murdered my father."

"Hold on. Asylum? You're an officer in their navy. If you stay here, wouldn't that be, well, some kind of desertion? Your mom knows about this?"

Matt stood easy. "No worries. I was a reservist. Not active duty. And I mean 'was.' I officially resigned just as I left. I mailed a letter to my reserve unit, with an effective date of today. It's no matter. Others have done the same. I told mom last night. She approved. Maybe she just wants me around. Guess I'll have to resign from my civilian job too. Didn't want to give the game away before I left, so I didn't resign beforehand." Matt chuckled a little, saying, "Unless my company will allow me to work remotely."

It took Roy a minute to get his bearings. There are procedures for this.

"Very well. Canadian policy allows the granting of asylum upon request for those fleeing political persecution. So, are you requesting asylum because of political reasons relating to your home country?"

"Ah, yes. I guess I am."

"Then, you have asylum. You know, lad, I think I'm off duty now. I'll have that drink. Whiskey and soda, bourbon whiskey, two fingers, on ice, if you please."

Matt quickly went to the bar and mixed Roy his cocktail. Handing it to Roy, they clinked glasses.

"By the way, Roy, wanted to ask about something. Is it true that Canadian Forces are now accepting noncitizens into their ranks? I'm surface warfare qualified in the U.S. Navy. Three years on an Arleigh Burke-class destroyer out of San Diego. Just wondering if I can help out in some way."

"I don't know much about that. We should get you in touch with Navy recruiting. And you need to call the RCAF. I guess you won't be talking that VIP flight back." Matt explained he had a contact number with the aircraft. He'd call them straight away.

"Alright, son. It's done then. Let's get your parent's solicitor over here. He's right over there, talking to Claude. Edward, Edward Donohue. He'll help you out. Immigration, residence status, employment, and the like. RCMP has their own reports to fill out for asylum requests. I'll get right on it tomorrow." Roy motioned to Edward to join them, who until then was quietly enjoying a martini. "Edward, I have someone who needs to talk to you." Roy then turned to Matt, offered his hand, and said, "Welcome to Canada."

As Edward met in a corner with Matt, George came over to Roy. "What's all that about?"

"George, it seems the Royal Canadian Navy might have just gained a new officer."

Later, on his way home that evening, Roy called LeClerc. He would want to know about the defection of a U.S. naval officer.

Robert caught his RCAF flight home two days later. He had a wife and daughter. Matt had neither. Robert had no choice but to go.

The Saint Andrew Raid: The Funeral

That evening, CBC broadcast a lengthy report of the funeral. Images of the funeral march, of the Prime Minister, and the readings by Robert, Matt, and Anna, the passage of the cortege through the town and the people gathered along the streets. Surprisingly, at least to Debbie, CBC replayed her memorial speech almost in its entirety.

She noted the banner at the bottom of the television screen showed the images as "Saint Andrews Raid Funeral." Raid, not incident.

The CBC anchor offered her opinion of Debbie's speech. "I have to say, she was a wife memorializing her husband, certainly. But it was also a call to arms, and, I think, a rather stirring one at that."

CHAPTER FOURTEEN
PLOWSHARES INTO SWORDS

Monday with the Commandant

"**G**ood morning, admiral."

As Debbie faced her first day after the funeral, Doug Miles was having breakfast when he got a call from the aide to the Commandant of the Coast Guard. The aide, a commander, told Miles the commandant wanted to speak to him about the board of investigation into the Saint Andrews incident. He said the commandant wanted to do this on a videoconference, where upon the commander handed over to a lieutenant the responsibility of getting Miles online.

Once the link was tested, the commander said, "Looks like it's working. Lieutenant, he will be ready for you in five minutes. Stand by. And don't touch anything!"

Suddenly, there he was.

"Good morning, lieutenant. I hope you're well. I wanted to talk to you about the findings of the board investigating the Saint Andrews incident.

"Bottom line. All the board members agreed you acted in accordance with our protocols with the government of Canada. And they agreed you helped avoid a serious international incident which would have tarnished the reputation of the Coast Guard. The board appreciated your forthrightness. I agree with their findings.

"So, I wanted to thank you personally for your initiative in resolving a bad situation for us. By the way, I've already spoken to your sector commander. I suppose he could've called you instead of me. But given the incident's unusual circumstances, and the unusual nature of your assignment to Eastport, I decided to call you directly."

"Thank you, admiral. Yes, sir. I understand. Yes, sir." *Well, that came out poorly*, thought Miles. *You think I'd be used to talking to admirals by now.* Then the commandant shifted to a softer, almost fatherly tone.

"Now it's time for the bad news." The admiral told Miles the Secretary of Homeland Security did not accept the board findings and has ordered all commissioned officers out of the stations with HSC units. An assignment officer would be calling Miles today to discuss a transfer. The commandant stressed this reassignment is not a punishment. Not from him at least.

"Ah, admiral, I'm not sure I understand."

The commandant told Miles he needn't worry. He said DHS is not going to pursue any action against him and, in fact, DHS is ignoring Miles' punching Williams. "One, they don't want any more attention directed toward the Saint Andrews incident. Two, that guy is dead.

"Oh, and as promised, that letter of appreciation from me is already on its way to your service record. And I think you'll be hearing from your . . . sorry, Admiral Miles today also."

Miles stumbled through another thank you to the commandant.

"Quite alright, Lieutenant. Goodbye."

With that, Miles got up from his desk, walked down the corridor and knocked on senior chief's door. "Got news I need to tell you about."

A Walk with the Asset

Since the raid, the old man kept watch over the station from his window and with more frequent walks. He messaged LeClerc at least once a day, sometimes more. So LeClerc knew about the evacuation of the HSC personnel, the demonstrations, and vandalism of the trailers.

LeClerc gave him a new assignment. That's why he was walking on the pier at noon of that Tuesday. He was to wait on one of the benches at the end of the pier. Thank God it wasn't raining or too cold.

The old man heard footsteps from behind. He turned, and saw Miles coming toward him.

"I take it, lieutenant, you heard from Robert."

Startled, Miles asked, "Who are you?"

"Just an old man who lives here. Nobody important." The old man got up and stood at the railing next to Miles and reached into his pocket.

"Who am I? Here, this will help explain. I think you already have one of these." He handed Miles a business card from Robert LeClerc, Canadian Security Intelligence Service.

"If you wish to confirm who I am, Robert said to give him a call. You'll see a further demonstration of my authenticity at roughly 1300 today. Anyway, I am to pass a message to you."

He's another spy, thought Miles. *A spy from Eastport? You just can't make this shit up.* "Okay, what is the message?"

"He'd like to meet with you. A place of your choosing. He suggested a coffee shop or a bar, which every you prefer. As soon as possible."

"And this demonstration?"

"Today, the *Corporal Teather* will leave Saint Andrews and pass right by here. At the same time, a Canadian warship, the HMCS *Glace Bay*, will pass by. Any further actions by the United States government in this area will be met by Canadian military." The old man went off script from the message for a moment. "Son, if anyone thinks the Canadians are going to give in, well, no. They're in no mood to beat their swords into plowshares.

"Anyway, there's the message. Call him. Please. It's important."

"Why are you doing this? I mean, here you are an, excuse me for saying so, an elderly man playing the spy in this tiny town. Like you walked out of a *Le Carré* novel."

"You've read *Le Carré*? Good stuff! Lately, I've found his stories pretty interesting. Almost like a training manual." The old man managed a little laugh.

"I'll bet you have. But why do this?"

"Well, son, I just . . . I just had to." The old man turned to look around, then started to explain. "You know, people around here are pretty conservative about a lot of things. They don't take to people from far away telling them what to do. They'll accept advice or help when needed. Mostly though, they just want to be left alone.

"But going after the Canadians, that's too much for a lot of people. And to use our town as a base for killing. Just too much. So that's why people around here got angry. Why they messed with those trailers. Probably a good thing those bastards left here.

"Anyway, that's a bit off track. For me, you know, I took the same oath as you did, only longer ago. Army during Vietnam. I like to think I'm a patriot. But those guys, the last thing they are is patriots. Those homeland security guys, to me they represent all that's gone wrong with this country. So, no, I just can't abide them. Any of them.

"I started watching them from the pier and from my house. Had a pretty good view of things. Kept tabs on the HSCs. Even got to know that Williams guy a little. Course, he's dead now.

"I should go. Already said too much." The old man started his walk back to his home.

When he was a few steps away, Miles called after him. "I'll call him."

The old man was good to his word. After lunch, Miles watched from the jetty as the *Corporal Teather* headed south as it passed by a gray warship that lingered for a while east of the station, as if showing off. Message sent and received.

Breakfast with the Spy

Two days later, Miles met LeClerc. Dressed in civilian clothes, Miles came early. He sat in his car and waited for LeClerc to show. And to watch for anyone else who showed up. At the appointed time, LeClerc went inside. Miles followed and met him in the foyer.

"Doug! Good morning! Kinda an out of the way place for you, isn't it?" Miles had asked to meet LeClerc for breakfast at a diner that sat aside Route 1 as it passed through the town of Perry, Maine. The kind of place that existed for regulars. No tourists passing through these days anyway.

"No, not really. Wanted to get out of Eastport. Let's take that table over in the corner, order something to eat, then we can talk." LeClerc nodded agreement.

Over coffee and after their orders were taken, Miles told LeClerc he'd have to fill out a report, of course. And this would likely be their last meeting. When LeClerc asked why they wouldn't meet again, Miles explained.

"I have to ask. Are you recording any of this? 'Cause if you are, I'd ask you not to."

"No. I, nor anyone else with CSIS, is recording any of this." LeClerc raised his right hand. "I swear. You are not being recorded. On my word as a spy."

They both had a laugh this time.

"Why last meeting? Pretty simple. I'm being transferred out of Eastport. DHS didn't like what happened at Saint Andrews. They didn't like what *I* did. Though, I have it on good authority they didn't want to draw more media attention by going after me, so they're pulling junior officers like me from all stations with HSC units. Guess they don't trust us. Wonder why."

"I'm sorry to hear that. Any idea where you're headed?"

"Maybe I shouldn't have told you that. Anyway, yeah. Headquarters, at least for now. Washington. Honestly, I think they want to find me a nice, out of the way place where I'll never be seen again. Especially by the news media. I'm still hoping for a ship, but . . ."

"May I ask if you're in any trouble?"

"It's okay. No. I've received assurances of that. I suppose if I keep my head down for a while, I might be able to salvage a career from all this. It's a big might though." Miles shifted the conversation. "May I ask, did you sneak across the border just to see me?"

"Yup. Didn't have anything else to do. I mean, what else could a Canadian intelligence analyst being doing these days?" Miles felt a tinge of sarcasm.

LeClerc said he'd be driving back to Fredericton to catch a flight to Boston, via Halifax. A matter at our Consulate. Routine thing. Security consultation.

Breakfast arrived. Both had ordered corned beef hash with two fried eggs. "Okay, so, what's so important?"

"You saw our ship, HMCS *Glace Bay?* Do you understand why we did that?"

"Yeah, I saw it. Impossible not to. Coastal defense vessel, Kingston-class. Commissioned 1996, homeported at CFB Halifax. I looked her up. Learned you guys rearmed them recently. A 25-millimeter chain gun. I can only guess its deployment off Eastport is a reaction to the Saint Andrews incident."

"And you would be correct. There's a special operations force aboard her. NTOG, or Naval Tactical Operations Group. They're Canadian Navy. Equivalent to your MSST teams. Maybe better. You can add that to your report. Another ship of her class will be patrolling the Canadian side of Quoddy Narrows. We've deployed two more to cover Vancouver. Another pair is enroute to the Great Lakes through the Saint Lawrence. I'm sure your government knows about all this."

"Tell Station Eastport personnel to stay well clear of Canadian waters. NTOG will shadow your people. I don't want to see anyone hurt. Our people are, well, pretty angry about what happened."

That was a threat, or something close to it, Miles knew.

"Wait, you do understand that raid was HSC's doing. My people, the U.S. Coast Guard, had nothing to do with it. Christ, I turned those bastards over to RCMP. You got them all. And the rest of them at the station were taken away. That unit is shut down!" Now Miles got a little mad. "Don't, just don't threaten my people when we were the good guys!"

"Easy, my friend. Yes, we know that. Everyone knows that. And I'm supposed to offer our off-the-record thanks to you. And we don't think the Coast Guard is about to invade Canada. But if the situation were reversed, that NTOG or RCMP went into your territory, tried to kidnap someone, but killed them instead, what would your Navy do?"

Miles mulled that over for all of two seconds. "Sink yours."

"Likely true. CSIS assesses a high probability that this situation will escalate. We base this mostly on the administration's past behavior. Aggressive. Decision making relying on ego more than analysis. Feel free to pass that along too. Tell anyone who will listen, we will defend ourselves."

A couple minutes past in silence as the two men continued eating.

"I'll pass that along. I don't know what good it will do."

"Maybe it won't do any good. We're hoping if the message gets out in as many ways possible, maybe someone toward the top will take things seriously."

Another quiet minute followed, during which the waitress refilled their coffee.

"So, Williams killed himself, didn't he?"

"Yes. Used his service pistol. Never saw . . . anyway, I guess he didn't see a way out. Stupid thing to say. That's obvious." Miles preferred to forget about Williams.

"Robert, I am curious about something. The old man. Tell me about him."

"Ah, yes, the old man." LeClerc took a fork full of his hash before continuing. "You have to understand I am constrained by ethics and law on what I can say about him. And please don't make a joke about spies having ethics."

"I'd love to, but I'll let that pass." Miles repeated what the old man told him about himself and his life in Eastport. "I think in your world, you call him a cut-out?"

LeClerc smiled. "Yeah, pretty much. You know, I was very conflicted about exposing him to you. Risky for him. But he thought you'd listen to him. He was on the pier when you slapped Williams that morning. You probably didn't see him. Just an old man out for a walk. He tends to blend in with the background.

"He insisted on meeting you. Said he was tired, just plain tired of the game. He would do it his way no matter what. He's a good man, and in the grand scheme of things he's a minor player, but I am concerned for him. Doug, I don't suppose you'd tell me if you reported your meeting with him."

Miles decided not to answer directly. "I haven't yet. I was waiting to see how this morning turned out. Course, I don't even know the name of the old man anyway. Let me ask, did you really use him to spy on the HSC unit?"

"Afraid you'll have to draw your own conclusions on that. No comment."

LeClerc felt it best to keep most things to himself for now. He was still uncertain where his relationship with Miles was headed. CSIS did use the old man to approach Williams, hoping to eventually turn Williams to their side. Perhaps as a source. Or get him to defect and use him as a propaganda tool. However, Williams decided on another course of action.

"Well, I'm about done. I mean with breakfast. Doug, there's one last thing I want to talk to you about before I head to Boston."

"Okay" Mike thought, here comes the real reason for all this.

"A young American naval officer defected to Canada the other day. In Saint Andrews. Actually, he's a reserve officer. He's much like you. Experienced at sea on a destroyer. Master's degree in mechanical engineering. You may have heard of him, though I doubt your news outlets will be fair to him. Already mentioned on CBC and such. Pretty dramatic story really. You know who I am talking about?"

"Not a clue, Robert."

"Matthew Whynot, former lieutenant of the U.S. Navy Reserve. You should know the name. He is the son of Michael Whynot, the man HSC killed."

Miles put down his fork and pushed his plate away, suddenly suspicious of LeClerc. "What are you getting at?"

"He's not the first U.S. military to leave their country of late. You could say Lieutenant Whynot left for personal and political reasons. He said he would not 'remain in a country that murdered my father.' But we in CSIS are wondering if and to what extent the U.S. military officer corps is disaffected by the actions of this new administration. I was wondering if you have any opinion on this matter."

Miles leaned back in the chair, folding his arms across his chest. "You must know that I cannot have an opinion on something like that. And even if I knew officers, or enlisted, who are disaffected, as you say, I certainly wouldn't tell a foreign intelligence officer."

Maybe you just did at least a little, wondered LeClerc.

"Of course. Now, assuming Whynot checks out, there's a good chance we'll allow him to join our Navy. He's not the only one. Not many, but we'll do the same for others. Doug, I have a kind of, let's say, suggestion? And I am dead certain you won't accept."

"Accept what?"

"You're hoping for a ship. You have doubts about your career. You've got valuable experience. Well, if things ever go bad for you, I'm sure we can find something for you in our Navy."

Miles, looking down and shaking his head, responded, "You really think I would defect?" He swore at LeClerc. "I'm done here. You can pick up the check." Miles marched out the door to his car.

On the drive back to the station, Miles listened to the car radio in a futile attempt to drown out his thoughts. *Christ, I'm in a box. Do I put the offer of defection in my last report? If I withhold that little nugget, what if it comes out later? If I include it, then I would be honest, but how would I be perceived? Will someone higher up think I sought the offer? Goddamn that LeClerc!*

The news came on at the top of the hour.

"A big story coming out of Washington. A shakeup in the Coast Guard. The Department of Homeland Security has confirmed the resignation of the Commandant of the Coast Guard, four-star Admiral Paul Wingate. The Admiral himself released his letter of resignation to the press and it is a damning statement against the current administration. We'll have more on that later, but the shakeup doesn't end there. The Vice Commandant of the Coast Guard refused promotion to Commandant and likewise resigned in protest. Four other Coast Guard admirals, all whom are known as district commanders, resigned in protest."

"Obviously, this is a developing story that we will be following closely."

Holy shit! Miles turned off the road. Taking out his phone, he searched news websites for more details, but there wasn't anything more detailed than the radio broadcast.

I gotta call her.

Hello Mom

"Don't you start worrying about me. I can take care of myself." In the history of parenting, how many mothers have said that to their children.

Rear Adm. Cynthia Miles, and as of yesterday, rear admiral, retired, confirmed to her son that she resigned as district commander in solidarity with the commandant and the vice commandant. She said she and the other admirals, six in all, would be holding a press conference the next day in Washington. "Only the press knows about the presser, so don't let it out. We want to surprise them."

She wasn't worried about what could happen to her. "It's a risk. They may want to refuse our resignations, stop our retirements, court martial us. I think that'll only give us a louder voice. I think they'll say nasty things about us, threaten us, which has already started, and then leave it at that."

"Now enough about me." Back to Mom. "How are you?"

"I'm fine. After I talked to the commandant, ah, the former commandant, I was happy to hear the board of investigation supported my actions off Saint Andrews. So did he. And I talked to the detailer and looks like I'm headed to headquarters, at least for now."

Back to admiral. "A couple of things. You won't be headed to headquarters. Captain Llewellyn interceded. He wants you at Sector Northern New England. You have valuable experience operating on the border. He's going to need that to deal with what is coming. He called the detailer. I called the detailer. The orders for the sector are coming out today. You know, that might've been my last official action as an admiral."

"Okay. Good to hear. But you said, 'what is coming.' Can you tell me what that means?"

"Sorry, no. You'll find out. And soon. Anyway, get your bags packed and get going to sector the moment you get your orders. I'd like to see you, but let's make it another time."

Goodbyes said, Miles almost called Capt. Llewellyn, but decided against it. And he decided to let the daily report slip his mind.

The orders arrived that late afternoon. Miles made the rounds of goodbyes to the crew and the senior chief. No ceremony. Just a last evening meal with the crew and leave it at that. Miles hated to make such a hasty departure. These were good people. He wanted to say and do so much more, but there was no time. Capt. Llewellyn wanted him at sector by tomorrow.

His bags were already packed. He kept a souvenir of his time here. A business card from a Canadian intelligence analyst.

He was on the road by early morning. Door-to-door, between 4 ½ to 5 hours, depending on stops. Enjoying the scenic route down Route 1 along the Maine coast had to wait for another time.

He was just getting on to I-95 at Bangor when he tuned into public radio for the news at the top of the hour. The Coast Guard was the lead story, again. The reporter began.

"There have been further developments about the leadership crisis of the U.S. Coast Guard. In a press conference this morning, the Secretary of the Department of Homeland Security himself announced Vice Admiral, that's a three-star rank, Vice Admiral Troy Bridges is the new Commandant of the Coast Guard. Last night, the president had promoted Vice Admiral Bridges to four-star rank, which makes him a full Admiral."

"According to the Secretary, replacements for the five other Admirals who resigned in protest, will be announced over the next few days. The Secretary reassured the public that there is temporary leadership in these positions. He said, 'There has been no operational degradation of Coast Guard capabilities because of the actions of these disgraceful and disloyal officers.' A harsh rebuke of the six admirals to say the least."

"Vice Admiral Bridges stirred controversy last month when he publicly referred to opponents of the current president as 'treasonous' and 'deserve to pay the ultimate price.' Also, in the past, Bridges was overflowing in his praise of the new president. For making such openly partisan political statements, the previous commandant, Admiral Wingate, issued a letter of reprimand to Bridges. Well, it seems roles may have now reversed."

"At two o'clock this afternoon, the six former admirals will hold a press conference to explain their actions. It looks like the administration is trying to set their narrative ahead of the admirals."

"This story brings to mind another change in military leadership that happened two months ago when there was a sudden replacement of the U.S. Army general commanding the United States Northern Command. That's one of the military's eleven unified commands. USNORTHCOM, as it is called, does not operate overseas. This one has operational control over military resources in the United States itself."

Miles shut off the radio, thinking there was no point in listening to the news and getting more pissed off. He tried listening to music. He tried to think of something, anything else. In his mind, he tried setting up the plan for his day. In about two or so hours, he'd be in Portland. Officially check in with his orders and then see the captain. And call mom after her press conference.

It didn't work. He was pissed off and knew he'd be that way all day. Without realizing it, he gave voice to his anger, ranting out loud in the car. "Mom lost, no, gave up her command. My career is gone. And why? Because of politics. Goddamn politicians did this. They wanted power, no matter what. No policies. No programs. Just power. Why? What happened?"

This went on until it dawned on him that he must be making a show of himself to the cars passing by. Miles decided to get off the highway and get some coffee. A roadside sign pointed to a Dunkin' a couple of miles away off the highway. Stop for a few minutes and get some coffee. Maybe a donut, too. Just as well because he didn't sleep that well last night.

Miles sipped his coffee in the Dunkin' parking lot for a minute, trying to calm down. He ignored the donut. He wasn't hungry. It then occurred to him that in his little tirade, he thought of no one but himself. He gave not a single thought of what happened to his country. A prescient conversation with mom the admiral, before he went to Eastport, came to mind.

Doug, we both took the same oath. To preserve and protect the Constitution of the United States, against all enemies, foreign and domestic. I'm really afraid our most dangerous enemies are of the domestic variety. And they have friends in the administration. Often wonder what kind of government I may be working for.

Meeting with the Captain

Miles went to the administrative office and handed over his orders. He found the captain's office on the same floor as the operations center.

The captain came out from behind his desk, welcomed Miles and offered a place to sit, while asking if he wanted a coffee or such. Miles took the chair, but politely turned down the coffee. Strange, Miles reflected, for all the times they've talked, he'd been in this office only once before, before they made that long car trip up to Eastport.

The captain closed the office door.

"Well, lieutenant, I'm very glad you're here. I mean that. I have to say too that I'm very sorry that Admiral Miles is no longer our district commander. She is an outstanding officer. Great leader. I am sorry it's all come to this."

Miles wanted to ask what he meant by "sorry it's all come to this" but decided to keep his mouth shut.

"So, tell me, how are things at Eastport?" Miles went quickly through the station's status and all that he knew about the HSC unit's departure. He confirmed the arrival of the HMCS *Glace Bay*. He then presented his written report of his contact over breakfast with LeClerc. In summarizing the report, Miles emphasized the tactical implications of the NTOG team on the warship.

"LeClerc's made an offer of defection. I refused, of course. In any event, before I sent it on, I wanted to fully brief you on these contacts and answer any questions."

"I appreciate that, but, yes, send it on right away. This contact may put you under the microscope again, with the defection offer and all, but your best protection is an honest report. Be hard for someone to accuse you of anything after you followed the rules."

"Aye, sir. I'll send it once we're done here." Miles had a moment of regret, remembering he decided to include a lie. A lie of omission. His report withheld any mention of the old man. *No, I will not rationalize it. I will lie. If that is found out, it will only be on me.*

The captain went through the report line by line, asking questions to check his understanding. That done, he raised Miles's new job at sector. He'd be taking over the Enforcement Division of the Response Department. Miles knew his predecessor was recently diagnosed with cancer and his treatment made him unable to fulfil his duties in the short term. "Your experience in the Persian Gulf, and at Eastport, makes you a good fit for running the division." Miles thought, *Enforcement Division. Enforcement of Laws and Treaties. Yes, I guess I am a good fit. Did a lot of boardings. I could even do boardings in Arabic. At least a little Arabic.*

The captain also wanted Miles put in the watch rotation in the operations center. He half-jokingly said, "Hope you don't mind starting tonight." As a lieutenant, he was expected to qualify as watch supervisor in short order.

"Now, don't get your hopes up, but this coming summer, there'll be an opening for the commanding officer of the *Finback*. Her skipper is rotating out. I expect I'll be able to recommend you."

Genuinely surprised, Miles blurted out, "Thank you, sir. That would be, ah, great."

A command. A real command. Not the sort of pretend commanding officer thing like at Eastport. Miles knew of the *Finback*. She's a Marine Protector Class cutter, 87-foot. He'd be the only officer aboard. Normally, they're commanded by a lieutenant, junior grade. Or a senior chief. So, a full lieutenant might raise an eyebrow or two. But the captain's recommendation might help. And he'd still be in the sector as the cutter was assigned to South Portland.

"Like I said, I'll recommend you. But please, temper your hopes with an understanding that you are, in some circles, a problem. I don't mean from within the Coast Guard. The board supported you in the Saint Andrews incident, the commandant supported you. But he is also the *former* Commandant. Do you understand what I'm trying to say?"

"Yes, sir. I think so." *That I may be too toxic for command. At least in the eyes of some political appointee or politician. Goddamn.*

"Well, if you do, that's more than me. Okay, well, let's go to the operations center. Meet the people there, get you access, and all that. We've got an operation coming down the pike. Operation order is coming on Monday. I'm told its pretty serious stuff, So, you need to get as familiar with sector operations and our people as quickly as possible. In other words, don't plan on going anywhere this weekend."

The Consulate

LeClerc finished his review of consulate security, working Friday and through the weekend. Auditing of personnel records, reviewing logbooks, checking security systems, and a thorough review of their contingency plans. How to evacuate, how to destroy classified materials and communication gear. All this was routine for LeClerc. The consulate security manager struck LeClerc as highly professional. No problems.

On Monday, LeClerc finished with the consul general by summarizing the report he would file and thanked her for their cooperation. She closed the meeting by asking LeClerc, "I hear Ken Lavoie is taking you to dinner this evening. Is that true? Ken knows the area very well, especially the finer places to eat. Have a good time. Oh, when is your flight tomorrow?"

"Ma'am, I have a flight from Logan Airport to Halifax tomorrow morning." Flying back to Canada these days was not easy. With the border closure, daily passenger flights from Boston to Halifax had fallen from about two dozen to just two.

"You're lucky. Well, thanks for your help." With that, LeClerc left the consul general to gather his things and get ready to sneak out to dinner. To accomplish the true reason for being in Boston. Spy stuff.

Upcoming Operations

Capt. Llewellyn directed his officers to the chart laid out on the large table in the operations center. "So, there you have it. *Operation Winter Harvest.* In less than forty-eight hours, Wednesday at 1200, we begin aggressive patrols of the international boundary, as directed by the Secretary of Homeland Security and Commandant Bridges. The stated purpose is to reinforce American sovereignty. Meanwhile, the same thing is going to happen in the 13th and 9th districts.

"We do not know if and how the Canadian Forces will react. Nor how involved our own Navy will be in all this.

"Yes, there're gaps in our view of the big picture. We don't need to know everything. It's our job to carry out these orders. We focus on the tactical. We leave the strategic questions to higher authority. Questions?"

The captain then outlined the tasks for his sector's assets. "Station Eastport will put a boat on the border and stop any vessel crossing. There will be no recognition of innocent passage. Deck guns will be prominently displayed at all times."

With the cutter *Finback* as escort, Station Jonesport's MLB would sail to Machias Seal Island and embark a team of Homeland Security Corps agents to occupy the island. They would arrest any Canadians present, who will be repatriated as quickly as possible. *Finback* would remain in the area, patrolling along the border off Grand Manan Island and Quoddy Narrows, until relieved by the sector's other patrol boat, the cutter *Sitkinak.*

Miles spoke first. "Captain, about Eastport. How shall we deal with merchant vessels coming in through Canadian waters headed for Eastport's Estes Head Terminal. Even during this border closure, Canada granted innocent passage to U.S. flagged vessels passing north of Campobello Island on their way to Eastport. No other way to get to that terminal. With *Operation Winter Harvest*, the Canadians may retaliate by closing their waters to U.S. ships headed for Eastport. Won't do Eastport a lot of good. They'll lose a lot of money."

"Well, you're right on all counts, Mr. Miles. Since I'm also the captain of the port, I have the legal authority to close Eastport to shipping traffic. And that is what district says I must do if the Canadians take that action. I'll have to issue a Notice to Mariners closing Eastport to any Canadian merchant ship. And yes, that will not make us very popular. But it is an order. I wish, ah, never mind."

"Captain, I also have a tactical recommendation regarding Eastport."

"Go on, Mr. Miles."

"Station Eastport's boats will get close to the HMCS *Glace Bay* and its NTOG team. Two heavily armed forces, acting aggressively toward each other, in close proximity. The operations order doesn't seem to acknowledge the *Glace Bay* at all. The order's rules of engagement are, in my opinion, vague."

The captain cut in. "That's an interpretation, not a recommendation."

"Sir, this is dangerous. Inherently dangerous. To avoid conflict, I recommend that our boats stay well away from the *Glace Bay*. And the NTOG team. And we stay in communication with *Glace Bay* to decrease the possibility of a misunderstanding."

The Response Department officer, a lieutenant commander by the name of Meyer, concurred with Miles.

Meyer then added his opinion of the Station Jonesport mission. "Captain, Machias Seal Island, we all know the Canadians dispute the boundary there. They claim it as their own territory. Their Coast Guard keeps a couple of lighthouse keepers there for no other reason than to reinforce their claim. If we send the *Finback* in there, put Americans ashore, and arrest Canadians, *Canadian Coast Guardsmen*, Christ, sir, the Canadians will see that as I would see it. An invasion."

"Invasion? That's a little strong, don't you think, commander?" The captain then looked up from the chart and smiled. He knew his Response Department head could be a bit blunt, thinking, *hell, nobody ever imagined they'd be doing anything like this.*

"Okay, invasion. Technically, I suppose that's true, commander. But don't use that word again. That'll only inflame things more. And I am very concerned at how the Canadians will respond to all this. Concerned enough that when I got the order, I called district. I shared the very same concerns. Even spoke with the staff judge advocate."

The captain bit his tongue when he was about to say the acting district commander didn't take his call. *That wouldn't help. My people don't need any more reason to doubt the chain of command.*

"It doesn't matter. We have our orders. I'm assured they are legal orders. That comes from the commandant and the attorney general of the United States. We will carry out our orders. Is that clear to everyone here?"

The Captain offered two modifications. "Eastport will stay well clear of the Canadian warship. And warn them, the Canadians, of their approach. Nothing in the operations order say they can't do that.

"If the Canadian Navy challenges us, anywhere, our forces will withdraw to a safe distance, and we will request guidance from district. Lieutenant Miles, your opinion of the operation's rules of engagement is well founded. I imagine you had experience on ROEs in the Persian Gulf. Write up how you would have the ROE. Have it on my desk by 1700. I can't say we can change anything, but your views might be useful to me if anything happens.

"Listen, tell all our people to stay calm, to act respectfully toward the Canadians, and for God's sake, do not use or display their weapons in a threatening manner. Station Eastport has to man a M240 machine gun on deck of their small boats. The op order is specific on that. But I want all deck guns under a canvas cover. Nothing threatening. Commander Meyer, make sure everyone understands the operations order does not explicitly say we must ready those guns.

"You've all got details to iron out. Let's get to work. Dismissed."

Before he left the operations center, the captain pulled Miles aside and quietly spoke to him. "Your concerns about cooperation with the Canadians on search and rescue were valid. I wish it was otherwise."

"Yes, captain. I saw that in the operations order. 'Suspend all SAR cooperation with Canadian authorities upon commencement of *Operation Winter Harvest*.' Jesus, Captain. I see it but can't believe it." Miles was about to say something more, but felt his composure weaken. He shook his head.

"Sir, I guess I need to see my division. If I may be excused."

Miles went to his division spaces, called his people together and went straight into the operation. He spent the next hour quizzing his staff on the sector's readiness, trying to find out if any problem loomed out there. He kept his doubts of the operation to himself.

Those tasks done, Miles went to his new office and closed the door. He put his head down, cradled in one hand. *My God, what are we about to do?*

Refocusing HSC

Late that same afternoon, a new troop of HSC officers arrived in Calais, Maine. With the trailers in Eastport uninhabitable, and the locals around there inhospitable, the new unit moved into a budget, run-of-the-mill motel on Route 1. They didn't need the Coast Guard anymore. They planned to use their SUVs to run land side patrols. No boats.

The owner and operator of the motel didn't like having HSC, but what could he do? It was steady cash in troubled times.

Former Comrade in Arms

When he accepted Lavoie's offer to make dinner reservations, LeClerc asked it to be made for three. The two of them and a third person. LeClerc explained, "I'm not familiar with Boston. I hear you know good places to eat around here." Upon reflection, LeClerc realized he should've been more specific about the cuisine.

A French bistro. He would've preferred Lavoie had picked a nice Italian place. LeClerc had heard the North End of Boston has more of those places than can be counted. But they both have French last names, so LeClerc chalked it up to a well-intended assumption. Besides, the place looks elegant. Expertly prepared cocktails and a fine meal is always something to look forward to. Could have been worse, he knew. Lavoie could've taken him to the one place in Boston that served poutine. LeClerc hated the stuff.

LeClerc told Lavoie they would go by foot. Staff there suspected HSC tailed their vehicles. Easy to spot with diplomatic plates. In spite of the cold air and light rain, they walked out through a back door and went to the nearby Prudential Center subway station.

Only they didn't take the subway. They went down into the station, bought their tickets, and milled around for a minute, watching the faces around them. Anyone tailing them would only go through the gate if they did. LeClerc tapped Lavoie on the shoulder, leading him up to a turnstile, but then pulled him away. They head back up the same stairway they had taken down. LeClerc stopped for a moment, looking back down the steps. He waited. No one seemed to be following. No one seemed to be hanging around.

Then down a residential street behind the Copley House Hotel. Unlikely anyone but residents would go down this street. A left along Braddock Park and Follen Gardens. A sudden right along another residential street. Another right along a public alleyway to Union Church. All along the way, LeClerc and Lavoie looked for anyone acting out of the ordinary. Nothing. The bistro was across the street.

Once inside the bistro, Lavoie told the receptionist they had reservations for three. The third person would be joining them in ten or fifteen minutes. Seated at a table toward the back, away from the windows, Lavoie just had to say something unnecessary. "God, that was fun! Been working at consulates for years now. Never did anything like that! Kinda like this spy shit. I mean, look at you. Fedora and trench coat. Anyway, all that walking and I'm really hungry too."

LeClerc wasn't pleased by Lavoie's cavalier attitude. Firmly, but quietly, he said, "Knock off that kind of talk. Do I have to remind you again of how important this is?

"Ken, one more time. I only needed you as a guide. When the gentleman arrives, you are not to talk aside from saying hello. And then goodbye. You will not say anything about any of this to anyone. It is classified. We hear you've said anything, your employment ends. Then we can discuss jail time. Am I clear, this time?"

Rightly sensing rebuke, Lavoie shut up, speaking only when he ordered a cocktail.

Five minutes or so later, a tall man in a woolen dress coat, gray suit, and umbrella walked over to the table. LeClerc rose to shake the man's hand, but wound up embracing him, ignoring the man's damp coat. As the man removed his coat, it occurred to LeClerc that he couldn't ever recall seeing Col. Henry Byron out of a U.S. Army uniform. *Impressive suit, Henry. Well done.* They sat down as LeClerc called over a waiter. "The gentleman would like a cocktail, I am sure." He did, ordering a bourbon on ice, saying "It'll take the chill out of the air.

"Robert, how long has it been? Really good to see you!"

It had indeed been an appallingly long time. Byron and LeClerc had been the same rank, captains, back in Afghanistan. Byron was an infantry officer, Ranger qualified, commanding a company of the 4th Infantry Division that was operating with the Canadian Army in the Kandahar region. LeClerc was there with Canadian Forces Military Intelligence. Third tour in Afghanistan for Byron. LeClerc was on his second. LeClerc first met Byron in the course of briefing him on intelligence about the Taliban in the area. Their friendship grew from there.

The sight of Byron triggered a slight bout of envy in LeClerc. Aside from the greying hair, in LeClerc's eyes Henry was still the tall and athletic young captain, while LeClerc's hair had also greyed, but thinned a fair amount. The softer middle didn't help.

Like many who served together, friendships formed fast and stayed deep. Though LeClerc hadn't seen Henry in years, they talked without awkwardness, as though they had seen each other only yesterday.

"Good to see you too, Henry." Updates of careers and family continued through the appetizers and until the entrees arrived. As well as a second cocktail all round. Lavoie stuck will nods and smiles.

"So what brings you to Boston, all the way down from Fort Drum? Is Nancy with you?"

"You may remember I have a younger brother, George. He's in hospice in Lexington, outside of Boston. Cancer. My hotel is out there. The hospice care place called me a week ago and said he didn't have much time."

LeClerc offered his sympathies, and Bryon continued. "Thank you. I wanted to see him one more time before he died. The division commander gave me four days leave. Have to drive back tomorrow."

"And Nancy?" Odd, felt LeClerc, that he didn't bring his wife, with a dying brother-in-law and all.

"She's back at Fort Drum. I didn't want to bring her. I think you'll understand why."

At the end of the meals, and before any mention of dessert, LeClerc leaned over to Lavoie to ask him to take a seat at the bar for the rest of the dinner.

Now alone, LeClerc got to business. "Henry, you called me. Why? I'm sure it wasn't just to reminisce about old times, no matter how good the bourbon."

"No, it isn't. I wish it was only that, believe me." Byron retrieved a small envelope from his suitcoat pocket. He handed it to LeClerc, sliding it across the table.

"I feel pretty silly about this. Maybe you're more adept at this line of work than me. Anyway, Rob, in that envelope is a thumb drive. Text and image files of an operations plan for my division. *Operation Northern Lights*. It's genuine. I promise you."

"*Northern Lights?* Why does that sound like it is directed at us? I mean, Canada?"

"Because it is."

"Can you talk about it now? Here?"

"Quickly. It's a plan for two regular army brigades of the 10th Mountain Division, plus the division aviation and artillery brigades. And engineers and support troops. They'll be augmented by an armored brigade combat team from the 3rd Infantry Division from Fort Stewart, Georgia.

"They'll move north across the Saint Lawrence bridges. Primarily, the Thousand Islands and Ogdensburg-Prescott bridges because they offer the shortest route to the objective. Secondarily, the bridges in Cornwall. Air assault troops will seize and hold them until the armor and mechanized infantry columns from Fort Drum arrive. That should take no more than half a day.

"Our fighters will keep your fighters on the ground. Broadcasts will tell your fighters to stay on the ground. Limited air strikes if there is resistance.

Your naval fleet will be ordered to remain in Halifax. U.S. Navy will be within striking distance of your fleet. Same deal. Resist and we sink your Navy. US-NORTHCOM wants quick action before the NATO allies deploy significant forces here." Henry anticipated LeClerc's first question.

"The objective is Ottawa. Two, maybe three days to get there. Essentially, it's a thunder run. We show you what we can do, hardly scratching the surface of our capabilities. Force your government to become a vassal state to the United States. We control your foreign policy, command your military, and get first dibs on all your natural resources. You become our colony."

My God. My God. They're really going to do this! LeClerc was shaken, unable to find the right follow-up question. Henry helped him out.

"Have your people confirm this intel. Give it to NATO. Have them confirm it. You don't have much time. Three weeks maybe. Assets are already moving. And remember. Surprise is the key."

"Your next question is, why am I doing this? Why am I betraying my country? The answer is because this operation is the betrayal. It's immoral and it's a war crime. A war of aggression, straight out of Nuremburg. They'll court martial me, but I've accepted that possibility.

"Funny thing, Rob. My dying brother offered me cover to come here. Pure coincidence. I wonder if I will ever be able to tell him about all this. Anyway, I saw a chance to do something. The same day I got the call from hospice, I called you."

LeClerc regained a measure of his composure. "Henry, will you . . ."

"No, Robert. I will not fight. If the order comes, I'll have my people stand down. Since my guys are tasked with the air assault on the bridges, maybe I can complicate things. Won't work, of course, but I will try. Then I resign, but probably be arrested before I can do that." LeClerc knew Byron commanded an entire Infantry Brigade Combat Team of the 10th Mountain Division.

"Do others in your command feel the same way?"

"I'd like to think that every damn senior officer in the division would refuse the order. But no. Feelings run from disgust to indifference to enthusiasm. And I've no idea what the Joint Chiefs are thinking, especially the new chairman. USNORTHCOM has operational control. None of this would have gotten this far unless he approved."

LeClerc drained the rest of his martini. Henry sat stone-faced before him.

"Jesus, Henry. Why? Why does the president want to attack Canada?"

"They didn't invite me to the Oval Office to ask my opinion or share their thinking. You guys will have to figure that out." It was Byron's turn to drain his bourbon.

"Maybe it's because your prime minister called him out, you know, especially after that thing in Saint Andrews, but by the looks of the operations order, and the troop movements it requires, I believe this was set in motion long before that. Even for the short action they're planning, it takes time to get ready. It's a pretty shitty plan by the way. Stinks of arrogance. Vague on reinforcement. The logistics planned do not support an operation of any long duration. And the whole thing lacks something else."

"Which is?"

"The commander-in-chief is about to send American men and women to fight and kill Canadian soldiers. Where is the rationale? The justification? There's no attempt to explain to our soldiers why they must kill your soldiers. No cause. No moral necessity. Nothing. Our soldiers are highly trained to kill the enemy but killing is very difficult to actually do. To overcome that, they need to know why."

"Your soldiers will know why they must kill our soldiers. They're defending their homes, their families. Ours, well . . ."

"Okay, Henry. Let's stop for now. I'm hoping you aren't under surveillance right now. Go out the back door and get back to your hotel. All I can say for now is I may be in touch. Thank you, Henry. Now go. I'll take care of the check." They shook hands for what LeClerc knew would likely be the last time.

As Byron walked away, LeClerc felt a tragic admiration for his friend. He didn't even ask for Canada to get him out. We could do that. We could do that tomorrow. Now. But he didn't.

LeClerc hurried to pay the bill. He almost pulled Lavoie off his bar stool. "Look, we have to get back to the consulate. Now. Call a cab. We're not walking."

LeClerc was near panic for the entire cab ride to the consulate building. *If Henry was under surveillance, was the FBI, or the Army, or HSC out there, ready to seize him in the cab? What if Henry was actually working for them? Was this a set-up?* A plan formed. He needed to make a copy of the files in the secure room of the consulate. He needed to send the files via the secure email to CSIS. He needed to copy them on another thumb drive. He needed to get past the HSC who guarded the building.

He needed to calm down.

CHAPTER FIFTEEN
FIRST MOVES

Disputed Territory

Wednesday noon. Clear and cold. Calm seas. On Machias Seal Island, a small, barren, rocky island about ten nautical miles southeast of Grand Manan Island, a lightkeeper inspected the island's ground array of solar panels. A routine inspection. He groused to himself, *everything we do on this goddamn rock is goddamn routine. I wish something would happen every once in a goddamn while.*

If not for the pair of lightkeepers, the island would be uninhabited, unless one considered the puffins. Hundreds of puffins. And the summertime wildlife biologists studying the puffins. And the tourists coming by boat from Cutler, Maine, to see the puffins. In fact, there was no practical need for the lightkeepers because the lighthouse was automated decades ago.

The island itself was a geological afterthought. At high tide, it was only about 20 acres of rock and grasses, barely enough to squeeze in ten misshapen football fields. Geology aside, the island just happened to be near shipping routes and therefore an excellent place to build a light house. The first one, a wooden tower, went up in 1832. The current lighthouse stood 65 feet on a concrete base. Built in 1914, it's a concrete octagonal tower with white walls and a red roof. Four single story, white walled and red roofed buildings completed the complex. Two were residences for the lightkeepers and summertime wildlife management staff.

Getting ashore from a boat wasn't easy. That meant leaving a big boat, getting into a little dingy, and then somehow getting ashore. There was no beach or dock, but there was a rather treacherous, half submerged concrete boat landing and walkway to higher ground. For the bird watching tourists, the best advice was to hold tightly to the safety rope strung along the boat landing.

Altogether though, it made an idyllic subject for any landscape artist.

International politics explained why the Canadian government always kept two lightkeepers there. Neither America nor Canada had settled the matter of ownership.

For nearly two centuries, both sides interpreted the border differently. And the border determined fishery rights, meaning the rich lobster grounds. Into the resulting political vacuum, Canada boldly moved. To assert sovereign control of the island, since the 1980s the Canadian Coast Guard had rotated two keepers in and out of the island. They flew in and out by helicopter every four weeks from the Saint John Canadian Coast Guard Station.

Today, the gods granted the bored lightkeeper his wish. Glancing over his shoulder, he saw two vessels approaching from the west, still too far away to identify them with the naked eye. He wondered, *way late in the season for the birdwatching tourists. Lobsterman? No, one boat seems a bit too big.*

He decided to give the solar panel inspection job a rest. He never found anything wrong anyway. He walked over to the residence building and called inside. "Hey, Mark." He kept at it until he found Mark in the kitchen, fixing himself a cup of coffee. "Yeah, Dave. What's up?"

"Two boats headed this way from the west." Mark grabbed his binoculars from the office desk. "Gonna have a look." Dave just nodded and followed Mark out.

Mark walked along the path to the west side of the light house tower and glassed the sea. He found them.

"Ah, shit. We might have visitors. U.S. Coast Guard. Two of their boats. Looks like they're headed straight here."

"You sure?" Dave knew the season for tourists coming out to see the damn puffins had passed. Despite all the border closure drama, the tour boats kept coming out all summer. The United States didn't recognize Canadian sovereignty there. So, no reason to stop the tourists. It's American territory, after all. The Canadian attitude was, no need to make a big kerfuffle over a bunch of bird watchers.

Mark replied in an irritated tone, "Christ yeah, I'm sure. Come see."

Dave saw. Yep, U.S. Coast Guard. He recognized the boats. A surf rescue boat and a cutter, one of their patrol boats over eighty feet long. He could see the crewmembers. They were less than a nautical mile away.

"Let's get back to the residence. I'll call Saint John. Dave, take a look around. See if any of our lobster boats are around. If they are, we'll warn 'em off."

Mark wasn't too concerned. He'd seen this before. The U.S. Coast Guard had come out there before to look at the lobstering around the island. Back in the residence, Mark used his satellite phone to call the station in Saint John. Standard operating procedure. As he was talking to them, Dave came in to say a lobster boat, a Canadian, was working off the north rock of the island.

Mark told Dave to use VHF radio channel 16 to warn the lobster boat of the Americans. Both knew that, on occasion, the U.S. Coast Guard would try to chase off any Canadian boats. Sometimes they'd threaten, politely, to board and seize the lobster boats, but the legality of that act was questionable at best. So, both sides abided with this little performance art. Political posturing of no significance.

"Okay, that's done. Let's go out and see what the Yanks are up to." Mark clipped the satellite phone to his belt.

They watched the patrol boat come along close by the east side of the island and launch their rigid hull inflatable. Mark thought that was a little unusual. Looking through the binoculars, the launch had two crew who looked like U.S. Coast Guard to Mark, but four others in black uniforms he didn't recognize. Then he saw those men carried rifles. Mark threw the binoculars to Dave and grabbed the satellite phone.

Mark frantically called Saint John to report an armed landing party about to come ashore. "Saint John, they have rifles. They're uniformed. The Coast Guard cutter is the *Finback*. Request assistance!"

"What do we do?" Dave was clearly shaken by the sight of armed men now coming up the concrete pathway from the shore, right for them.

Mark was about to say there was nothing they could do. Maybe call them names. Say bad things about their mothers. "Let's lock the door. Barricade it. Keep talking to Saint John." They could buy time.

"What do we say to these Americans?"

"Plan B. Tell 'em to go screw themselves. Think that'll scare 'em off, eh?" Mark was in no mood to be polite to their uninvited guests.

Dave and Mark locked the front and the back doors and moved a file cabinet and a desk in front of the door. At most, it would buy them a couple of minutes, but they could spend those minutes calling for help on the satellite phone and the VHF marine radio.

"U.S. federal agents! Homeland Security! Open the door." A pair of agents banged on the doors at the front and the back.

"We're Canadian Coast Guard! This is Canadian territory! You have no right to do this!" In accordance with Plan B, a colorful string of obscenities from Mark and Dave followed.

The back door gave way first. Two American agents, guns up, rushed to the office. They grabbed Dave and Mark, put them on their knees and zip tied their hands behind their backs. Mark felt one agent root through his pockets until he found his wallet. The agents demanded to know if anyone else was on the island. Mark said yes. "There's a company of Canadian Army soldiers in the next cabin. Why don't you knock on the door and find out?"

The other Americans paid no mind, but kept going through every room, door, and drawer in the cabin. Looking up at the agent questioning him, Mark angrily said, "You do realize, Yank, you've invaded Canada. But then, that's what you guys do. Like at Saint Andrews. So, screw you!" The agent looked away, unresponsive. Mark demanded their release and continued proving his profound expertise, even artistry, in the use of obscenities, in English and French.

To Mark, time became a lesson in relativity. Hands bound behind their backs, painfully kept on their knees on the wood floor, time seemed almost frozen. To the Yank agents busy with their invasion, time must be passing quickly.

"Name's Mark, right?" His tormentor got within inches of his face. "Look, Mark. You and your partner Dave are under arrest for unlawful trespass. A Customs and Border Protection helicopter will be here in 20 or 30 minutes. They will take you to a facility in Houlton, Maine. No harm will come to you. We're going to help you up off the floor and onto that couch over there. Are you going to cooperate, or do we leave you where you are?"

Christ, my knee hurts. "Alright, we'll cooperate."

Mark kept up with Plan B. "First, Mr. American agent. Go screw yourself. Second, we called for help. Third, I said we'll cooperate, but I won't be nice about it, you dick. Before that helicopter of yours gets here, maybe you'll have some visitors."

Aboard the Motor Lifeboat

Sr. Chief Chabot, officer-in-charge of Coast Guard Station Jonesport, had gone along on the mission to Machias Seal Island. Aboard the 47-foot Motor Lifeboat, he kept a close eye on their "guests," a four-man detachment of Homeland Security Corps. Earlier, Lt. Cmdr. Meyer, response division chief from sector, made things clear.

"Senior chief, be careful around HSC. Hard to trust them after Eastport. Make sure they don't endanger our people. Watch them closely. Keep our crew focused on the mission. Escort the *Finback* and once HSC is done, come back.

"The HSC on the *Finback* will take control of the island. The Canadian Coast Guard personnel there will be detained and then repatriated to Canada by CBP. The HSC on your boat, their job is to challenge and arrest any Canadian lobstermen. If that happens, bring the lobstermen and their boats back to station."

Senior chief had two questions for the commander. "Sir, CBP does have boats of their own. Why aren't they using them?"

"They aren't saying. I can only guess they wanted boats with a larger presence."

"Another question, commander. Is the 47 still my boat?"

"Yes, senior chief, it's your boat. Everything that happens on or in the 47 is under your command."

After requesting to speak freely, the senior chief went on a short rant. "I know this mission is not of your making, or anyone in the Coast Guard's making. I know we have no choice. But this mission is wrong. Dead wrong."

"Senior chief, I hear you." The call ended right there and then because Meyer didn't want to let the senior chief keep talking.

Chabot had taken this trip before to Machias Seal Island. He knew all the background. When the station's boats went out there, they'd challenge any Canadian lobsterman, but otherwise let it go. The CBP boats at times took a different tack, boarding the lobster boats to check for illegal immigrants. Chabot just shook his head when he remembered the first time he spoke to a CBP officer about their boardings. "Seriously, son, illegal immigrants are going to come through Canada aboard a lobster boat by way of this rock? What bullshit have you been sailing in?"

Before going out that morning, Chabot did something he rarely did before as officer-in-charge. He picked up an equipment belt with a sidearm.

Standing in the boat's cockpit, Chabot watched the HSC team land on the island and chase after the two Canadians. He watched as the HSC officers broke down the door. He saw an HSC officer walk over to the flagpole and haul down the Canadian flag, dropping it to the ground before taking out an American flag from his pack and hoisting it up. Chabot felt only shame at that sight, whispering to himself, "This is wrong. Dead wrong."

"Hey, Chief! I think I see a boat over there!" Miller, the HSC team leader on the MLB, pointed to a boat by a small rock outcropping on the northern end of the island. "Get us over there!"

"It's senior chief."

"Huh? Whatever. Senior chief. Happy? We want that guy. That's a Canadian lobster boat. He's illegally fishing in American waters. Get this boat over there!"

Chabot didn't acknowledge Miller. Instead, he directed the coxswain to bring the MLB to intercept and come alongside the lobster boat. Chabot then used the VHF marine radio to ask the lobsterman about his activities.

"Coast Guard. Look. I'm a lobsterman on a lobster boat. Just what do you think I might be doing?"

Chabot couldn't help but laugh. "Captain, I have U.S. agents on board who want to talk to you. Will that be a problem? Over."

"Coast Guard. No. Shouldn't be a problem. Been through this before."

As they came within twenty yards of the lobster boat, Chabot turned to face Miller. "My crew will bring this boat alongside the lobster boat. I want to know your intentions."

"Our intentions? Arrest them. Take the boat. Now uncover 240 and put a man on it."

"No need for that. The M240 is just fine. It stays covered. Captain's orders."

Now yelling, Miller was red in the face. He threatened to put one of his own men on the machine gun.

Chabot didn't back down. As calmly as he could, he said, "Miller, this is my boat. The guy on that lobster boat is no threat. If you guys get too excited, if you can't execute this in a professional manner, I will withdraw this boat. Is that clear?"

Cornered, Miller grunted and said, "Just get us alongside. We'll take it from there."

"That's not an answer. Are you going to board him?"

"Well, shit, Chief. How else would we inspect his boat?"

Chabot didn't answer, but instead directed the coxswain to stand by. He used the secure communication system to talk to the *Finback's* commanding officer, a lieutenant, junior grade, informing her that HSC wanted to board the lobster boat. With the headset on, Miller couldn't hear what *Finback* had to say.

"47, *Finback*. The op orders say we are to support them in boarding any Canadian fishing boats. Will inform sector. Stand by. Over." Chabot acknowledged Finback and then told Miller to stand by.

"Chief, are we boarding that boat, or what?"

"Well, Miller, we are standing by. Unless you think you can swim the twenty feet, of course."

What Chabot did not know was that a leadership change had taken place that morning while he and the *Finback* were underway to the island. A new district commander in the form of a rear admiral from headquarters. From the district operations center, he had taken personal command of the operation.

The order came down within minutes. From district to sector to *Finback*. Do what the HSC directs.

When Chabot got the word from *Finback*, he told the coxswain to bring the MLB alongside the lobster boat. The crew put the fenders out and prepared to secure the two boats. Tying on to the vessel to be boarded wasn't standard operating procedure. Normally, the Coast Guard vessel came alongside to allow the boarding team to transfer, and then stand off a short distance. But this time, Chabot wanted to keep a close watch on the HSC officers. On the VHF, Chabot apologized to the lobster boat captain for the delay and asked for his continued cooperation.

"I take it, Chief, you understand now who's in charge." Chabot kept silent in the face of Miller's insult and kept his attention on the boarding.

The boats secured, Chabot finally spoke to Miller. "We're secured. You can go aboard the boat. Miller, have you ever done a maritime boarding before?"

"How hard could it be?" Chabot could only think, *what a prick*. The only enjoyment Chabot would get that morning might be if Miller stumbled trying to get aboard the lobster boat deck. *Shame the seas aren't a little rougher today*.

Two HSC officers remained on the MLB. Miller and another officer awkwardly got aboard the lobster boat. Chabot could see Miller on the boat's aft deck, waving his hands to call the skipper and his crewmen to come talk to him, while he sent the other officer to look below.

Chabot couldn't hear it all, but he saw things were getting heated. He was just leaving the cockpit when he heard the shot. He saw Miller had his pistol out, holding it in a two-handed grip, pointing it lower toward the deck. He couldn't see the lobsterman until he reached the MLB's gunwale. A man was down on the deck. It took a couple of seconds for Chabot to realize that Miller shot the man.

"WHAT HAPPENED? WHAT DID YOU DO?" Miller didn't answer. He stood frozen in place.

Chabot ordered the MLB's EMT crewmember to the lobster boat. He yelled at Miller to put his gun down. The other two HSC officers on the MLB stood there, stunned by what had happened. Chabot yelled at them, "You two stay right where you are. Do not move." He told the coxswain to radio *Finback*, brief them on what happened, and then contact sector to request MEDEVAC by helicopter.

The EMT was already treating the man. Miller backed away toward the stern, slowly holstering his weapon. Chabot called out, "Is he alive?" He yelled twice to be heard over the engine noise and yelling men. "Yes, senior chief. Alive, but serious. Maybe shot through his right lung. Exit wound out his back. He needs MEDEVAC now! Get the litter over here so we can bring him aboard the MLB."

While the EMT was talking, the other lobster boat crewman decided on a different course of action. He grabbed the second HSC officer on his boat, wrestling him to the edge of the boat. For a second or two, Chabot entertained the idea of letting him throw the HSC guy overboard. *But no. That wouldn't help. And we'd have to rescue him. Too much trouble.*

Chabot leapt onboard the lobster boat, ignoring Miller. He grabbed the Canadian from behind and struggled to pull him away from the HSC officer. Chabot wasn't a big man. Hardly 5 foot 8 inches but fit for his age. The Canadian wasn't much taller, but much heavier and much, much angrier. "Easy, easy son. We want to help your skipper. We're getting in the way of the medic. We need to get him on our boat. We've called for a MEDEVAC." Chabot kept repeating himself, speaking softer and softer each time. The crewman released the officer. The HSC officer thanked the senior chief. Chabot swore at him. "You dumb bastards. You did this. Get off this man's boat. Now! Miller, you too! Get off this boat!"

"Senior chief, *Finback* wants to talk to you! And MEDEVAC's here!" The MLB coxswain pointed to the southeast. A big Canadian CH-149 Cormorant rescue helicopter, easily recognizable in its brilliant yellow paint scheme. Chabot had two near simultaneous thoughts. *Yeah, I'll bet she wants to talk to me. How'd that helo get here so fast?* Chabot let that question go for now, ordering the MLB to prepare for a helicopter evac while he contacted the *Finback*.

"*Finback*, 47-232. HSC officer shot a Canadian lobsterman. We're preparing for an evac to the helicopter. Over." Chabot was about to supply more details, but he saw the helicopter move off, to hover over the island. As the helicopter rotated, he saw something strange. *A door gunner? What's going on?*

"*Finback*, 232. Are you in contact with helicopter? Over."

"232, *Finback*, Negative. We did not call for MEDEVAC. The helo just showed up. Stand by."

Half a minute later, *Finback* radioed Chabot. "232, *Finback*. The helo was unaware of the MEDEVAC. They dispatched in response to HSC taking the island. The helo will now assist in MEDEVAC. Be advised, more Canadian forces are enroute. Over."

Chabot acknowledged the message, but the part about "more Canadian forces" didn't register in his mind. He was too busy seeing to the MEDEVAC. By then, the wounded Canadian was aboard the MLB and being prepped in the litter for a lift up to the helicopter. With the Cormorant helicopter now hovering above the MLB as they both pointed into the wind, the helicopter's hoist lowered a cable. An MLB crewmember used a special wand to discharge static electricity before grasping the cable and attaching it to the litter. It lifted off the deck and into the helicopter. In a matter of seconds, the helicopter headed for Nova Scotia.

Chabot now turned his attention to the HSC officers on the lobster boat and the MLB. Miller was still standing on the aft deck of the lobster boat, with the other HSC officer close by. The two on the MLB found a corner in the MLB cabin to hide away. *What do I do with these guys?*

At almost the same moment, a warning came over VHF channel 16. "U.S. Coast Guard, U.S. Coast Guard operating near Machias Seal Island. This is HMCS *Summerside*. Acknowledge. Over" *Finback* acknowledged the Canadians. Chabot got the order to maintain position while *Finback* contacted sector.

Chabot checked the MLB's radar. It showed the image of what must be the Canadian warship. He looked up with his binoculars. There she was, on a bearing of forty degrees from their position. She was passing the southwest point of Grand Manan Island. In his head, Chabot calculated the warship was only eight nautical miles away. Using the radar to plot her progress, he mentally calculated their new friends on the *Summerside* would arrive in 30 minutes or so.

Issues with the Canadian Navy are best left with an officer. *Finback* will handle it. Chabot had something else to deal with. He went back aboard the lobster boat. He asked the second lobsterman if he could pilot his boat back to port. Though clearly shaken by the shooting, he told Chabot he could.

Chabot wasn't so sure. He asked the lobsterman again. This time though, he asked for his name. "Eddie. I'm Eddie. Eddie Gladstone. You know that man you shot. He's, my father. You shot my father."

My God. Jesus. What do you say? Chabot could only tap the man on his shoulder before turning to head back to the MLB. He saw Miller and the other guy still on the lobster boat. Chabot went aft. With barely controlled anger, Chabot said "I told you to get aboard the MLB. Go. Now."

Miller and his partner finally unfroze themselves and clumsily climbed aboard the MLB. Chabot directed the MLB crew to let go the lines tethering the two boats together.

Chabot watched as the lobster boat sailed away toward Grand Manan, thinking, *Jesus. Yeah, we shot him. Miller shot him. Miller shot your dad. Never should have happened. I will not let this go any further.*

Chabot told Miller to gather his officers together on the MLB's fantail. An odd sense of detachment came over Chabot. He brought two other armed MLB crewmembers with him.

"Miller, you and your team should know the condition of the man who was shot. My EMT tells me he suffered a gunshot wound to his right chest, piercing his lung, and creating an exit wound. A sucking chest wound, he said. He treated him, but his outlook is doubtful. In one way, he's lucky. It's SOP that those Canadian helicopters have crewmembers aboard called SAR technicians. SAR Techs, for short. Very highly trained. Expert combat medics. They're as good as our Air Force Pararescuemen.

"My EMT says he saw the whole thing. You went aboard and confronted the man. He objected to being boarded. You yelled back and swore at him. You drew your pistol and pointed it at him. The man started to back up a step, but you kept yelling. He yelled back. He yelled for you to put away you gun. You didn't. Then you shot him. He didn't attack you. He was moving away from you. That's what the EMT saw and that is what he is putting down in a written statement right now. You better hope that lobsterman doesn't die."

Until then, Chabot kept his cool. No more.

"Miller, you know who you shot? His name is Gladstone. That other crewman? That's his son Eddie. You shot his father! Why did you shoot his father?"

Miller didn't answer and Chabot was in no mood to wait. For the first time in his career, Chabot drew his sidearm in a confrontation, holding it in a two handed grip, but aimed to the deck. The two Coast Guardsmen with him followed his lead. Chabot ordered the HSC to disarm.

"You and your people are a danger to my crew. You and your men will surrender your weapons. Unbuckle your equipment belts and slowly drop them to the deck. Then move to your right, to the starboard side, away from the weapons."

The HSC officers looked back and forth to each other. None spoke. Finally, one officer, the one who was on the lobster boat with Miller, unbuckled his belt and guided it slowly to the deck. The other two followed his lead. The MLB crew motioned for them toward starboard side, and ordered them to get on their knees, hands clasped on their heads. The three complied without a word.

Miller didn't comply. He somehow regained his inflated sense of importance. "Chief, no goddamn way. Like hell I will! I . . ."

Chabot aimed his weapon at Miller's chest. Center mass. "Miller, do as I say!" The two other MLB crewmen did the same. One of the HSC officers, Chabot didn't see who, pleaded with Miller to give up his weapon. It didn't matter. Miller moved his hand to the weapon's grip.

Chabot again loudly said, "You will drop your weapon! Drop it!" He repeated it. And again.

"Screw it. Doesn't matter. We won't face charges." Miller slowing moved his hand away from his holstered pistol. He unbuckled his equipment belt and let it crash on the deck. Keeping his weapon aimed at Miller, Chabot ordered him to join his fellow officers at the starboard side, on his knees, hands on his head.

With the officers disarmed, Chabot told the Coast Guardsmen to handcuff the officers.

"Hey, chiefy." Miller was back to his old self. "You know who'll face charges. You. No doubt." Chabot tried his best to ignore Miller. It was hard, though, to dismiss the thought.

Finback and the MLB remained on scene as it seemed the whole Canadian Navy arrived all at once. There was the HMCS *Summerside*, standing only a hundred feet away, with her guns out. Its main gun, a 25-millimeter autocannon, and at least one fifty caliber machine gun, trained on the Coast Guard cutter. There were also sailors on deck, armed with rifles aimed their way.

Two large gray helicopters arrived. Canadian Navy for sure. Chabot couldn't identify the type, but they looked like the Cormorant. These had two door guns. He watched as one circled the island as the second sank in altitude to hover just a foot or so off the ground, about fifty yards south of the helipad. Out leapt troops. Lots of troops with lots of guns. At least a dozen.

Once they were out, the helicopter lifted up to circle the island with door guns aimed on the buildings.

Over the VHF radio, came the message, "U.S. Coast Guard, HMCS *Summerside*. Canadian forces are landing on Machias Seal Island. An incoming U.S. helicopter of Customs and Border Protection was warned away. Do not interfere with our landing. Repeat. Do not interfere."

In the distance, Chabot could see troops fast roping to the ground from the second helicopter, just north of the lighthouse compound. At the same time, the other helicopter provided cover while broadcasting for the HSC agents to surrender.

The HSC agents on the island apparently concluded the fight wouldn't end well for them. With the building surrounded by troops, Chabot saw a white bedsheet waving out one of the windows. First, the two Coast guardsmen, Mark and Dave, came out. A minute later, the four HSC officers marched out, hands on their heads. Not a shot was fired.

Stripped of their gear and handcuffed, the HSC officers were led onto a waiting helicopter.

A Canadian soldier went over to the flagpole. He saw his nation's flag caught on the ground, wrapped by the wind around the base of the pole. The soldier called over his comrades. They hauled down the U.S. flag and saluted as they raised the Canadian Maple Leaf. Another had idea to record it all on his mobile phone.

Chabot reckoned, *not exactly Iwo Jima, but still a pretty good look.*

Mark and Dave, reinforced by four soldiers, remained on the island as the two helicopters left for Nova Scotia with four more HSC officers in custody.

Stand Off

HMCS *Summerside* kept the *Finback* and the MLB in place for the next two hours, demanding the Coast Guard turn over the HSC officers held in custody on the MLB. *Finback's* commanding officer briefed sector, who briefed district, who briefed headquarters, who consulted with Homeland Security, the State Department, and the White House.

The Canadians thought their position was straightforward. Miller shot and seriously wounded a Canadian citizen in Canadian waters without any imaginable justification. Therefore, he and the others must be turned over to Canadian authorities. Aboard the *Summerside*, an RCMP officer was ready to do just that. In addition, the landing of HSC officers on the island was a violation of Canadian sovereignty. The HSC officers captured on the island would face charges which may include kidnapping the two lightkeepers stationed on the island.

The American government thought differently. They refused to turn over the HSC officers. They were on a United States vessel, which was sovereign territory. No Canadians would be allowed to board the U.S. Coast Guard vessels. In addition, the Coast Guard vessels were not in Canadian waters as the United States had claims to the island and its surrounding waters.

Chabot's position much simpler. Let the Canadians have them all and let's go home.

Finback's skipper took the cutter's rigid hull inflatable over to the *Summerside* to meet face to face with her commanding officer. Chabot mentioned to the MLB coxswain that was a lot to put on the shoulders of a lieutenant junior grade. The petty officer's response startled the senior chief.

"Yeah, senior chief. Jesus. I don't like this. That HSC bastard back there, he shot that Canadian. No reason at all. I mean, I saw it!"

Chabot could only say, "Yeah, I know."

"Senior chief, have a look out there! There's a very big gun pointed right at us. Can you tell me why we might have to fight, fight and die, just to save that guy's sorry ass? Can you?"

"Petty officer, we will carry out our orders. Doesn't matter what we think."

"Yes, senior chief. We will carry out our orders. No matter if they are absolutely wrong."

Chabot almost started to chew out the coxswain but held back. It was as if his own words to Meyer echoed back to him. All Chabot could do was put his hand on the coxswain's shoulder, to reassure him that all would be well.

The next hour passed quietly as both sides waited for instructions from the higher authorities who, conveniently for them, didn't have their lives on the line. Then Chabot saw the main deck gun on the Canadian warship turning its aim away from them. At the same time, the *Finback's* commander was headed back to her ship. The answer came a couple of minutes later.

"232, *Finback*. We have permission from the *Summerside* to withdraw. You may return to the station. The HSC officers on the MLB will remain on board. Upon arrival at the station, they will be taken into custody by the FBI. Over."

Chabot slapped the coxswain on the back in a small gesture of the relief he and his crew felt. *Christ, we almost went to war, over what? A tiny island with a lighthouse, puffins, and lobsters.* He went below to tell Miller they'd be handed over to the FBI once they reached Jonesport. Miller didn't seem to react. But yeah, Chabot came around to the idea that Miller was right. He had a feeling the bastards would get away with this.

Senior chief later learned that negotiations resulted in a promise by the American government to investigate the shooting and if justified, the officer involved will be prosecuted under U.S. law. It wasn't at all satisfactory to the Canadians, but now they had other immediate concerns.

Freedom of Navigation

Until Chabot's return to Jonesport, he was unaware that what the Canadian media was calling the Battle of Machias Seal Island was only one element of a campaign launched by his commander-in-chief against Canada.

That Wednesday night, after turning the HSC officers over to the FBI, Chabot and the commanding officer of the *Finback* called sector to report on the Machias Seal Island operation. That done, Capt. Llewellyn said, "I'm meeting with the staff here in a few minutes, so I have to cut this call short. One thing though. I don't know if you heard. News out of Canada. That lobsterman. He died. I'm, ah, sorry to tell you that. I know you did all you could."

In the sector operations center, the captain met with Meyer and Miles. "Gentlemen, let's go over what we know is happening. Keep it to our area of responsibility. Commander Meyer?"

"Sir, I'll start with Station Eastport." Meyer reviewed their patrol activity, focusing on the boarding of a Canadian vessel that ventured into U.S. waters. The Canadians responded in kind, ordering a U.S. cargo ship headed for Eastport to stay out of Canadian waters. The Canadian Navy's NTOG team off the HCMS *Glace Bay* shadowed the station's small boats wherever it went.

CBP Blackhawk helicopters, based out of the former Loring Air Force Base near Limestone, Maine, were patrolling the border, from Quoddy Narrows all the way north to Fort Kent, Maine. They flew very low over the Saint Croix River. One helicopter hovered close to the *Glace Bay*. That prompted a warning from the warship.

"I have to admit to frustration here, captain. Here we are, keeping our people a respectful distance from their ship. We alert them by radio whenever our boats came nearby. Now these CBP, ah, pilots, maneuver near the *Glace Bay* in a threatening manner. Our crews confirmed their helos had mounted door guns. *Glace Bay* warned CBP by radio. When CBP did not move away, *Glace Bay* turned her main deck gun toward them."

"Commander, sounds like you wanted to use a word other than 'pilots.' Frankly, I can think of a few myself. For now, I'll call them irresponsible. *Glace Bay's* captain did exactly as I would. Defend the ship."

"Captain, CBP's tactics and the Canadian response could spill over onto our people. I recommend we contact district and request they talk to CBP. Get them to stop these, frankly, foolish tactics."

"I'll call district about CBP after this meeting. Obviously, we can't have them threatening the Canadian Navy. Endangers our people. Next." Meyers continued.

"Sir, on the chart we've plotted the current position and course of the *Sitkinak*. She's in position along the Maine coastline, as we planned. *Finback's* preparing for a quick turnaround."

"We've also plotted the *Escanaba* and the *Campbell*. Atlantic Area ordered they take position in international waters at the mouth of the Bay of Fundy. They should be there by first light tomorrow." The new commandant sortied the 270-foot cutters from Boston and Newport, Rhode Island.

"Perhaps knowing the 270s were enroute, with greater firepower than their ship, may explain why the Canadians backed off on their demand for the HSC officers. But that's speculation on my part."

"You might be right, commander, but let's leave speculation out of this for now. What else?"

Mildly admonished, Meyers went on.

"Captain, the Navy, excuse me, the United States Navy, diverted a destroyer to take position in the Bay of Fundy. Another U.S. destroyer is taking position off Halifax. Watching CBC, there's video of one of their frigates leaving CFB Halifax. CBC said their Navy announced this as a response to our destroyer.

"Then we have CBC reporting of a near collision between one of their long-range maritime patrol aircraft, a CP-140 Aurora, with a U.S. Navy P-8 Poseidon. We don't know if this incident was intentional or simply accidental. The P-8s are patrolling international airspace around Nova Scotia. They're staging out of Air National Guard Base Cape Cod."

"Any other ship movements we know of, commander?"

"That's the thing, sir. We aren't in the loop for U.S. Navy ship or aircraft movements. Or Canadian Navy. Or NATO ships. I do remember a news item about the French carrier, the *Charles de Gaulle*, and her escorts, operating somewhere off Newfoundland. Plus, NATO's Standing Naval Forces Atlantic is reportedly operating more on this side of the Atlantic. It's a multinational task force of four to maybe six destroyers and frigates. No information on anyone's submarines, of course. Anyway, we'll have to rely on the news media, and, of course, Atlantic Area."

"Any public statements from our Navy?"

"Only one. Essentially, it says the U.S. Navy is conducting Freedom of Navigation patrols in disputed areas. Hence, the two destroyers and the P-8s." Meyers stopped himself from offering his opinion of the situation. He needn't have. The captain did.

Staring down at the chart table, the captain said in a quieter voice, as if he didn't want anyone else in the room to hear, "Commander, somehow, I wouldn't have thought you conduct Freedom of Navigation patrols in areas where there is not a disputed boundary, like around Nova Scotia."

He went back to his command voice.

"Very well. I think I have a good picture of what *we* are doing. But when I call district, I'll also ask about U.S. Navy actions around here. See if we can't be put in the loop. If war comes, it'd be nice to know since we're on the front line."

Meyer and Miles both snapped looks at each other, as if they had the same thought. The duty officers in the operations center did the same. The captain said, war.

The captain looked up at them, and realized his mistake. Should not have used that word. "Relax, everyone. I doubt, seriously doubt, it would come to that. And in comparison, to the destroyers and such, I guess we're just a bit player."

The Captain redirected himself to his staff.

"Gentlemen, talk to your people. Don't downplay the seriousness of these events. But don't make the mistake I just did. Don't inflame emotions right now. We carry out our lawful orders. Understood?"

Now Miles spoke. "Captain, may I have a word with you? In private?"

"Sure. Let me call district first, then I'll see you."

Would They Follow Orders?

"Well, Mr. Miles. You wanted to speak to me?"

"Captain, I didn't want to talk about this in front of the other staff."

"Very well, go on."

"Sir, what if something else goes wrong in this operation? A mistake is made. Like what if that P-8 even accidentally collided with the Canadian plane? Or the *Glace Bay* fired on the CBP helo? There could be a reflexive response, a misinterpretation, by one side. A fight could start."

"Yes, that's always a possibility. For our forces, we just have to do everything we can to avoid that. Your memo on our rules of engagement helped. I assure you I am aware of the danger."

Miles realized he may have overstepped. "No, sir, I do not mean to doubt your awareness of the situation. Not at all."

"Then, Mr. Miles, let's get it out. What are you most concerned about?"

"Captain, I'm worried that a fight will start. By accident or design. I don't doubt the outcome. The U.S. Navy can overcome any potential adversary. That's not the issue. The issue is that those potential adversaries out there were until recently, our allies. Our friends."

"Lieutenant, I share your feel . . ." Miles cut off the captain.

"Captain, we've already directly supported, well, sir, I don't know how else to put it, an attack on the Canadians. Ferrying those HSC guys out to Machias Seal Island. They shot and killed a Canadian lobsterman."

"Mr. Miles, those men were handed over to the FBI. *We* handed them over. It'll be investigated and if warranted, those men will be charged. You know how this works." The captain leaned forward across the desk. "You know I have no love for these HSC people, but we have to trust that the judicial system will act."

"Captain, I'm not sure I can. If the administration felt any responsibility over that man's death, then why are they still deploying Navy ships and aircraft? I would think they'd pull back. Allow the diplomats and lawyers to sort this out. No, sir, Machias Seal Island was just one part of it. Deploying destroyers and our 270s makes me believe a larger plan is being conducted. To threaten the Canadian with military force."

"Lieutenant, I have to say, that sounds rather conspiratorial on your part."

"Captain, if the order comes to fight, I can't do that. I cannot, directly or indirectly, support firing upon the Canadians. Or the NATO allies." Miles wasn't sure he kept his tone in line with military decorum.

"Stop right there, Miles! If the order comes, a legal order, against a legitimate military target, you will obey orders!" The captain uncharacteristically showed real anger toward the young lieutenant.

Miles reached into his blouse pocket and withdrew a folder piece of paper. He handed it to the captain. "Sir, this is my letter of resignation."

The captain unfolded the paper and read the letter. It was only one line of text. No explanation. The captain felt his anger dissipate and he wasn't sure why. When Llewellyn looked up, he started to talk, but Miles interrupted him once more.

"Captain. Please, I did not reach this decision lightly. I have the greatest respect for you. I do not in any way mean my letter as criticism of you or the Coast Guard. But a man died out by that island. I'm afraid others will die. That seems likely given the deployment of Coast Guard and Navy warships. This government is directing us to participate in a fight that is without any justification. Without any sense of morality. Sir, it's wrong." He wanted to say criminally wrong, but he held that back.

A long, awful moment passed before the captain spoke. He admitted to himself, *the young man is right. This is all wrong. But right now, I don't have the luxury of opting out. I am the commanding officer. My job is to hold all this together. To see that orders, lawful orders, are carried out. Then again, I wonder how many others feel the same way as Miles.*

"Lieutenant Miles. Douglas." *That was the first time he ever called me by my first name,* Miles thought. "You're a top-notch officer. Accomplished. An expert in what you do. I don't want . . ." Llewellyn stopped, struggling to find the right words.

"Doug let's step back. Can you allow me a few days before I accept the resignation? Can you hold off, officially, till let's say Monday? We'll meet Monday morning, 0800. It's almost Thursday, so that'll give you, what, four days to think it all over. By then, if you want this to go through, I will endorse it. I'll hate doing that, but I will. Then again, if you change your mind, let's burn the letter and forget we ever talked."

"Yes, captain. That makes sense. Monday then. 0800."

"Good." The captain leaned back in his desk chair, rubbing his hands over his face. "A long, difficult day." Miles remained silent. Almost without thinking, the captain released the tension in his mind.

"You know, I've been wondering the same myself. Kinda the same thing that's troubling you."

"Sorry, Mr. Miles. I'm not being clear. Let me try again. Suppose it does come to a fight. Let's say that U.S. Navy destroyer off Halifax is ordered to sink a Canadian frigate. I wonder if the destroyer's commanding officer would carry out that order. Might refuse. And if he or she did not refuse, I wonder if the ship's officers would refuse. And how would the crew react?

"Frankly, I don't think our national leadership has considered that possibility. I think they're moving headlong into this without any thought of its effect. Its morality. You're right in that."

For just a moment, Miles thought he saw the captain's eyes well up. "Lieutenant, don't repeat what I just said to anyone else."

The Power of an Image

Reports of the engagement between U.S. and Canadian forces swept across Canadian and world media. The Battle of Machias Seal Island, as it was first called, was a clear Canadian victory. The island was retaken, the U.S. Coast Guard sent on its way, and Homeland Security Corps had four more of their officers in a Canadian jail. Canada, 14. HSC, 0.

On Thursday morning, the Prime Minister spoke from his office, condemning the raid and the killing of a Canadian civilian. He demanded the extradition of the other HSC officers involved. A futile gesture perhaps to extradite these men, he admitted privately, but one that must be taken. Meanwhile, the captured HSC officers would be charged under Canadian law.

The PM said there would be more moves and countermoves by the government, but such things can take time.

As it turned out, social media lead the counterattack.

In the hours that followed the Battle of Machias Seal Island, LeClerc and his team set aside time to browse the internet for the news and popular reaction. He remembered the director saying, ". . . it is the public opinion of Americans that might be our greatest defensive weapon. A way to stop conflict before it starts." LeClerc knew CSIS had weeks ago engaged a dedicated team in Ottawa to become social media influencers in support of Canada. As it turned out, that team was like a dingy trying to outrace a cigarette boat. No contest. The social media consuming public zipped ahead.

Never underestimate the power of a manipulated picture mated with witty dialogue. Almost immediately, memes raced across social media. One showed a puffin emblazoned with the Canadian Maple Leaf across its white feathered breast, with the caption "Care to try again?" Another captioned the puffin with a quote from Shakespeare's *A Midsummer Night's Dream*, "And though she may be but little, She is fierce!"

Amusing, thought LeClerc, and that was the point. Ridicule the opponent. Gather people who are "in" on the joke, and they will spread the message faster than a novelist's post-apocalyptic virus. Twitter Likes soared into the tens of millions. Instagram and Facebook spread the brave little puffins just as quickly.

But the most popular meme might have been a matched pair of photographs, not intended at all to be satiric. One showed the Canadian flag lying on the ground, wrapped by the wind around the base of the island's flagpole. The photo paired with it showed Canadian soldiers raising the flag back up, while soldiers saluted. Video of those moments, taken by the soldiers them-selves, played again and again on televisions across the world.

Amazon soon reported a surge in sales of Pro-Canada merchandise. Ca-nadian flags and pins. T-shirts with the Maple Leaf. T-shirts with the puffin memes.

The memes and paraphernalia helped shift public opinion toward Can-ada, LeClerc had no doubt. But public opinion is fickle and short-lived, to say the least. There must be other things. Again, the world moved faster than he could have imagined.

The sport born in Canada made the next move. The closed border did not stop Canadian athletes and teams from playing their league opponents in the United States. After all, there were championships to be won and money to be made. Now that would change.

It was one of those moments in history when most everyone remembers where they were and what they were doing. On Sunday, LeClerc was in Hal-ifax that afternoon to discuss with the director the review of *Operation North-ern Lights* by CSIS and Canadian Forces Military Intelligence. NATO was like-wise ready to render judgement on its authenticity. A secure videoconference among all the intelligence players was scheduled for the next day, and the Director wanted LeClerc to be ready to participate. So far, no leaks to the press, but all knew that wouldn't last. At least as far as LeClerc knew, his asset Col. Byron hadn't been found out.

Henry had said we had three weeks at most. That was six days ago.

As LeClerc and the director were taking a break from their preparations, the announcement came over the television. The players of the league leading *Montreal Canadiens* would suspend their season play with any teams in the United States, in protest of the Saint Andrews Raid and the Battle of Machias Seal Island.

The director, LeClerc and three others in the break room stood silently as they watched the news. It was LeClerc who spoke first.

"Did we have a hand in that?"

"No. I am certain we didn't. But I wish we had."

"I thought something like this might happen. Still, you don't believe it until it happens."

"You know, there could be more of that coming our way. But this hockey thing. Might hit people hard. Harder than anything we could have said."

By the late evening, the other six teams with home ice in Canada followed suit. Canadians playing for the U.S. based teams quickly joined the walkout.

Given that approximately 40% of NHL's players are Canadian, the league had no choice. Four days after the battle, the entire season was suspended.

Authentic: Monday Morning After Machias Seal Island

The major general commanding Canadian Forces Intelligence Command put it well, in LeClerc's opinion. Via secure teleconference that linked Ottawa to NATO headquarters in Brussels, he was briefing selected members of the NATO Military Intelligence Committee.

"We have high confidence in the intelligence confirming a build-up of U.S. forces at Fort Drum, New York. We have U.S. news reports, local television, radio, newspaper, and social media postings by persons living in the area, confirming the deployment of the 2nd Armored Brigade Combat Team of the U.S 3rd Infantry Division out of Fort Stewart, Georgia, to Fort Drum. Armor, artillery, engineers. Plus, the 3rd Division's Combat Aviation Brigade and its sustainment brigade for logistical support.

"We can also confirm the movement of supplies by rail and cargo aircraft. Fuel, food, and munitions. Medical supplies. And the vehicles necessary to logistically support a division sized formation in the field."

Satellite images obtained from a commercial source flashed across the videoconference screens. They showed shipments by rail and air of munitions of all types, trucks bringing the munitions to the base weapons depot, as well as temporary weapons depots set up in the base's woodland training fields.

The next images made a before and after comparison of the Fort Drum area. "Tanks and other vehicles of the armored brigade continue to arrive, being off loaded from the rail cars and from transport aircraft. Here are four C-17 cargo aircraft on the airfield's tarmac, plus a significant number of helicopters. Quite crowded there. The flights are continuing around the clock.

"We estimate that a third of the armored brigade has reached Fort Drum. In one week, it will be fully deployed.

"U.S. Army public statements say they will be conducting winter maneuvers on the base. We do not find that credible. To move so many resources forward, off all types, at such an expense, supports the conclusion this is not merely an exercise. Maneuvers do not require munitions in these quantities. And the build-up is continuing."

The major general turned to the director of the CSIS Ottawa Region.

"We have human sources in that area of New York. Not in the base, but in nearby Watertown. These sources confirm the build-up. I hope you will understand that I cannot go into any detail on those sources."

LeClerc and the Atlantic Region director, both sitting out of sight at the CSIS director's secure conference room in Ottawa, nodded in professional admiration of the CSIS Ottawa Region for that little nugget. The major general continued by pointing out that the deployments match the order of battle called for in their order *Operation Northern Lights*. The general then summed up.

"I've served ten years working with the Americans. NATO, Afghanistan. I've seen countless of their operations orders. This order, *Operation Northern Lights*, matches their style, format. How it specifically identifies actual military units and the timetable. The detail of the logistical planning. This does not match an operation order for an exercise. This is not conceptual. This is more than contingency planning. This took time to put together. Yes, Canadian Forces Intelligence assesses the plan as authentic, and it is being executed."

He began his summation. "We project a force of approximately 14,000 soldiers, fully equipped and provisioned, positioned only 150 kilometers from Ottawa.

"Let's hypothesize that America achieved strategic surprise. That we did not know of *Operation Northern Lights*. Their air assault elements of the 10th Mountain could seize Parliament Hill in two to three hours. Assuming they capture intact at least one of the bridges over the Saint Lawrence, their tanks could join them in two days, maybe one."

NATO Military Intelligence Committee Chair was equally forthright in his assessment, flatly stating there was a high level of confidence in the authenticity of the document and agreement in the buildup of the American forces.

The committee chair went on to say, "Tomorrow, NATO will invoke Article Five in response to the American administration's attempted seizure of Machias Seal Island and their aggressive naval maneuvers. This is no secret. They know this will happen. Yet, their buildup and their naval activity continues. Common sense tells us they were not deterred by Article Five."

"At the request of France and the United Kingdom, the United Nations Security Council will meet on Wednesday this week to discuss American aggression toward Canada. The U.S., of course, objected. However, Russia and China did not object."

LeClerc recalled an analysis of the U.N. votes then making the rounds. Why didn't Russia and China join with the United States' objection? After all, the president was doing all he could to befriend Russia. No one knew for sure, but the analysis offered a fairly simple hypothesis. The humiliation and isolation of the United States by her former allies was too sweet a prize for them to pass up.

The meeting ended somberly with the committee chair saying, "There we have it. We all agree the document is authentic." The chair then added a cautionary note.

"We have their operations plan. We know the details of their buildup. Yet, I must point out what we lack. We do not know why the Americans are preparing to invade Canada. That is a serious deficit. However, we are left with no choice other than to take their plan and capabilities seriously and prepare for our collective defense. We do not have much time. The timetable of their means that NATO could be at war with the United States in one to two weeks."

Before thanking the attendees, the chair said he would personally brief the NATO secretary general within the hour and recommended the Prime Ministers of the NATO members be immediately briefed. "Decisions have to be made very soon indeed."

As it turned out, no one questioned LeClerc or his regional director. They were only there in case any of the senior participants asked how this intelligence coup came about. LeClerc had already faced hours and hours of interrogation by skeptical CSIS and Canadian Forces Intelligence, as well as by the intelligence services of Great Britain and France. Like skilled anatomists removing organs from a cadaver, their agents dissected every moment, every word, every movement of LeClerc's meeting with Byron.

LeClerc survived the questioning. The entire intelligence establishment of NATO verified the documents. LeClerc felt somehow vindicated. His country had their adversary's attack plan. There would be no strategic surprise. No Pearl Harbor. No 9/11. Canada and her allies would be prepared. Canada would act.

Well, maybe. Their political leaders and generals had to believe the intel was real and then have the courage to act. Often, leaders did not. McClellan always imagined Lee's army to be far larger than it actually was. Stalin refused to accept intelligence warnings of impending Nazi invasion. Even days after it happened, he couldn't believe Hitler betrayed him. After hearing of Pearl Harbor, MacArthur in the Philippines went inexplicitly silent for a day. He left his Air Force without orders and on the ground when the Japanese destroyed his planes at Clark Field.

They had to be sure LeClerc wasn't working for the other side. They had to be sure the document wasn't a ruse designed to trap NATO. They had to sure enough of their conclusions if they were to convince the heads of state of the world's remaining democratic powers.

The Old Man

"Robert, I appreciate the offer, but I think I'll stay."

LeClerc's CSIS team in Fredericton was spending the bulk of their working hours scouring media outlets for any hint of a leak. Any news about any U.S. military unit in all of New England relevant to the operation. Any word about his asset Colonel Henry Byron. So far, nothing.

There was someone else LeClerc worried about. The Monday evening of the NATO videoconference he called the old man.

"Listen, my friend. You've already done a great service. We shouldn't expect more. We could easily get you here. You can join your family. I'm saying this because things are not good. Things could get dangerous. Dangerous for you."

The danger was no secret. LeClerc didn't divulge any deeply classified intel. Turn on the cable TV and it was all there. Extensive, round the clock media coverage of aggressive U.S. Navy forays around Nova Scotia.

And more in the Pacific. A U.S. destroyer took position south of the Canadian Navy's main naval base, CFB Esquimalt, British Columbia. Another destroyer waited in international waters where the Strait of de Fuca met the Pacific Ocean. Navy patrol aircraft ran along the coast of British Columbia, flying only barely outside Canadian airspace. Day and night, U.S. Coast Guard, U.S. Navy and CBP helicopters patrolled the boundary from the Strait of Georgia to the Pacific. In media video of their night operations, they were seen flying low and using their high intensity searchlights to broadcast their presence to all.

In practical terms, a blockade of Canada was only a single order away.

"Please remember. I can't be sure Lieutenant Miles didn't include mention of you in a report."

The old man's stubbornness anguished and frustrated LeClerc. The old man wouldn't budge. He would stay where he's always been and where he is going to end. He thanked LeClerc and hung up. As he put the phone down, he said to the empty room, "I'm sorry, Robert."

The evening of the next day, the old man called his son in Halifax and his daughter in Boston. He kept the conversation light. Everything's fine. Just wanted to chat. How's my grandkids? Yeah, a lot's been happening around here, but it doesn't involve me. I pay it no mind. He planned to make a more truthful phone call, some day.

The old man regretted putting LeClerc in such a difficult position, but he couldn't bring himself to leave his home. This is where he grew up, married, and raised his children. His wife died in this house. Should they come for him, so be it. His last decision may be how to make proper use of his deer rifle.

CHAPTER SIXTEEN

SURPRISE

The United Nations

Debbie hadn't returned to her clinic yet, though by this Wednesday morning she knew she should. I need something to do. Stay busy. Back up my words at the funeral. How long had it been since Mike . . . since Mike died?

Last Sunday, Anna returned to Ottawa. It was not an easy parting. The realization that her mother would be alone hit her hard. Oh, yes, Matt was living there now, but Anna knew that would end soon. Eventually, all his immigration paperwork would go through. And maybe he'll soon be in the Royal Canadian Navy. Matt explained that given his surface warfare experience, "I might get in as what they call a Direct-Entry Officer. Skip the Royal Military College in Ontario and get commissioned as a sub-lieutenant. Then to one of the Naval Fleet Schools at CFB Esquimalt or CFB Halifax. Kind of hoping for Halifax. 'Course, it's a big decision for them. I mean, they might see me as coming from an adversary. Kind of hoping for anything, really."

In the meantime, Matt could run all the household errands, fix anything that needed fixing, drive Mom wherever she needed to go, and keep the house in order. Mostly in order, Anna supposed.

And then there was Roy and Marge. And George and Cheryl. They came over as often as they could to check on her, but there'd still be long days when she was all alone. And nights. Anna began looking for work around Saint Andrews. She and Debbie talked a about it. As mothers do, she said she'd be fine, and it would be so much trouble and worried how that could affect Anna's career. Anna reminded her mother, "Mom, I have a Doctor of Optometry. There're eyeballs everywhere. I'm sure I can find a clinic around here to hire me."

At least her foot was healing up nicely. And the rib pain was gone. Mostly gone. And the house was fixed up. The smashed deck door was replaced, as Cpl. Jenkins promised. Not that they spent time these days looking out across the deck to the water. Looking out to where Michael died. Was killed.

Back to work, George seemed to be in better spirits. Cheryl told Debbie that George could have taken more time, but he just showed up one day and demanded to be put back on shift. "You know, Debbie, he needed to get back to work. He was underfoot around here. Maybe, I needed him to get back to work!"

To Debbie, the best thing that happened in the past few days was the departure of the Canadian Army soldiers. She and Anna had a nice send-off party in the house for them, thanking each of them. The soldiers were needed for her security, but for now Debbie felt a sense of privacy was just as vital.

Besides, a pretty good-sized Canadian warship was right out there, hovering around Saint Andrews. She often caught sight of it passing just beyond Navy Island, heading north, and then south, right through that spot on the river. Where she was taken. And then rescued.

Then there was that invitation from the Expat Committee. Maybe out of guilt, or need, or both, they invited Debbie to assume her husband's former role on the committee. She knew it'd be an added burden, given her medical duties. Given her grief. She called Morgan, who was temporarily in charge, to accept. "Morgan, I want you to know that Mike held you in high regard. He often said, if any expatriate needed something, you would do all that was possible to help. Well, let's get to work. When's the next meeting?"

She called her clinic right after she hung up with Morgan. "I'm coming back to work." She would hear none of their concerns that it was too soon, that maybe she needed more time, etcetera, etcetera. "Thank you, but I'm coming back Monday. Open up my appointments, please." So, for now, a few last days at home.

After she shared a lunch of roast beef sandwiches, pickles, and chips with Matt, they went to the living room. A live event on CBC and televised around the world. The United Nations Security Council was meeting in an emergency session to discuss the tensions between the United States and Canada.

Beforehand, Matt did a little research online. Though not a permanent member of the Security Council, last June Canada joined as a nonpermanent member. That in itself was a bit unusual since it should have fallen to another nation. Accusations that Canada "jumped the line" were particularly amplified by the United States, but the matter died down after a while. Especially after the other members, including Russia and China, made quite clear their support for Canada's new status.

In a display of expected theatrics, the White House had threatened to quit the United Nations.

"Well, mom, that threat didn't go too far. Someone must've reminded the White House that without a permanent member chair at the table, the Security Council could vote to send U.N. peacekeeping troops to protect Canada. But stay on the Security Council and they have the power to veto any resolution. But they can't use veto power to deny a member a nonpermanent place on the council. That would be like overturning an election. Not that, that ever happens."

According to the news anchor, only minutes ago the Canadian U.N. ambassador announced the Prime Minister himself would speak at the United Nation Security Council.

The Prime Minister's appearance was a carefully guarded diplomatic surprise. Appearance of a head of state was rare and usually done as a ceremonial gesture.

Looking for something to fill the time before it all started, Matt threw in a little history. "Even during the Cuban Missile Crisis, Kennedy didn't attend. Used his U.N. ambassador. Ah, Adeli, ah, no Ad*lai*, yeah, a, d, *l, a, i* Stevenson. Strange first name. Anyway, guess Kennedy was too busy. You know, with a nuclear war about to happen."

"Where'd you learn all that?"

"Saw it all in a movie. Oh, wait. Here's the Prime Minister."

After the introductions and the usual courtesies, the Prime Minister didn't waste time.

"The government of Canada has undeniable evidence that the government of the United States is preparing a significant military attack against Canada. I am here today to inform the world of the evidence in our possession."

Staff members began distributed materials to the council members as the Prime Minister announced Canada had the actual operations order. He went on to say Canada and NATO unanimously verified the authenticity of the document.

"Right now, the document is also being uploaded to the websites of Global Affairs Canada and NATO for all the world to see. The plan is called *Operation Northern Lights.* I welcome all the members of the United Nations to closely examine the plan.

"Let me be clear. This is not a conceptual outline of a far-fetched contingency plan. I only wish it were. No, it is precise. It is specific in its targets, the military units, the logistical needs. And the attack is being prepared at this very moment. The forces necessary for the attacked are assembling at Fort Drum, a U.S. Army base near Watertown, New York.

"We know the timetable. The attack is scheduled to start in less than two weeks, on or about December 1."

"It's objective. Ottawa."

Diplomatic decorum in the hall collapsed. Murmurs lifted into loud voices, even yelling. Ambassadors and their staffs frantically looked around. Other attendees stood up, moved randomly, called on cell phones, wandered from their seats as if they were searching for something. An astute observer would note that the ambassadors of Russia and China, after recovering from their initial surprise, seemed to enjoy the spectacle.

All the while, the ambassadors of the United Kingdom and France, both permanent members, sat stone-faced. They calmly waited for the Prime Minister to continue speaking.

Not so with the U.S. Ambassador. He turned frantically to his aides seated behind him, who immediately started calling on their cell phones. He raced through his copy of the plan, flipping pages madly back and forth. His face left no doubt. Panic.

The President of the Security Council called for order. Repeatedly. Once restored, the Prime Minister resumed. "Allow me to explain the elements of the plan and then show you the evidence of its implementation."

Point by point, the Prime Minister reviewed the military intelligence. On easels placed alongside the PM, the world saw the satellite images of the Fort Drum base and its airfield. Images of a growing number of armored vehicles and helicopters. An ammunition dump carved out of the woods. Fuel trucks. Self-propelled and towed artillery. He listed by name the military units now at the base, confirmed by local news reports in New York and Georgia. He emphasized the identified units precisely matched those called for in the operations plan.

"To move these enormous quantities of military resources, the decision to execute the plan must have been made long ago."

"Jesus, Matt. Like Stevenson. During the Cuban Missile Crisis."

The Prime Minister summed up this portion of the presentation by calling the evidence "incontestable, undeniable, and damning." He went on.

"The United States is about to execute a war of aggression against Canada. It continues to prepare even in the face of an invocation of Article Five by NATO. It continues to prepare, positioning its own warships to threaten our naval bases. It continues, as their forces aggressively patrol near our waters and airspace. It continues, as the United States attempted to solve a trivial, decades long border disagreement by force. I refer, of course, to what we in Canada call the Battle of Machias Seal Island.

"And what is the ultimate goal of *Operation Northern Lights*? I can tell you because it is explicitly stated in the plan. It arrogantly assumes a quick military victory following a surprise attack. Canada, then defeated, would be forced to subjugate its foreign policy to the United States. Canada would be forced to withdraw from NATO, be forced to accept trade policies that would cripple Canada economically and be forced to grant the United States access to our natural resources on terms little different than outright theft."

It was at this point the U.S. Ambassador abruptly left his seat and started to storm out of the hall. The Prime Minister called him out. "Mr. Ambassador! Go back to your seat! How dare you leave when you face an issue of such importance. An issue of peace . . . or war!"

The ambassador did return to his seat, but not of his own volition. One of the ambassador's aides followed after him and within a few steps grabbed the diplomat's arm, nearly dragging him back to his proper place. The aide wagged a cell phone in the ambassador's face.

"I wonder, Mom, if that guy is telling the ambassador someone wants him to stay put."

"Mr. President," the Prime Minister began, "may I offer my sincere apologies for my outburst toward the American ambassador. It was not behavior one should expect in a place of such importance and in such a moment in history." The council president assured the Prime Minister he may continue.

"Now it is time to say what Canada is doing to prepare."

The Prime Minister announced a full mobilization of their reserves. He had ordered Canadian Forces to a higher alert level. The Canadian Army had begun fortifying the bridges over the Saint Lawrence River, key to the American invasion plan. The bridges would be "defended, and if necessary, destroyed." Air defenses are being deployed in Ottawa. In the coming hours, NATO would announce a surge of reinforcements to Canada.

The Prime Minister then turned toward the U.S. ambassador.

"Mr. Ambassador, your colleagues from the United Kingdom and France are about to introduce a resolution that will ask members to institute economic and diplomatic sanctions against the United States. That resolution will also ask members to contribute troops to a peacekeeping force.

"No doubt, you will be instructed to veto those measures. So be it."

"Let me assure my countrymen and all who cherish their freedom across the globe, Canada will not become a vassal to the ego of one man's government. In the words of another Prime Minister, Canada will defend itself 'whatever the cost may be.'"

"None of us in Canada view the American people as our enemy. None of us at all. The American people are not the aggressors. They are our friends. And in uncounted instances, they are our family. We share a common history. All Canadians share the hope that the American people will demand a peaceful end to this crisis."

"No, it is not the American people who threaten Canada. It is the current U.S. administration that decided on this dangerous course of action."

"And honestly, even though we have the operational plans, we do not know why. Mr. Ambassador, perhaps you can answer that simple question. Why? Why are U.S. military forces being marshalled near our border? Why are naval forces now positioned off our naval bases? Why are warplanes flying so near to our territory? These things have never been done before. Again, Mr. Ambassador, why?"

The U.S. ambassador refused to answer the question. He sat silently in his chair, pretending to read papers.

"Since, Mr. Ambassador, you will not or cannot answer that question, allow me to suggest an answer." The Prime Minister halted to see if the ambassador reacted. He didn't but kept staring at the table.

"The United States, having established a near autocratic government has now discovered the mortal weakness of all such governments. Autocracies cannot sustain themselves as long as democratically founded governments exist, whether they be nearby or far away, to inspire their own people who hunger for freedom. Democracy anywhere is ultimately fatal to autocracies everywhere.

"A democratic Canada is a reminder to the people of America. A reminder of what they long ago created for themselves and the entire world. A reminder of what they once fought to defend. Of what they once cherished. And because of that, the autocratic government of the United States must end democracy in Canada.

"Let me end with the words of a past American president. 'That we here highly resolve that these dead shall not have died in vain—that this nation, under God, shall have a new birth of freedom—and that government of the people, by the people, for the people, shall not perish from the earth.'

"Well, Mr. Ambassador, shall democracy perish from the earth? I await your answer."

The Prime Minister did not wait long. He departed the hall accompanied by thunderous applause. The American delegation sat silently.

The CBC anchors, experts and commentators launched into their analyses. One analyst said something that struck Debbie hard. "The Prime Minister, by using America's own words, Lincoln's Gettysburg Address, he has elevated a dispute into a crusade. He has sent those words into battle once more."

My God! As the shock of the speech lessened, Debbie realized how dangerous things could become for her community, thinking *if Canadian soldiers are killing American soldiers, would her people support Canada? Will they switch back to that fascist? If American soldiers are killing Canadians, how would Canadians then regard American expatriates? As enemy aliens? Agents? Potential terrorists?*

"Matt, I've got work to do." She called Morgan and told him to call the others Expat Committee members. They must meet tonight.

The President Reacts to NATO

"Let's sum up the president's response to the Prime Minister's accusation that his administration is planning a military attack on Canada. A rather short but animated statement at that, from the White House. I'll add the president himself spoke live from the White House Press Briefing Room and he took no questions."

The anchor started to go through the bullet points of the statement. The president said the accusation is false. The Prime Minister is unhinged. American forces are on maneuvers. With all the criticism the Prime Minister is hurling toward the president, he wondered aloud if it is Canada and NATO that are planning to attack the U.S., saying 'After all, the Prime Minister just ordered his military to full mobilization. That's a threat directed at us.'" Unable to hold back, the CBC co-anchor chimed in, "Patently absurd!"

"The president said he will sign an executive order this evening ordering all U.S. defense contractors to immediately cease all business with Canada and the NATO allies. No training, no technical advice, no spare parts. The legal justification of this action, he claimed, falsely, is that Canada is aiding domestic terrorists in the United States."

The anchor introduced three guests to the coverage. "We have retired Admiral Roland Leveque, Royal Canadian Navy, here as our military analyst. We also have Dr. Louise Carruthers, a historian and author of two books on authoritarian leaders who is also a retired major of the Canadian Army. And an economist, a Canadian, working on Wall Street, Dr. Michael Andrews. Admiral, let's start with you."

The admiral stressed that the president's claim the build up at Fort Drum was for maneuvers, but the depth of the logistical commitment is not what is done for field exercises. "This looks very much like the president's preparing for war."

"And a very troubling thing from the president. He said, and I am quoting, 'War isn't only fought with tanks and planes and ships. It's also fought with computers and over the internet.' Did he just threaten a cyberattack on us?"

The anchor came back saying, "Though he denied preparing a military attack, it is clear the president is preparing an economic attack on Canada. He said the U.S. is preparing new and much more painful economic sanctions and tariffs against Canada. Commodities, such as lumber, minerals and oil were specifically mentioned. Even with the border closure and new tariffs, trade in those things continued to a degree. Now, it looks likely these new tariffs will bring us to a near embargo. Dr. Andrews if you would speak to the economic side."

The economist painted a horrifying picture. The president's latest executive order prohibits all Americans from transferring their money to the banks of Canada and the NATO allies, a tactic used by millions as a hedge against disruption and disorder in the United States.

"He's not stopping there, saying he is considering banning Canadian corporations from participating in U.S. stock exchanges. That threatens over two hundred Canadian corporations."

Then he summed up the reaction by the financial markets in a single word. Panic.

He noted the market just closed and all the indices, Dow Jones, S&P 500, NASDAQ, have hit new lows. The Dow, for instance, was off 6% since just this morning. Since the presidential election last November, the markets are down roughly 35 to 45% in value since then, erasing trillions of dollars in lost value.

"It's not just the Wall Street hedge fund managers losing out. It means in the last year and a month the retirement funds and pension funds of most Americans have been hammered.

The anchor directed the discussion to the historian. "And now, I think we should hear from Dr. Carruthers to give us a sense of the political history being made before our eyes. Dr. Carruthers."

"We've known for a long time how to characterize the president's world view. He lives in a zero-sum world. For him to succeed, another has to fail. That's how he sees every dispute or disagreement, monumental or trivial. He fails to grasp the give and take of legitimate negotiation. As he sees it, negotiation means he takes, and the other side gives. Finding a win-win situation in dealing with him is a foolish hope."

"That's a hallmark of every authoritarian or dictator I have studied. The president is not the ruthless authoritarian, or autocrat, that we've seen from other historical figures. There still are vestiges of constitutional government in the U.S. But look at what he's done. He created his own political police force, the Homeland Security Corps. He's put sympathetic senior officers and political appointees into the military. He's sent his Department of Justice out to investigate major news networks for their critical coverage, falsely alleging their coverage aids domestic terrorism. No, he is not a Hitler, or a Saddam Hussein, or a Stalin. Or a Putin for that matter. But he is on his way. Our mistake is to under . . ."

The anchor's frustration showed itself as he cut in. "But none of this makes any sense. Where is the sense in attacking us? Where is the logic?"

"Listen. There is no sense or logic. And looking for any is a fool's errand." The historian went on to explain. "We fail to understand the autocrat's mindset. This goes beyond autocracy versus democracy as systems of government. It goes to the autocrat himself. Let me explain.

"An autocrat's foundation of power is strength. He must always appear strong. He must be without weakness. Even in imagery, like being seen playing a vigorous sport or carrying a gun. Decisions, actions must convey his strength to his country and the world. His life depends on that. And I mean that literally. Remember, autocrats surrounded themselves with the like-minded. Show weakness and your advisors will quickly become your adversaries.

"Therefore, when it comes to the current conflict between the president and Canada, I, and many of my colleagues, believe this conflict will continue until, in the president's mind, he has a clear win and Canada is clearly the loser. Barring regime change in the states, Canada's only option is to resist."

From his office in Fredericton, LeClerc watched all this on that eventful afternoon. He sat there processing the president's words. None of it helped LeClerc find an optimistic mood. We're all going to be poorer soon, on both sides of the border.

The phone rang. A text message. His primary reserve unit, 3 Intelligence Company, 5ᵗʰ Canadian Division, has mobilized. Report to CFB Halifax by 1200 tomorrow.

The Old World Comes to the Aid of the New World

The next morning, LeClerc joined in the Atlantic Region's secure video conference before reporting for military duty. The director opened with a review of events and war preparations. To LeClerc, the director seemed almost to be in good spirits.

"Until now, NATO limited its deployments to Canada, designing them to send a signal to the United States. What we are about to see is something quite different." He then went on to describe NATO military deployments.

NATO Standing Naval Force Atlantic is now within sight of the U.S. destroyer off Halifax. The French carrier *Charles de Gaulle*, escorted by four destroyers and frigates, was providing air cover with her wing of Rafale fighters. In two days, the HMS *Prince of Wales*, with a full air wing of thirty-six F-35 Lightning stealth fighters, and a large escort force, would set sail from the United Kingdom

"Strangely, the U.S. Navy hasn't sortied a carrier from Norfolk. Lords knows they have more than a couple there. That could change quickly. I expect local media down there will notice if they do."

NATO's early warning aircraft, E-3 AWACS, already operating out of CFB Gander, would increase to six aircraft by tomorrow, enabling round the clock aerial surveillance of the Maritimes, the Northeastern United States, and more.

Three squadrons of Typhoon fighter aircraft were enroute to Canada and should be deployed and operational by Sunday. Spain was sending two entire squadrons of their own F-18 fighters. All told, over a hundred additional fighter aircraft. The Royal Canadian Air Force said they'll have ninety CF-18 fighters operational in a week. That includes a number taken out of storage and others being repaired as quickly as they can.

NATO was putting together an air bridge of cargo aircraft, both military and civilian. "Remarkable, since no one ever envisioned reinforcements going from Europe to North America. Always been the other way around."

"Ground forces will take more time." The French-German Brigade of the Eurocorps, light infantry with limited artillery support would deploy here within three days. To help defend Ottawa, Canadian C-17s and Royal Air Force C-17s were transporting British Challenger tanks and Warrior fighting vehicles from their training base at CFB Suffield, Alberta, as quick as they can, "but at one tank per aircraft, and only six dedicated aircraft, it'll take time. Four, possibly five days just to get all the tanks, their crews, spare parts and munitions. The rest of the Brits will come by train but have to take a longer route to stay in Canada."

"Next, NATO's secured U.S. military resources still in Europe and the UK." The director explained the U.S. was still withdrawing equipment, supplies and personnel from their bases in Germany, England, Italy, and Norway. Within the past hour, those host nation governments ordered all U.S. military aircraft be grounded and assumed control of their air traffic control systems. No incoming U.S. flights permitted. Equipment cannot leave NATO seaports and could not be shipped by rail to a port in a non-NATO state.

"That includes the U.S. base in Greenland. Thule. Denmark's taken control of the base. And Iceland has stopped any American aircraft from using the air base at Keflavik." The director almost chuckled at that.

"There are more deployments happening, but I think that gives clear indication that NATO is supporting us with something more than words and token deployments. I, for one, am encouraged. In a week, we could have a sizeable deterrent force.

"Oh, yes. King Charles will speak to the British nation tomorrow. He has already sent a personal message to all the Commonwealth nations to support Canada in any way they can.

"You may have seen this. The NATO secretary general decided to go off script, I guess. In response to a reporter's question about the U.S. president stopping all shipments of U.S. made military systems and spare parts to the NATO allies, he said, 'All the president did was reinvigorate our European and British defense industries.'

"If you're thinking that's unnecessary bluster, you'd be right, but the CEO of a huge U.S. defense contractor just tweeted out a pretty harsh protest of the embargo. So maybe, maybe corporate America is not at all pleased. We'll get a better picture of things when Wall Street opens tomorrow. Futures are down, way down across the globe."

"I don't care to speculate if he, I mean, the NATO Secretary General, will ask NATO members to respond in kind. Put a military supply embargo on the U.S. The U.S. military needs stuff from across the pond, too."

An analyst from the Ottawa Region interrupted the director with a question. Together with the Quebec Region, they started holding joint videoconferences, restricted to the senior personnel. *Poor guy* thought LeClerc. He doesn't know that our director does not like to be interrupted. "Sir, any actions taken by Russia or China that are concerning?"

"Excellent question. And no, they haven't. They seem to be very cool about all this. Maybe they'll wait to see what advantage will develop. Now, let me finish what I was saying."

"Sir, if I may, another question. Aside from Fort Drum, have we seen any other U.S. military buildups along the border?"

"No, with the exception of a U.S. naval force off Esquimalt. Of course, that could change quickly."

Well, that guy got off easy, judged LeClerc.

"Now, what about our forces?" The director went down his list. Recruiting offices are very busy. Reservists are reporting for duty. Veterans are being taken back in. Regular forces secured the Saint Lawrence bridges. Video of which is already playing on all the news channels.

"We're giving the media as much access as possible, especially television. The feeling is it will build support among our people. And maybe diminish American popular support for the administration. So, you'll see TV video of our Leopard tanks and LAV-IIIs leaving CFB Gagetown and CFB Valcartier."

Since he mentioned tanks, the director reviewed the balance of armored forces. He explained that one U.S. armored brigade had about ninety tanks. If the Canadian army concentrated its own Leopard tanks, add in the twenty Challenger tanks from the British Armored Training Unit Sheffield, NATO forces could match the Americans, tank for tank, in Ontario.

"That might force the Americans to delay. Force them to reinforce with additional armor. Sure, they have tanks to spare, but it buys us time."

Once the director started briefing about the naval side of things, LeClerc sensed in the director an elevated tone of pride in his former service. "Our frigates and submarines at both naval bases are being replenished and making all preparations for sea. Best to get them all to sea before anything happens.

"Again, the media is watching our naval preparations. Frankly, I'm glad they're watching. Might help convince the Americans that we are serious.

"There you have it. All of this is either already out in the media or will be very soon. Nevertheless, I thought it important to review what is happening. I want everyone to understand what all this means.

"We are preparing for war. If we do this right, the United States will see that the cost will be too high and beg off. They'll think of another way of getting at us, but we'll buy ourselves time." He went silent for a short time before continuing.

"I must, however, keep a realistic outlook. I ask you, throughout history, when has a large army ever been assembled on the border of an enemy, only to be called back from the brink?" The director seemed to look at all the attendees, awaiting an answer. Then he spoke. "Let's just say history provides few examples. Any questions?" None were offered.

The Ottawa director took her cue. "Thank you, Director. Before we break off into our regional groups to discuss region specific taskings, I want to address a concern about these developments that have come to my attention."

"Is it possible *Operation Northern Lights* true intent was to frighten Canada into appeasement, to give in to U.S. political and economic demands? Yes, something short of war may be their goal. We must consider that possibility. Put the forces in place, leak the plan deliberately, and scare us into submission."

LeClerc remembered being grilled about Byron's veracity. Why did this friend that you hadn't been in touch with for years suddenly call you? He knew you were with CSIS, making you a perfect conduit for disinformation. Why would a man with a sterling career and headed for a general's star turn informant? Turn traitor? Looks like they were ultimately satisfied.

"Like my colleagues, we arrived at a simple place. Having confirmed the buildup of military forces on our border, we had no choice but to mobilize. We had to act. To do otherwise would have been foolish, even immoral.

"And our mobilization, plus NATO reinforcement, may have surprised the Americans. Certainly their U.N. ambassador was surprised. Add to that, we've uncovered no other buildups. The Americans may have put all their eggs in this one Fort Drum basket. Does that reflect sloppiness, arrogance? Perhaps, but we have no solid evidence to support that hypothesis.

"There's another consideration. Polls and public demonstrations happening here and in Europe are in our favor. That may not last. If the NATO allies start to suffer casualties, public support will weaken. We're also seeing large pro-Canada demonstrations and protests in the U.S. That sentiment too, may weaken with time."

To himself, LeClerc put it more bluntly. The U.S. has strategic and tactical superiority, in the air, on the land and the sea. They can always add more troops and planes and ships. We can't match them. Not even close. If we lose NATO support, it's over.

"Finally, we have no answer to the question the PM posed to the U.S. Ambassador. Why? Hell, for all I know, maybe the PM just pissed off that president."

The Ottawa director wrapped it up. "Okay, it's time to break up this conference so the directors can review tasking with their staff. That should start in about ten minutes. All I can say is, hold fast."

On their own videoconference, the Atlantic director went through tasks for his staff. When the director came to LeClerc, he pushed him to further develop his contact with the Coast Guard lieutenant. He promised the Director he'd do so, even while joining his reserve unit in Halifax.

"You know, I could ask for your exemption from call-up, with your CSIS duties and all."

"Thank you, but please don't. I've considered it, but it looks like we're coming to a fight. I'd rather fight in uniform. They'll need all the help they can get."

"Robert, I understand. Right now, I wish I was back commanding a frigate again. *Bonne chance.*"

CHAPTER SEVENTEEN
UNPOPULAR

Change of Mind

Miles took the scenic route along the coast back to Eastport. Route 1 all the way. Past Bath, then Belfast, on to Ellsworth and the final leg to Eastport. It would take him all day. Maybe more if he was lucky.

All day. Alone in his thoughts. As much as he tried to distract his mind with the radio, listening to the news didn't help. The confrontation with Canada only seemed to be getting worse. *At least I was right about that.* After half an hour of that, he switched to music.

The music didn't work. Over and over again in his mind, Miles replayed his meeting two days ago with Capt. Llewelyn.

Miles hadn't wasted time. He asked, "Sir, you saw the news about this *Operation Northern Lights*? The Canadian Prime Minister's speech at the U.N.? And the President's statement?"

"Yes, I did, Mr. Miles." The captain sat himself in his desk seat, his arms across the desk surface. He knew in his mind the lieutenant wasn't going to stay. "And I think I know you well enough to guess you're not here to talk about current events."

"Then, sir, I hope you will understand why I have decided to resign my commission. Here is another letter." The captain took the letter Miles handed him.

"Very well, Lieutenant Miles. I will accept this, reluctantly, very reluctantly, but I will endorse it and send it on. As I promised. Our personnel people will take care of the rest. It may take time to process."

Miles felt compelled to explain his reasoning. "Captain, I cannot . . ." His voice began to break. The captain held up his hand, to signal Doug to stop talking.

"Please, Doug. I think I understand why. No need to go into all that." But the Captain felt his own conflicted need to go into all that.

"I believe you're doing this out of moral conviction. You're doing what you believe is the honorable thing to do. I understand that. Frankly, I wish you'd stay on. You're a fine officer. Right now, the Coast Guard needs officers of your caliber. But I respect your decision." He held out his hand.

That day and the next were horribly awkward. No surprise the gossip got around. Just staying out of the operations center drew a lot of questions. Meyers got a little too insistent about knowing what was up. Miles brought him into an empty office and closed the door. He told Meyers of his resignation. He said it was a personal matter, but Meyers wouldn't let it go. Miles finally let fly.

"Look, for one, it's none of your business. It's personal and it was my decision to resign. The captain understands my decision, so I don't give a rat's ass what anyone else thinks! But have you given any thought to what's happening? That we're about to go to war with the Canadians? The Canadians, for God's sake! Have you?"

Miles didn't wait for an answer. "No, I bet not. To me, you even seem a little excited by it all. Like you're enjoying this." When Meyers started to protest, Miles cut him off. "Maybe I owe you this. I told the captain I wouldn't be a part of this. I will not be a part of an attack of Canada in any way. What is happening is wrong. Absolutely wrong!" Miles stormed out and slammed the door behind himself, thinking, time for a long lunch. Maybe I'll stretch lunch into dinner.

He spent his remaining time arranging his departure. No need for a mover. He hadn't bothered with an apartment in Eastport or here in Portland. Truth be told, Miles hadn't accumulated any property. Nothing during his academy years. Then he was aboard a cutter. He never rented an apartment then, instead just joining in with a couple of shipmates at a place rented by a shore assigned academy classmate. And while in the Persian Gulf, he had the cutter and the visiting officer quarters. Before joining the cutter there, he sold off most things on Craig's List.

His minimalist lifestyle did allow him to accumulate a healthy set of bank accounts and investments. Yesterday, he took out six thousand dollars from his bank account. That left about $53,000 in his portfolio that he had to somehow move without too much attracting attention.

On Friday, the only person Miles gave his last goodbye was Capt. Llewellyn. Doug preferred to leave quietly and unseen. He took his remaining days as leave. Terminal leave, as in the end of service, though technically, for the next twelve days, he'd still be a lieutenant. He had passed his five-year obligation of active duty while in Eastport. He didn't elect to transfer to the reserves.

That evening, he checked into a waterside hotel along Route 1 about twelve miles north of Eastport in the little road stop of Robbinston. He didn't want to be seen around Eastport and have to explain himself to anyone who recognized him. But tomorrow, he planned to cruise around Eastport looking for the old man. Maybe he would find him. For no other reason than to talk to him. Even then, he wasn't sure why he wanted to do that.

Sleep was difficult. He obsessed over his decision to resign. *Was it the right thing to do? Why did I do it? Really, why? No doubt, it would be this way for some time. Months, years maybe.* Now he was without a home. Without a job. Driving a six-year-old car. With only enough possessions to fit in a couple of seabags and a garment bag. Even his uniforms seemed superfluous now. And the worst part, he knew, he would have to call mom.

Before he made any big decisions, he needed to contact someone to discuss his future.

The Almost Former Lieutenant

Miles had one thing to do before he slept. A little before midnight, Miles took out a cheap cell phone he bought yesterday. He texted a message to a number from the business card he kept from Eastport. "Want to talk. Call me tmw. Breakfast Friend."

The screen said, *Delivered.* Miles knew he may have just committed a crime. Hardly a way to start a new life.

Contact

"Hello, is this my friend from breakfast?"

Miles was about to leave the hotel that cold Saturday morning to start his search around Eastport for the old man. The call came in as he got into his car. The caller's number matched LeClerc's. To Miles, it sounded like LeClerc, but he couldn't be sure. He needed to say something that only LeClerc would recognize.

"I didn't mention the old man."

"Thank you. That's good to hear. I'm hoping we can meet again for a breakfast of corned beef hash and fried eggs. Myself, I can't get enough of that. You want to ask me something?"

It struck Miles as a bit odd to bring up their breakfast order, but then again, he guessed LeClerc was trying to reassure him of his identity. *Who else would know that little tidbit?*

"Yes. Rather do this in person. But you're probably busy and can't get away. So, I'm using this prepaid cell phone. Do you think it's safe?"

Better than your own phone, thought LeClerc. *He's using a burner phone. At least he understands that. And he's not using names. Trying to be vague.* "Yes, reasonably so. Go ahead."

"I want to discuss your offer of future employment."

LeClerc had a moment of guilt. *This is your job, Robert. You sometimes persuade people, good people, to ruin their careers and risk imprisonment. The old man. Henry. And now Miles. Who knows? Maybe no one will find out and he can still go on to a great career. No, the worst is that he will know. For the rest of his life, he will know that he broke the laws of his country. I hope this is worth it to him.*

You're forgetting someone else, you dumb bastard. Michael Whynot. How much are you to blame for his death?

Never mind, I can't think like that. His country is preparing to attack my country. If stopping that costs Miles everything, I'll accommodate him.

"We can. To get the job, you have to travel here, on your own. Can you do work for us where you are now?"

There was a long silence on the other end. LeClerc finally said, "Hello? Are you there?"

Miles responded in what he knew was a half-assed code.

"No, I'm offline. I can start work only when I'm done travelling. Can you help with transport? I can travel in twelve days." Miles preferred not to leave the U.S. until he was officially no longer on active duty. Waiting for

LeClerc to answer, he thought, *That's it, Doug. You just hinted at defection to a foreign country while still technically in service. You are a criminal.*

"I'll check on that. I'll text you the next time we can talk. Be patient." LeClerc hung up.

LeClerc knew the chance U.S. authorities intercepted their conversation was extremely low. Possible, but highly unlikely. For now, he'd operate on the assumption that Miles wasn't compromised, and the call was genuine. He knew he had little choice. CSIS desperately needed more sources. But now the question was, is Miles still a potential source? When Miles asked about "transport," that was easy to decipher. He was asking for help across the border. That led LeClerc to conclude Miles was more a potential defector than a covert source of intelligence. CSIS could smuggle a high value defector into Canada. But he questioned if Miles was anything approaching high value. And LeClerc wasn't clear on what "offline" meant.

He tried to put his thoughts in order. *An officer who was involved in the Saint Andrews Raid, and perhaps the Battle of Machias Seal Island. Disaffected? Possibly. Is he an indication of dissention in his military's officer corps? Put that together with Henry. Doug's mother as well. An admiral. And those other admirals. Is Doug a way to her? To them?*

LeClerc's mind suddenly shifted to another important issue. *Jesus. We've got to do better than call it the Battle of Machias Seal Island. Really does not roll of the tongue. Need something like, Battle of Puffin Island? The Great Puffin Fight?*

Doug Spies the Spy

What troubled Doug most that Saturday was being spotted by one of Eastport's Coast Guardsmen. There he'd be, out of uniform and not where he was supposed to be. Maybe they already heard about his resignation. He muttered to himself *I just don't want to explain myself. Get this thing done and get out of here.*

The trick was to find a place to watch and wait for the old man. Doug had no idea who he was.

The old man said he kept tabs on the HSC unit. He watched them on his walks on the city pier. He watched them . . . he said from his house. His house. He lived here all his life. An old house. Where is there an old house that has a good view of the station?

Water Street. Has to be able to see the station from his house. The lower part of Water Street is shops, diners, and other businesses, like the brewery he had dinner with the senior chief. The upper part of Water Street then. There're homes up there. He lives in one of those old homes.

Doug decided to drive slowly on Water Street, looking at each home, trying to judge which ones had a clear view of the station and the parking lot where the HSC trailers were. Maybe eight homes fit the bill.

Doug stopped at the intersection of Adams and Water Streets. Someone in such a small town would know him. *Well, I could ask around. Describe him to random people. I could go door to door, asking the occupants if there was an elderly spy for Canada living there. Stupid idea.*

Another option was to pull over, camp out along the street, and wait for the old man to come out. Not that anyone would wonder why a stranger was sitting in his car for hours on end. He could call LeClerc, but was certain he wouldn't betray the old man's identity.

Well, Doug, you didn't think this one through, did you? He decided there were two options. Option A. I wait around here and get lucky and not get questioned by the local police. Option B. I ask for help. That's the worst option. Until you realize it's the only option.

Doug got out of the car and walked up to a B&B on the corner. Looked like a nice place, though he never went in there before. He'd say he was checking out places for a trip in the spring, then shift the conversation around to the old man. *It won't seem at all odd, right?*

Turned out, the owner of the B&B knew exactly who Doug was talking about. "Sure, young fella, I know him. Just a couple doors down. You say your father was an old Army buddy in Vietnam? Here, I'll call him and let him know you're coming." He gave Doug the house number.

The house was across from the Eastport Port Authority parking lot. Doug saw it had a direct view from the house to the station and the HSC. He walked up the front doorsteps and before he could reach the door, the old man was already there, all smiles and with an outstretched hand.

"This is a surprise! Hello, lieutenant, how are you? Please come inside, it's a bit chilly out here."

The old man ushered Doug inside, pointed in the direction of the kitchen, saying he had just brewed some fresh coffee. The two found themselves sitting at the kitchen table, stirring in creamer and sugar. Doug explained why he was there.

"I remembered what you said to me on the pier that day. I did meet with Mr. LeClerc for breakfast after I saw you. Since then, I was transferred to our base in South Portland. Had something to do with that incident on the Saint

Croix with the HSC." Doug stopped for a moment to sip his coffee. The old man nodded his understanding. "You know, I don't even know your name."

The old man smiled at that. "Yeah, you're right! Course, in my new line of work, you don't give your name out all that readily. Anyway, its Jonathan. Jonathan Young. Most people I know call me Jon. Jon without the *h*, I like to say."

"Okay, well, Jon, I'm here to let you know I didn't report our meeting on the pier. When you told me about the *Glace Bay* coming. Not a word of it." Doug, paused, looked away, then continued. "I don't know why I felt I had to tell you that, face to face. Maybe so you don't spend your days wondering or worrying. I already told LeClerc. But I'm sure you already knew that." Jon nodded in return.

"I appreciate the gesture, son. A long trip up from Portland. But maybe, there's something else on you mind."

Doug poured himself another cup of coffee, putting in the sugar and creamer before continuing. "Jon, I resigned my commission."

"In heaven's name, why?"

"It's complicated. You heard about what happened that night on the Saint Croix?"

"Yes, everyone has."

"I think it started with that. Those HSC people went across and shot an American to death. Planned or accidental, it doesn't matter, at least to me. Then they had us ferry some HSC officers out to Machias Seal Island. They shot, murdered a lobsterman. No reason. A fiasco. I was at Sector Northern New England, that's our base in South Portland, when it happened. I helped prepare that mission. Then there's all the other things happening. The U.S. Navy threatening the Canadians. You heard about this *Operation Northern Lights?*"

"Yes, Doug." Jon decided to let the boy talk it out.

"It was too much for me. Maybe I'll never be able to explain why, but it was too much. It's just wrong. This country, our country, may go to war with Canada. I say it, but still can't believe I said it. Long story short, I talked to my commanding officer and resigned. I told him I couldn't be a part of it. I think he understood. Eventually."

A silent minute passed before Jon spoke. "It's a real shame what's happened to us. I mean to all of us in this country. I have to tell you I had the same kind of ... what's the word I'm looking for? Revelation. Yeah, I guess that works. Doug, I spent a year in combat in Vietnam. Saw my friends killed. I killed their soldiers. And for what? I mean, we were defending us from Communism. Defending our freedom. I still believe that, even now. My Dad and my uncle fought the Nazis. I had an uncle who died fighting in Korea. But if all that we did ends with our country becoming what it is today, we're no different from our enemies back then. My uncle, my friends, what did they die for?

"I just had to do something."

"Something? Well, most people will join a protest or something like that. Me, I just quit."

Doug decided it was time to take the conversation on a different course. "How in the world did you ever get into the spy business?"

"Happenstance. Not like there was an ad in the paper. Help Wanted: Spy Work. Elderly Applicants Preferred. No Experience Necessary." Doug smiled at that.

"No, my son is a friend of LeClerc. LeClerc heard of the HSC unit coming here. My son put LeClerc in touch with me. Simple, really.

"You know, it suddenly occurs to me that perhaps I shouldn't be so open with you. After all, you could be working for HSC now. You wearing a wire? Is that what they call it?"

"Yes, I'm sorry. I shouldn't have asked. I promise you I am not doing that. And I left my cell phone in the car."

"Well, no matter. You found me pretty easily. So, if the feds want to arrest me, it wouldn't take any effort. Besides, I have a plan B for that." Jon pointed to a deer rifle leaning against the door frame and a revolver on the kitchen counter.

"I see. Well, let's hope it doesn't come to that. All I can say is, again, no one but me on this side of the border knows about you. And in fairness concerning our disclosures, I don't intend on staying on this side of the border."

"How's that?"

"I've contacted LeClerc. Another ten days and I'll be officially off active duty. I asked him about getting across to Canada. Others have done that. He, well, discussed an option for me. I'll leave it at that."

"You know, I can get you across. That's easy. Anytime you like."

Revolt

Having little else to do but drive around town that Sunday, the four teenage boys, ended up at a local pizza place near the bend of Main Street in Calais. Nearly next door was a cinema. The plan was simple. Pizza first. Then a movie.

The pizza finished up with time to spare. So, the car driver decided to stop by the gas station just up Main Street, maybe 250 yards. Anyone at the pizza place could look up the road the see the station. All agreed and they headed up Main Street.

Filling up his old, barely passed inspection sedan, the boy could see the border station building just fifty yards away, on this side of the Ferry Point International Bridge. The bridge itself wasn't even a football field in length. Many times, he imagined himself standing on the American side of the bridge and throwing a football all the way into another country. From Calais to Saint Stephen. The boy promised himself. Someday, I'll give it a try.

Almost done gassing up, he saw his friend get out of the car. His somewhat less than bright but extraordinarily impulsive friend. Another vehicle was starting to fill up. An SUV. Black. Government plates. Homeland Security Corps. One of them was outside the vehicle attending to the gas hose. A second officer sat in the driver's seat.

The boy saw Impulsive was giving shit to the HSC cop manning the gas hose. All morning Impulsive had gone on and on about how the president wanted a war with Canada. He ranted about the American kidnapped and shot dead by the HSC from Eastport. Then there was that lobsterman. He was pretty upset by all the news. Impulsive had two uncles just over in Saint Stephen that he wanted to go over and see, like he used to. Like many families around here used to do. Couldn't see them because the President was pissed at Canada and closed the border. He talked about how the HSC set themselves up in a motel down the road and running patrols all over the place. He let them all in on his plot to get revenge against the HSC cops. He'd go over to the motel, wait for a couple of the HSC cops to come out, and maybe throw eggs at them. Stuff like that.

Now there was Impulsive, yelling and swearing at the HSC cop at the gas pump. The boy knew Impulsive was headed for serious trouble. Jesus, he's right in that HSC cop's face. The boy's two other friends were too busy on their phones to notice. The boy finished filling his car, hung up his gas hose and started walking over to pull his friend away. He was too late.

The other HSC cop got out of the SUV, gun drawn. He yelled at Impulsive, swore at him, and ordered Impulsive to back off. Impulsive just kept yelling at both of them. The HSC cop with the gas hose used his free arm to push the jerk of a teenager away. The other HSC cop brought up his gun to firing position, trained on Impulsive. He yelled at Impulsive to get on his knees. The kid didn't obey. Instead, Impulsive swore at the cop and walked toward the cop with the gun out. The cop fired. Impulsive fell to the ground. Impulsive was dead.

The boy froze in place as the gun went off. He was only ten feet away. Without thinking, he walked slowly over to his friend lying on the oil and now blood-stained concrete. He tried to wake him. He tried to pick him up off the ground. There was blood. Lots of blood.

His two friends on phones did what anyone would do in their situation. They recorded the whole thing on their cell phones, even while the boy started yelling for help. It was the store clerk who called 911.

The HSC cop who fired the killing shot now aimed his weapon at the boy who had knelt on the concrete, cradling his dead friend. The second HSC cop yelled at his partner to put the gun down.

By now, patrons of the gas station had come out. The boy yelled to no one and everyone the HSC cop shot his friend. Two customers came over to the dead boy, futilely trying to give aid. They immediately saw there was no helping Impulsive. One customer tried to break the boy's hold on his dead friend, speaking as gently as he could to the boy as they both eased the body to the ground. He led boy away to the inside of the store.

The other customer rose to his feet, stood between the shooter and the body, and faced down the gun. He cursed the HSC cop. "I saw the whole thing from inside. You shot him! You killed him for nothing!"

A small crowd gathered. Passers-by and customers. A couple of cars stopped on the road. Someone by the store threw a plastic soda bottle at the HSC vehicle. Another bottle followed in seconds. Two more headed for the shooter. One glanced off the shooter's face.

The shooter backed away, still with his gun drawn, but now not aimed at any targets. He got back into the SUV. His partner drove them back to the Customs and Border Protection building next door. As they fled, the Calais police arrived along with an ambulance. The EMTs scooped up the boy's friend off the concrete as the police started to quickly interview all the witnesses.

Even quicker than the Calais police got there, the two teenagers in the back of the car uploaded the entire shooting to social media. Within an hour, most of their friends saw the killing. It would spread throughout the day, going well beyond the small city of Calais.

It didn't take long for the small crowd of witnesses to build into a mob. By car and by foot, people came from all over town. At first only tens of people, then hundreds from a town that numbered just over three thousand.

The mob shifted focus from the gas station to the border station. The city cops tried to get everyone to get away from the border station building, but citizenry was in no mood to obey. At first, it was curses yelled toward the front door entry. Then banging with fists on the building's locked doors and windows. Then rocks. Windows cracked under a barrage of larger rocks. One man used a baseball bat against the door with great effect. Another used a crowbar against windows. Every available officer in the Calais Police Department came to the scene, but they didn't have the numbers to put themselves between the mob and the CBP building. They were overwhelmed.

The mob's attention shifted to the CBP and HSC vehicles in the parking lot behind the border station building. The inevitable happened. One, then another, and then another, were set on fire.

All the while, the CBP and HSC officers remained locked in the building.

A chant arose from all around the building. "Send him out! Send him out!"

Then someone, from somewhere, made use of a deer rifle, firing at the border station windows, four, maybe five times. The city cops drew their weapons, desperately looking for the shooter. Some in the mob scattered, but most continued their assault on the building. The rifle shots could be heard over half the town and across the border to Saint Stephen, echoing up and down the river. Sirens could be heard all around town. All the noise brought more people.

A smaller mob drove over to the motel housing the HSC cops, led by someone who screamed he knew "where more of the bastards are!" They were there in minutes, using their cars and trucks to block in the HSC vehicles at the motel. Men banged on the room doors, demanding they come out. The motel manager called 911. One man started stabbing the HSC vehicle tires with a large hunting knife.

Two HSC cops charged out of their room, guns in hand, yelling "Get on the ground!" They fired shots into the air and then leveled their pistols at the crowd.

Bad fortune followed. An ordinary looking man perhaps in his fifties drew his own handgun and exchanged fire. In seconds, one HSC cop was dead. And so was the ordinary looking man. The unwounded cop retreated back into the motel room. The mob stayed in place, uncertain of their next move. But they would think of something.

Cavalry Arrives

From across the Saint Croix River, George LeBlanc kept at his post at the Canadian border station. They had no protocol for dealing with a riot and gunfire coming from the American side. So, they made up their own. Close the station to traffic. Get people under cover. Call for help. Keep watching. Fortunately, for now the gunfire seemed to stop.

By now, George saw a big white van with the satellite dish arrive at the CBP building. Through his binoculars, he could see the news truck was from a station in Bangor. All that way, he thought, and they still got here ahead of the military, even though he knew the National Guard had an armory right there in Calais. The 1136th Transportation Company, Detachment 2. Not hard to figure that out. They're in the book, as they say.

The sun was setting as Army National Guard helicopters landed at a baseball field almost directly across Calais Avenue from the Calais Armory. Other guardsmen with the Transportation Company met the platoon of military police carried by the helicopters and brought them in their trucks to the epicenter of the riot, the CBP building by the Ferry Point International Bridge.

For the next hour, there was a lull in the violence, but the mob didn't disperse. They waited and watched. Two National Guard trucks rolled up as close as they could get to the building's front door. MPs got off the trucks to form a tight perimeter around the building's front entry and the trucks. A captain with the MPs went into the CBP building. Having no argument with the National Guard, the mob didn't interfere with them, but remained nearby. All the while, the Bangor TV news crew went from one person to the next, asking questions of the locals for their live broadcast.

What happened next enraged the mob.

They saw MPs escorting the HSC officers to the trucks. The shooter was with them. The mob's chants returned. A few ran toward the trucks but were tackled by the MPs. Many in the crowd struck out with hurled rocks and anything else that would fly, trying to hit the HSC cops, but often hitting the MPs instead.

The trucks pulled away, escorted by a single Maine State Police cruiser. They quickly drove to the ball fields to meet the helicopters waiting to fly the HSC cops back to the Bangor airport. HSC took away only what wore. They left behind all their equipment. And they left behind their colleagues at the motel, both alive and dead. Maine State Police dispatched to the motel took them all out in their vehicles. The dead ordinary man was left to the city police.

CBP officers remained in the border station building. Faced with a crowd furious at the escape of the HSC cops, the MP captain knew she only had bad options. She chose the least bad. She disarmed and walked outside of the reestablished perimeter and called over three people from the crowd. She explained her orders to them and presented her troops as the only force there protecting the citizens of Calais. Her MPs stopped those CBP and HSC officers who wanted to come out guns blazing. Her people disarmed all the CBP officers and took away the HSC officers.

"It's simple. We're here to protect their lives and your lives. We can only do that if I can get cooperation from you all. They aren't a threat to you now. We aren't leaving. But I need you to talk to your people."

When one of the few accused her of letting the shooter get away, the MP captain replied, "If I stood by and let you burn this building down, let you grab the shooter and the other HSC cops, well, you'll only make yourselves look like a lot of rioters. You're better than that. As it is, all those HSC cops will be handed over to Maine State Police. Governor's orders. That's the best chance of holding the shooter accountable."

They agreed to talk to the others in the crowd. It took time, but over the next few hours the crowd went home a few at a time.

Well into the early morning hours, the MP captain stayed outside the perimeter the whole time, answering questions, thanking those who decided to go home. One older man came up to the captain and said, "You know, the boy they killed. Good boy. I don't think this fight is over yet. Don't let those murderers come back here."

"Sir, I understand. That's the shame of it. I hope there won't be other dead boys before it's over."

Taking the Bridge

The obstacles and other fortifications set up on the American side of the bridge to Campobello Island were impressive. Concrete jersey barriers, steel fencing and razor wire. CBP must have figured that would be enough. Months ago, they closed the border station in Lubec and sent their people elsewhere, leaving the people of Lubec with a blocked bridge and no summer and fall tourists that many here depended on.

The bridge and border closure did leave Lubec with more than their fill of resentment. Most everyone suffered from the bridge closure, economically, and emotionally. Walk into any café or tavern in the area and the conversations had a recurrent theme. The unfairness of it all, to take the brunt of the punishment all because of politicians in Washington.

News of Sunday's shooting and the riot in Calais spread quickly among the people of Lubec. The fuel of rebellion was well seasoned by that day. It needed only a spark to ignite.

The spark came in the form of two HSC officers who appeared at the closed border station only hours after the teenager was shot dead. They parked their van by the building and went inside on a routine inspection of the building. They had no inkling of what was about to happen.

The first brick smashed the van windshield. Within seconds, more struck the passenger side window. A couple more hit the building windows, cracking the glass. The cops, lucky for them, were in the building as almost fifty people marched toward the bridge, armed with chains, long pry bars and two powerful farm tractors.

In no more than fifteen minutes, a gang of determined Lubec citizens, dragged the concrete barriers to the side, cut away the steel fencing, and threw the razor wire into the waters of Lubec Narrows, suffering only a few lacerations in the process.

They opened the bridge to Campobello Island. The deconstruction gang leader, a woman who owned the charter boat service in town, set off three blasts from a hand-held air horn. Immediately from the town, sounds of car horns, boat horns and cheers. Hundreds began leaving their homes and locking up their cafes and shops.

The citizens of Lubec were about to take back their town.

The two trapped HSC cops called their unit in Calais for help, but couldn't get through. Help wasn't coming. All they could do was lock the doors, crank up the thermostat, and watch the growing crowd through the windows. One said to the other, "Look what's happening. They had this planned. Maybe it's just chance we were here."

Half the town of Lubec came to the bridge. Armed with horns, beer and spirits of all kinds, they passed by the now barricaded customs building to begin a loud and slow march across the bridge. A couple pickup trucks had gas grills in the cargo beds and coolers of hamburgers and hot dogs. Another pickup had burn barrels, steel fire pits and a lot of firewood. From the Canadian side, a smaller, but no less enthusiastic crowd walked across the bridge to join them.

REFUGE

The Revolt of Lubec climaxed in a party on the FDR Memorial Bridge. More people, more food, more drink. Fire pits got going up and down the bridge. The HSC officers were not invited.

Word spread to Eastport and by sunset a flotilla of Eastport boats made the short trip south to Lubec. From the Station's RB-S, Sr. Chief Jones shadowed the flotilla of civil disobedience. He assured sector that he was only going to observe, not join in. But watching the party from the heated comfort of the RB-S's cabin didn't suit him. He spent as much time as he could, on the open deck, waving at the revelers on the bridge. He remarked to the seaman, "Guess they haven't done any real harm. Just having a little bit of fun. Kinda wish I could join 'em. But it can't last much longer."

The party lasted longer than the senior chief thought it would. Just before midnight, lighted candles and flashlights appeared throughout the crowd. Senior chief could make out a Bangor TV news crew on the bridge, videoing Canadians on American soil. Americans on Canadian soil. At midnight, a four-blast signal from the same air horn. Someone on a bull horn asked all the Americans to join in an anthem. *O, Canada* could be heard over the Lubec Narrows. The Canadians followed with *America the Beautiful*.

As the crowd finally started to thin out a couple of hours later, a lone Maine State trooper arrived at the border station. The trooper asked a couple of the partiers still hanging out by the border station building if anyone was in charge. The two laughed before saying they would escort the trooper to who they thought was in charge.

Walking together to the middle of the bridge they brought the trooper to the charter service owner, the lady with the air horn. She gave the trooper a run-down of events. "I was in charge. Planned the whole thing. Decided to do it, finally, when we got the news of that kid getting shot in Calais. It's all my responsibility. I want to say too, trooper, nobody got hurt. Everybody got a chance to put things right."

The trooper said that could be looked into later. Right now, she was there to take away the two HSC cops. That she had the authority to arrest them all didn't matter to the people on the bridge. They greeted her as one of their own. She met no resistance. A couple of the more joyful protestors asked her to join them in one last celebratory drink. Happy drunks. The trooper declined.

Once in the cruiser, the HSC cops asked if they were headed back to Calais. No, the trooper explained, they wouldn't be going to Calais. "You guys go back to Calais, they might throw you into the Saint Croix. Both the border crossings are locked down. Called out the National Guard. Hell, the

319

town is under curfew." When the HSC officers asked why, the trooper answered succinctly. "One of your type shot and killed a boy in Calais. Just because the kid mouthed off. People rioted. One of yours was shot and killed later. You people are lucky you're still alive."

The trooper headed out on Route 189. "I'm taking you two clueless idiots to our troop's office in Ellsworth. It'll take a while. You might as well shut up and relax. And stay out of sight."

At the Northern Most Point of U.S. Route One

The people of Fort Kent could remember a time when they would, on a whim, walk or drive over the Clair-Fort Kent Bridge into the small thumb of New Brunswick that ran east to west under Quebec. Same went for the people of Clair, the tiny, rural French-Canadian town opposite Fort Kent on the Saint John River. They'd often do no more than wave at the CBP officer as they passed. In places like this, everyone knew everyone.

The economies were so intertwined they were essentially a single town. People would live on one side of the border and work on the other. They shared a history. They shared a language, as most of the Fort Kent Mainers could speak what was known as Valley French.

After September 11, that easy stroll across the border ended. In the spirit of patriotism typical to the region, the people of Fort Kent adapted to the tighter security. They learned to tolerate the few extra bureaucratic steps required to go across. Inevitably though, the rules proved more powerful than even the river in dividing the two peoples. Fewer and fewer locals took the trouble to make that trip across.

This year's border closure hit both sides hard. Especially when it came to emergency medical care for the people of Clair. Before the closure, an American ambulance from Fort Kent brought medical emergencies to the Northern Maine Medical Center and its Level II trauma center. This continued even under the border closure, though the ambulance had to stop to get clearance from the HSC.

With the ramped-up conflict between the president and Canada, that all changed. No cross border medical emergency services. Inevitably, that stupidity led to tragedy.

Three days after the Battle of the Puffins, an elderly woman of Clair suffered a stroke. The RCMP detachment received the 911 call and, as they had always done, called for the Fort Kent Police Department, who dispatched the ambulance. The ambulance responded as it always did, but at the bridge the HSC officers denied it permission to cross. "No, not allowed now. New policy." The HSC cop turned his back on the ambulance driver and went back inside.

That was too much for the ambulance driver. He told the EMT to call RCMP and advise them of the situation. The driver got out and marched up to the station door, slamming his fist against the door glass again and again, swearing at the cops, demanding they let them pass. He could see the cop, sitting behind the counter, acting as if he was not there.

The driver got back in the ambulance. Screw it. He said to the EMT, "Let's go anyway. You in?" The EMT nodded.

The ambulance backed up and then sped through the ungated lane and onto the bridge. Within ten minutes, they had the patient and headed back. The driver hoped to go around the border station the same way. It didn't work out as planned.

Unknown to the ambulance driver, the HSC cop strung a line of tire spikes across the lane. The ambulance lost three of its tires. The abrupt stop broke loose the patient gurney with the old woman. The EMT treating her went crashing forward.

The HSC cop hauled the driver and the EMT out of the ambulance. He held them at gun point and then cuffed them He ignored the elderly stroke victim lying on the gurney. She died within the hour.

The news reported the whole incident. HSC offered no comment. The Fort Kent hospital issued a furious complaint. The town manager and the province of New Brunswick issued its own complaints.

The HSC cop reported as usual for his next shift.

The world moved on. Not so the people of Fort Kent and Clair. It began with the shunning of CBP and HSC officers. People saw the uniform and moved away. Restaurant waitstaff and shopkeepers ignored them. Garages were always too busy to repair their vehicles. Walking past the border station while giving the middle finger salute became to local thing to do. Posters of the deceased elderly woman appeared all over town. Someone put up a huge sandwich board bearing the woman's picture at the tiny park next to the bridge, America's First Mile. It read, YOU KILLED HER!

Keying their vehicles came next. Someone had the bright idea to do a drive-by with a paintball gun. CBP and HSC complained to the local police department who did investigate, though no one could say they did so with enthusiasm.

There was talk in town about more dramatic protests of the border closure and the death of the old lady. Protesting anything that had to do with the HSC. A committee formed – The Committee to Normalize the Border, or CNB. An odd mix of town business leaders, students from the University of Maine Fort Kent campus, and two or three well-known local politicians. Petitions were signed and sent to their congressional representative and the governor. More petitions were sent to the state attorney general and the U.S. district attorney to investigate the ambulance incident. All politely received and quietly put aside. Nor was the media interested in an old story. Their efforts seemed to be coming to a dead end.

All that changed with the news of shootings in Calais. Anger at the stricter border closure and the HSC cops who enforced it ignited into rage.

That late Sunday afternoon, people gathered around the CBP border station. Some drove up in cars and trucks, blasting their horns, and blocking the station's entry lanes. More joined the crowd. The CBP and HSC cops secured themselves inside their building. The crowd chanted "HSC, OUT! HSC OUT!" More people came. The sirens in the background meant the police were on their way.

The confrontation could have burned itself out right then, but it didn't. A protester reached inside the bed of his truck, produced a three-pound sledgehammer and calmly walked up to the front entry of the CBP station. Others followed him, though they kept well behind, as if they were unsure of the wisdom of what may happen.

The man bashed the door glass, spiderwebbing the impact resistant glass. It didn't break, so he kept at it. Smashing and smashing until the glass finally broke through. He raised his hammer in victory. Cheered on by the crowd, he moved on to another window to add to his conquests. Four CBP and HSC officers came out, guns up, ordering him to drop the hammer. He turned to face them with his hammer still held up. They fired. He died on the spot.

Hammer man's compatriots retreated in a panic. Maybe it could have ended then. But one of the HSC officers aimed this weapon at the retreating protestors. He fired.

The other three federal officers reflexively joined in, targeting one person after another, indiscriminately, protestor or not. A Fort Kent police SUV arrived. The cop leapt from the vehicle into the open, yelling at them to cease firing. They kept firing. One and then another reloaded. They kept firing.

They fired at the cop. The police officer spun to the ground as a round clipped the side of his bullet resistant vest. From the ground, he returned fire before crawling to take cover beside his patrol car. He called for back-up. Any back-up.

Back-up of an unexpected form came immediately. Someone took a rifle from his truck and fired back at the CBP and HSC cops. One CBP cop fell to the ground. The Fort Kent officer could only hear the rifle's distinctive sound but could not see where it came from.

The CBP and HSC cops retreated inside their building, dragging their wounded comrade with them.

The engagement last one minute. Maybe two. Lying against his vehicle, the Fort Kent police officer could see five or six people on the ground. He kept checking on the federal cops. And on himself. No blood, but breathing was near impossible. With his field of vision rapidly collapsing, he slipped into unconsciousness as the locals dragged him to a car to take him to the emergency room.

It took over two hours for Maine State Police to arrive from their Troop office in Houlton. By then, it was well past sunset. The state police came with their lieutenant, eight troopers, plus their Evidence Response Team. At the scene, they found Fort Kent's four remaining police officers, plus others from surrounding towns. An RCMP vehicle stood by at the crest of the bridge. The Fort Kent Fire Department directed what little traffic there was away from the scene and evacuated the buildings along West Main Street that were in a possible line of fire. The local police and fire department had set up powerful lights toward the border station.

Mixed in with the police were twenty or so of the local citizens, armed with shotguns, hunting rifles, and more than a few AR type rifles. The state police lieutenant was not pleased to see this kind of public support for police. With the Fort Kent Police Chief, he called the local volunteers together in a parking lot behind a building across the street from the border station.

"Let me say first, I appreciate your help. It can take time for us to get here, but now the troopers are here. For your own safety, and the safety of my troopers, I want you to go home now. I know you've seen your people hurt. And killed. But we know how to end this without any more bloodshed."

"I promise you, those CBP and HSC personnel will be taken into custody. They will be our prisoners. They will face prosecution by the state. Thank you again for your assistance. So, okay, let's get you home."

Most started to walk away, but five made clear their desire to stay. Especially a pair with the AR rifles. One of them started yelling at the lieutenant and refused to leave.

Another voice came from the crowd. A middle-aged man, in jeans and a green winter coat. "Charley, will you just hush. The trooper is trying to do his job. He's the professional. We did what we had to do. Now we need to leave. Besides, Charley, as I recall, you just got here maybe half an hour before the troopers showed up. Long after the shooting stopped. I guess you needed to go home first and get all dressed up in your camo and vest and fancy rifle."

Charley shut his mouth, slung his rifle, and started to walk away.

As the lieutenant started to head back to the scene, the middle-aged man approached him. His hunting rifle now slung over his shoulder. "Ah, officer, I have something to say. Something I want you to understand." The lieutenant stopped, and said, "Yes, sir, go ahead."

"Name's Eddie. Sorry about Charley. He's a little off today. Most days he's like that, as a matter of fact. He's been trying to put together one of those militia groups for the past few years, so I guess this was his dream come true. Anyway, been talking to all these guys. You know, around here, most everyone supported these Homeland Security guys back when. Going after them protesters in the cities. We were fine with that. We're patriots. A lot of us are vets. Me included. Marine Corps. We didn't protest. We just wanted to go about our lives. With nobody telling us how to live our lives.

"But look where we are now. What, half a dozen of our people shot dead by them. Maybe twice as many wounded. We heard about what they did to that kid in Calais.

"Officer, those guys were supposed to protect us. Us! Instead, they've hurt us. Hurt us bad. Most of the guys around here are outta work. Most people around here have come to hate those federal bastards. Closing the border took away a lot of jobs. Even before this shooting. Me, I'm sorry I ever . . ."

The lieutenant could only gently grasp the man on his arm, and said, "I understand. We'll take care of this. Please go back to your people. We'll likely need to talk to them about what they saw. Let them know that."

The CBP and HSC refused to come out at first.

Maybe it was the departure of the vigilantes. Perhaps it was the sight of the troopers getting into tactical gear and arming themselves with assault rifles. But after a brief negotiation from the lieutenant, the federal officers filed out, unarmed, hands up. Five of them. A sixth one had died. The troopers took them into custody.

The eleven people wounded had already been evacuated to the hospital up the road. Seven bodies lay at the scene. Five men, a woman, and a teenage boy.

The Governor's Statement

Doug felt himself fortunate to get a room at the hotel in Robbinston. Nice place, clean, and inexpensive. Only half an hour from Eastport. Best part, good wi-fi. He knew he needed that if he was to start making arrangements.

Their dining room had been closed for a while, so he Googled restaurants in the area. Not many. Doug wanted a decent place with table service and cocktails. A steak would be nice. Instead, he'd settle for takeout and maybe a couple cold beers. Any such places in Calais were off the table. Lockdown and curfew and all. So, what's south along Route 1? He decided on a burger joint in Perry. A convenience store was also along the way. He felt he'd need for snack items and such.

Before he left the motel to head to Perry, Doug went to the property edge. When the place got named The Cliff, they weren't kidding. Walk too far and it's a quick trip into the Saint Croix River. The sun was setting, but the buildings across the river could still be seen. That's Canada. About a mile and a quarter away. He remembered that he'd come along this side of the river with the Coast Guardsmen from Station Eastport.

Someday, I'll have to explain to them why I did what I am about to do.

Doug took a look as directly south as he could along the Maine shoreline. Yes, he told himself, that's where it all happened. That's when things started. Right out there off of Saint Andrews. He could see the lights from Saint Andrews coming on. He thought he'd like to visit that place. That place where *the life I planned ended.*

He got in his car and headed toward Perry.

Change of plans. He could get table service. And it had a small counter that doubled as a bar. He chose the bar. Burger, fries, and a beer. Driving, he'd keep it to one beer. Doug finished the food, which he found was pretty good. Doug was nursing his beer when he saw one of the waitstaff switch channels on the television to the Bangor news station. A customer objected leaving football for the news. "Yeah, yeah, look, honey. The governor is coming on. She's got something to say about what happened in Calais and Fort Kent. With all the shit that's going on, maybe you oughta watch and learn something."

That shut that guy up, reckoned Doug.

"Good evening, I wish to speak to you about the serious violence that has happened in Calais and Fort Kent. I will review of the facts we have been able to confirm. Obviously, the attorney general and the Maine State Police continue in their investigations, and I urge Mainers to cooperate with their efforts. I urge all Mainers to put aside violence and put their trust in the judicial system of Maine."

Doug watched and listened closely as the Governor reviewed the facts of Calais and Fort Kent. To Doug, the speech so far seemed somewhat disjointed, as if hurriedly written. Of course, it would be. All this started only hours ago and was still going on. She seemed nervous, tripping over words here and there. When she included the Saint Andrews incident, Doug came within a nanosecond of yelling to the restaurant, "Hey, everyone! I was there. I took care of those HSC guys!"

Then the governor found her footing.

"There is a common thread throughout these horrific events. That thread is the Homeland Security Corps officers deployed at our Ports of Entry with Canada, Coast Guard stations and the regional offices of the U.S. Customs and Border Protection."

"In Calais, a boy of seventeen was shot and killed by an HSC officer. There was no justification for deadly force. A massacre of seven unarmed citizens of Fort Kent was perpetrated by HSC. Twice that number and more are being treated for gunshot wounds inflicted by HSC. There was no justification. Only last October, a raid was launched from Eastport by HSC to gun down a dual citizen in Saint Andrews, New Brunswick, a clear violation of Canadian law and sovereignty. Only days ago, the HSC shot and killed a Canadian lobsterman during their illegal and ultimately failed seizure of Machias Seal Island. There was no justification."

She promised the HSC officers in the state police custody would be prosecuted.

"All the facts known to us leave with this conclusion. The presence of the Homeland Security Corps officers in Maine are a danger to its citizens. Homeland Security Corps used our state as a launch pad for illegal acts. The question is, what is to be done?"

Someone in the bar said, "Support the president, that's what. Be a patriot!" The other customers groaned in disapproval. A couple threw in choice curses.

The governor demanded that the HSC be removed from the state. She singled out the HSC force at the former Loring AFB special attention. "We tried to cooperate with the federal government on the deployment of HSC and CBP resources at the long-closed air base. However, closure of the air force base means, in every legal sense, the land there belongs to the State of Maine. We have ownership. We have jurisdiction. So, as their landlord, so to speak, I am sending them a notice of eviction."

She said that until they go, the Maine State Police, with help from the Maine National Guard, will "quarantine" all the HSC teams in the state, including Loring. Any contracts between the state and the federal government to provide any support for the HSC are terminated. Unless the situation changes, CBP officers and operations will not be interfered with.

"Our attorney general has sent a formal demand to the Department of Homeland Security to immediately evacuate HSC from Loring and all other places in Maine. If HSC is not evacuated from Maine, I am prepared to order their removal by the State Police and National Guard."

Doug's mind raced to interpret what she just said. Does that mean she is laying siege to Loring? What happens if that idea spreads to other states?

She wasn't done yet. The governor said she would do everything in her power to prevent Maine from being used as a base of operations for an attack on Canada. "In addition, we demand the reopening of the border with Canada. Tomorrow, the State of Maine, with the support of New Hampshire, Vermont, New York, Massachusetts, Connecticut, and Rhode Island, will file suit to that effect against the federal government."

The governor end with a plea for calm and repeated her wish that Mainer's put their faith in the state judicial system.

Doug thought, *did a rebellion just start?*

"What's the matter, honey? You look like you're all upset by what the governor is up to?"

Startled, Doug realized the barkeep was talking to him. "Ah, yeah. Sorry. Just surprised she's gone that far."

"Surprised? I'm not all that surprised. Not surprised people around here went after them HSC thugs. Bastards killed people. Bastards ruined the economy in Maine. Especially around here. Calais, Fort Kent, Eastport. Let me tell ya. Next time they shoot at us, we'll shoot back."

"I see." That's all Doug could muster in the moment.

"I'll bet you ain't from around here. Well, ask around. You know, on Facebook, lots of protests being organized. A big one in the works for Boston. Guess the feds haven't got round to shutting Facebook down. Anyway, there's word of a protest caravan heading up Route 1 to Houlton. There's HSC cops up there at the Border Patrol building. It's just south of the town.

No one saying this online, but people are going, and I heard they're going with their guns."

Doug and Jon

Half an hour after leaving his motel that Monday morning, Doug was at the front door of Jon's place in Eastport. Jon welcomed him into the old parlor of his house, thinking most of the furniture there was definitely older than this young man. There was a nice fire going in the fireplace.

Jon brought his finger to his lips to quiet Doug. He turned on a small black speaker on the mantel, brought out his phone and started his Pandora playlist. "What's the matter, Doug. Just because I'm old, doesn't mean I don't know how to use technology." Etta James started singing "*At Last.*"

"Got a call from our, ah, your breakfast friend. He suggested I take steps to keep things, well, safe. I guess he's just worried about me."

This old guy is a marvel, thought Doug. "I understand. Let me get to the point." Once again, Jon shushed Doug and handed him a pen and paper notebook. Doug nodded and wrote. "Time for me to leave. When and how can you help me get across. LeClerc can't be of help."

Late last night, LeClerc had contacted Doug on the burner phone. He couldn't help anyone across but can help once they get into Canada. He promised Doug to look into getting him some useful words, though after a thorough debriefing.

Doug handed the notebook back to Jon, who tore out Doug's note, threw it into the fire and started his reply. Awkward as it was passing notes back and forth, in an hour they had a plan worked out that answered *how.* The sticking point was *when.*

"It's the weather. Forecast is river will start freezing soon. In three days. Must go Wednesday." Doug wanted more time to make sure his two mutual fund IRAs got transferred to a local bank branch office so he could cash out, but he finally relented. Before coming to Jon's, he'd withdrawn another sizeable chunk of money from his bank. It'll have to do.

The last thing Doug wrote before they could switch to safe conversation was, "Will you come along?"

Jon didn't write his answer. He said, "Yes, I think I will. I want to see my family."

CHAPTER EIGHTEEN
DECEPTION

Webb

The best thing Webb could say about his new home was the food wasn't that bad. Better food than at Gagetown. And the interrogations had slackened off. He was just starting his third week in his new reality, sitting at the prison dining hall with two of his fellow HSC officers.

Former HSC officers. Are they now former officers? The thought stuck in Webb's mind. Webb knew the United States was picking a fight with Canada. If they go through with it, Webb imagined they would be liberated and able to resume our old jobs. Perhaps. Webb's cynicism about higher ups brought him to only one conclusion. *HSC will need someone to blame. It'll be us. Maybe they get us out of jail, but we'll be out of work. So, yeah. Former officers.*

For their own safety, Webb and the others tried to stick together. As one prison guard explained to Webb, "We've some of our worst here. Violent guys, but guys with a warped sense of patriotism. You could've come in here charged with murder or rape or robbery and these guys wouldn't give you a second thought. But they've heard you attacked Canada. So, watch your back, eh?"

Sitting there, Webb did as he did almost every day. In his mind, He began to trace what happened since he was first arrested.

Webb and the nine other HSC officers captured at Saint Andrews first went to CFB Gagetown. The army put them into makeshift cells slapped together in one of their warehouses. Basically, heavy plywood boxes with eight-foot-high walls and furnished with a cot and a chemical toilet. No ceiling, other than heavy steel fencing laid flat. The guards at Gagetown, a mix of army MPs and Mounties, watched them from the floor and from elevated catwalks that allowed them to see their charges below.

On their first day there, they were examined by a doctor, put into orange jumpsuits with matching orange slippers, fingerprinted, photographed, and kept in solitary confinement. Yet in Webb's opinion, it wasn't really hardcore solitary. Real solitary confinement was something familiar to Webb. During his active-duty army days, he did a tour with the 15th Military Police Brigade at the United States Disciplinary Barracks. Leavenworth to the uninformed. No steel bar cell doors. At Leavenworth, there was a very solid door and a thick glass window. Clean, efficiently designed and run with a precise routine. They called a state-of-the-art facility.

At Gagetown though, if they were careful and quiet, they still managed to communicate with each other through the plywood boxes. Webb urged his men to get their stories straight, but for the most part they seemed uninterested. Mostly they griped about this or that thing about their comfort, or the lack of reading materials or no television. Or they bitched that it was the other guy who screwed up. Webb eventually gave up on his leadership role, thinking *those selfish bastards. No unit cohesion. Every man for himself.*

For Webb, the worst part then was the total news blackout. No television and certainly no internet. He had no idea of what was happening outside or what the news was saying about the Saint Andrews incident. The most they allowed was a couple of phone calls back to family in the states. Something Webb never bothered with as he had no family.

Whatever the U.S. government was doing to get them out was a complete mystery. No one from the U.S. Embassy in Ottawa or any of the consulates had bothered to pay them a visit, real or virtual. That's their job, Webb often complained to the uninterested guards. Nothing gave Webb a greater feeling of abandonment and isolation than that.

From the moment they finished being processed in at Gagetown, the interrogations by the RCMP and army intelligence began. In cuffs and leg restraints, they faced their interrogators in a special room set well away from the cells. It was fully enclosed, with steel walls on the outside and sound-proofing on the inside. Interrogated at least twice a day, he and the others faced the same questions over and over again. Webb knew the RCMP was looking for inconsistencies, making sure whatever was said was corroborated by the evidence and by the other prisoners. Cooperation might bring leni-ency, they would say. Maybe they'd be sent to something less than their toughest prison. Webb just kept his mouth shut.

His first interrogation introduced Webb to the Canadian legal system. His Canadian lawyer explained his rights and the charges he was facing. Webb remembered the guy didn't pull any punches.

"We don't do Miranda in Canada in the same way as in the states. Under our law, specifically the *Canadian Charter of Rights and Freedoms*, you can remain silent, pretty much like under the U.S. Miranda rules. You also have a right to a lawyer. Hence, me. You'll soon receive a hearing during which the formal charges against you will be made known to you. They're going to do that on videoconference. It's being set up now. The Canadian government is taking these steps to safeguard your rights."

Webb wasn't impressed. "I want an American attorney. Someone from the Department of Justice."

The lawyer held up his hand, shaking his head. "Stop right there. That will not happen, so forget about it." Waiting to make sure he had Webb's attention, the lawyer continued, "Department of Justice Canada is preparing the formal criminal charges against you and your team members. That could take time, days certainly, but it's only been two days since the Saint Andrews. For now, you're being held on murder, assault, and kidnapping. There's a whole list of other charges relating to burglary, illegal entry into Canada, firearms, and so on. As your lawyer, I must say you're facing very serious charges. If convicted, a civilian court by the way, you could face life in prison."

At that point, the lawyer said that DOJ Canada had, in fact, given the U.S. government the chance to provide them with American lawyers. They turned down the offer. That crushed Webb. He knew then they had been abandoned.

"Release prior to trial on bail is extremely unlikely. The Crown prosecu-tor, that's what we call them here, will argue at a hearing the day after tomor-row that you meet all the grounds for pretrial detention. The seriousness of the charges, the risk of flight, and the needs of public safety. Given the vio-lence associated with the charges, don't hope for bail.. It's a security consid-eration.

"Before questioning by RCMP begins, they're allowing me time to meet with you, to get your side of the story, as it were. Give me the facts. Explain to me what happened as you saw it, experienced it. And if you have information that could mitigate things, I need to know that."

Webb cooperated, going through every minute of the raid. When his lawyer asked him if he had any information that might influence his sentencing, Webb just shook his head, saying, "Maybe, but I'll let you know later."

His lawyer was right about one thing. Three days into his confinement at Gagetown, they were informed of the charges. The probability that he'd be in prison for the rest of his life began to dawn on Webb.

One week after their capture, Webb and his fellow ex-officers were transferred to a maximum-security prison. A Canadian federal prison. A real prison. The Atlantic Institution in Renous, New Brunswick.

It was a real cell. Clean, off-white painted cinder block walls. A thick glass window on the far wall. A single bed shoved into the corner. Kitty-corner from the bed was the stainless-steel single piece toilet and sink. Home.

As he sat there on the bed for the first time, he put his head in his hands, and started to sob, doing he best to keep it quiet.

In that moment Webb decided to let his attorney know about the American agent in Saint Andrews.

Plotters

Debbie was not happy. One whole week had gone by since the Prime Minister told the world about *Operation Northern Lights*. One whole week since she called the Expat Committee members to start planning for a possible war. That long for the Expat Committee to do a town hall meeting. And they were so pleased with themselves for doing it so quickly! Jesus, quickly my ass!

For the town hall's first hour, the committee ran through what they knew from media reports before offering advice to the expatriates on what they should do to prepare. Simple stuff like have an evacuation plan. Make sure cash is on hand. Get food and clothes ready. Their message ended with a plea for calm. They spent the next hour taking questions, and often providing few or vague answers.

Debbie was front and center, having been granted committee leadership, the post once held by her late husband. Outwardly, they projected unity. The committee must have seemed so peaches and cream to the Americans attending the meeting.

The truth was far different. Over the past days, Debbie argued, yelled, and cursed her way to get the town hall meeting to go. She thought the members too timid, too cautious. They, in turn, were terrified she'd lead them over of cliff. None had forgotten her eulogy of Mike. And she was only too quick to remind them of her willingness to fight. No, she assured them, she did not want to grab a gun and start killing Americans. Morgan, however, was quick to point out to her, "Yeah, I believe you, but all that tough talk. Someone is going to take what you said too far."

The town hall wound down. To Debbie, the expatriates seemed sullen. A resignation to their fate. As one woman said, "We'll hunker down and hope for the best."

Debbie had little patience for the woman's attitude, replying "How'd that hunker down plan work out for you last time?"

Debbie was about to get up from the table at the front of the hall when two younger men approached her. She recognized their faces but couldn't remember their names. One, black hair, in his thirties, who stood about 5 feet, 8 inches at most, was familiar to her. Yes, of course. A laceration across the palm caused by an errant fillet knife. Patient cases she could remember, but names? No so much. She did remember stitching up his hand sometime about the mid-summer. "Doctor Whynot, I haven't seen you since, well, the funeral. 'Course, I was in the crowd. I'm so sorry for what happened."

"Thank you. Thanks very much, Mr., ah, I'm sorry. What is your . . ."

He smiled and said, "It's okay. I'm sure you see lots of people. It's Keith. Keith Madsen. Oh, and this is Tom, Tom Anderson."

Debbie shook hands with both in turn. Anderson was a bit taller by a couple of inches. Blond hair cut short. Also looked to be in his thirties or so. "So how can I help you guys?" Anderson started talking.

"Doctor, or should I say colonel, we want to help."

"What do you mean by help?"

"We're working with other people. We all want to help. Help fight back."

"Go on." Debbie retook her seat and motioned for the men to drag a couple of chairs to the table. They sat down close to her.

The two nervously looked around for anyone else in earshot. Madsen spoke up. "Ma'am, both of us are veterans. Both of us have combat experience. We figure we can put that to use."

Debbie interrupted. "Good. I hear the Canadian Army opened enlistments for nonCanadian citizens. I suggest you go talk to them. If not, figure out some charity work to do."

Anderson spoke. "Yes, Ma'am. We might do that." He looked once more around the hall before talking. "But we have something else in mind. Something more in the line of direct action."

Madsen struck her as at least somewhat personable. This Anderson guy was another matter. To Debbie, there was something strangely cold about Anderson. Never met him before and he's starting to sound like trouble. She took an immediate dislike of Anderson.

"Alright. I think it's time for you guys to speak plainly. What's your idea?"

Anderson spoke. "Ma'am, we've formed a small unit of resisters from among the expatriates. Younger people. Military experience. We've got the first ones organized now. Enough to make trouble. We're hoping you could help us identify more candidates."

"And just what would this unit of yours do?"

"Hit back. Cross the border and hit back. Like you said, 'Today, I fight!'"

Fear began to well up in Debbie. *Maybe Morgan was right after all. Maybe my little speech might provoke a few hotheads to do something really idiotic.*

"Okay, stop right there. No, the Expat Committee, myself included, will not in any way support you. And I'm telling you right now, stop this fantasy of forming, what, a little guerilla unit to raid the United States. That will not work!"

Anderson's cold retort struck hard at Debbie. "And your meetings and television broadcasts. Are they working? Not that I can see. Or is your weapon of choice is just talk. No action. Talk only. Your husband tried that." *Anderson is not shy about hurting someone,* Debbie could see. She stood from her chair. The two reflexively did the same.

"Listen, let's bring things down to reality. Right now, just speaking to me about your plans violates Canadian law. If the Canadians find out about you, they'll throw you into jail. If Americans start shooting Americans on the other side of the border, that will end our lives here. It'll only help the far right back home. You'll give them a reason to invade. Don't you see that?"

"Both of you go away. I won't talk of this anymore. Go home."

Anderson was not done. He slipped a handwritten business card across the table in front of Debbie. "Ma'am. Here's a card with my name and number. Call me if you change your mind. Call me if you want to do something effective against the people who killed your husband."

Debbie stood in place as the two men walked away. She took the card. *Now what do I do?*

Roy

Debbie didn't go straight home. She stopped at Roy's place and knocked on the door.

"Hi, Roy. Hi, Marge. Christ, I'm sorry really for barging in like this, so late and all, but there's something I need to talk to you about."

"Sure. Of course, Debbie. Come on in. How can we help?"

Debbie started to go over her encounter with Madsen and Anderson. Roy stopped her and asked her to have a seat at the kitchen table while he got himself a notebook and pen from a kitchen drawer. As Roy made tea for the three of them, Marge excused herself. "Sounds like you two have some business to discuss."

As Marge left for the living room with tea in hand, Roy said, "Marge, whatever you hear, please, don't discuss this with anyone. Anyone."

"Jesus H. Christ. After all this time, you think I haven't learned to bottle up all sorts of things I've heard from you?" Marge winked at Debbie as she left for the living room.

When Debbie finished her story, Roy said, "I'm glad you cut short the conversation with them. And glad you told them they were breaking the law. Did anyone else witness all this? Did you talk to anyone else?"

Debbie said there were no other witnesses and no one else knows. She handed Anderson's card over to Roy. "The Madsen guy. I treated him for a laceration a while back. The other guy, Anderson. Never saw him before. Kind of a creep if you ask me."

Roy ran through his notes once more with Debbie to confirm their accuracy. "I have a contact with Canadian Security Intelligence Service. I can't remember if you ever met him. Robert LeClerc. Well, I'll call him tonight. CSIS will have an interest in this matter. You did the right thing in telling me."

"Yes, Roy. I know that. And I heard of LeClerc. If you wondered if I had any reluctance in turning in Americans, well, no. Not in the slightest. Not for these guys. I've done a lot of thinking about how I should respond if something like this came up."

"Why do you think they approached you?"

"Maybe they think I'm angry enough about, about Mike. That I'll do anything to get back at them."

Roy took a final sip of his tea. "Are you sure they're both, ah, both Americans? That is, Americans on your side?"

For a moment, Roy's question perplexed her. Then things became clearer. "So as far as I know. Wait. You think they're, well, working for the other side?"

"Always a possibility."

"I can get you what information we have on them. Tomorrow. At least, the forms the Expat Committee has on every expatriate." Jesus, Debbie remembered that's the stuff Mike tried to turn over to LeClerc. "We never had the resources to do background checks on our people, but at least it's a start. If you want, I'll bring over the files we have on everyone."

"Yes, for now, RCMP will start more thorough background investigations of these two. You said Madsen and Anderson said they had others that are part of this?"

"Yeah, they claimed they did. That's what got me so worked up about all this. I don't know how far this thing might go."

"I understand Mike pushed the Expat Committee to turn over those same files to CSIS and they refused. If they ask, you can tell them RCMP demanded the files."

"Or I can tell them to go screw themselves."

"Okay but try it my way first." Roy began tapping his pen on the paper as he tried to get himself to think. "It's late. Let's get you home. Try to get some sleep. I'll call LeClerc and I'm sure we'll talk about all this. I'll call you in the morning. Can I call you at seven?"

Preparations

The next morning, Debbie called Anderson saying she wanted to hear more of their plans. She set down certain conditions. They'd meet at a public place outside of Saint Andrews in the late afternoon and only Anderson and Madsen would come. To set them at ease, she let them choose the place to meet.

They chose a brewhouse in Saint Stephen, one near the waterfront along the Saint Croix River. Good pub food and quite good beer. To avoid the Friday evening crowd, it was agreed they'd meet at four o'clock. Find a quiet table somewhere in the brewery. One round of beers should allow enough time to talk about things.

Roy's plan was fairly simple. Debbie would try to get them to explain their plans and capabilities in as much detail as they were willing to say. She would make no promises other than to say she'd think it over. Debbie would call it quits at the appropriate time and leave for her car. Drive around for a while, then meet Roy at his RCMP Detachment building in Saint Stephen.

LeClerc told Roy he couldn't make it, explaining he was too busy with his military duties. "You know. Getting ready for a war." In his place, LeClerc arranged for another CSIS officer from his Moncton office to accompany Roy. "Her name's Sue Jenkins. I'll text you a picture of her. She's very professional, Roy. But try to act natural. Think of her as your date." Roy didn't appreciate the humor.

"No Roy, I'm serious. We should assume that these two guys will be there well ahead of time to scope out the place and observe anyone going in before they do. So, if you go flashing your RCMP badge around, you might blow things. Make it look like you and Sue are friends. She'll meet you at the Tim's where we met before. You both drive in to the brewhouse in the same car. Get there one hour before the meeting. You go in. Order a couple of beers. Sip them slowly. And wait. Mrs. Whynot will arrive first, unescorted. She'll see you, I'm sure. Try not to react."

"Christ. You know, this type of work isn't unknown to me. Anyway, our people put in a set of surveillance cams in the place this morning, before it opened. The owner is being very cooperative. Well, cooperative in the sense that a stack of minor parking violations will be made to go away. We tested the camera system. It's working well. I also got a couple more of my people to hang around the brewery in case they're needed."

"How's Mrs. Whynot?" Roy said she was fully briefed and drilled on the use of the recording device she was going to wear. "That's good, but how is she?"

"Hard to say. Keeps up a pretty tough exterior. I'm sure she'll get this done for us, but, I think, she's still hurting. Who wouldn't? Anyway, who do you think these guys really are?"

"Okay. Snap assessment. Possibility one. A couple of wannabe commandos who fantasize leading an attack on the United States. If that turns out true, RCMP can roll them up with an arrest. Possibility two. The two are as skilled as they say, combat veterans, and are genuine in wanting to attack the United States. Again, RCMP can arrest them.

"Possibility three. One or both are agents working for U.S. intelligence. They may be trying to entrap Mrs. Whynot. I suppose if they could hook her into their planning, their DOJ could make a strong case for her to be indicted and extradited. I'm leaning toward possibility three.

"Possibility four. That's the possibility we don't know about yet. Let's hope we find out tomorrow. There's something else that backs up possibility three. You remember that American HSC agent we captured on Joes Point. Name of Webb?"

"How could I forget."

"Yes, well, he's up at Renous prison with the rest of his bunch. Guess he doesn't like the idea of life in prison. Anyway, he told his lawyer he had information. On the night of the raid, Webb says they got a signal from someone on shore that had the Whynot's home under surveillance to make sure they were at home. That contact used an HSC secure communications link. Webb gave us the code words. What this means is that the Americans already might have at least one agent in Saint Andrews."

"And so," Roy got to the conclusion. "Is this Anderson or Madsen the agent? Or both?"

The Voyage of Doug and Jon

High tide, calm, and very cold. Ice was starting to form along the rocks on the shore.

As the old man said, it was simple to get across the boundary. By eight in the morning, Jon had left his dock at the Sullivan Street pier and was rounding Margie Rock, heading south for the short trip to the boatyard at the end of Sea Street. He'd fuel up there. Doug should be there to meet him.

Jon had everything on board he wanted to keep. Really wasn't much. Albums of family photos, important financial documents, his will, and his passport. A framed picture of his wife. A few cherished books. His army medals. He packed all the clothes he needed, extra food, and his two guns. And a complete set of fishing gear for two, including bait.

"You're not going to sell the place?"

"No. Not yet. Kinda hope things'll change so I can come back. Some day. Oh, yeah. I went to the town hall yesterday. Paid up my property taxes in advance for the next year. I think they thought I was crazy. Did the same for the insurance."

"Jon, well, I guess you'll be needing some help loading the boat tomorrow."

"Yes, I appreciate it. One thing more. A friend of mine has a car to sell. Your boy is looking for one, right? Gotta be a cash deal. Get to the bank. Offer two thousand dollars. The blue book is six. He'll take it. Here's a blank bill of sale. He has the title. Free and clear."

Doug arrived at the boatyard in a new foul weather coat and black watch cap. He greeted Jon and helped him tie up and get the boat fueled up. Once that was done, Doug went back to his car and brought down to the boat his two military seabags filled with all his worldly possessions, plus a couple of garment bags, and a backpack with a laptop and such.

The boat impressed Doug. The *Shirley Anne*. A deep red hull with a white cabin and standing shelter. Fiberglass, but with the lines of an old-style wood hull Maine lobster boats. All the boat gear was neatly stored and the electronics were in working order. Doug couldn't help but fiddle with the radio and radar.

"Real nice boat, captain. Is she named after your wife?"

Jon said, "Thanks, and yes, and knock off the captain shit."

Dan and his boy were in the parking lot. Doug signed the bill of sale and title and handed the boy his keys. Even selling at a loss, Doug was pleased not to simply abandon the car.

Jon and Doug paid the boatyard for the fuel, let go the boat lines and headed out into the Saint Croix River, north at about eight knots. At most, the border was only seven tenths of a mile away. Three, maybe four minutes at eleven or twelve knots. But a dash from the dock wasn't part of the plan. They went southeast from the dock, about three hundred yards or so and slowed to a crawl. From that point, they had a good view north, south and east. A last chance to see if there was trouble. Or to abort. Or to simply wave goodbye to a former life.

They saw it. The RB-S. And the RB-S saw them. It had just cleared Margie Rock when they saw Jon's boat. Doug could see their blue light pulsing, coming on fast. Doug estimated they would hit 24 knots within seconds. They had maybe a minute.

"Jon, we can't outrun them."

"So, we'll try to fool 'em." Jon turned northward, taking a leisurely speed. "Remember the plan?"

Doug went below to get the fishing poles and gear all laid it all out on the platform. Bait, too. Jon's rifle was locked into a gun rack below and the pistol in a locked drawer. If the Coast Guard boards them, they were better off keeping the guns in the open. They hid a few things before leaving the dock, such as passports and financial documents in a small, hidden compartment in the forward cabin space. As for the duffle bags and such, they'd just have to hope.

As Doug came up from below, the RB-S was alongside, fenders out, with two boarding officers ready to come aboard Jon's boat. Doug recognized one of the boarding officers and waved. The surprised petty officer waved back, saying, "Lieutenant? Lieutenant Miles?" Not knowing what to do next, he saluted Miles. Doug, still a few days shy of his official separation day, reflexively saluted back.

The boarding officers leapt aboard Jon's boat and Doug greeted them.

"Petty Officers Sinclair and Lewis, how are you this fine morning?"

Lewis spoke first. "Well, fine, ah, sir. We're fine. Excuse me, I didn't expect to see you again. I thought you were at sector. What're you doing here?"

Doug had dreaded meeting up with anyone from the station and having to answer that question. Time to trot out one plausible half-truth.

"Nothing much. I'm here with a friend of mine, Jon. I got to know him while stationed here. He's got this nice little boat and wanted to get in some fishing before he has it hauled out for the winter."

Now it was Sinclair's turn. "How did you manage to get leave, sir? I mean, all leaves were cancelled because of what going on with Canada."

"Plead my case. Use it or lose it. Had almost sixty days when I got here. Lost some here. So, the Captain quietly gave me leave, just a few days, to make up for things. Or, I'm here on an undercover mission watching the border. Which do you prefer?"

Lewis and Sinclair looked at each other and smiled. "Well, I like the undercover story, sir."

"Good. Then there's no need to tell anyone I'm out here."

Jon changed the conversation. "Gentlemen, what can we do for you? If you want me to open up any compartments, be happy to do so. Oh, and be mindful, there's a rifle and pistol locked up in a rack and drawer just below. I know you guys always ask about that."

The petty officers were successfully diverted back to their duties. Even then, their boarding inspection was a bit cursory, at least in Doug's eyes. That worked to their purpose.

The RB-S came alongside once more and picked up the boarding officers. Both sides wished each other well. The RB-S departed to the south. Doug said to Jon, "Continue north along the coast. Any other course might draw suspicion. Once we get to Gleason Point, we make our run east. Set your speed at 10 knots."

"Aye, aye, sir." Doug's military demeanor amused Jon, thinking, *I'll bet he doesn't even realize how he sounds.*

As they passed the station, Doug couldn't help but have a look. He saw someone standing behind perimeter fence. Doug grabbed the binoculars for a better look. It was Sr. Chief James. Doug waved. James waved back. *I wonder if he knows?*

Passing Gleason Point, Jon brought the boat to a stop. While Doug checked the radar, Jon did a 360 look. Nobody. Four tenths of a nautical mile from the boundary. Standing beside each other at the wheel, Doug said, "Well, Jon?"

"Doug, take her across if you would please." Turning the wheel to starboard, Doug brought the throttle up as he turned. The boat responded smartly. In two minutes, they were cruising into Canada. "Well, Doug, I'm a refugee and political dissident seeking asylum now."

"Jon, no. You're a grandfather going to visit his family."

Doug looked straight ahead. "And I'm about to be forever known as a defector." Doug's tone troubled Jon.

"You know, my friend. We can still turn around. No harm."

Doug shook his head. "No, Jon. Please don't. I have to start a new life. Back home, just can't do it. Let's keep going."

To the north, only four nautical miles away, they saw the patrolling HMCS *Glace Bay* heading toward them. Once again, Doug brought the lobster boat on a northerly course to meet the *Glace Bay*. This time, there would be no need to deceive.

The *Glace Bay* slowed and then stopped, only fifty feet way. Over a bull-horn, one of her officers asked the *Shirley Anne* of her intentions. Doug answered back, "We are two Americans. We're headed for Back Bay. We are seeking political refuge and asylum."

Told to standby, Jon and Doug watched as the Canadian boarding party came aboard and searched the vessel thoroughly. Every drawer, every cabinet, every bag. They questioned Jon and Doug separately, asking about their identification, their destination, and intentions. Before allowing them to proceed, the lead boarding officer tore off a copy of his report.

"Gentlemen, you will need this to accomplish legal entry into Canada. Please note that it documents your request for asylum. Everything is in order, it seems. Remember, you must report to a Border Services office tomorrow at the latest. If not, find an RCMP detachment office. That's it. All I can say is, welcome to Canada."

Jon's son met them at the Back Bay marina and boat yard later that afternoon. Arrangements had already been made there to pull the boat tomorrow and winterize it. All packed, the three drove to Saint John straight away, but arrived too late to go to the Border Services office on Canterbury Street. Instead, they checked into a downtown Marriot hotel.

Tomorrow, after seeing Border Services, they would all go to Halifax and stay with Jon's family. Doug included. Jon's son happily covered the hotel fare and treated them to a fine meal that night, telling them they needed "to celebrate their escape."

Doug knew he meant well, but the word "celebrate" just didn't fit his mood.

Doug called LeClerc just before dinner. "I'm glad you and Jon are safe. I mean it. When you get to Halifax tomorrow, ah, Thursday, call me again. We need to debrief you and discuss your future."

Just One Beer

Debbie saw the two of them walking into the pub. She called the pair over to her table in a corner, away from the other customers. When Madsen started to talk, Debbie hushed him, saying, "Let's wait for the beers." She struggled to keep her focus on the two and not on Roy and his CSIS partner.

The beers arrived. She was in no mood to waste any more time. "Well, we're here. I want to hear what you're planning. Then I'll decide if I want to help."

Madsen spoke first. "Sure. But I hope you understand we won't tell you everything. We can't. I mean, operational security and all."

Operational security? OPSEC? Jesus, Deborah thought. *These guys really like playing Army.* "Look, everything? No. Of course not. But enough. I'll say when."

"What the hell does that mean?" Anderson sat back in his chair, crossing him arms. Debbie was pleased she'd already pissed him off. *Good. Might keep him off balance.*

"It means you will tell me your plans. Tell me what you think you can, but I need enough information to decide if your plan is feasible. That it is an acceptable risk. Then I'll decide if I help." Debbie shifted to a tougher approach. "What did you guys think? You'd just ask, and I'd say, sure, no problem, not knowing what you were going to do?"

Madsen looked at Anderson, jerking his head toward the exit. Anderson shook his head no.

"Okay, boys. Let me be blunt. If you could do whatever you want to do, you wouldn't have approached me. So, from that, I could conclude that you two are all there is. Just you two wannabe secret agents or commandos. That's one possibility. Why should I take the risk helping out a couple of boys with Rambo fantasies? You do understand Rambo, or is that before your time? Anyway, it's up to you to prove me wrong."

"There's a second possibility. That you're genuine. That you've designed an operation that stands a reasonable chance of success that is worth the risk to me. And not just me, but the entire American expatriate community here."

Anderson decided on a frontal attack. "Mrs. Whynot, are you afraid? You talked tough at the funeral, but I guess those were just words. Fighting means risking. I thought I was listening to a patriot."

"In this fight, Anderson, patriots who throw away their lives are of no value. There's a third possibility. You two are agents for the American government. Your job is to entrap me, get evidence that I am violating Canadian law, forcing them to extradite me back to the states. Again, prove me wrong."

Madsen didn't like hearing that. "That's pretty paranoid."

"You didn't have American agents kidnap you and murder your husband. What's that old saying, just because your paranoid doesn't mean people aren't after you."

There was a long, uncomfortable pause. Debbie broke the silence. "Tell you what. I'll give you a minute to talk things over. I'll go look over the food menu on the wall over there. When I come back, we can talk."

She came back to the table and sat back down. "Well, gentlemen?"

Anderson spoke. "We're planning two operations. The first op, we lead a team to raid the former Loring Air Force Base. The base is only five miles at most from the border. We take a small team, squad size, in by land. Our targets are the CBP and HSC Blackhawk helicopters. We get close enough to damage them with rifle fire. Deer rifles with telescopic sights will do. Shoot out the windows. That won't destroy the helicopters. We'd need mortars for that. And sneaking on the base with explosive charges is not possible. They put up a very good perimeter fence. There're lights, dog, sentries. But putting a few holes in their helos will cause them to devote more resources to protect the base."

Debbie interjected. "Harassment, in other words. How do you get within rifle range?"

"We've reconned three routes in by foot. Matter of fact, we've crossed the border twice. Made it to as close as fifty yards to the base fence. Used camouflage gear we put together from scraps of burlap and cloth. Obviously, we made it back undetected. We got within rifle range of the helicopters. I mentioned at the town hall that we're both infantry. Combat experienced. They aren't running any foot patrols beyond the perimeter. Further out, they only patrol in their vehicles. Our fallback to the Loring op is to ambush their vehicles. Improvised explosive devices."

"You say you're combat experienced. Explain."

"Both of us were in Afghanistan, Army."

"What year was that?" They both answered 2018 and into 2019.

Debbie asked them to run down their military units, training, occupational specialty and ranks. "You guys have your DD214s?" They both said no, having left their service documentation and discharge paperwork in the states.

"But you need more people. You still need my help in finding more people. Is there just the two of you after all?"

"We're looking for four more people."

Debbie had enough. She leaned forward.

"You've already lied to me. At the town hall, you said there were others. That was a lie. There's just you two. You said you're combat experienced. U.S. combat operations stopped before 2018. By 2020, the U.S. was in peace negotiations with the Taliban. So, I suspect you're exaggerating your experience. And you haven't got any documentation to support your claims. Pretty careless to say you just left all that behind. How do I trust you?" Debbie paused to take a sizable slug of her beer. She then continued.

"The Loring operation sounds, to me at least, feasible. Shooting helicopters may do something. But it's like a mosquito bite on an elephant. Significant resources and risk for little payoff. No, I won't help you there. And using IEDs against their vehicles is a bad idea if some innocent family out for a Sunday drive is killed. What else you got?"

Anderson spoke this time. "We've got a couple of motorboats. Outboards. We take them across the border, at night, hit the Coast Guard Station in Eastport. That is, we burn and sink their boats."

"Those Coast Guardsmen saved my life. And they turned over the people who murdered my husband to the RCMP. Don't attack them. Leave them alone."

Madsen was about to argue, but Debbie got ahead of him.

"You know, Anderson. Madsen. I was right the first time. You're both just a couple of commando wannabes. Or for all I know, you're working for the Americans and you're trying to trap me. My first advice was my best advice. You want to fight? Enlist in the Canadian Army."

Debbie got up from her chair and headed for the door.

Anderson and Madsen stayed long enough to order a second round for themselves. When they finished, the surveillance began.

The Bridges

The Thousand Islands Bridge was the nearest and first bridge the Army planned to seize and cross into Canada. Only the bridge wasn't one bridge, but a system of bridges. On the American side, less than 20 miles from the base as the crow flies, the first of the bridges was at the small New York town of Collins Landing to Wellesley Island. Interstate 81 ran through town and over the 150-foot-high suspension bridge that, shore-to-shore, crossed almost a thousand feet of water.

Interstate 81 was the main route for the invasion forces.

A state park took up most of Wellesley Island right up to the border where I-81 became Canada 137. At the border between the opposing border stations, there was a short double span concrete bridge of less than one hundred feet in length that linked Wellesley Island to Hill Island. Past that, there was roughly a mile of roadway into Canada before reaching the bridge.

The bridge crossing the Saint Lawrence River was a combination of high suspension spans and elevated roadways. All in all, a half mile trip to Ontario. The span from one river island, Georgiana, ran just over two tenths of a mile.

On D-day, air assault battalions would hit the entire length of the bridge system. Engineers would search for and disable any explosive charges. As fast as they could, more engineers and mechanized infantry would spearhead the ground assault, going up I-81 and across the border. Humvees and L-ATVs would lead as scouts. Tactical trucks outfitted as wreckers would then follow to clear any obstructions, themselves escorted by a screen of armored Bradley Infantry Fighting Vehicles and Abrams tanks fitted with dozer blades. The heavy stuff, more Abrams, more Bradleys, and self-propelled artillery would follow them. All covered by helicopter gunships.

Operation Northern Lights called for a second invasion route. Thirty-six miles to the east, the plan targeted the Ogdensburg Prescott International Bridge. The Army would take it at the same time in the same way. Sixty miles away from Fort Drum, the ground force would travel along US 11 and NY 26 to reach the bridge. The bridge itself was a single span suspension bridge that stretched over 2,000 feet of water, shore-to-shore.

The Canadians could drop the Thousand Island and the Ogdensburg Prescott bridges at any point, drowning the invaders. The advantage lay with the Canadians if they knew what was coming. Which, as it turned out, they did.

345

Unpopular War

It was a week ago when, like everyone else on the base, Col. Henry Byron watched the Prime Minister's speech at the United Nations. Unlike everyone else, he knew how it all came about.

Only minutes after the television coverage ended, the division commander's aide called to say there would be an immediate meeting of all his senior officers. Byron acknowledged and hung up, thinking, *the day ought to be interesting.*

The general's briefing was a bit disjointed, like someone reading down a disorganized grocery list. Byron realized the man had no idea this was coming. *Good. Guess that means I'm not about to be arrested. At least not today.*

His overall message was simple. The division would continue preparations for *Operation Northern Lights*. "If changes are authorized, that will come from USNORTHCOM. If ordered, the op will be executed. Of course, there'd be an investigation of the leak of the operations plan."

What struck Byron more than anything else was the general's seeming disappointment, fear even, that *Operation Northern Lights* might be called off. Quite of few of Byron's colleagues echoed that sentiment. Byron remained as silent and unemotional as he could be. What really surprised him was when the colonel commanding division artillery spoke.

"General, frankly, I am hopeful this news will result in the cancellation of the operation."

Astonished, the general could only sputter out, "What? Colonel Mac-Donald, what do you mean?"

The colonel rose to attention from his chair at the conference table. "Sir, this plan to attack Canada was wrong from the start. It is a war of aggression. Plain and simple. I had planned to resign my command and my commission if the order to execute ever came. Well, in the last few minutes, I accelerated my timetable. Take this officially. I resign my command and my commission effective immediately. You'll have my letter within the hour."

"Colonel, you are relieved. And consider yourself under arrest as a suspect in the leak of the operation plan. Restrict yourself to your office." The colonel saluted and turned to exit the conference room. The general turned, furious, to face division artillery's executive officer. "You, Lieutenant Colonel Matthews, now command division artillery. Anyone else have something to say? No? Meeting is over. Dismissed."

Until that very moment, Byron had no idea MacDonald would do this. They weren't friends, more professional colleagues. Yet, Byron believed

MacDonald was the most apolitical officer in the room in comparison to the others. He never said anything that Byron could remember that betrayed his political sympathies. Byron immediately thought, *if MacDonald could do this, how many others are thinking the same way?*

Byron sat at the table, silently admiring MacDonald's courage. *Could I do that?*

Now a week had passed since the Prime Minister's speech. Though Byron concerned himself with the readiness of his brigade during working hours, he directed all his private moments to the news.

On the military side, NATO reinforcements were still coming in. They might face parity in tanks and armored vehicles. The Canadians were fully mobilized and deploying with knowledge of U.S. plans. The Canadian Army had fortified the Canadian side of bridges and made damn sure the media saw them setting up bunkers, placing barriers across the bridges and roads, moving armor and deploying air defenses. The Canadians made not so subtle hints they were prepared to destroy the bridges. Strategic surprise was lost. This would not be the cakewalk so many planned it would be.

Startling news came from the civilian world. Public demonstrations sprang up in cities across Canada, Europe, Japan, Australia, and more. In the United States, the cities once again exploded in demonstrations against the war. Hundreds of thousands of protesters marching on Washington, D.C., and were only turned back with the use of deadly force by a mixed force of Homeland Security, the National Guard and regular troops.

In New York, something more surprising happened.

In the late of night, heavy earth moving equipment and huge dump trucks from a sand and gravel site alongside Interstate 81, Wellesley Island Park, went to work on the highway, just south of the Customs and Border Protection Station. They spent the night dumping huge boulders, sand and other debris across the road.

A local television reporter interviewed the owner of the sand and gravel pit. "No. It won't stop army tanks. Maybe they'll just go around. But no way I was going to sit by and watch a war start right where I live. Saw on the news the Canadians put up really big barriers on their side of the bridges. I guess our army might have to come this way. Like I said, maybe I can't stop them. But at least they'll know how I feel." He went on to accept responsibility, saying his employees helped him, but he ordered them, so he is responsible.

He was arrested right away, of course. But, getting the rocks, gravel piles, and trucks out of the way proved more challenging.

Byron could only admire the man's courage. And the courage of those he inspired. New Yorkers, local and from far away, drove up to the border bridge. They set up camp on the American side, vowing to the reporters to form a human chain if the tanks came. Within days, their numbers approached a thousand.

There weren't enough CBP and HSC officers around to organize clearing of the road and arrest the demonstrators encamped near the bridges. Human blockade groups then appeared at the bridges near Ogdensburg and across the river from Cornwall, Ontario. The media reported caravans of protestors from as far away as New Jersey and Massachusetts headed to the bridges and to Fort Drum. The President demanded the New York governor order the highway department and the National Guard in to clear the road and the bridges.

She did order the New York State Police to the bridges. Not to arrest the demonstrators, but to prevent their arrest by CBP and HSC officers. The highway department, she said, was busy with other things.

Meanwhile, the administration announced HSC units would intercept "these caravans of radical anarchists." Byron wondered where they found the authority to stop people from driving together on an interstate. Freedom of assembly and all.

The rebellion spread far beyond the streets and into the legislatures. The governors of Maine, Massachusetts, Rhode Island, Connecticut, New Hampshire, Vermont, and New York jointly announced their intention to refuse their states as a staging-areas for an invasion of Canada. Byron agreed with many of the online and television analysts that the legality and practicality of this move was open to question. It looked like it would be backed up by overwhelming votes from their legislatures.

In something Byron never imagined happening, legislators in each of those states announced their intention to file articles of succession should military action commence. Perhaps half-seriously, one legislator from New York even suggested that Canada annex his state. Purely symbolic, and highly illegal, but to Byron it reflected the depth of public disfavor with the military and the administration.

True, there were many counterdemonstrations in support of the president. Right wing governors offered up their National Guard to support the action and keep order in the Northeast. Political opportunism by those governors, Byron supposed. He couldn't imagine the governor of Maine, or New York, allowing the Texas National Guard to police their constituents.

All this heightened Byron's anxiety about *Operation Northern Lights*. To him, it showed plummeting support for the Army and increasing likelihood of events getting out of control.

The biggest news of public resistance came that day during the division briefing. To counter the NATO deployments, days before the President ordered more armored forces to Fort Drum. Forgotten was the fact there is only one rail connection to Fort Drum capable of handling tanks and armored vehicles. A CSXT line running roughly north and south from Syracuse.

The general somberly announced the Teamsters Union, specifically the Railway Workers United union members who worked the CSXT line, went on strike. "CNN says they refuse to man or service any train that is carrying military equipment destined for Fort Drum or any other base they believe may be involved in *Operation Northern Lights*. That means that two loaded trains already enroute will have to be turned around or sent to some alternate site where their cargos can be redirected."

The general tried to put the best face on things, saying the equipment of the reinforcing battalions could be brought in by aircraft direct to Fort Drum's airfield, Wheeler-Sack. At the same time, Army prime mover trucks and contractors could take armored vehicles and equipment from rail depots further away and bypass the CSXT line from Syracuse.

Good luck with that, thought Byron. In his mind, he began laying out the logistical challenges. Leaving aside the rerouting problem for the two stalled trains, these air and road options would take much more time.

The base airfield could handle the Air Force's biggest cargo aircraft. But the problem is rate of delivery. The typical armored brigade combat team has 87 Abrams tanks, plus some 200 other armored vehicles. One C5-M Super Galaxy cargo aircraft can take two tanks per round trip. There's fifty-two C5-Ms in the entire fleet, but there's always aircraft in maintenance. Usually, the whole fleet's mission capable rate is around 75%. So, Byron estimated at most forty operational aircraft. Of those, some will be committed to other missions. And all that assumes they'll call up reservists. Aside from two active squadrons, most of the aircraft are in the Air Force Reserve. Call ups might be a sensitive issue. Even calling up Air National Guard in any capacity hasn't been discussed. Maybe forty is too generous. Byron adjusted his C5-M estimate down by half.

Adding in the C-17 Globemaster fleet offered brighter prospects. There were somewhere around 150 aircraft in the active-duty fleet. Even at one tank per aircraft, they would be a big help. But those numbers dwindle for the same reasons. Other commitments, maintenance, upgrades, and so on.

Even an Army type like Byron understood that only one aircraft can land at a time. Land it, park it, and unload it. Then refuel it and launch it. Our airfield had only so much capacity. And don't forget the airfield where the tanks are coming from.

The nearest usable airports are at Syracuse and Rome. Even using the former Griffiss Air Force Base outside Rome would mean offloading from planes onto flat-bed prime movers for a long road trip to Fort Drum. He remembered their Wheeler-Sack airfield finished an expansion about thirty years ago. Why did they do that? Simple. Trucking all their troops over eighty-five miles of road to Griffiss Air Force Base took the rapid out of the old Rapid Deployment Force.

Byron wondered about the truck driving private contractors the general mentioned. *How many are with the Teamsters?*

Which brought up the land option. The Army has a least a thousand prime movers capable of hauling an Abrams tank, but right now they're spread out at bases all over the country. It would take days just to get enough of them in place to pick up tanks bound for Fort Drum. Not to mention all the diesel fuel they'd need.

Using public roadways may be problematic anyway, believed Byron.

The State of New York could order the prime movers with 74-ton Abrams tanks off the road. Above weight limits. After all, reasoned Byron, if the governor uses state police to safeguard protestors, using them to keep roads and bridges from collapsing didn't seem far-fetched. Another thing. The only land route might be I-81. Byron asked himself, how difficult would it be for protestors to block the roads? Not difficult at all. Protestors could easily create their own traffic jams.

Even a maximum effort would take the better part of a week to get a complete armored brigade combat team to Fort Drum, assuming nothing went wrong. And something always went wrong. And the President wanted not one, but two additional armored brigade combat teams.

More time. Too much time. And all the while, NATO reinforcements arrive unimpeded. And we're already playing catch up.

Byron decided he'd ask the big question. In front of everyone there, he asked, "General, our D-day is seven days from now. Is that still the case? Or are we going to delay?"

"Nothing has been changed." *Stupid answer. He doesn't know. Damn him!*

"General, we do not have strategic surprise. My air assault forces will now face serious antiaircraft fire on their approach to the bridges. The bridges themselves are likely readied for demolition. We do not have a backup plan to deal with the loss of the bridges. Thousand Island Bridge's widest stretch over water is about 300 meters long. We've only a handful of armored bridge launching vehicles. Not enough at all. Obviously, the Navy can't ferry us across."

"Sir, we're facing a mobilized opponent. The two additional armored BCTs won't get here in time. And if we look at the news, it is doubtful the American people support this operation. General, as our best option, I recommend we delay our assault."

The general slammed his fist on the conference table. "Colonel, we do not have the authority to delay. That's with USNORTHCOM. I should think you understand that!"

Byron didn't like being yelled at in front of his peers. No one does. But he kept his calm, knowing that the general's anger only betrayed his own insecurity. Byron softly countered, saying, "General, you could call them." The general did as Byron expected. He exploded.

"DON'T, BYRON! DON'T PRESUME TO TELL ME WHAT I CAN DO! Byron, I've already relieved one brigade commander! I can do the same to you!"

Thank you, general. You made things easier for me. "My apologies, general. I overstepped."

The room was silent as the general calmed himself and called on his officers to refocus on the problem of finding alternate routes to the buildup. Byron kept quiet, hashing out alternatives for himself.

Should I Stay or Should I Go?

Later that evening, sitting at his desk in his robe, Byron started writing his letter of resignation. Today's conference left him with no hope. In the letter, he explained all his objections to *Operation Northern Lights*. He ended it with a respectful request to be relieved of command and retire. That was the first version.

The second version went through his objections once more, but this time he added his culpability in passing the operation plans to Canadian intelligence. More of a confession than a retirement letter. "A request for transfer to Leavenworth," he muttered to himself.

Leading his brigade into this battle was unthinkable and unforgiveable. Byron was already fixed on that. It was always only of matter of how and when to resign. As was his habit when facing difficult decisions, he scribbled a list of options, matching pros and cons.

He considered following MacDonald's example. Brave as it was, it seemed ineffectual. No one else followed his example. Another officer took his place. The operation was still proceeding. The general already had him flown out of the base. Rumor had it MacDonald was in custody somewhere in Washington.

Another option was to resign as the attack starts. Until then, he thought he could put a little sand in the gears. Not literally sabotaging equipment or anything like that, but by persuading other officers to join him. He quickly dismissed that notion. *Refusing orders that I argue are unlawful, I may have the backing of law. If I bring others to my side, then I am engaging in a conspiracy that leads to charges of fomenting a mutiny. Might was well pick out my style of blindfold for the firing squad now.*

He decided to make his resignation known to everyone at a division briefing. Maybe give a little speech. Maybe example will be the sand in the gears.

Which version of the letter should I use?

Not the first version, he thought. Someone will eventually find some trace linking me to the document passed to the Canadians. Foolish to expect they won't find out. He knew he'd look worse if he resigned on a claim of principle and morality, then only to be discovered as a traitor.

Byron decided to use the second version of the letter. While sitting in my prison cell, if the war is called off, I can always assuage my guilt with the knowledge that hundreds of American, and Canadian, mothers won't be greeted by an officer at their door telling them their child was killed in action.

Or my soldiers will go into action against a prepared foe and hundreds more died because I told the enemy.

What about my wife? Christ. What have I done to Nancy? He felt his head fall to his folded arms across the desk. *What a fool I am. What a cruel bastard I am to leave Nancy like this. She had no idea what was about to happen. That she'd see her husband arrested, tried, and sent to prison. For treason.*

Before he handed over the operations plan to LeClerc, Byron decided he did not want Nancy connected in even the remotest way to his crime. Passing classified materials to a foreign government. He had no doubt the investigators will be rough on her, but her best defense was to not know.

He'd already planned his own defense if he was arrested. No defense at all. Plead guilty. Explain his reasons in court. Pack his bags for prison. At least, Nancy would still be left with our savings and investments, enough to grant her a fairly comfortable life, even without his military pension.

There was always another way out. Byron looked away from his desk to the safe in the corner of the room where he kept his personal firearms. No, that is not an option.

In the morning, he would talk to Nancy.

Nancy

Before breakfast, he shared only the first version of the letter with Nancy. At first, she seemed shocked by the resignation. Nancy knew he was headed for general stars. It was all so unfair, she knew. Then the moment passed. She recovered. "I think I understand, Henry."

"In fact, I'm feeling quite relieved. Yes, resign. I don't see you have any choice. Stay in command of your brigade and lead them in this attack, you'll be committing a crime. A war crime. So, get out. I want you out."

They embraced. For the first time in many years, Henry started crying. *She probably thinks I'm crying over the end of my career,* he thought. *No, I'm crying because of what I've done to her. How I lied to her.*

Hearts and Minds

Since the publication of *Operation Northern Lights*, Debbie and Matt spent hours obsessively watching cable news. CNN, CNN International, BBC, Fox News, CNBC, and CBC. The stories were often terrifying. And sometimes absurd. Today was no different.

CBC showed many videos of Canadian and NATO forces on maneuvers, on land, air, and sea. The RCAF setting up contingency airfields on highways. Antiaircraft missile batteries manned by Canadian, French, and British soldiers being set up at RCAF bases and around the naval base at Halifax.

Calling in to a rightist news outlet that morning, the President used the Canadian buildup as proof of his claim Canada and NATO were preparing to attack the United States. He went on to demand the release of the HSC officers held by Canada, perhaps slipping when he called them "my police." He hinted at cyber retaliation and the imposition of an embargo and blockade of Canada.

Then the president stumbled into the ridiculous, claiming that Americans living in Canada were being arrested and attacked. By Canadians. Matt quipped, "Mom, guess that's news to us. So far, it's only been Americans attacking us up here." Matt immediately regretted the remark, fearing he just reminded his mom of her husband's murder.

"Matt, he's building a new justification for invasion. 'I have to invade Canada to rescue persecuted Americans.' When have we heard that before?"

Yesterday, CNN International announced a new poll of Americans. Support for the war was in the low 20% and opposition almost 70%. In Canada, the numbers were reversed. CBC covered the same poll and went further, showing images and interviews with the thousands of Canadian reservists reporting for duty, and thousands more waiting their turn at recruitment centers. Though the polls in Europe showed somewhat weaker support for war, just over 50% favored defending Canada.

Matt noted then that the most telling poll might be Wall Street. At noon yesterday, the President suspended trading indefinitely as the Dow Jones, NASDAQ and S&P 500 went into a brief free fall, losing almost 20% of value in less than two days.

As to be expected, the President's supporters in Congress came out in favor of war, but to varying degrees. Some seemed to revel in the prospect. Others kept their comments to generic statements of support for the troops. Then there were the elected idiots.

A senator demanded the White House arrest and deport all Canadians in the United States. Or intern them in camps.

A congresswomen called for the execution by firing squad of whoever leaked *Operation Northern Lights* and the arrest of anyone in the media connected with divulging any information on U.S. military deployments.

Three senators held a press conference where they somberly demanded the U.S. Department of Justice, for reasons of national security, arrest the governors of the New England States and New York.

A congressman from Florida introduced a bill that would require the U.S. Fish and Wildlife service change the name of Canada Geese to Traitor Geese and issue a permanent federal open season on the bird.

Debbie and Matt got a good laugh out of that. "Matt, you think anyone told that moron that the geese were named after a scientist, John Canada?"

That evening, the news moved on from absurdity to tragedy.

A story first reported on Bangor TV news, but picked up by CNN, CBC, YouTube, Fox, Twitter, Facebook, and hundreds of other media outlets, large and small, spreading the story across the world. A firefight between protestors against the war and militia supporters of the President at the CBP Sector facility in Houlton, Maine.

Fourteen protestors' dead. Twenty-three wounded. Six militia were dead. Five more wounded. One State Trooper caught in the crossfire suffered a leg wound that severed his femoral artery. He died enroute to the hospital. There weren't enough ambulances in that half of Maine to carry all the wounded.

Colonel Byron saw the report too.

No Plan Survives First Contact

Four days until D-Day. The daily senior officer briefing with the general was about to begin. The general opened with a startling announcement.

"Gentlemen, USNORTHCOM accelerated the operation by two days. The Friday after Thanksgiving. H-hour is 0500. Here are the changes to the plan."

"We cannot stop Canadians from fortifying and mining the bridges and we must have those bridges. The Canadian Army defends the bridges now. Antiaircraft missiles and guns are deployed. They set demolition charges on the Canadian side of Thousand Islands Bridge and the bridges at Ogdensburg and Cornwall. They've zeroed in artillery on the entire stretch of the roadway. We must assume they've also assigned aircraft to target the bridges. If we went in as originally planned, they'd slaughter the air assault force. Even if U.S. forces secured the bridges intact, the long columns of tanks and armored vehicles would be in the open, arrayed in a long thin line, vulnerable to attack by infantry antitank weapons, artillery, and air strikes."

"We've lost the strategic surprise essential to *Operation Northern Lights*, but USNORTHCOM and the commander-in-chief are determined to see it through, at least to some extent."

Byron thought otherwise. *The administration doesn't know how to back down. Politically, they feel they must do something even if they can't thunder run to Ottawa. At least they're not having us go on Thanksgiving.*

The general announced USNORTHCOM had modified the plan. Ground forces would move right up to the border but stop. The Canadians and NATO would not attack forces marshalling on U.S. soil. Just before they reach the border, the administration would tell the Canadians and NATO of our intentions to stop.

For the briefest of moments, Byron felt relief. *Christ, thank you. We won't invade Canada.* That moment passed as the general continued.

"But we will demand the bridges remain intact and open. Ground forces will remain in position to threaten invasion until such time as the administration extracts certain concessions from Canada. Engineers and special forces will covertly reconnoiter the bridges to locate demolition charges and uncover their defenses. Reaper drones will also keep a constant watch over the bridges."

So, thought Byron, *someone in the Pentagon thinks they can seize the bridges through a special forces assault. High risk. Might work, but most special ops don't work. Does anyone think the Canadians are not thinking of that possibility?*

"However, if they destroy the bridges, if they resist at all, U.S. Naval Forces will strike their Naval bases in Halifax and Esquimalt. We will sink their warships at sea and in port and destroy their fuel and weapons depots. If necessary, we will attack any other NATO warships at sea in the position to defend Canada. At the same time, U.S. Air Forces will strike Canadian Air Force bases and shoot down any Canadian and NATO fighters, achieving air supremacy. Additional Air Force wings are getting their assignment now. That includes Air National Guard.

"After destroying Canadian air and sea power, administration will then offer the Canadians terms, based on the objectives of the original *Operation Northern Lights*. The demilitarization of Canada and their withdrawal from NATO would be almost entirely achieved even without having to take Ottawa.

"Keeping our troops on the U.S. side of the bridges, fixes in place the bulk of Canadian and NATO forces. USNORTHCOM believes we can then regain the initiative. The two armored brigade combat teams that were destined for here will shift to other points of weakness. If we threaten in enough places, NATO will start to run out of assets. Remember, they have to deal with the Russian threat."

Byron couldn't believe what he just heard. *Did the General intimate that our actions are being coordinated with Russia? You goddamn . . . they should charge you with treason, not me.*

The general suggested that there may be an advance on Montreal or Quebec City. Or from Maine, going through New Brunswick and then to Nova Scotia with an objective of Halifax.

"Personally, I like the Halifax scenario. Might be a role for the Marines if we go that way."

Any hope Byron had for sanity to prevail evaporated. *Our move to the bridges is now a feint. Christ, it could work if we move quickly. It would mean a longer war.*

"USNORTHCOM nixed leapfrogging the bridges with an air assault troops against Ottawa. Without support from ground forces, it would end in defeat."

Securing the roads and bridges along their line of march to the border, the general explained, would largely be the responsibility of Homeland Security Corps.

"The Army does not have the necessary legal authority to deal with civilians. USNORTHCOM has concluded the New York State Police will not be of any assistance in this matter."

A colonel sitting next to Byron broke protocol, leaning toward Byron, saying "Well, to hell with the State Police." The general overheard the comment. "Yes, colonel, I quite agree."

Everyone at the briefing knew two days previous the governor of New York had issued an executive order closing the New York bridges to heavy military vehicles, claiming they would cause severe damage. She ordered the state police to the bridges and had the highway department to deploy sand filled dump trucks at on-ramps and on the bridges themselves.

The general then asked Byron to brief on the readiness of his brigade. Byron went to the podium. From his blouse pocket, he took out a sheet of paper. He looked straight at the general.

"General. *Operation Northern Lights,* at least the original version, assumed an unprepared foe. Instead, the Canadians and NATO are well-prepared and are motivated to fight. We can't cross the Saint Lawrence against a prepared defense. They knew of our plans. How did they know? I can tell you."

"They knew of the plan because I told them. Weeks ago, I passed a copy of the operations plan to a contact with the Canadian government. I hoped this would stop this foolish and unlawful war. I was wrong. I misjudged the determination, no, depravity, of our leadership."

Byron was surprised he got so far in his speech before the general and several of the other officers exploded in rage. The general leapt up to the podium. For a moment, it looked to Byron the general might take a swing at him. Instead, he raged and swore at Byron, before ordering his aide to call the MPs.

"Byron! You are under arrest! You goddamn traitor! Troops are going to die because of you!"

Byron let them rage. When their anger seemed to sputter for a moment, Byron continued.

"None of our troops need to die! General, here's my letter of resignation. My confession. I stand by what I did, and I will accept the consequences. You execute this operation, even this new version, and you and everyone here will be committing a war crime! And if any of our troops die, it's because of you."

Byron stopped, thinking, *I'll save whatever else I want to say for my trial.*

CHAPTER NINETEEN
H-HOUR. D-DAY.

First Engagement

D-day. The division's first engagement that very early morning was against its own citizens.

Protestors had stationed themselves outside the base and along the roads leading to the bridges. I-81, NY 12, NY 26 and NY 11. They weren't there to block the Army, but to warn of their departure. The shortest, most direct, most unpopulated route to the bridges from Fort Drum was along I-81, leading to Collins Landing. Twenty-five miles.

Ahead of the advanced D-day, HSC promised the Army and the White House their officers would prevent demonstrators from hampering the Army's line of march to the border. They overpromised. The widespread demonstrations in so many of America's cities, towns and universities had already thinned the number of officers available to support *Operation Northern Lights.* Advancing the invasion timetable didn't help either.

An hour before dawn, two CBP Blackhawk helicopters landed twenty HSC officers in a field nearby the Thousand Island Bridge Authority tollgates in Collins Landing. HSC couldn't put together a larger force and they were already behind schedule. HSC reinforcements in tactical vehicles were still hours away.

Once HSC got to the tollgate building after walking across a sodden field, they found themselves facing a couple dozen New York State Police having their morning coffee. A conflict was inevitable. However, one side forgot the key personnel needed to win the day.

Bureaucrats.

The HSC officer-in-charge argued to the Troop Commander of the New York State Police that federal jurisdiction took precedence, as the federal officers were supporting a military operation being conducted on a federal highway. The HSC leader argued the Supremacy Clause of the U.S. Constitution allowed them to override state law and government. He waived a letter from the Secretary of Homeland Security at the State Police. He was rather pleased with himself.

The New York State Police had their own view of Federalism, arguing the bridge and the interstate roads were state assets and had been since the Eisenhower administration. Troopers enforced law on the interstate. State public works departments maintained the interstate. Ipso facto, the state had the jurisdiction necessary to close the bridges to vehicle traffic that would likely damage the structure. Like seventy-ton tanks.

Then the troop commander introduced the HSC leader to a lawyer with the bridge authority. The lawyer handed the HSC leader a copy of the bridge authority's rules and regulations. In the thoroughness that only a professional bureaucrat could muster, she explained why tanks are not allowed.

"As you can see in the section I highlighted for you, Section 5503, Point, 2, page eleven, there is a list of excluded vehicles. Most pertinent to this situation is Part d. It excludes any vehicles with tracks. As Army tanks have tracks, they cannot use the bridge. Also, Part n of the same section grants the bridge authority the authority to exclude, and I quote, 'Vehicles determined to be unsafe by an Authority.' The bridge authority has determined that the U.S. Army tanks are, in fact, inherently unsafe to traffic and the bridge structure itself.

"Continuing, vehicles over forty-five tons require special permitting and an escort by bridge authority personnel. Army tanks run, I believe, around seventy tons. And they are oversize. The Army failed to secure the necessary permits and no bridge authority personnel are available to provide the required escort, nor to inspect the vehicles to ensure their compliance with the bridge authority rules and regulations.

"Therefore, the Thousand Islands Bridge Authority will not allow the Army vehicles on the bridges. The New York State Police will enforce this prohibition, as they normally do in this situation. Violation of this prohibition could result in the arrest of the vehicle operators and impoundment of the vehicles in question. Do you have any questions, thus far?"

Exasperated, all the HSC officer-in-charge could come up with was, "Christ! Are you seriously saying a United States Army armored column is going to be stopped because they didn't get the right permits?"

She replied, "Yes, that is exactly what I am saying. They must apply for the permits, await our decision, and then wait for our personnel to inspect and escort. Otherwise, the Army and Homeland Security Corps will face penalties and prosecution under the laws of New York, as I stated previously."

The troopers nearby broke out into laughter. Bureaucrats: one. Army: zero.

To close things out, she produced her own cease and desist letter from the New York attorney general. It was a legal stand-off. Then again, the troop commander had no idea how a handful of troopers would arrest thousands of soldiers.

The military planners missed something else. In the 1950s, less than a mile south from the cloverleaf ramps at the foot of the bridge, the I-81 builders blasted out a path through the hills, leaving rock walls as high as twenty feet on either side and the median of the highway for over 500 feet. No secondary roads ran parallel to the highway. To the immediate east was a huge bog. To the immediate west, dense woods. It was a man-made bottleneck the protestors didn't miss.

The spotters for the protestors waited until the main Army columns fully committed to moving on the interstate after they left Fort Drum. They signaled their compatriots in Collins Landing, who raced south on I-81 in old trucks and cars, most driven or some towed, to block both sides of the interstate's bottleneck. Army helicopters above could only watch as the protestors jammed their cars and trucks together in a barrier below the highest point of the rock walls. As a final touch, they punctured the barrier vehicle tires before retreating and hiking up to watch from the rock walls.

They knew the barricade couldn't stop the tanks, but it could delay them. Besides, by hiding people in the trees, some excellent video propaganda would be theirs for the taking.

When the column arrived, it faced two choices. Turn around hundreds of vehicles and go about three miles back down the interstate. Get off at the exit for Route 3. First right heading north on Route 13 through the village of Omar to Route 180. That would get them to NY 12. That'd take them into Collins Landing and the bridge onramps. The downside? They'd be in full view of the awakened citizenry and their cameras. And there's no guarantee the protestors don't have another little surprise waiting for them.

Or bulldoze straight through the line of junk cars, out of sight from the public. So, it was this highway, or find another way.

They bulldozed, knocking aside the barriers. All the while, protestors looking down from the rock walls hurled down insults. And very loud music. Really loud music from obsolete but functional boom boxes. They played only one song, over and over again. The troops below withered under the assault of the theme music of *It's a Small World*. One protestor said, "You know, it'd be more humane if we shot them. That music has to be a war crime."

As the Army's heavy vehicles attacked the barricade, a handful of light tactical vehicles took covering positions. The infantry they carried took covering positions, and the gunners directed the vehicle machine guns up toward the top of the cliff walls.

One young woman at the cliff's edge urged her fellow demonstrators forward. They looked down and waved at the soldiers. On the other side of the bottleneck, others did the same. One soldier in a vehicle waved back and let his machine gun's aim fall to the ground. Other soldiers in the infantry screen then stood up from firing positions and held their weapons in a more relaxed manner. Others yelled greetings to the people above them.

At the cost of a fine collection of junk vehicles, the protestors forced the Army to waste an hour as the tank dozers and wreckers cleared the road. A stunning victory of asymmetric warfare.

While the Army engineers cleared the bottleneck, a second battalion of demonstrators ran drove themselves up on the Thousand Island Bridge – Alexandria Bay span itself. When you have defied the United States Army by blocking their passage on a major interstate, scooting around a bridge's tollgate without paying somehow didn't seem so serious a crime. Had the bridge authority attorney the opportunity, she would have informed the occupants that demonstrations on the bridge were prohibited under Section 5505, Point, 3. Instead, she decided to leave that to the troopers. As the protestors passed, they honked and waved at the HSC officers. They didn't wave back.

Tipped off by the protestors, a satellite news van and reporter stood by the tollgates and caught the whole scene. When an HSC officer tried to block their camera, a trooper pushed him away.

Parking their vehicles on ahead, protestors got out to form a human chain at the first bridge tower. Only a few hundred people were needed. They didn't block the bridge to everyone, letting the few commercial trucks and commuters pass unmolested. The mood among them was almost festival like. They waved banners, played music and sang songs. Most everyone had a cell phone out, ready to take video for the world to see. The Army and HSC would have to meet them head on. This was the protestors' main line of resistance. Stopping the Army was out of the question. Instead, delay them. Embarrass them. That was their goal.

Orbiting the scene in a helicopter leading the air assault elements, the general kept his eye on the armored column, as any good battlefield commander should. But then in his mind, he unwisely took the counsel of his own frustrations. The resignation of MacDonald. The betrayal by Byron. The protestors at the rock wall bottleneck on I-81. HSC's failure to secure the bridge. The constant media attention. Now all he had left to command was the equivalent of a Sunday morning drive up to grandma's house at the border. Nothing that would further his career. And even that was looking farcical. *Jesus, his troops waved at the protestors on 81! Now look at them protestors! Getting up on the bridge. Goddamn it!*

Being under fire was nothing new to the general. He commanded combat troops in Afghanistan and Iraq as a junior officer and had a Purple Heart and a Silver Star to prove it. In his first engagement, he remembered all those lessons on leadership at West Point. And in the second before his first shot in anger, a memory of one of his professors came to mind. He had quoted Emerson. "Keep cool, and you command everyone."

The general forgot that lesson this morning. And this action was wholly different. It was one thing to combat enemy soldiers and terrorists. It's entirely another thing to face down your fellow countrymen. Only then he began to realize how ill prepared he was, in training, professional experience and his own psychology. The general's composure began to collapse in front of everyone.

He diverted one company of air assault infantry to land by the northern end of the bridge. The general ordered the captain commanding the company to clear the bridge. "Captain, march your troops down the goddamn bridge and arrest every goddamn protestor there. I want that bridge cleared! Now!"

The captain should have advised the general that regular troops had no authority to arrest civilians engaged in an exercise of their Constitutional right to protest their government. He should have reminded the general that HSC does have the authority to arrest civilians and the small unit of HSC officers was already marching toward the protestors. He should have told the general it was not a lawful order. Instead, he went along.

From a loudspeaker mounted on an orbiting helicopter, the captain had the pilot warn the demonstrators to move out of the way. No harm will come to them if they peacefully walk down the bridge. After the company dismounted from the helicopters, the pilot lifted off and continued his messaging to the crowd while orbiting the bridge. The captain led his company up the northern bridge span.

The HSC officer-in-charge would have none of this pleading for compliance. Already feeling humiliated by the state police, he led his officers on a march up the bridge, in a single line across the roadway. Batons and long guns at the ready.

At fifty feet from the first human chain, he used a bullhorn to warn the demonstrators to leave. They refused. He kept yelling. They kept singing. He drew his sidearm and fired several warning shots into the air.

The warning shots startled an HSC officer who then brought up his carbine and fired. Reflexively, others started firing.

Four, five, then six demonstrators fell. Horrified, the HSC officer-in-charge ran out in front of his men, yelling "CEASE FIRE! CEASE FIRE!" Confused, frightened, they kept firing. Only a hundred feet behind the line of demonstrators, the air assault company took cover from the rounds that missed the demonstrators.

The Army helicopter pilot radioed the captain. "Jesus Christ, captain! HSC is shooting those people. I saw it! HSC started shooting!" Without waiting for the captain, the pilot called over the loudspeaker, "CEASE FIRE! CEASE FIRE!" HSC finally stopped shooting.

The captain moved forward among the demonstrators who lay dead or wounded. He almost broke down as he stepped into a pool of blood, realizing it came from a boy. A boy of not more than ten, dead, his parents holding his body, pitifully trying to cover his head wound. *My God. What happened here?* His sergeant brought him back.

"Captain, I've got our medics working on these people, but we need more help. We've got to get these people Medevac'd. We've got more than a dozen wounded. Half that number dead. Captain? Captain!" He grabbed the captain, shaking him to get his attention. He got it.

"Sergeant, over there." He pointed to where they had landed earlier. "Take the wounded over there. Grab the troopers as you need. Get help from the people here to carry the wounded or use their cars. I'm ordering the helos to prep for a MEDEVAC. Our medics will go with them."

As he called the helos, the captain called over to a lieutenant platoon leader. "Get your people over here." The platoon assembled, the captain led them toward the HSC officers, who now huddled in against the side of the bridge. The captain ordered the lieutenant to disarm the HSC officers.

"Captain, if they resist?"

"I don't think they will." He pointed to the state police cruisers racing up the bridge. "If they resist, defend yourselves. But I'll ask the state police to place them under arrest." The captain then pointed to the TV crew who followed the state police up the bridge. "And if the TV news people try to talk to you, tell them exactly what you saw. Tell them that we're evacuating the wounded but ask them to stay back." The captain stopped for a moment, held the lieutenant's arm, and said, "They don't need to see that boy. No one does."

The general was already screaming when the captain radioed him. "Get that bridge cleared, captain! Get it done right now!" The general wouldn't stop. He didn't acknowledge the dead and wounded. He just kept screaming to get the bridge cleared.

The captain looked down to his blood-stained boot as the general ordered him to halt the MEDEVAC.

"General, that is an illegal order. I will not stand down the MEDEVAC. Those are American wounded. My troops will help the wounded. Over." The captain threw down the handset. He ordered his soldiers to keep helping the injured.

"Excuse me, captain." The captain looked behind and saw a state police trooper. "Captain, I'm commanding the state police detachment here. We know HSC did the shooting. We saw it happen. We'll be taking them into custody. Anyway, I, ah, couldn't help but overhear you and your general. Is that the guy in charge of Fort Drum?"

The captain nodded and said, "Yes, commanding general, 10th Mountain."

"Captain, please tell him to land his helicopter. The New York State Police would like to speak to him."

"Officer, you can talk to him directly on our radio if you wish. He's up in a helicopter observing this, all this."

"Yeah, that'd be great. Won't get you into trouble, will it captain?"

The captain thought, *I'm already hip deep in shit with him. So, what difference will a little more make?* "Standby and I'll get him on the radio."

From a couple of feet away, the trooper heard the general yelling at the captain. *Kid's got balls,* thought the officer. The captain handed his handset over to him and stood nearby.

"General, I am Major Silva with the New York State Police. We need to talk to you now about what happened here. I'm not going to do that over a radio set. Land your helicopter in the vicinity of the tollgate."

The general refused, to which Silva replied. "Land it here. Land it now, or the state police will come onto Fort Drum and arrest your star-studded ass. What's your pleasure?"

The general landed in the field near the tollgate.

The first helicopter began to lift off with the wounded.

The first social media posts were up before that.

CBC Breaking News

At his garrison headquarters in Halifax, LeClerc watched as CBC announced breaking news coming from New York.

"Moments ago, these scenes came to us on a live feed from a New York television news crew. In Alexandria Bay, New York. There's been a deadly incident where the Thousand Islands Bridges begin in Collins Landing. It involves American demonstrators and the U.S. Army. We must say we do not have all the details, but we do know a number of the demonstrators are dead. More are wounded. They were shot down as they tried to block the movement of the U.S. Army onto the bridge.

"As you know, U.S. Army troops are moving toward our border in two places. An armored column, supported by helicopter borne troops and gunship, is approaching the Ogdensburg-Prescott Bridge. Another column is approaching the Thousand Islands Bridges. The same spot where the shootings happened. As unbelievable as it sounds, we are seeing the opening stages of an invasion of Canada by the United States.

"We expect a statement from the Prime Minister within the hour. However, a statement just released from the Defense Ministry affirms that Canadian and NATO forces mobilized to resist the American forces if they cross the border.

"As to the Thousand Islands Incident, we're also monitoring various social media sites. Video of the incident have shown up on many sites. Some of the video is very graphic. But we have some now, can we play it? Yes, okay, here it is . . .

"There, it looks like video taken from the demonstrators, facing south, down the bridge into the town, and there we see a line of troops advancing toward the demonstrators, toward the person taking this video. If we can, can we confirm who these troops are? The ones in black. Are they U.S. Army? Are they civilian police?"

Popping noises rise above the video's background noise. "Yes, right then, we saw one of those troops, perhaps the leader out in front, take out a pistol and fire into the air. A warning perhaps. But . . . right then, another soldier or whatever he his, starts shooting with a rifle. Then another and another." The video ended.

By then, LeClerc was surrounded by his fellow military intelligence soldiers. Throughout the night, his people had processed the reports coming into CSIS that originated from sources around Fort Drum. They also had an ally in social media. Constant uploaded video showed the armored column coming up Interstate 81, plowing aside the barricade, and the mocking chants from atop the rock wall.

As the senior officer present, LeClerc felt he had to say something. Something profound to suit this moment in history. All he could come up with was "Well. Shit."

A corporal across the room rescued history. "We all saw that in the first engagement of this war, Americans killed Americans. They killed their own."

CHAPTER TWENTY
ONCE MORE, UNTO THE BREACH

Kidnapped

Debbie did her best to provide for the Thanksgiving holiday. The American Thanksgiving, rescheduled for Saturday. There was Matt and Anna. Marge and Cheryl, with James, came over and helped with the preparations. George and Roy were at work. After all, war doesn't allow for holidays.

Debbie was out of her medical boot. She remarked on that more than once during the cooking.

They were joined by her RCMP guardian angel, Constable David Kalinowski, one in a line of RCMP officers who still stood a security watch over the Whynots, though their number dwindled to only one officer at a time. His shift would expire at midnight. They normally stayed in their RCMP vehicle outside, parked just up the driveway to Joes Point Road. But this day, this holiday, Debbie would not leave her protector out in a cold car when there was a feast in the works.

Turkey, a small one suited to six and a half people. Mashed potatoes, squash casserole, green beans cooked in salt pork, baked carrots with onions, meat stuffing and bread stuffing. A small hill of home-made rolls. They ate their pumpkin pie with vanilla ice cream while seated in the living room, watching college football. Cocktails would wait until after dessert.

The only thing lacking in the meal was joy.

Constable Kalinowski politely declined the cocktail, thanked them for the wonderful meal and begged to resume his duties outside.

She knew, they all knew, this would be a tough day. The first holiday without Mike. Inevitably, mention was made of Mike. A memory. Something he would do on the holidays. Something he would say or what dish he really liked. It helped. And it hurt at the same time.

The celebration ended with the football game. Debbie and her kids did their best to enjoy the game. Marge and Cheryl politely pretended to do the same, but instead spent the last quarter cleaning the dishes and the dining area. Debbie tried to help, but Marge steadfastly barred her from the kitchen, and in a steely voice ordered Debbie to sit down and rest. Marge and then Cheryl hugged them before leaving. Even little James gave them all big hugs.

By ten that evening, they all started to doze off in the middle of a Christmas movie they always watched on Thanksgiving. Then off to bed. After checking the door and window locks and setting the alarm, Debbie looked at the constable sitting out there as he waited for his relief.

It was one in the morning when her cell phone rang. These days, she allowed most calls to go directly to voice mail unless she recognized the caller. The ID identified the caller as RCMP.

"Ma'am. RCMP Constable Jones. I relieved the constable who was here earlier. I'm calling from out front. Could you please come out to the door? There's something important I need to inform you about."

Unconcerned, Debbie got up. *It's RCMP. He said it was important.* She put on a heavy robe over her pajamas, slipped into a pair of thick slippers, and went to the door. She let Matt and Anna to sleep.

On the porch stood a tall figure, but hard to see with the light from a flashlight shining in her face. All she could make out was the silhouette of the RCMP cap and what was a man with a heavy coat. She stepped forward outside onto the porch, allowing the door behind her to fall shut.

"Jesus, officer, could you get the light out of my face?"

"Yes, Ma'am." But in the next second, Debbie felt twisted around, a gloved hand over her mouth, shoving something inside at the same time. *A ball? Wrapped in a cloth?* She felt her arms being grabbed, brought down in front. A sticky, tearing sound. She couldn't move her arms. *Held together, at her hands?* Then the sticky sound again. Something wrapping around her head, covering her mouth.

Now being dragged, lifted. A car door. She realized she was inside a car.

The man grabbed her head to face him. He spoke. "Not a sound. You yell for help, and I will go inside and kill everyone there. Understand?" The man showed a gun. Black with a long barrel. Then things went dark. She guessed, *a blindfold or something. Legs. He's grabbed my legs. The sticky sound again. He's taped my legs together. At the ankles.*

Jesus, they came back! They came back to get me!

She heard the thud of the door closing. Then another door opened, and the car started. He drove away. In what must have been just a couple of minutes later, Debbie sensed the car stopping again. She heard the door open and immediately felt the man grab her, dragging her out, pulling her upright. She couldn't walk. He lifted her almost entirely off the ground and walked her a few feet to . . . slam! Metal. Another car. The door opened again. Shoved in the back, lying on . . . a car floor? The car started moving.

Settle down. Settle down, Debbie. Think. Process. What do I sense? What does this feel like? Rubbery. I'm in the back seats, no, lower, where the feet go. I'm being driven. I'm facing . . . yeah, my feet, they're on the driver's side. Okay, keep going. I'm facing forward. Every time he speeds up, I feel it. I feel the back of my head going backwards. Don't stop. Move the arms, up. Tight. Hard to move. Twist a little. Yeah, that's better. Keep doing that.

The man's voice. Think. The man's voice. Heard it before? Yes. Sometime before. Somewhere. Get him to talk again. Kick the seat. No. No room. Get him to talk. Moan. Moan as loud as you can. As long as you can. Get him pissed off. It worked. "Enough, Whynot. Shut up."

He knows my name. Not random. He slipped up. I know that voice . . . Anderson! That guy Anderson!

Fantasies of Glory

Anderson was an agent behind the lines and out of communication. He had done everything his handlers in HSC asked of him. He passed them intel on the expatriate community. Their names, addresses, and their stories. More than once, Anderson told them he knew more about the Saint Andrews Americans than anyone else. Short of getting on the Expat Committee, he'd done everything HSC asked of him and more.

Since October's Joes Point fiasco, he'd received zero assignments. No calls incoming on his HSC provided satellite phone. When he did call HSC out of frustration, they told him to cease calling until they called him. All they said was, "Just maintain your cover until we need you again."

He followed his orders. He tried to keep the proper mindset, almost becoming his own preacher. *I am a true believer. A believer in the new America we're trying to create from the ashes of her failures. Strength. Power. God. The righteousness of their cause. The moral failure of democracy. Their treason against his race.* He did all he could to discipline himself, to shield himself from doubt.

But with each passing inactive day that task become more difficult. His work began to seem altogether futile. Useless. Alone. No one to talk to. Nevertheless, Anderson kept his cover, even to his despicable roommate Madsen. He submerged his thoughts. *Jesus, the stuff that Madsen believed. That I had to pretend to agree with. Acting like a parrot speaking to his master.*

HSC still hadn't called. Anderson's anxiety grew, supplanting the faith he once held in the cause.

Those HSC fools, those incompetent fools from Eastport. I did my job. I watched the Whynots. I gave them accurate intel in real time. I did everything well. But they screwed it up. And so, who is cut out now? Who's out . . . what was that expression from that old spy movie he saw a couple of weeks ago . . . out in the cold?" Me. I suffer because they blew it.

A little over two weeks ago, the solution to his problems came to him as he walked alone one unseasonably warm morning along the Saint Andrews shoreline. Finish the operation. Do what the others failed to do. Kidnap Whynot and forcibly return her to the states. Grab her and bring her over the border to face justice. Don't wait for HSC's bureaucracy. Don't ask for permission. Use initiative. Anderson convinced himself that then HSC will finally realize his value.

Anderson's mind flashed through the heroic possibilities. *Hell, there's a war about to start. They'll see I removed a traitor. An effective traitor I'll grant her. That funeral got widespread coverage. She hurt our cause. Time to get her off the stage. Silence her. I've got the sat phone and a pistol with a suppressor that they gave me. HSC must want me to use them somehow. Maybe I'll get a promotion. Sent on another assignment. An important assignment.*

Tactics. Anderson imagined how he would do it. A tactical plan. Take her in a boat across to Maine? He dismissed that. He had no experience with boats. *Look at how that HSC assault ended.* He took a lesson from the expatriates who got here after the border closed. Grab her and escape in a car. Find a forgotten road near the border. Lots of places to cross. And if necessary, walk across dragging her all the way.

Into Action

Now an hour into his mission, Anderson began to think it would work. As he turned north on to Highway 630 near the few buildings that were Andersonville, he reviewed the evening's events in his mind.

Turns out, ditching the RCMP surveillance wasn't that hard for Anderson.

After the meeting with Whynot, at the pub in Saint Stephen, apparently RCMP decided the best approach was to simply confront Madsen and Anderson. They picked them up and brought them in to the Saint Stephen detachment for a short talk. RCMP told them they had likely broken the law. As their plot hadn't advanced beyond just talk, the police decided to keep things to a warning. However, any further planning would result in immediate arrest. RCMP believed the warning and interrogations would deter them. That and two unannounced visits by RCMP officers to their rented cottage off Highway 127.

It certainly worked on Madsen. He got cold feet. He was terrified about doing anything. Anderson played along. For now, the two agreed to lay low.

After a pitiful holiday meal of turkey sandwiches and potato chips at their cottage, Anderson stayed up late watching television, waiting for Madsen to go to sleep. After midnight, Anderson tied up a loose end. He shot and killed Madsen while he slept. Anderson wasn't sure why he killed him, thinking there wasn't any good reason, other than perhaps he just didn't like Madsen. He settled on the idea that Madsen was just another traitor who deserved what he got.

Anderson took their compact car and drove toward Joes Point Road.

Anderson had stopped the car well before getting to the road leading to the Whynot home. Dressed in dark clothes and winter coat, with suppressed pistol and sat phone tucked into its pockets, he had walked through the woods until he saw the RCMP sedan parked on the side of the road. Past the vehicle he could see the house, all lit up by the exterior lights. He low crawled through a line of bushes and then across the grass until he was within an arm length of the passenger side of the RCMP sedan.

Anderson had never killed anyone before that night. Not even in Afghanistan. He had worried how he might react to killing a man only a foot away. Killing Madsen helped allay his concerns. Anderson rose up and shot the constable three times through the front passenger window.

He found it was easy. Anyway, had to get the job done. No other way.

Punching through the fractured window, Anderson unlocked the car, opened the door, and pulled the officer's body out and on to the ground. He stripped the uniform heavy coast from the body and, for good measure, the sidearm and spare magazines. Anderson dragged the body into the trees.

He got into the driver's seat, ignoring the blood on the front seats but wiped away blood spatter on the windshield with a cloth he found on the floor. He started the engine and drove as quietly as he could toward the Whynot's house. And then called Whynot on the constable's cell phone.

Once Whynot was secured in the RCMP sedan, he drove back to his own car, transferred Whynot to the compact and headed north on Highway 127. He planned on a brief window of time, maybe an hour or so, before the RCMP sedan or the dead cop was discovered. He could go a long way in an hour. He figured the police wouldn't have a description of his car and likely wouldn't connect him to the kidnapping.

Anderson headed for Highway 540, a much more rural road than the one he was on and one that almost paralleled the border. Getting past Richmond Corner worried him. He had to cross a major road, Highway 95, but if he got past that, he should be alright. Just north of there, 540 takes a sharp change in direction to the east and intersects with Highway 550. Then go north until just before the road turns toward Good Corner. From there, it was less than a half-mile to the border. Farmer's fields. A stand of woods for cover. And nobody around for miles. It'll still be dark.

Once over the border, call HSC on the sat phone for a pickup. Use the authentication code and there shouldn't be any problem. All in all, two more hours. Maybe three, but no more.

He thought, *this is going to work.*

Best Laid Plans

Anderson forgot one thing as he bathed in his own self-satisfaction.

Another expatriate renter at the cottages had driven in as Anderson was driving out. The man had just been getting back from a party with friends. He knew Anderson by sight and had talked to him a couple of times in days past but thought Anderson an odd duck. As he parked his car, he wondered, what is he doing leaving now, this late? He then saw Anderson's cottage had the front door cracked slightly open with the lights on.

Being a natural busy body and slightly drunk from the party, the man decided to check on things. Hell, maybe those two guys are still up, and we can keep the party going! He knocked on the door and it swung open wide. From the entry way, he could see into Madsen's bedroom. Anderson had left that door open too. The man saw someone was in the bed. He called out. Without thinking he walked in. He saw things more clearly. He saw the blood more clearly.

The man panicked, almost running backwards out the door. He rooted through his pockets for his cell phone. It took a couple of tries before he hit the right buttons to call 911. RCMP responded to scene. Twenty minutes later, the man faced questioning from two officers.

Yes, officer, a dark grey Toyota. A small four door, but I don't know the model. No, only got part of plate. Definitely New Brunswick plates. The first three letters, LMK. Yeah, his name's Anderson. No, didn't touch anything. The dead guy, he's Madsen. Both Americans.

The constables phoned in the plate fragment and car description for matches. Of the six that match the description, one stood out. Registered to the expatriate Madsen.

Then came word that the RCMP officer watching Joes Point had been found dead. Shot. And Mrs. Whynot was missing. A working hypothesis developed. For an unknown reason, Anderson killed Madsen as he slept. Took the car and likely killed the officer and kidnapped or killed Mrs. Whynot.

As Anderson and his victim turned on to Highway 540, an alert went out to the RCMP units throughout the province.

I Fight

Feeling around with her bound hands, she found an exposed metal edge underneath the front passenger seat. Working in the blind from the hood over her head, she had scraped away at the duct tape. It cut through. Twisting her wrists back and forth, she freed her hands. Even with her feet still bound by tape, and a gag taped across her mouth, she had a chance. Debbie took this moment to think through her situation.

If he wanted to kill me, he had plenty of chances. He wanted something else. Where am I? Where is he headed? Hood's off now. Can't see beyond the back of the seat. Streetlights flashing by. Can't make out road signs. I can't let him get to where he's going. I can't let him take me out of this car. He's most vulnerable now. I can get to him. He can't get to me. I need a weapon.

She started to feel around wherever she could reach without giving away her free hands. *There, something under the seat.* She drew it closer into her right hand. A small cheap ice scraper. A knife would have been better, but this will have to do.

374

There would not be a second chance. Debbie slowly took hold of the scraper in her right hand and used her left hand to grab the edge of the driver's seat. She pulled herself up and took off the hood.

Debbie struck Anderson from behind, slashing him across the bridge of his nose until the scraper found something soft and wet. He screamed. She held it there even as Anderson grabbed her hand to pull her away. But the damage was done.

Anderson reflexively slammed the brake. Shrieking from the agonizing pain in his eye, he covered it with his right hand. He fell over to his right side. His left hand followed and jerked the wheel hard around to the right. The car slid into the roadside ditch, and then flipped onto the driver's side.

Another driver happened by only minutes later. She called 911 for help as she tried to free the now unconscious passengers from the car. She couldn't move them. That's when she noticed something odd. The woman in the back. A woman wearing pajamas and who had tape across her mouth. She reached down inside and ripped the tape away and pulled the cloth piece from the woman's mouth, thinking maybe she'll breathe better.

All through her extraction from the car by the fire department and RCMP, Debbie stayed unconscious. As an ambulance took her away, the Good Samaritan pointed out to the officer the tape and gag. "Ma'am, yeah. Thanks for helping out. You might have saved her life."

"Okay, but the tape. What's going on here?"

"The guy, the driver. We think we know who he is."

"And the woman?"

"I think you'll hear all about it on the news. That's all I want to say for now. But really, thanks for what you did."

As the ambulance took away Anderson next. He wasn't spared of the pain by unconsciousness.

CHAPTER TWENTY-ONE
LAST WORDS

Impeachment and Conviction

Perhaps it was the shootings at Thousand Islands Bridges. Or Houlton. Or Fort Kent. Or the nearly fifty other places around the country where Americans shot down Americans.

There were rumors of mutinies among the troops who refused to continue with *Operation Northern Lights*. One rumored revolt, which turned out to be true, came from the Vermont Air National Guard's 134th Squadron. Every squadron member, from most junior to command, refused the order to attack Canada.

Then there were the humiliating news images of U.S. Army columns in New York held up by unarmed protestors. All of it caught on cell phone video by celebrating protestors and citizens. It didn't help that the soldiers were seen waving to the protestors.

The last order the commander of USNORTHCOM issued before he resigned was to order the tanks back to base.

In other places, the protests continued. On their televisions, smart phones, and computers, Americans saw constant video of protests across America's

REFUGE

major cities, most peaceful, some violent, that continued unabated despite the use of regular troops. Sometimes they lead to more deaths. More than a few soldiers interviewed claimed they refused orders to attack the protestors.

The threatened imposition of economic sanctions already prepared by the European Union didn't help the President.

D-day plus two, the governors of the New England states and New York signed bills of secession that would go into effect if the President was not removed from office. The legislatures of California, Oregon and Washington debated their own secession bills. The President countered with threats of arrest against the governors and military seizure of their governments. The governors stood firm, ordering their National Guard to protect their legislatures. Tens of thousands of citizens stood alongside their Guardsmen.

The next morning, an opposition congressman filed a bill of impeachment against the president, accusing him of conducting a war of aggression. Against all expectations, it flew through the House Judiciary Committee, a committee controlled by the President's party, and passed in a near unanimous committee vote. The next day, the bill went to the full House where it passed in the early morning hours with a thirty-four-vote margin. The President was impeached. The President's closest ally in the Congress, the Speaker of the House, sent the bill to the Senate.

Faced with a Constitutional crisis that threatened the very existence of the United States, the President's party decided to rescue itself.

One after the other, the President's allies in the Senate advised him he faced certain conviction in the Senate. Their existence as a political party, their political agenda, and their hold on power required the President leave office immediately. Otherwise, the United States faced the very real possibility of a break-up and even civil war.

The President resigned. Only hours later, the Attorneys General of Maine and New York announced they would investigate the now former President in connection with the deaths of the demonstrators at Collins Landing and Fort Kent.

The vice president resigned at the same time, announcing he was doing so for health reasons. The chief justice swore in the Speaker of the House as President. His first act was to formally order the U.S. Armed Forces to stand down from hostilities with Canada and NATO. A request to Canada to begin negotiations to reopen the border and end sanctions followed.

The Prime Minister

The Prime Minister of Canada addressed his nation on live television.

"Good afternoon. As most of you, most of the world, knows by now, this morning the President of the United States, and the vice-president, resigned from office. Succession to the Presidency, under the U.S. Constitution, fell to the current Speaker of the House of Representatives.

"While I certainly do not mourn the end of his presidency, I caution everyone not to conclude that the threats have passed.

"Yes, we can confirm that United States Army units have moved away from our borders and have returned, or are returning, to their home bases, and that U.S. naval and air forces have stood down and sailed away. That is good news in itself. A serious war has been averted. And for that we can thank the Armed Forces of Canada and the militaries of our NATO allies. And in no small measure we can thank the actions of Americans themselves, who put themselves in harm's way to protest and impede the reckless and criminal actions of the former President. We mourn those who died in protest of those actions.

"We should all be grateful for this outcome. We can be encouraged that the new President has pledged to reopening the border between Canada and the United States.

"Nevertheless, we must be realistic. The newly ascended President is known for his loyalty to the past administration. The former President's far right party still controls the U.S. Congress and the Presidency. That political party is still largely intact and in control of critical electoral states. As well, the new President's past comments on many issues are disturbing. His initial support for a war against Canada is well documented. He's made no mention yet of holding accountable those who planned this war of aggression.

"The fact remains that the United States threatened the sovereignty of our country and the lives and liberty of all her citizens. It threatened war.

"I will remind the President of another fact. Those who died during our recent troubles were almost entirely Americans. Killed by other Americans.

"I will acknowledge the new President's first comments may indicate a change of heart. Perhaps all Canadians can hope that this new administration seeks a path to peace. Perhaps we can allow our American friends the chance for redemption.

"And yet, while I hope we may forgive them someday, but there must be confession and contrition from the transgressor before we can reconcile and forgive.

"Until then, we must not delude yourselves. We must be realistic. American expressions of peace and hope must be met with actions.

"Democracy in the United States has been nearly extinguished. If democracy finally dies in the United States, it will surely die everywhere. Therefore, democracy in Canada is still under threat. We must therefore still be prepared to defend our nation."

EPILOGUE

I t was the first Wednesday morning in a new September. Debbie waited for George at the SunRise Café. He texted he'd be there in about ten minutes.

Debbie took up Mike's habit of meeting with George for breakfast. She even drove up in the MGB, only these days she brought a passenger along. Cheryl LeBlanc. It was a welcome break for her now that school for James started back up.

Claude was of a better mood these days. With the border reopened, trade and tourism resumed, though the American tourists were still few in number. Claude remarked, "Guess they don't know how we'll treat them. Maybe they are embarrassed by all that happened. Maybe they should be."

Debbie knew all was not well. She allowed herself no wishful thinking. True, since the war failed, American expatriates could return to the United States. But few did. The Expat Committee estimated roughly 95% of her community stayed in Canada. They had made new lives, new friends, and now could go back and visit America whenever they wished. Debbie could never to go back. The indictment against her had not been dismissed.

Attempts to repeal the *Overseas Americans Act* failed. The national state of emergency remained in effect. The Homeland Security Corps was going through a series of reforms, but it still existed even in the face of its bloody failures. The former President's political party still held the White House and the Congress, and likely would through the next elections. Though emboldened by the resignation of the former President, and his indictment by New York and Maine, the opposition seemed to lose momentum. At least, that is how Debbie saw things.

With help from the European Union, Canada vastly boosted its defense spending. NATO successfully met its greatest challenge and was keeping forces permanently stationed in Canada, but renewed threats from Russia strained the alliance.

Her son Matt was doing his bit. His experience at sea with the U.S. Navy proved valuable to the Royal Canadian Navy. Now a renounced American citizen and naturalized Canadian citizen, Matt served on His Majesty's Canadian Ship *Saint John's*, a frigate homeported at Halifax. Commissioned as a full lieutenant, he was one of the warship's engineering officers. Best part for Debbie, it wasn't a long drive to Halifax from Saint Andrews.

Anna moved closer to Saint Andrews, having accepted a new optometry position with a hospital in Fredericton. At the same time, Robert and family found a new home with the large American expatriate community in Ottawa. The preparations made to smuggle Robert, his wife Christine and her granddaughter proved unnecessary. They simply packed up and moved once they found employment as teachers in Canada.

Robert's case was another lesson is how things were not well. Given the awful celebrity the murder of Mike created, Robert faced continuous harassment at work from right wing parents and students, as well as just plain fascist nut-jobs from all over. He and Christine went public with their story, hoping it would dampen the hatred somewhat. It only got worse. Debbie stepped in, taking advantage of her new celebrity, and secured them a future in Ottawa.

On CBC that morning, Debbie caught a breaking story about a U.S. Army colonel, locked up at the U.S. military's prison at Leavenworth. The details of the charges had only now been uncovered by investigative journalists from *The New York Times*. Apparently, the colonel was charged with turning over the plans to *Operation Northern Lights* to Canadian Security Intelligence Service. The Prime Minister's office was not offering a statement at this time.

The CBC anchor went a bit off script, saying "I wonder if this American colonel, who pled guilty, if he is the hero in all this. Is he the guy that saved Canada?"

Debbie thought immediately of LeClerc. *Did he have anything to do with that? Would be interesting to ask him sometime.*

George came in the restaurant door. George these days was more like the old George. Not fully healed, Debbie was sure, but better. Much better.

Claude came over to take the orders. Eggs benedict all around.

While sipping their coffees, Roy came in, accompanied by a younger man in the uniform of an officer of the Canadian Coast Guard. After the good mornings and handshakes, Roy motioned to the young officer and said, "Debbie, this man wanted to meet you. Actually, you've already met."

"Good morning Mrs. Whynot. I'd like to talk if you don't mind. I'm Douglas Miles."

THE END

AUTHOR'S NOTE

'm older. That is a fact. Wiser? That is often debatable. Now that I've arrived at the legally magical age of sixty-five, I carry a Medicare card in my wallet and can claim eligibility for the innumerable museum and tourist discounts available to me simply because I lived long enough.

Just before the pandemic, I retired after fifteen years as a high school science teacher. I did other jobs before that, but none was as worthy. Except when I served as a junior officer in the United States Coast Guard. With retirement, however, it dawned on me that I needed to do something with this time.

Take it from a science teacher. The second law of thermodynamics requires an increase in entropy over time; that is, an increase in disorder and randomness of the matter and energy of the universe. Meaning with every action I take, at any time, in my body and within my surrounding environment, I break down complex things into simpler things. Things must fall apart. In other words, I get older. Same goes for you. No exceptions.

Entropy is, in a word, a bitch.

So, I could wait for entropy to do its thing, leading to the inevitable knee or hip replacements and countless other medical procedures and maladies. Or I could do something I always wanted to do before I couldn't. I decided to write this story, my debut novel.

I've been trying to pigeonhole it into an accepted genre of fiction. Dystopian? Yes, there's a good deal of that. I don't end civilization in a nuclear war or with a virus that leads us to zombies, extinction or vampirism. Thriller? Check that box too. Military with a bit of spy stuff? Got it. Political? Definitely.

I've settled on this: political horror. Without supernatural demons. We've managed to elect enough perfectly natural and mortal demons already. The horror of this story is that it is plausible.

Maybe all that genre stuff isn't important to you, the reader.

I hope you will like this story. I hope you will believe losing our democracy could really happen. I pray it never does.

Almost forgot. Let me end this part the way authors are supposed to end this part.

I live in Rhode Island with Cathy, my wife of forty-two years. I could not have done this without her encouragement and her help in reviewing my drafts. She is the most brilliant person I have ever known. She is also the love of my life.

Made in the USA
Middletown, DE
25 August 2024

59171027R00216